THE PAPER BIRDS

ALSO BY JEANETTE LYNES

The Factory Voice

The Small Things That End the World

The Apothecary's Garden

The
PAPER
BIRDS

A NOVEL

JEANETTE LYNES

An Imprint of HarperCollinsPublishersLtd

The Paper Birds
Copyright © 2025 by Jeanette Lynes.
All rights reserved.

Published by HarperAvenue, an imprint of HarperCollins Publishers Ltd

FIRST EDITION

No part of this book may be used or reproduced in any manner whatsoever without written permission.

Without limiting the author's and publisher's exclusive rights, any unauthorized use of this publication to train generative artificial intelligence (AI) technologies is expressly prohibited.

HarperCollins books may be purchased for educational, business, or sales promotional use through our Special Markets Department.

HarperCollins Publishers Ltd
Bay Adelaide Centre, East Tower
22 Adelaide Street West, 41st Floor
Toronto, Ontario, Canada
M5H 4E3

www.harpercollins.ca

HarperCollins Publishers
Macken House, 39/40 Mayor Street Upper
Dublin 1, D01 C9W8, Ireland
https://www.harpercollins.com

"Sometimes, When the Light" is reprinted by permission of Louisiana State University Press from *Alive Together: New and Selected Poems*, by Lisel Mueller. Copyright (c) 1996 by Louisiana State University Press.

Library and Archives Canada Cataloguing in Publication

Title: The paper birds : a novel / Jeanette Lynes.
Names: Lynes, Jeanette, author.
Identifiers: Canadiana (print) 20250174375 | Canadiana (ebook) 20250178087 | ISBN 9781443472814 (softcover) | ISBN 9781443472821 (Ebook)
Subjects: LCGFT: Historical fiction. | LCGFT: Novels.
Classification: LCC PS8573.Y6 P37 2025 | DDC C813/.54—dc23

Printed and bound in the United States of America

25 26 27 28 29 LBC 5 4 3 2 1

Again, for Mike

Sometimes, When the Light

Sometimes, when the light strikes at odd angles
and pulls you back into childhood

and you are passing a crumbling mansion
completely hidden behind old willows

or an empty convent guarded by hemlocks
and giant firs standing hip to hip,

you know again that behind that wall,
under the uncut hair of the willows

something secret is going on,
so marvelous and dangerous

that if you crawled through and saw,
you would die, or be happy forever.

—Lisel Mueller

THE PAPER BIRDS

PART ONE

THE *BARRACUDA*

1943

Shall I compare thee to a summer's day?
—WILLIAM SHAKESPEARE

ONE

GEMMA SULLIVAN HAD barely stepped into the foyer, hadn't yet shaken rain droplets from the umbrella she grasped like some soggy pelican with collapsed wings, when her aunt's question lofted, clarion-like, from the kitchen:

"8 Down crossword clue: *'Baked beans or*—blank—*cream pie'*? What think you, niece of mine?"

Aunt Wren's epithet—"niece of mine"—always amused Gem, who laughed then called back from the foyer, where the umbrella now perched on the drip mat, her own moniker of endearment. "Birdie, can't you at least let me get through the door first?"

After prying off the pumps that had pinched her heels crimson then flinging them beside the umbrella, Gem padded with her straw satchel into the kitchen, where her aunt sat hunched at the table, spine curved, ladle-like, tackling a crossword. Because Aunt Wren's spectacles had a cracked lens, they weren't much use. She held the magnifying glass, like some flattened crystal ball, close to the puzzle. Sometimes Gem helped, even if just by reading aloud the clues. She'd learned scads of new words this way. How her aunt loved crosswords; they were a portal, a pleasurable escape, mode of travel, dream realm rich with words that often surprised and tickled the tongue.

Escape, yes, but increasingly, Gem suspected, a way to sidestep problems—like the overdue rent for their upstairs flat. The letter about this hadn't moved from the kitchen table since yesterday, but had been shoved farther away to merge with other mail: bills, flyers, newspapers. Gem's high school graduation diploma lay among these papers, too. Its ink barely dry. Only a week had passed since Gem skittered across the stage festooned with bunting and received her diploma. She'd barely begun to ponder what to do next. But whatever she did, it needed to bolster the household income. Near the stack of papers, soft mounds of Aunt Wren's sewing and mending, badly backlogged. Her seamstress work had become more taxing on her eyes yet was Birdie's main livelihood.

Gem was too distracted for puzzles—her own day had puzzled her enough. It was a day that would alter the course of her life. She hadn't told Aunt Wren about the telephone call that started it all. Yesterday, while Aunt Wren had been out grocery shopping, Gemma answered the phone. It was her English teacher, Mr. Keane. A colleague of his oversaw a new office looking to hire young women "with aptitude in language, a literary bent." He thought of Gem immediately; she'd been one of his best English students. He gave her the phone number to call for an interview. Gem didn't tell Aunt Wren about the interview. What if she wasn't offered the job? Why raise hopes only to deflate them?

Aunt Wren hadn't noticed Gem, dressed for her interview, scoot through the kitchen, saying she'd be back in time for supper. Birdie had been bashing away at a hem, humming along to radio music, and didn't glance up as Gem left the flat.

Now, cooked turnips with their unmistakable whiff suffused the kitchen, mingled with meat loaf in the oven. Aunt Wren put much stock in daily rituals like crosswords while supper cooked. Gemma had observed her aunt grow even more attached to routine since the war had begun, nearly four years earlier.

Aunt Wren glanced away from her crossword for the first time. "Why so spiffed up, Gemma, summer gloves, jacket, skirt? Where have you been that called for such a fancy getup?"

"Give me a minute to catch my breath first, Birdie," Gem said, peeling off her gloves. She sat down across from her aunt, noting the usual props on the kitchen table: teapot, cracked eyeglasses, tarot cards fanned, one lone card jutting from the deck. Auntie drew a card every morning that she believed, for good or ill, would direct that day. So absorbed she must have been in her crossword she hadn't even opened that day's *Lake Shore Dispatch*. Normally, Birdie would have read the news by now, its stories blown wider by her magnifying glass. But the real reason her aunt subscribed to the paper, Gem knew, was for the crossword puzzles.

A headline caught Gem's eye: ENEMIES AMONG US: TOWN COUNCIL OPPOSES LOCAL POW LABOUR OUTSIDE INTERNMENT FACILITY. She read: "Until now, the *Dispatch* has been largely silent on the conversion of Mimico's reformatory to a wartime internment facility several years ago, but a situation has arisen about which the public has a right to know." Gem's mind, still flustered from her job interview, skimmed the article: *robust debate in town council . . . labour shortages . . . nearby tannery lobbies for prison workers, insists prisoners will be escorted by armed guards . . . in the end, despite strong citizens' grassroots opposition the outcome will likely be settled by Ministry of National Defence.*

Gem didn't want her aunt to read this; it would only make Birdie more anxious. Everything about the war unsettled her, triggered memories of the last war, her fiancé killed in action. The overdue rent was burden enough, along with Aunt Wren's eye problems.

So, while the meat loaf baked and Birdie plugged away at the crossword, Gem tucked the *Dispatch* in her handbag. This was a stopgap measure, she knew; before long, her aunt would ask for the paper because a new crossword lived within its pages.

Gemma studied the tarot cards on the table. She found the cards' images spooky, with their outsized stars, weird waterways, and gnarled trees, but like the crosswords, the cards evoked new worlds. For she and Aunt Wren rarely went anywhere, couldn't afford it, except Sunnyside Amusement Park, Mimico Beach, and, for

Gem's fifteenth birthday nearly four years ago, Aunt Wren took her to the Exhibition, where they'd sampled the latest treat—ice cream sandwiches—and cracked up with the hilarity of it; imagine, *ice cream in a sandwich*! They'd enjoyed the mist from the Gooderham Fountain as it cooled their faces. It was a rare instance when Gem didn't mind being near water, her nemesis. Outside the Pavilion she and Aunt Wren swayed to the music of Tommy Dorsey's orchestra. It hardly mattered that they didn't have entry tickets to the concert; the divine music wafted wide and far through the warm night. Auntie, in a festive mood, had twirled Gemma around, right there at the foot of that grand pavilion's steps. But mostly their world was the flat on Pidgeon Avenue. And Gem thought, how much more stooped her aunt's posture, since that night. They didn't know it then, but it was fun's last gasp, because a few days later Canada entered the war.

Gemma noticed, too, on the table near the spectacles with their cracked lens, a bottle of Bayer Aspirin. Aunt Wren must be battling one of her headaches.

Yesterday's tarot card had revealed a naked figure, enwreathed, floating above the earth.

"*The World*," Wren had explained. "Means setting out on a voyage of some kind."

Let's just hope the "voyage" isn't our eviction from the flat, Gem thought.

The desk lamp beamed a ray down on the puzzle's black-and-white squares, and Aunt Wren's face, half shadowed by the lamp's angle, appeared haggard. But Gem's news, if she phrased it carefully, would surely bring her some cheer.

She took a teacup from the shelf then sank back gratefully onto her chair. She poured herself some tea, not without guilt. Gem worried they'd exceed their ration allotment. Lately, Aunt Wren always had a pot steeping with tea. Earlier that week, Gemma had suggested they might hold back, guzzle tea with less abandon. Her aunt had shrugged, a wistful flick of her bony shoulders, saying, "Oh, let's *live* while we can, niece of mine." But a moment later, Aunt Wren conceded that they should re-steep the tea several times, to conserve their supply. The newspapers didn't help, either, with their constant harangues that this was a time of sacrifice, not luxury.

Rubbing her sore heels, Gemma scanned the kitchen, with its clean but threadbare tea towels. Birdie's patched gingham apron. Chipped dishes drying on the rack. Setting aside her teacup, Gemma fished the rent notice from the stack of papers on the table and unfolded it. Unlike her aunt's vision, Gem's eyesight was strong. She read the handwritten words, with their loops and swirls:

Wren,

I'm sure you know we're a few days into July now, and I still haven't received your rent. You and your niece have been good tenants for 7 years; this won't change, I hope. Please drop off rent at your earliest convenience.

We have too many beans to pickle. I'll give you some when you bring rent.

Grazie in anticipo,
Rosa D.

As alarming as Gem found the overdue rent note, and as much as she longed to spill her job news, she still didn't have the heart to disturb Birdie's peace as she worked on her crossword.

Gemma gazed again around their flat. It was the upstairs of a house and basically one large room, kitchen at one end, living room at the other. An archway marked the between. Three small bedrooms sprouted from a hallway. Under the archway, clothing of all kinds—jackets, dresses, shirts—slumped over an ironing board, awaiting Wren's expert needlecraft. And yardages of fabric. People stretched their clothes' lives; Depression-era frugality had become engrained with the current wartime restrictions. The soft stack of clothing had swelled since last week. Soon it would topple and spill over the ironing board onto the parquet floor. This distressed Gem; her aunt took pride in prompt, quality work, wielding the needle like a dervish so her customers' garments would be repaired promptly, and payment be received with equal speed. The wall calendar confirmed what Gem already knew: It was after the first of July, as Mrs. Deluca's letter pointed out. If Mrs. Deluca turned them out, where would they live?

Which was why Gemma had signed those formidable papers at the job interview a couple of hours earlier, papers that, despite the day's heat, chilled her very spine: the Official Secrets Act. It felt like writing one's name in blood. Gemma had written her name in the space beside *I understand the severity of any offences I have been deemed to commit under this Act in accordance with the Criminal Code, Part XV*. When Gem had hesitated at first, pen hovering above the signature line, the stern, cigarette-wielding lady interviewer asked her a question, like a flame flaring from a dragon, across the desk: "Do you want to help end the war, or not?" There was only one answer to this question, so Gem had inked her name.

Finally, Aunt Wren looked up from her crossword. "So?" she probed. "You've caught your breath, taken tea. Can you help me solve 8 Down?"

"Banana," Gem offered. "As in banana cream pie?"

Wren flicked her pencil about, then set it down. "Right number of letters, but doesn't fit with the other clues hooked to that word. Let's give it a rest. Maybe the answer will strike us. Tell me where you've been, niece of mine, all smart in my old cornflower-blue Sunday jacket and skirt I remade for you—from when I used to go to church. When I still believed. And day gloves! How unlike you. But today, so grown-up—is that *lipstick* you're wearing? Such a pretty shade!"

"Our rent worries will soon be over, Auntie. I found work today." Gem glanced at her aunt's worn spectacles with their cracked, spiderwebbed lens. "And you can get new eyeglasses!"

It took several seconds for this news to register, it seemed. In the interval, the meat loaf's pleasant meld of onions, celery and ground beef intensified. Wailed mirth reached them from downstairs; the Delucas must have tuned in to *Fibber McGee and Molly.*

Aunt Wren flashed her distinct grin. Front tooth canting sideways. "You don't say. That's tremendous for someone who just finished high school. What a lifesaver you are—and this isn't the first time you've saved my life. Bless you, niece of mine! What sort of work? Please tell me it's nothing to do with this awful war."

Gemma knew the root of her aunt's anguish around war; even years after the death of Adam, her fiancé, Wren hadn't fully healed, and she'd never taken another sweetheart. So, Gem needed to be tactful around this delicate topic. The dire words of the Official Secrets Act rebounded into her mind as well—*imprisonment, hard labour, steep fines.* She was not at liberty to disclose her new job. She clutched her teacup harder to steady her quaking hands. *Be careful, Gem.*

"At the soup company? Tire and Rubber?"

Gem shook her head. She sensed that her aunt enjoyed the guessing game, rather like a puzzle.

"Tell me it's not at that terrible place where they slaughter animals so the ladies who live in the Estates can lavish their own hides and closets with finery," Birdie implored.

Knowing her aunt meant the tannery and the posh summer homes nearby, along Lake Ontario, Gem said wrong again.

Aunt Wren mused. Then gave up guessing.

"Office work," Gem breezed. "Filing. Typewriting." (That's what she'd been told to say.) "Government branch. They're just setting it up, so I'm scant on details. But related to communications."

"You were always good at that," Aunt Wren said. "You used to write the birds little notes and deliver them into the notches of tree trunks or stabbed through branches, so adorable. I recall you'd even devised a language—chirpy-brogue, or some such thing. How you even knew a word like *brogue* is beyond me."

Gem smiled. "No doubt I learned it from one of your puzzles, Auntie. The birds probably used my notes for nesting material—everyone needs a home. And now I can support us in keeping ours."

"Where is this office?" asked Birdie.

The office was a lakeside cottage repurposed for the war effort. But to say she now worked at a "cottage"—more precisely, the *basement* of this cottage—would only confuse her aunt and spawn further questions. Gem cleared her throat. "Just down on the lake's shore, not far from here."

This seemed to satisfy Aunt Wren.

"I start tomorrow," Gem said. "Let's hope I'm paid soon."

Aunt Wren reached across the table and clutched her hand.

The ancient, ticking oven timer buzzed, jolting them both. Gem got up and said she'd serve the meat loaf and turnips.

"That would be grand," Aunt Wren replied.

Gem obliged, and they ate, contentedly.

Suddenly famished, Gem spooned herself a second helping of meat loaf.

Aunt Wren dabbed at her mouth with a napkin, then circled back to the crossword puzzle that was still on the table. "'*Baked beans or*—blank—*cream pie*'? Answer just came to me."

Mouth stuffed, Gem beheld Birdie's gleeful face.

"Boston," Aunt Wren chirruped. "Sure as this day is long I'm right." She reached over for the newspaper, turning to the answer page. "Correct!" She drum-rolled her fingers on the table, a gesture Gem recognized as her victory code. At moments like this Birdie became a child again.

That day's upturned tarot card still lay at the table's far end, a little too distant for even Gem's sharp eyes. "And today's card, Birdie? What does it say?" Gem didn't always ask, but that day felt different; being employed, she supposed, made her officially an adult, so she should probably take more interest in other adults' concerns, especially her aunt, who'd raised her since the age of three, filling the mother role. Gem adored her to her very core.

In a strained yaw that suggested creaky joints, Wren reached for the card. "Today's message is the Moon." She showed Gemma the card.

Gem scraped her plate clean. "Meaning what, Auntie?"

"Trickery. Deception."

The gramophone downstairs roused loud, all bright brass, bubbly clarinets, then Ella Fitzgerald's pure strains: "Little White Lies." As if the song knew about the scowling moon face on the tarot card.

Sighing, Aunt Wren cleared away the dishes. "Maybe the card knows I'm a pretender in my work as a seamstress—more so every day. Trying to deceive my customers. Ah, my poor tired eyes. I can hardly manage it anymore."

Wren filled the sink with water, detergent, swabbed away with the cloth. Then she turned to face Gem, dripping cloth in her hand, a look sodden with woe. "You know, I admire people's willingness to remake their clothes, repair them, fashion new ones from material they've kept on hand. But I'm overwhelmed just now. Someone wants a man's suit made into a woman's, a tablecloth turned into a blouse, even a jacket made from a bedspread. Then there's all the ripped seams and missing buttons, hooks and eyes."

Gemma was hopeless with the needle, a butterfingers, and had once almost stabbed through her finger on the treadle sewing machine, so it wasn't like she could provide any help. And at her new job at The Cottage she'd have to pass a trial period, a probation, before she was assured of the job. All Gem could suggest to her aunt was maybe taking a short break from the mending and sewing, a rest, before diving back in refreshed.

"Perhaps," Aunt Wren replied, sounding unconvinced.

"Once I get on my feet, and am paid, you'll be able to buy new eyeglasses," Gem reiterated.

"In the meantime," Wren murmured, "I must mend for a while tonight if I can. Keep me company?"

"I wish I could, Birdie. But tomorrow I rise at six a.m. for work, and tonight I'd better iron my blouse and hand-wash my underthings, then maybe I'll read a few pages of my romance novel before sleep. I need to be clear-headed and rested to make a good impression on my first day on the job."

"Ah yes, you're a working girl now," Wren quipped.

"Tomorrow, Birdie, can you tell Mrs. Deluca I found employment? And we'll have the rent for her as soon as I'm paid. Hopefully that will satisfy her."

Wren agreed, adding, "Good night, then. Dream well."

But Gem *didn't* dream well. Instead, she fretted all night about her new job, until darkness unfurled its thick curtain down over their town.

TWO

As she loped, in her sneakers, towards the lake, she thought about yesterday's interview. Gem didn't have anything to compare it with—it had been her first one. She was fairly sure that other jobs didn't involve signing a contract about what you could and couldn't say—even on your deathbed.

But she'd done what she'd done. And after helping Birdie steer a strand of thread through a needle's eye earlier that morning, she'd kissed her aunt's forehead and left the flat.

Gem replayed yesterday's events: She arrived at the interview a minute or two late. After checking the address she'd been given, she remembered that during the phone call she'd been directed—by a woman's voice—to go around to the "cottage's" back door. This took Gem very near water—a mere hop, skip down to Lake Ontario. She shuddered.

The word *cottage* fell far short of the handsome house Gem stood before, with its pretty dormers and low wrought-iron fence running along the front. Where she and Aunt Wren lived in St. John's Ward in Toronto's core was called a cottage, too, but it was nothing like this; theirs had been a tiny workers' cottage. If this posh place—for it *was* posh, to Gem's eyes—was a family's summer home, what was their *regular* house like?

The gate was unlocked. She clicked it open and tottered through. Went around to the back door, as instructed, and knocked.

The woman who greeted Gemma had coppery, crimped hair that had mostly fallen from its pins and looked like an assemblage of electric wires or a tree where fireflies nested. She wore a rayon crepe dress, rumpled, like she'd slept in it. The woman, who appeared to be about forty, soared above Gem, and on her feet she wore fuzzy bedroom slippers.

She led Gem down a few steps into a large basement room. Then settled into a wooden chair with wheels, behind a huge desk, also wood, with a badly pocked surface. She motioned for Gem to take the chair directly across from her on the other side of the desk, which floated like a raft between them.

The woman lit a cigarette, inhaled and scrutinized Gem. "So, you're the new high school graduate Boyd Keane sent me."

Gemma hadn't known her English teacher's first name, so she sat, stunned, for a few instants. The woman must have thought her very dense.

"Oh. Yes. Mr. Keane suggested I call about the job opening." Suddenly very nervous, she chugged forth, "I'm Gemma. Sullivan. But I go by Gem, usually."

"And I'm Beatrice Fearing," the woman said, exhaling smoke. "Miss. I realize you're fresh out of high school, but have you ever worked before, even part-time?"

"Yes, as a milliner's assistant," Gem replied. "I helped my aunt make hats. When I was little. Mostly plaited straw." To distract from her jitters Gemma studied the desk's surface, where there were numbers and weird symbols carved right into it. While Miss Fearing, having stubbed her cigarette, rifled through a drawer, Gem cast her gaze around the basement. Its small windows were covered with dark, heavy cloth.

Gem struggled to adjust to the room's dank humidity and dim lighting.

Batting a strand of hair away from her eyes, Miss Fearing bantered, caustically, "Well, there are plenty of mad hatters in our line of work." Then she apologized for "the state of things" while her long fingers switched on a nearby table fan that wheezed and croaked, circulating little air. Miss Fearing rose long enough to turn on a floor lamp, then returned to her chair.

In addition to Miss Fearing's desk, there were four others, spaced apart, against the wall. Above one desk hung an Irish cross. Another held a wilting peony in a jar. Some kind of behemoth machine squatted on a cart between two of the desks. There were large rolls of paper. Half-opened boxes belching wires, cables. Two file cabinets. An expansive chalkboard on one wall, peppered with mumbo-jumbo. On the opposite wall, a huge map jabbed with red pins. Tied to each pin a string, taut across the ocean. The nearby walls splattered signage, in thick black letters: *Do not talk about your work at home. Do not talk in the diner. Remain silent on the streetcar, the bus. The enemy does not get his Intelligence by great scoops, but from a whisper here, a tiny detail there. English proverb: "Wicked tongue breaketh bone, Though the tongue itself hath none."*

Gem shifted her gaze to the other side of the basement, where there was a small sink and a hot plate with a tea kettle. A simple cot was tucked into a far corner. Had Miss Fearing slept in this dungeon-like place overnight? That might explain her creased dress and the sacks beneath her eyes, as prominent as orange segments.

"We're still getting this office operational," Miss Fearing said. "They've sent me here to be in charge, and I've no time to fritter away. I've been toiling night and day getting everything afloat. Ottawa and Whitby are swamped. They're drowning in work; we take the overflow."

Gem didn't like all the watery words. Water frightened her badly; her parents had drowned in a northern lake. She couldn't imagine anything worse than drowning.

To steer her mind away from water, Gem pointed to a portrait on the wall, a lady with ringlets, in an old-fashioned gown worn low on her pale shoulders.

"Who's that?" Gem asked.

Miss Fearing inhaled her cigarette deeply and smiled for the first time.

"*That*," Miss Fearing said, "is the Enchantress of Numbers, Ada Lovelace. My heroine. Her functional equations leave me breathless. The genius of her analytical engine, her poetical science." The eye-mist thickened to a rolling droplet down Miss Fearing's cheek. "My own age now exceeds, by four years, Ada's death. She died not even forty. Who knows what further computational marvels she might have struck upon had she lived."

Miss Fearing stubbed out her Pall Mall and said they'd best begin the job interview in earnest. "Boyd Keane told me of your adeptness with words, with language. He praised your linguistic dexterity, called you a highly articulate young lady."

Gem stared at her silently. She didn't feel very articulate.

"Here we work with language and numbers. Can you give me an example of a code, Miss Sullivan?"

Her hands damp with sweat, Gem ventured, "A telephone number, maybe?"

Miss Fearing leaned forwards, looming closer to Gem. "Everything is a code," she began. "Stars in the night sky. The camber of a swallow's wing. A soldier's wink. Mayday. The colour blue. A pulse, a gong, a chime. A poem. Seven short blasts from a ship's horn. A musical score. Slashes of paint on a cave wall. A stained glass window. A white flag. Bloomers pegged to a wash line, sorrowed with coal soot, greyed, unrequited. And bells, always bells. A shriek between jaws. A bone. A heart. Column of smoke from a fire."

She paused—for effect, Gem supposed.

Then more. "*Dit, dah, dot, dash*. Ave Maria. Wilco. A girl riding a bicycle, her hand signalling a turn. A raven's swoop near your shoulder some consider a sign from a departed one. A cross. The messages contained in our cells that scientists are only now starting to discover. We're living codes. So, the whole world is a code, infinitely more abundant than a mere phone number."

Gemma didn't sense a question here, so she pressed her damp palms together, as if in prayer.

Miss Fearing looked straight at Gem. "What do you think this war's most important weapon is, Miss Sullivan?"

A lake gull mewled out in the summer day. How Gem wished its cry held the answer. She fumbled again. "Guns?"

Miss Fearing's lips flattened. "Intelligence. Information. A million signals whizz through the air on any given day." She paused, as if to reflect. "All this is so simple, yet so complex," she went on. "We're trying to get supply ships over to Britain through the perilous, shark-filled waters of the Atlantic. The sharks are German submarines, U-boats, but they, too, need supplies, fuel. A couple of months ago, thanks to work like ours, our ships dodged numerous U-boats. This work takes grit. Do you possess grit, Miss Sullivan?"

Gem honestly didn't know, and said as much.

Miss Fearing looked perturbed. "Then tell me a situation where you persevered and conquered a tough challenge."

"Water," Gem said. "I'm rabidly averse to it. Before the war, our class took a school trip to Niagara Falls. I forced myself to climb out of the bus and stand by the railing. It was the hardest thing I've ever done."

Miss Fearing seemed satisfied with this answer. "So, you've overcome an obstacle. Good. Any chance you speak German?"

"Sorry. Only word I know is *schnitzel*."

"How about Cree?"

Gem shook her head.

"I didn't think so. Navajo?"

"No, Ma'am."

"Too bad. Let's move on then," Miss Fearing said. "We'll now test your recognition skills." She took a large black-and-white photograph from the desk drawer. Slid it across to Gem. "What do you see in this picture, Miss Sullivan?"

The inter-webbed white vectors in the image reminded Gemma of embroidery work, but with a purposeful gauze, procedural coldness.

"Winter?"

"Be more specific," Miss Fearing urged.

"Doily?"

"You were closer to the mark the first time, Miss Sullivan. Look again."

"A snowflake."

"Good. Now, what do you notice about this snowflake? I refer to its composition."

Gem's heart panged with hope. "Is this office a weather forecast station?"

"No. Sometimes. Answer the question."

"It has a design," Gem ventured. "Tiny, repeating triangles." With this response she sensed a warming from across the desk.

"Indeed. These are renderings of the Koch snowflake. Fractals." Then, verging on delight, Miss Fearing rousted from her chair and wrote madly on a nearby chalkboard—numbers and letters, some tiny, raised, brackets, fractions, equal signs.

Gem's heart plunged into her too-tight shoes. She wouldn't get this job. She didn't have the slightest inkling what the weird symbols on the chalkboard signified. She might as well confess this, to save them both time. She hung her head. "I don't know what any of that means."

Turning to face Gem, Miss Fearing sent her a wistful smile, an indulgent preamble to dismissal, Gem guessed. But instead, the copper-topped conjuror said, "I didn't suppose you would. It's only one of the most elegant pieces of conceptual geometry known to man—and woman."

"I didn't score high in geometry," Gem confessed. "I missed some classes. My aunt went through a rough patch, and I stayed home to take care of her."

"That shows humanity. As for the computational side of our operation, it might not matter. I've hired Cora-Lynn Ponder. Mathematics is her forte. The girl positively lives for number theory. She studies at the University of Toronto; I taught her a course. She works here through the summer. And, hopefully, part-time after that, between her classes. I call her Ponder the Wonder. And Hester Hobbs, the other new hire, possesses acumen in logic. What I need now is someone *not* shackled by logic—instead, intuitive, starry-brained, to complement skills covered by Cora-Lynn and Hester. Someone Alice-minded."

Gem was lost. "Who's Alice?"

"Alice from Mr. Carroll's book. When no logical path led her to the garden, instead of letting the obstacle confound her, she kept devising new methods to reach her goal, roundabout, unorthodox stratagems, a most resourceful girl. Ponder and Hobbs are bright, but the cognitive compasses of both veer towards the shores of logic rather than imagination."

Those two desks, the one with the peony, the other the cross, must belong to them, Gem assumed. "Where are they?" she asked. "Ponder and Hobbs?"

"In training out at Whitby," Miss Fearing replied. "At The Farm. They'll be back tomorrow."

What Ponder and Hobbs were doing at a farm in Whitby, whether learning to milk cows or something else, Gem couldn't begin to speculate. She didn't think she was shackled by logic. Logic meant knowing that if you didn't go into the water, you'd be safe from it. But Gem believed that if you were close enough to it, a monstrous, watery arm, like a wave, could reach out, icy and wet, and pull you under.

"Miss Sullivan, stay present, please. Let's return to your strengths. Tell me more about your language skills—what do you excel at in this area?"

"Reading. Composition. I wrote a few pieces for *The Peptimist*, our school paper."

"Good. Your teacher told me as much. But I must test your aptitude for language, to verify this."

The fuzzy feet sloshed over to a screen on a roller that lowered from the ceiling, like the large maps in geography class. Even the noisy, decrepit fan couldn't smother the officious snarl made by the heavy sheet of paper as Miss Fearing pulled it down then snapped it into place. It was filled with words printed in a magnified typeface legible from some distance.

"Read out loud what you see, Miss Sullivan."

Gem cleared her throat, and began: "'Alas, poor Yorick! I knew him, Horatio, a fellow of infinite jest, of most excellent fancy. He hath borne me on his back a thousand times. And now how abhorred in my imagination it is!'"

She paused for breath. Since she wasn't likely to get this job, and was in fact a dunce who couldn't tell a snowflake from a doily, she'd go down with a flourish of drama.

"Continue, please," Miss Fearing urged.

Gem ratcheted up the emotion, injecting anguish into her delivery: "'My gorge rises at it. Here hung those lips that I have kissed I know not how oft. Where be your gibes now, your gambols, your songs, your flashes of merriment that were wont to set the table on a roar?'"

She'd reached the end of the words on the screen and was surprised to see Miss Fearing scoot a tear from her eye.

"I sense you know this passage you've just read with such expressive conviction?"

"*Hamlet*. Act 5, Scene 1."

"Correct. Your delivery reveals a literate person with performative dexterity, intuition in human psychology and a precise eye for detail. You stumbled not once."

"We studied the play in English class," Gem explained, not wishing to appear boastful.

Then Miss Fearing asked Gemma to scramble the words and phrases and reconstitute the passage whilst maintaining its overall gist. Gem didn't find this difficult. After all, *I knew him* bore the same import as *him I knew*. And Shakespeare's phrasing often held up backwards as well as forwards. She scrambled. She juggled, like a word puzzle, voicing her new configuration.

Miss Fearing seemed pleased. Then she slid a small book across the desk to Gem. "Open it at page 137 and read Emily Dickinson's poem numbered XLIV."

Gemma found the page. She read. Waited.

"Well executed, Miss Sullivan. Can you decode this poem? Do you know what it means?"

Gem quivered with nerves; much hung in the balance of her answer. She sighed, and thought she'd better be honest. "I'm sorry, I can't make head or tail of it."

Instead of the dismay Gemma expected, Miss Fearing laughed, a single wallop of drollery. "Neither can I, Miss Sullivan. What a shame Emily Dickinson can't return from the dead; she'd be wondrous as a codebreaker."

Before Gemma could agree and join the moment's jocularity, Miss Fearing became sombre. She pointed to a framed needlepoint on the wall, finely crafted alphabet letters, in rows, some obsessive linguist-crafter's dream. It also reminded Gem of a test on an eye doctor's wall. "Do you know what this diagram is?" Miss Fearing asked.

Gem shook her head.

"I didn't suppose you did, having attended a parochial high school in Mimico. It's a *Vigenère Square. Tabula Recta.* Quite a cock-a-doodle over its validity, but I still think it's beautiful. And my sole attempt at needlepoint."

Gem was about to compliment the interviewer's handicraft when the telephone rang.

Making a "wait" signal with her finger, Miss Fearing answered it. Gem heard a muffled male voice. Then Miss Fearing: "*No*! How many times do I have to tell you? That's a null, a dud, meant to trick us." The exchange ended shortly after that.

The interview resumed.

"I must pose this question: Would you say, Miss Sullivan, that you rattle easily? I ask because—I'll say this straight—our work here can cause illness of the mind, could drive one to insanity." She sparked another Pall Mall. Then: "I don't mean the lunacy of attempting to prove that Bacon penned Shakespeare's plays, or that *The Iliad* or *The Odyssey* contain deep encryptions. I mean the madness brought on by knowing another Allied fighter could have been saved if you'd solved a problem sooner, that another life was lost while you muddled about. Do you have the courage and stamina to withstand such a burden, to hold a life, many lives, in your hands?"

The question *itself* unnerved Gem. She thought hard. "I may have some tiny practice at that, Miss Fearing, because these days I rather hold Aunt Wren's life in my hands. She can hardly work, so it's up to me to help her if I can, and support us."

Miss Fearing forged ahead. "Fair enough. I'll need you to be, above all, trustworthy. When someone has told you a secret, have you kept it? Can you think of an instance?"

Would this interview *never* end?

"Aunt Wren told me things, some scandalous, sordid even, her millinery customers revealed to her in confidence, and my aunt made me promise not to tell anyone. I never did."

Miss Fearing stared hard at Gem, then drew some papers from a drawer and slid them across the desk towards her, along with a fountain pen.

"After you have read this document, Miss Sullivan, you won't be the same girl you were when you stepped into this office. If you agree to its terms, I'll hire you on a probationary basis. Even if your probation doesn't work out and you leave us, you must never tell anyone about this place and what we do here. Not even on your deathbed. But you can't work here unless you read this first, accept its terms and sign it. Take your time. Read carefully."

Gem read. The Official Secrets Act and its severe proclamations:

Any person who is guilty of an offence under this Act shall be deemed to be guilty of an indictable offence and shall on conviction be punishable . . . and if so prosecuted, shall be punishable by fine not exceeding five hundred dollars, or by imprisonment not exceeding twelve months, with or without hard labour, or by both fine and imprisonment.

Run while you still can, Gem thought. The pen shook in her hand.

"Do you want to help end the war, or not?" Miss Fearing prickled at her.

Gem signed.

"Now I can tell you more," declared her new boss. "Please treat everything I say as though it's part of the Official Secrets Act. You're never to disclose any words spoken in this office. If anyone asks about your work, tell them filing, typewriting, that sort of thing.

Can't emphasize that enough. I'm a naval cryptanalyst. And this place called The Cottage is a Signals Intelligence Office for the Allied war effort. We're an offshoot, a satellite office, of the Examination Unit in Ottawa, which is itself a branch plant of Bletchley Park in England. We're also affiliated with The Farm at Whitby. We're an outpost of an outpost of an outpost. Regular civilians don't know about any of these places. Intelligence officials who are, surprise surprise, men call us the lipstick bureau, ladies' lake-hut or, more crudely, the henhouse. And we inherited Whitby's castoff furniture, too, as you see by this wreck of a desk, broken lamp and ruined chair. As for the intercepts, we take the overflow. Everyone's swamped. Thousands of radio signals are intercepted every day. Our boys'—and women's—lives depend on our efforts. Here at The Cottage, we don't have the luxury of the big machines they have in England, or America, or even Whitby. It's all manual here. We're like a broom closet of Bletchley Park. Their facility is astonishing. I trained in England, at the Government Code and Cypher School, then worked at The Park for a while before being stationed here. Quite a place, Bletchley, everyone from punch-card grunts to geniuses. So many dazzlingly sharp girls. Here we're like the scullery maids of this operation—but I'll wager we'll surprise them yet. Revelation can rise from the lowliest corners."

Cottage. Farm. Park. How innocent these places might strike ordinary ears. Which Gemma no longer possessed; she'd signed them away.

Miss Fearing grew, in Gem's estimation, more magnificent, and scarier, every second.

Gem supposed, after this sermon, Miss Fearing would leave off. But there was more.

"We aren't the only small operation, either. Often, it's where you'd least expect. They've been doing brilliant intelligence work above a fruit store in Ottawa. Imagine the soaring intellect at work mere feet above your head while you're buying bananas. Just down the road from here, at Humber Bay, war boats are being built. Smaller vessels, but no less crucial. All of us together, we're a vast solar system with a common North Star guiding us—the star of good triumphing over evil."

Adrift in this dizzying solar system, Gem saw no other course than blunt directness. "Am I hired, then, Miss Fearing? Even though I couldn't decipher the snowflake or your . . . symbols on the chalkboard?"

"Probation, as I've said. I need staff with a range of skills. There are word girls and number girls. And girls somewhere in between, hybrids. It takes every bent of mind to crack enemy codes. Lots of codes use literary works as keys. Poems, even. The work we do will tax your heart and mind. I should have asked earlier—are you single?"

"Yes," Gem answered.

"Less distractions that way," Miss Fearing said. "And no eager ears to bleat top secret intelligence to, in a moment of weakness—or passion. That being said, a sweetheart in uniform can be a valuable motivator, or a relative in the service—do you have any?"

Gemma shook her head.

"Have you ever been convicted of a crime?"

Again, no.

"Now that you've signed the Official Secrets Act and its confidentiality clause, you must never tell anyone what you do, or where you work—not even your own mother."

"It's just me and Aunt Wren."

Miss Fearing pressed on. "Do you understand the gravity of this, Miss Sullivan, the trust placed in you?"

Gem nodded, solemn.

"You're now a keeper of state secrets, Miss Sullivan. If you betray your country's trust, they'll cut out your tongue. That's one way to think about it, to keep yourself in check."

Gem wanted to change the topic. "Who lives upstairs?"

"No one," Miss Fearing answered. "The government has taken over this commodious cottage. Upstairs is my office. I work down here sometimes, but I've got my own set-up above, for confidential meetings, phone calls, that sort of thing. There's a buzzer system so you girls can reach me. No one goes upstairs without clearance from me. I touch base every morning and issue that day's orders, updates, priority tasks. And I come downstairs at each day's end to debrief and log what you've accomplished."

Then Miss Fearing told Gem the salary. She was shocked. It was surely much more than the tannery or soup factory. But those places had no secrecy oath, no strings attached, or threat of harm or jail.

Taking the papers and fountain pen, Miss Fearing's demeanour softened. "Report back here at seven a.m.—be *on time*. Dress in regular, civilian clothes. We don't wear uniforms; it would draw attention. Mimico is still a town, after all, and people are nosy. And don't ever take work home with you, for security reasons. Right now, we're faced with the toughest assignment thus far: tracking the Atlantic's most menacing killer—a German U-boat we call the *Barracuda*. You'll learn more details tomorrow. Your co-workers will be back then, too."

Miss Fearing's intense peering unnerved Gemma. It was as if the new boss peeled away her outer layers, to decode her core. Gem felt sweat spackle her forehead.

"I expect you'll be good at codebreaking, Miss Sullivan. Being a word person, as you are, helps us. Bletchley hired numerous scholars of language—morphologists, phonologists, syntacticians, you name it. Besides your linguistic skill, you possess humility, I can tell. Too many codebreakers' downfalls stem from overblown egos. *Hubris*. And this job is one situation, a rare one, where gender works in our favour; we women are naturals at intelligence work—we're *perfect* for it, in fact, having been told, since girlhood, to hold our tongues. But *here*, I'm in charge; I can speak."

Her words rasped caustic, sour as raw rhubarb. Truly, Gem had never met anyone like this dishevelled, charismatic cryptanalyst.

Lighting another cigarette, Miss Fearing continued. "Yes, they'd prefer us silent, like statues, dolls—but now they *need* us." She took a hard pull on her Pall Mall. Smoke fogged across the desk. "The Allied forces can't win this war without us. Any last questions, Miss Sullivan?"

There were, in fact, *many* questions. One was when Gem would be paid. The rent notice back home loomed large in her mind. But, as if yanked by marionette strings, Gemma only shook her head and thanked Miss Fearing for the opportunity, adding she'd do her best not to let the Allied forces down.

Miss Fearing reminded Gem again about her oath of secrecy, then concluded the interview. "All the same, there are advantages to being quiet. If you're not talking, it's more likely you're *listening*. War demands attentive ears. Tune in to the world, Miss Sullivan. And nature—hearken to the birds' gabble. Study their codes. Be all ears. This exercise will sharpen your mind." Then another non sequitur, which, Gem began to grasp, was Miss Fearing's habitual mode of thought.

"Miss Sullivan, this interview never happened. Got it?"

"Yes, Ma'am."

Gemma ascended from the basement into the summer day's shimmer. Naval cryptanalyst. Signals intelligence. *Not even on your deathbed.* Gem wasn't sure what any of it meant, only that, somehow, she'd snagged a job that might keep her and Aunt Wren alive, with a roof over their heads.

But she must learn to tolerate being near water. Why not start now? In a few short steps that involved picking her way in the drastic pumps over scruffy grass, smooth stones, through The Cottage's back garden in ruins with its crumbled lady statue, then coarse sand, then past an enormous fallen log, weathered, bleached silvery, smooth, like a giant's bench, Gem approached the lake's roiling swell. Like some menacing, reverse sky. Just looking at it made her stomach pitch. She couldn't go any closer, out of fear, but even from where she stood, she saw, bobbing on whitecaps, two gulls. *Hearken to the birds' gabble.* These two pontificated loudly. What code was that? What could they be telling each other? Their noise grew raucous. Scoffing at her, Gem imagined, for getting in over her head, more bewildered by her new job, almost, than frightened of the lake before her eyes.

THREE

THE NEXT MORNING, Miss Fearing towered before Gem and the two other girls back from Whitby. Just before their boss descended the stairs, before her thudding footfall which, to Gem, sounded heavier than bedroom slippers, the girl with the pert ginger ponytail and cute sloping nose took the desk with the wilted peony and introduced herself, Cora-Lynn. So, that was Ponder the Wonder. The shorter, bespectacled, dark-tressed girl sat under the Celtic cross. "I'm Hester Hobbs," she told Gem. "Welcome to Crypto-Cottage." This raven-haired one appeared so earnest that Gem didn't know if this welcome was meant as a joke. So she strove for a neutral expression.

"You can take the desk between Hobbs's and mine," Cora-Lynn told Gem. So the Wonder was also a take-charge type, perhaps even a sub-boss.

Gem settled where she'd been directed.

"Here comes Lady F," Cora-Lynn said, tight-faced. "At attention."

All three girls swivelled in their chairs to face the door.

Miss Fearing wore a tailored suit that day, oxford shoes. Her crimped hair had been tethered into submission with pins. She carried a bundle of papers she dumped on her desk, then stood, sentinel-like, as if some orator about to launch a speech. Which she was. She cleared her throat. "Today the real work begins. I assume you've met Gemma Sullivan, our new hire. She's a word person, a regular alphabet crackerjack, which rounds out our skill set."

Not waiting to have this confirmed, Miss Fearing forged ahead.

"I expect you three girls—and hopefully, soon, a fourth—to comport yourselves with civility. We're different from Bletchley, day and night. Bletchley was so immense, one hut didn't know what work was carried out in the others, for the most part. They were so many silos. But here you're all in one room. You can help each other. In fact, I *encourage* a co-operative spirit."

She let this notion sink in. "As recently as three years ago, Canada was a baby, an *utter diaper-swaddled infant*, in global intelligence. But that baby has matured very fast, sprung into grown-up trousers with almost superhuman speed. But I'm not here to give you a history lesson."

Hester shifted in her chair, and it squeaked a lament.

"Hobbs, Ponder, you girls have been here for over a week, so you've heard some of this before. Bear with me. Last year was very tough for us," the boss said. "All those poor innocent people killed on the Newfoundland ferry. Everywhere our progress stalled. The *Kriegsmarine* added a new rotor to their Enigma. But now, in the Atlantic theatre, we've been gaining ground."

She paused to light a cigarette with the lighter stashed in her suit pocket. "But there's no time to be complacent. The battle isn't over yet, and our fortunes could turn for the worse again. We've taken out numerous U-boats—so many, in fact, that the German naval commander-in-chief has pulled their wolf packs from the waters and adopted a different tack. Rather than moving in packs, the enemy now dispatches lone wolves, solitary rogue U-boats that troll the Atlantic. One of these submerged killers can be just as destructive as a whole fleet of submarines. There's one *very deadly one* in particular—"

While Miss Fearing inhaled her cigarette, Gem glanced at Hester and Cora-Lynn. They'd turned pale, keenly attentive. Gem clutched her chair's wooden arm.

"U-boat 195, which our side has dubbed the *Barracuda*," their boss declared, as she tramped over to the large map on the wall and swept her hand across the Atlantic Ocean. "It lurks, somewhere in this cold sea, or skulks, hovering on the surface, a stealth executioner lying in wait to torpedo our supply ships. And its commander, Karl Hans Krause, is one of the *Kriegsmarine*'s best—on par with Otto Kretschmer, before his capture. Scuttle goes, they call Krause the Long-Haul-Liquidator because of his lengthy patrols and how many Allied ships he's sunk. Can you imagine if we help capture his submarine? They might even seize Krause's *code book*. Do you know how *epically* that would put our little office on the map?"

Not waiting for an answer, Miss Fearing pivoted away from the large paper ocean and snuffed out her cigarette. "This stack on my desk contains hundreds of new intercepts gleaned everywhere from coastal listening stations to some anonymous Joe's ham radio. The intercepts could be any code species. See what you can find. Don't discount anything. Divide up the intercepts. Ponder, orient the new girl. I'm off to conduct an interview at The Castle, a young lady I'm trying hard to recruit. I'm hoping they can spare her for part of each week. If you find anything that looks urgent, call this number"—she passed the slip of paper to Cora-Lynn—"they'll patch it over to me. Take your usual lunch. You need strength. I'll be back before day's end. Questions?"

Hester shook her head. Cora-Lynn had already leapt to her feet, dividing the stack of intercepts.

"Hunt down that *Barracuda*," Miss Fearing said. "Get its coordinates out there in the briny deep before it gets *us*. I'll add *four dollars* to the pay of whoever finds something first."

Then she scooted away, officious in her oxford shoes.

Hearing the bounty, a look crossed Cora-Lynn's face that suggested the money was as good as hers.

Four dollars would go far towards Birdie's new eyeglasses. Gem silently cursed her own ignorance. The handicap of starting this job after her two co-workers. A thick wad of paper thudded onto her desk. The only other objects on its surface were several pencils, a sharpener and a pad of stenography paper.

A moment later, a deafening din nearly startled Gem out of her chair.

Seeing Gem's sudden jolt, Hester said, "That's Beatrice Fearing's Norton motorcycle."

"Like the witch roaring off on her broom," added Cora-Lynn.

"Don't you like Miss Fearing?" Gem asked.

"I like her well enough," Cora-Lynn replied. "As well as one *can* like one's teacher. But we've only been here a short while and she's already busting our chops. Being trained in England gives her a high-and-mighty complex. She's ambitious, if you haven't gathered that by now, and she resents being stationed here in our tadpole-puddle colony. So, she's out to prove herself. She lives on air and tobacco and doesn't sleep except maybe a few winks over there on the cot. It'd be better if she stayed upstairs in her fancy office, but she's often down here, breathing smoke down our necks."

Hester popped a stick of chewing gum into her mouth. "Let's get to work."

"Right. Suppose I'd better teach you some fundamentals, new girl," Cora-Lynn groused, adding, "Guess *I* won't be catching Captain Barracuda today," as she moved her own chair over beside Gemma's. "Because I have to train you, it throws a wrench in my four-dollar bonus."

"Don't be mean, Cora," Hester urged, sharpening her pencil. "And she has a name—Gemma."

"I usually go by Gem," she said, weakly. Casting her eyes on the top sheet of paper, Gemma decided to initiate her training. "What is all this?" she asked Cora-Lynn.

The Wonder snatched the top sheet and studied it. "Someone at a listening station picked up radio signals in Morse code, then translated it into this text. Looks like a monoalphabetic substitution cipher," she said. "So, it's not Enigma, which uses a polyalphabetic one. Which means this message is likely low-level importance. Bush league. But Lady F told us to not overlook anything. So, a decent starting point. Don't worry about rotors, keys, spindles or compression bars for now. I'll start you off easy. See if you can find letters that are repeated—Gemma."

"Here's *M*," Gem chirped. "And here again, and again."

"First fundamental," Cora-Lynn said. "A letter will never be encoded as itself. So, *M*, I'm guessing, is *E*, the most common letter in the German language, followed by other frequent ones, *N*, *I*, *S* and *R*, *A* and *T*. Once you've mapped these, you can begin to guess the words. But there are also nulls, or duds—symbols the enemy uses to throw us off, or sometimes to signify a space between words. If you've half a brain, you'll begin to see patterns and recognize words. For example, *wetter*. Weather. Sometimes, even if you don't know German, you can guess. Whatever stands for *E* will occupy slots two and five of six. You'll begin to get a feel for words used often, they're called cribs, commonly used words and phrases. Pick away at this— it's called frequency analysis—and see what you can do. There's an English-German dictionary on Miss Fearing's desk, for our use. I'm going back to my own desk now, to rack up my four-dollar bonus."

Bouncing her ginger ponytail over to her work spot, Cora-Lynn settled there and lit a cigarette that puffed out a cloying, minty smell.

Hester sighed, audible, dramatic. "Cora, is it only about the *money* for you, rather than the higher moral cause—saving the world? And really, must you smoke? Lady F's noxious blasts are hellish enough."

More cloying mint odour.

"These mentholated cigarettes, Kools, are less harsh and they're for ladies. Besides, they help me concentrate," Cora-Lynn barbed back.

As a gesture of compromise, Gem supposed, the Wonder expelled her minty clouds in the opposite direction. Through the haze, Gem noted, for the first time, the intricate print of Cora-Lynn's dress—very pretty. Tiny bluebirds.

Gem spotted more repeated letters. Such long words. The first word alone appeared to contain ten letters—unless one or more was a null, a trick. Not many of Aunt Wren's crossword clues had ten letters. The second word—eight letters. It was hard to determine the location of spaces. One mercy, Gem thought, was that so far she was dealing with words, not numbers, albeit foreign words.

The minutes heaved onward.

"Got anything, Hobbs?" Cora-Lynn called across to the desk with the Irish cross over it.

Hester leaned back in her chair, stretching her shoulders, which had been hunched. "First thought I had a bifid cipher, fractionated stacks. But how could I be so thick? Now I think it's a grille, I'm looking at it as quadrants. Fleissner grille?"

"Unlikely," Cora-Lynn replied. "That's very last war. Used in the field. In any case, they abandoned it."

"And you?" Hester lobbed over to Cora-Lynn's desk.

"Menthol didn't help," the Wonder griped. "I might as well be back in the nineteenth century, staring for the first time at Babbage's Difference Engine."

Ada Lovelace looked down from the wall; her eyes had changed, Gemma could have sworn, animated to a disdainful glare. A tightening seized Gem's temples, foretelling a headache. The tiny bluebirds on Cora-Lynn's dress blurred to blobby dots. Perhaps it would help to turn her mind elsewhere. Gem laid down her pencil. "What did Miss Fearing mean when she told us she's off to The Castle?" She directed her question so either co-worker might run with it.

Cora-Lynn issued forth a groaning noise like some sour baritone horn, not ladylike at all. Annoyed at being interrupted, Gem supposed.

Hester sneezed. Plucked a handkerchief from her purse. "Hay fever."

The Wonder eyeballed the clock on the wall, above the Atlantic Ocean. "We've done our best all morning." She shrugged. "Only five minutes until noon. Let's knock off early." She rose, smoothed the blurry bluebirds on her dress and retrieved her purse from the desk's drawer.

"We eat lunch down by the lake," Hester said. "Gets us out of this stuffy cave. You should come, Gemma—Gem."

Cora-Lynn added, "Join us, and I'll tell you what I know about The Castle."

Gem rose from her chair, gratefully, and took her straw satchel, her lunch wrapped inside it. Lunching by the lake would mean venturing near water, but she was desperate for fresh air, light, sun. So she followed her co-workers out into the brilliant high noon, traversing the scruffy grass, smooth stones, ruined garden with its few last struggling perennial stalks, and sand. Cora-Lynn and Hester had already stationed themselves on the mammoth log, weathered and smooth. Hester took her spectacles off and rubbed her eyes. Cora-Lynn donned sunglasses and perched prettily on the log. She looked like a star from Hollywood.

Feeling suddenly shy, very much the new girl, Gem seated herself a couple of feet away, as if to signal a respectful distance. She unwrapped her canned meat sandwich from its waxed paper, wishing the basement office had a refrigerator instead of a hot plate; her sandwich smelled overripe, like some doomed picnic. But it's all she had to eat.

Hester crunched on a dill pickle.

Cora-Lynn drank from a thermos, turning her face to the sun

between swallows. Gem noticed for the first time the pretty red sandals she wore.

Lake gulls wheeled in closer to the silver beach log where the girls lunched.

So welcome was sunshine, light, air, it was enough. For the time being, no words felt needed. Besides the gulls, summer's sounds punctuated noon: the lake's rhythmic slosh, which that day was gentle, so it didn't alarm Gem too much. Notating repeated letters all morning had sharpened all Gem's senses; she heard summer as if for the first time. Cicadas. Distant caterwauls of children tossing a ball farther down the narrow strand of sand that fringed the lake, swishes of balmy breeze, somewhere a radio. And, closer, the unmistakable rumble and bell of the streetcar along Lake Shore Road. She detected, too, the sweet scent of phlox, clove-spice perfume of dianthus from other houses along the lake's shore with better-maintained gardens than the one behind their workplace.

Gem noticed that Cora-Lynn hadn't eaten anything. "Don't you have lunch?" she asked.

The Wonder shrugged. "Don't need it. I've got this instead." She brandished a small pill from her dress's pocket. "This keeps me sharp. This and my brain tea, a mix of ginger, turmeric, lemon. And menthols. Food bogs me down."

No wonder Cora-Lynn maintained such a trim waist, Gem thought.

Hester chomped a muffin.

Gem polished off her sandwich in no time, then bit into a hard-boiled egg.

"You asked about The Castle," Cora-Lynn said.

Gem recalled the secrecy code she'd signed. "Are we . . . allowed to talk out here?"

"Look around you," Cora-Lynn urged. "See how far apart these 'cottages' are?" She made little quotation marks with her fingers with their coral-painted nails around the word *cottages*. "And tall fences or lush thickets between them. No one can see us, and if we keep our voices down, no one will hear us—those chainsawing insects blot out our voices, too."

"Cicadas," Hester said.

"Sure," Cora-Lynn agreed. "Lady F tells me things no one else here is party to—she trusts me because I was her student at the University of Toronto, in the city." She waved in an easterly direction.

"There's no logical equation there," Hester countered. "Between student and trust."

A dragonfly blew in from nowhere, swooping near Cora-Lynn. She batted it away and ignored Hester's remark.

"Are you likely to stick around, Gemma Sullivan?" Cora-Lynn probed. "This job, I mean."

Gem kept her voice low. "I've got to try my hardest. Aunt Wren and I haven't paid our July rent yet—any money I earn keeps our home. And she needs new eyeglasses—badly."

Hester sent a kind, pitying look in Gem's direction. "I'm saving up for my own apartment," she said. "Living with my parents and brother drives me to distraction."

Cora-Lynn's eyes stayed shuttered behind the sunglasses, so nothing could be read there. But her voice registered a solemn note. "And I'm out to impress Miss Fearing so she'll recommend me for graduate studies in mathematics." Then the Wonder looped back to an earlier topic. "About Fearing riding off to The Castle—it's Casa Loma. Such splendour, with its ballroom. But in its bowels are tunnels—and now I'm letting *you* in on this, Gem, so you'd better not betray my trust or cross me—where they're making"—she muted her voice still more, and near whispered—"equipment for Allied *spying*."

Gem gasped, surprised, then wondered if this was guff, if

Cora-Lynn was having a little fun at her expense. Haze the new girl. She remembered to keep her voice low. "Are you sure?"

"It's true," Hester said. "I *was* let in on this. Miss Fearing works with Station M, which is Casa Loma's operation. A few days ago, Cora-Lynn and I devised a code that screen printers there placed on a scarf. We named it *The Mimicode* after this town, Mimico. We were proud of it, and Lady F was pleased—actually *praised* us. But mostly, Gem, be fearing Fearing. She's fierce, a formidable genius."

"Do either of you know when my probation ends?" Gem tried to toss this question out casually, as if chucking a breadcrust to a gull.

Cora-Lynn removed her sunglasses and shrugged. "It ends when Lady F *says* it ends."

Hester glanced at her wristwatch. "We'd better head back to Grindstone Cottage, it's almost one o'clock. Usually, Fearing's bell beckons us back."

How had an hour flown? Gem reached into her straw satchel, brought out her lipstick and dashed some on her lips.

Cora-Lynn gawked at her quizzically, with a touch of scorn. "Why wear lipstick, new girl, when nobody ever sees us?"

"Lipstick helps me think," Gem said, as the three of them returned to their desks in the airless cavern. "And makes me feel grown-up."

Gem had no idea why she'd blurted the lipstick assertion, nor any idea if it was even true. She'd begun to feel not like herself, odd words babbling from her mouth.

THEY SLOGGED THROUGH the afternoon, pausing at intervals to compare notes. On one such brief, unofficial break, Cora-Lynn thwacked her pencil down on her desk, exasperated. "I've tried quadratics and co-primes, but I can't get anywhere. Same goes for additives. Cycles. Loops. But I can't piece anything together. Hobbs?"

The room's swamp-like humidity kept making Hester's glasses slide down her nose, and hearing this question, she shoved her spectacles back in place. "They might as well be waving flags at night for all the sense I can make of any of this. All I've gotten so far is what looks like a woman's name, maybe someone's girlfriend. Heidi."

"Or Heidi is code for a military operative. Or the whole book, *Heidi*, the children's classic, you know, is an encryption of some kind. Keep working on this."

Hester groaned.

Cora-Lynn turned towards Gemma. "And how's your frequency analysis?"

Gem straightened to attention. "I've found most of two words I think may form a phrase," she replied cautiously. "One part of a word seems like English. Chicken, maybe? I've got everything except two letters I can't figure out."

"Let me have a look." Cora-Lynn rolled her chair over to Gem's desk. "German has some odd letters. Maybe you've hit an eszett or umlaut. And their syntax is different. I've dabbled in the language as a hobby."

Of course you have, thought Gem.

The Wonder lived up to her moniker; it didn't take her long to complete the phrase Gem had grappled with.

"*Leberpaste schicken!*" Cora-Lynn brayed. "*Eureka!* You were only missing the *c* and *k*. Means 'send liver paste'—a nutrition staple on U-boats, especially long-haul patrols like Krause's. This message could have been issued right from the *Barracuda*'s bowels. If we can find coordinates, dates, we might really have something."

Just then Miss Fearing, still wearing her motorcycle helmet, gusted into the office. She removed the helmet and sank down at her desk—not a defeated sinking, rather as someone satisfied, though windblown after a long ride. She lit a Pall Mall and gazed around the room. "My recruiting mission was a success—the brilliant Ada

Swift will soon join us as many days a week as they can spare her. I'm sure she'll make an impact here. Now, what progress have you girls made on those intercepts? Any closer to clues that will cook the *Barracuda*'s goose once and for all?"

"Yes!" Cora-Lynn vaunted. "Just before you arrived, I uncovered a message quite possibly from a U-boat, maybe even *the* U-boat: *send liver paste*."

Hester chimed in. "But to be fair, *Gemma* had already unlocked the thing except for two letters. Quite good for her first day, I'd say."

"Yes, I—" Gem began.

But Miss Fearing heard none of this. She rose, came close to jumping up and down in excitement. Rocked back and forth on her oxfords' heels and clapped her hands. "*Top effort*, Ponder! I haven't forgotten the four-dollar bonus. In fact, why don't I award you right here and now?"

Again, Hester interjected. "But oughtn't it at least be split evenly between Gem and Cora-Lynn?"

Gem started to say something, but Cora-Lynn coughed loudly. Several seconds later, Miss Fearing pressed the rolled bills into the Wonder's open palm.

Miss Fearing floated on cloud nine. She applauded again. "All right! I'm going to chase this, telegraph it to Ottawa and dig deeper for any coordinates, dates, to narrow it down. It's quitting time for you girls, though, so *fly away, paper birds*!"

A most peculiar dismissal, thought Gem.

Cora-Lynn had gathered her things and dashed out in no time. Hester took a minute longer, but soon she, too, took her leave.

A sudden fatigue swept through Gem's bones, causing her to move slowly. As she was about to leave the office, Miss Fearing called over to her: "You made it through your first day, Miss Sullivan—kudos to you!"

Gemma thanked her boss. A minute or two later, as she headed north on Church Street, towards the flat on Pidgeon Avenue, with each weary step her conviction grew that those kudos would have meant more in the tangible form of four dollars. Or even two. That sum, as a promissory gesture, would have reassured Mrs. Deluca that the remaining rent would soon be paid. So much for "co-operative spirit" at The Cottage.

The tarot card Aunt Wren had drawn earlier that day faced Gem on the kitchen table. She looked at the card with its figure in red boots. "What is it? *Who* is it?" she asked her aunt.

"Seven of Swords," Birdie said. "It's a thief."

Cora-Lynn Ponder had worn red sandals that day.

FOUR

GEMMA SOON DISCOVERED that the daily walks to and from her lakeside job opened a precious dream-space; while her feet moved, her mind ranged, free to chase whatever notion or whim or worry or memory surfaced there. Until her aunt's recent reminder, Gem hadn't thought about the little notes she'd printed in her childish hand, to the birds. This was when they still lived in the Ward. Downtown Toronto. Back when Aunt Wren worked at Munro's Millinery. The lone tree behind their rented rooms was a hickory loved by chickadees. Gem also left notes in a nearby park when her aunt took her there. Once, Aunt Wren had asked, gently, what Gem's *avian dispatches*, as she called them, contained. "Always the same message," Gem had replied. "I beg the birds to ask their water-bird-relations to urge the lake bosses or gods or whatever they are to please return my parents from the watery depths." These words had turned Aunt Wren's eyes to water, and Gem felt so rotten for making her sad, she abandoned the notes.

SOON ENOUGH GEMMA discovered what Miss Fearing meant about cryptography's potential to cause disorders of the mind. By noon of each day, Gem's temples throbbed from staring at the strings of garbled alphabet. Meaningless numbers. She kept forgetting to bring some of Aunt Wren's Aspirin with her to work. The previous night, she'd checked employment ads at the soup company, also Tire and Rubber. Her hunch that The Cottage paid higher wages had been correct.

Miss Fearing posted her daily heralds on the basement's blackboard. Fresh-chalked words filled the large slate: LIVES DEPEND ON OUR SHARP MINDS—FIND THE BARRACUDA! Another new addition to the office Gem noted was a mousetrap placed below one of the small shuttered windows. The rest of the subterranean room seemed untouched, the cot with its rumpled sheets still in the corner.

The office had become noisier, though. Quite the racket. Hester Hobbs was tasked with answering the phone's shrill, frequent summons while Miss Fearing took over Gemma's training. Gem soon learned that the *rat-tatting* machine that chucked paper from its maw was a teleprinter. Then there were the knocks at the door when Luther, the messenger, delivered documents apparently too sensitive to risk sending by telegraph. Across the room, the Wonder wore earplugs, and Gem could see why.

As a teacher, Miss Fearing was intense, relentless. Gem felt sure her boss didn't mean to be this severe, it was just that knowledge tumbled out of her in a torrent she seemed not to know how to dispense in smaller sprinkles or droplets. And Gem, trying not to choke on cigarette smoke, struggled to absorb the onslaught of information. Miss Fearing had ferried her cup of coffee over to Gem's desk, saying they'd "start simple. Take small steps, like Marconi did, then proceed bit by bit." Context, the boss called it, pivoting back in time to the Greeks. Romans. Medieval monks discovering codes in the Old Testament. After a few minutes, Miss Fearing stubbed out her cigarette and reflected on her approach. "I'm going too quickly. I'm sorry. In England, so much was crammed into a few weeks at the Government Code and Cypher School—before Bletchley. *Elementary Wireless, Introductory Morse, Fundamentals of Cryptography, Listening Station Basics,* lectures on U-boat tracking. I shouldn't inundate you. Those were such heady days." Her eyes glassed over.

"And such grand times we had, boarding at Woburn Abbey, despite those cold, draughty rooms, despite eight of us crammed, in bunk beds, bats swooping over our heads."

Gem cringed at the image of swooping bats, then said, "Maybe I'm not bright enough for this."

"Nonsense," the boss countered. "Absorb this above all else, Miss Sullivan: The enemy is human, like us. They can become complacent, downright lazy. *The enemy will make mistakes*—those slippages are our entry point, our way in." She downed her remaining coffee. Then said, "Let's try something different." She drew a diagram. Numbers 1 to 5 along the top, down the side, alphabet letters in rows. Quite tidy. "This is a Polybius square." She explained how it worked. Then asked Gem to decode the following:

44 23 15 23 34 35 51 24 33 15 43 11 42 15 42 34 12 45 43 44
44 23 24 43 43 45 32 32 15 42

Gem stumbled along with her pencil. Some numbers appeared more than once. The most popular 15, 43. Others only once. Unpopular 51. This helped her guess. Thinking out loud, in murmurs, also aided. "I might have it," she said. "*The hop vines are robust this summer.*"

"Correct, Miss Sullivan."

The Wonder had popped out her earplugs and tongue-clucked across the office, carping, "If only what we're doing was *that simple*. Polybius is for babies—and dead Greeks."

Ignoring this, Miss Fearing carried on with the lesson. *Kriegsmarine. Wolf Packs. Milk Cows. Beetling. Rodding. Stecker pairings. Key blocks. Substitutions. Transpositions. Rod positions.* The concept of redundancy. Frequency tables. Which letters recurred most often in German, in English. Cora-Lynn had already relayed some of this, but it bore repeating, Gem supposed. Cribs for officer titles, salutations, weather. Statistical norms were gold. How so much rested on the letter *e* with its wheel and tray.

Gemma glanced across the office at the Wonder, whose pencil flashed forward like lightning. Her feet clad in those red sandals. Ears plugged again.

Hester Hobbs was speaking on the telephone, writing notes.

"Do you know," Miss Fearing asked Gemma, "what codebreaking is, at its essence?"

"A game? Like a puzzle?" Gem ventured.

"Worse," answered the boss. "It's eavesdropping, a trespass, smashing through a wall. Discovering a crack through which to peek. Reading someone's mail. It can make you feel a bit tarnished. Or it can be . . . intoxicating. The thrill of the transgressive. Either way, right now it's for the greater good."

The boss paused the lesson long enough to light another cigarette, then launched into "some linguistic theory. Basic philosophy. You will be one of two types here, drawn to noumena or phenomena."

Gem had no idea what she meant.

"I'd pegged you as starry-brained, and you may *yet* be, but you're also the concrete type, Miss Sullivan. What tipped me off was how ably you seized upon frequency, pattern. Materiality. You prefer solidity."

This was true. Also, why water daunted her—as if it devouring her parents wasn't enough, it wasn't solid unless frozen to ice.

"Or you're a hybrid," Miss Fearing said, "supple, able to slide from one realm to another. That works well here. But mostly you're a word girl, so I'll keep you on frequency analysis, what you've been doing thus far. But first, more basics." The boss showed Gem a simple monoalphabetic substitution cipher. "Really a child's game, and of course the enemy would never use anything so obvious. For high-level stuff they use polyalphabetic ciphers with constantly changing settings." Then Miss Fearing explained more elements of encryption: columns, grille ciphers, square ciphers, transposition ciphers, periodic systems, grids, wheels, loops. The stacking method, how some cryptanalysts laid codes on transparent paper, on top of each other, to get a feel for depth; it was like peering into the ocean, depth upon depth, seeing if certain fish recur at various levels, their boss explained.

Gem hoped never to peer into the ocean. For that's where the sharks lurked, and the U-boats. There was death in the depths.

Then Miss Fearing wrote what she called a simple cryptogram, and said, "Try solving this, Miss Sullivan."

So much for the Polybius square success. Gemma struggled. She failed and began to cry.

Miss Fearing stiffened. "Here at The Cottage, we *don't cry*." She urged Gem to keep trying, to show some grit.

Gem snuffled into a handkerchief, strove to compose herself. By morning's end her head felt about to split open.

Then, mercy at last—noon hour.

"Fly away, paper birds!" Miss Fearing told them. "Lunch break—get some fresh air."

There was a rasping of chairs against the floor as Hester and Cora-Lynn rose, stretched their arms and rolled their shoulders as if it was morning and they'd just risen from bed.

Hester laid her glasses on the desk and picked up her lunch box. "Coming, Gem?"

Cora-Lynn had already bolted.

All Gem wanted to do was run away.

"Not today," she told Hester. "I need to clear my head. I'm going for a walk."

Gemma took her satchel with her lunch. She might be lousy at cryptograms, but she could eat and walk at the same time. Shame coursed through her as she soft-shoed, in her sneakers, past Miss Fearing. The morning had gone so rockily she couldn't make eye contact with her boss, who seemed to read Gem's mind, saying, through the smoke, "It gets easier, Miss Sullivan."

Not seeing how this could be possible, Gemma left the office, emerging into daylight so ablaze she squinted, like some vole who'd lived underground too long. She didn't know where she'd go, didn't care, really, anywhere away from The Cottage, the lake, the ever-so-smart Cora-Lynn, who made Gem feel small and deeply inept.

She crossed Lake Shore Road, chomping a carrot. Eat. Plod. Breathe. Such relief. She gobbled one of her sandwiches. Scarfed down great gulps while she walked. Every step, each bite, took her farther from the lake. She picked her way across railway tracks, reached a forlorn field, factories nearby. A weedy field rife with ragweed, creeping charlie. But also patches of baked, bare earth. Several worn paths that perhaps animals used, or tramps. The paths reminded Gem of those carved by cows' hooves; her class had taken a school trip to a farm. Some animals, like her, preferred familiar patterns, worn paths. Solid things.

Imagining herself a cow, Gem chose one of the narrow paths and pulled the remaining sandwich from her satchel. Weeds bordered the path. She'd always enjoyed exploring the wild corners of places, much to Aunt Wren's disfavour. "You'll land yourself in a scuffle," Birdie always insisted. "Stick to the main road. Otherwise, it's begging for trouble."

Gem didn't see it that way. For one thing, off-the-beaten-track often brought discoveries. During her Mimico rambles she'd found tiny bird bones, an old apothecary jar, beach glass. She was glad for the second sandwich as well as the Vulcain cricket watch Aunt Wren had given her for her fifteenth birthday. Birdie must have scrimped and saved for ages to buy that watch. Gemma knew she must keep a close eye on it and return to the office on time. She wasn't exactly acing her job; tardiness would push her closer to the doghouse, perhaps get her fired. Gem recalled her co-worker's warning: *be fearing Fearing.*

The day heated suddenly, like a punch from a furnace. Gem's white blouse, her only white blouse she'd washed by hand last night, scrubbing at the underarm sweat stains with baking soda, dampened. She undid the blouse's top two buttons. So grand, breeze against her throat. Then rolled up her sleeves, pressed her way along the path until it thinned, fizzled out into a swath of unkempt ground. Rampant switchgrass, dog-vine, burdocks. In the bare-earth patches, bits of old brick and shards of shale poked through the ground—remnants of earlier industry, Gem supposed. Then blue-star galaxies of chicory blooms. She should remind Aunt Wren that they could make coffee from chicory. Several empty, rusted cans were stranded in the grass, from the soup factory likely. Grasshoppers clacked and chirred in their vertical forest, their legs frantic rotors revolving at high speed, with messages more easily fathomed than the strands of code back in the basement. *Live your grasshopper lives*—clack, clack—*to the fullest*—clack, clack—*summer fades fast.* She heard distant sawing. No, not saws, those insects. Cicadas. A school science lesson came back to her. Courtship, that was their continuous drone. Their code.

Gem dodged around knee-high burdock plants. Foxglove blooms, seeded by the wind, flown from some garden, now lavish among the weeds. She adored their spired bells around which bees bumbled. She might pluck a pretty stem to cheer the basement office; Cora-Lynn's expired peony freed up the Mason jar. A touch of beauty couldn't hurt the decoding effort, could it?

She turned her face to the sky. Breathed. Opened her mouth to bite into her sandwich.

A rustle in the high grasses nearby startled her. She gasped, fearful of snakes, and nearly dropped her sandwich. She backed away, onto a gravelled mound, left, perhaps, from an industrial deposit. The thing swishing through the grass emerged.

It was only a cat.

Gem caught her breath. A harmless cat, amber-marble eyes, coat the shade of smoke except for a furred white tuxedo in front, murky stripes through the hocks. Off-centre white splotch near the nose. The cat navigated the grasses with nimble agility, so it—*she*, Gem decided, given the delicacy of movement—couldn't be so very old.

The cat stopped in front of Gem on the gravel mound. Mewed.

She mewed back, two cheerful syllables. "What're you doing out here, kitty? Lost? Hunting mice?"

The cat must have sniffed Gemma's sandwich. It stood there, ears perked, eyes beseeching. So, because she'd already eaten the first sandwich, Gem supposed she could afford a little generosity. She broke off a bit of crust with some of the potted meat clinging to it and fed it to the feline.

After munching down more offered food, the cat trotted away from Gemma, then scampered back, towards her, marble eyes lit with hope, then away again. Plain as a pikestaff that the cat was beckoning Gem to follow.

So she did.

The large building towards which the cat gambolled with purpose, tail pluming above the grass, loomed closer. It was the old reformatory, but surrounded now with a barbed-wire fence higher than a house. It resembled a giant, gloomy cage.

The smoky cat scurried straight for the barbed-wire fence.

For a hair-flick of time Gemma reasoned it would be best to turn back, not go any closer. It must be some type of prison. Which meant guards. It didn't take a cryptanalyst to guess visitors weren't welcome. The large signs on the fence indicated this: *Danger. Keep Away. No Trespassing.* (How could one trespass even if one wanted to?) But the cat mewled, coaxed in a compelling cat way. It *really* wanted Gem to come along. So Gem moved one sneakered foot in front of the other, against her better judgment.

The cat kept a measured-out space in front, almost as if she used a metal rule.

Then Gem heard a man's plaintive, calling voice:

"Head-Vig! Head-Vig!"

At least that's how it sounded to Gem. She wondered what a *head-vig* was, then, seeing the cat lope faster towards the fence, reasoned it must be the cat's name.

She really should turn back.

She'd reached the tall barbed-wire fence. A young man stood there, behind the fence, wearing a drab grey shirt with a number, *1007933*, on the front pocket and trousers in the same dull tone, with a stripe down each leg. She quickly gathered that he was locked inside that place. He appeared to be in his mid-twenties, or close to it, with hair the colour of a sandbar along Lake Ontario. His open, angular face regarded her with wariness and curiosity in equal measure.

The cat slipped easily through an opening at the bottom of the wire fence and the young man scooped her up in his arms. He muttered something to the cat Gemma couldn't decipher, though it struck her ears as a chiding endearment. His hand stroked the cat's fur.

"Guten Tag," he told Gemma.

Gem stood staring at him. He stared back at Gem, his face taking on kindness and warmth.

The cat nuzzled against the prisoner's neck, purred.

He hadn't spoken English, but Gem wished to discover if he could. "What is this place?"

The prisoner, still stroking the cat, looked surprised. "You can't tell just by looking, Miss?" So, he spoke English. With no trace of a

German accent. Yet he'd called the cat and hailed her in German. Then, tight-lipped, he pointed in a restrained way, finger barely raised, behind him, and higher, to a little hut with windows jutting above a large building. Gem saw, too, many other smaller buildings scattered around, all inside the soaring barbed wire. A cacophony of sounds from the large building—piano music, radios blaring, men huffing loudly in hard syllables.

So, all those men, including this open-faced young man with the cat at the fence, were locked within this compound. No doubt this was the prisoner-of-war camp she'd read about in the news. Later, Gem would wonder at her own naivety, and why she didn't instantly turn on her rubber heels and run. Because surely the man high in the hut was an armed guard. Had he seen her, straw satchel hooked over her arm, sandwich in hand, approach the fence?

The young man must have noticed the fear in her eyes. Because he said, again in fluent English, "It's all right, Miss. You can talk to me for a minute. Me and my cat." He smiled.

"But what about up there?" With a restrained gesture towards the hut perched high like an eagle's nest, she told the prisoner, "If a guard sees us, will he shoot me?"

"He's a guard, all right, old-timer from the last war. Don't bother about him—his hearing's not so good. And he's not paying attention. He listens to *The Happy Gang* cranked to full volume every lunch hour with his feet up on the ledge and his back to where I stand now. Some afternoons, especially warm ones like today, he falls asleep with the radio blaring. The codger in the guard hut is the least of my worries. It's the *other* prisoners." The young man moved as close as he could to the barbed wire, to Gem, without it piercing his nose, which was, she thought, nicer even than Ponder the Wonder's pert proboscis.

"They call this place Camp M," said the prisoner.

While Gem took his word for it, about the guard—for surely the prisoner knew the daily rhythms of his confined world—her nerves stayed knotted and she kept her voice low.

"What's the cat's name?" she asked. "Sounded like a funny word."

The prisoner ruffled his pet's fur. "Hedwig. I'd been standing at the fence, calling her. Sometimes she wanders off. Unlike us, she's free." Then he near whispered, through the wire: "I'm not supposed to be here."

Gem's mind spun and wheeled. What did he mean? She stared at the young man.

"What I'm saying is"—his voice riddled with anguish—"I'm no Nazi."

Just then the certainty that she'd never done anything this intriguing—no, *exciting*—walloped Gem's rib cage. She longed to learn more. About him. *Why* wasn't he supposed to be there? Why could he switch so easily between two languages? But, *blazes*, the hands on her watch accosted her eyes. "I have to go."

Thankfully, she wore running shoes; she'd need to sprint fast to make it back to The Cottage on time. As she turned to leave, he said, "*Wait*—who are you, Miss? And what do you do? Still in school?"

"Done school," replied Gem. Then, the secretive nature of her work smacking her conscience, she added, "I'm just a girl in an office."

Gemma, you nitwit. Why "office"? Why not diner, cannery, tannery? Long Branch Racetrack? Anaconda Brass? Anywhere but "office." And you're still standing at the fence.

She noted the young man's slender build beneath his prisoner uniform. Maybe he needed the rest of her sandwich more than she did. She held it out to him, about to squeeze it through the spaces between the wire.

"It's all right," he said. "They feed us. In fact, some say, gossip finds us—we're fed better than many civilians who live on rations, and people resent us for that. And they haven't shackled us, like they did at another Ontario camp. But"—his striking cheekbones shadowed—"try living on one shared bar of soap that must last a whole *monat*—sorry, *month*. Sometimes German words escape from my mouth. They're all I hear all day."

His soap disclosure tugged at Gem's heart. But her wristwatch ruled. She'd need wings on her sneakers now. She shoved the sandwich through the wire anyway. "Feed it to your cat, then. Hedwig clearly likes canned meat, it's probably why she ran to me so eagerly."

"Hedwig likes girls," the prisoner said. "Especially pretty ones with potted meat. She's tired of living with us louts."

Gemma felt herself blush. She'd never thought herself pretty, with that mole parked near her upper lip. Aunt Wren called it a beauty mark, likely to make Gem feel better about the blemish.

More heat reached Gem's cheeks. She turned and ran. She hadn't even properly said goodbye. A police officer strode past her on the street, nodded a greeting. Would a girl running like a mad thing arouse suspicion? Gem hoped not.

When she careened, breathless, into the office several minutes late, Cora-Lynn and Hester were drudging at their desks. Facing the wall. They didn't turn to look at Gem. But Miss Fearing, looming over the teleprinter machine, shot Gemma critical eyes, saying: "Afternoon work starts at one o'clock, Miss Sullivan. Bear in mind, too, that you're still on probation."

Gem muttered sorry. Sank down at her desk. Her marathon through the scraggly industrial wastes, then along Lake Shore Road, then back down into the fox-burrow office, had overheated her. She forced her mind back to the task at hand, scribbling a few repeated letters (promising!), but her body couldn't cool down. Between the strings of letters, the prisoner's face emerged. How, Gem wondered, could someone with such kind eyes be dangerous? A monster, even, for she recalled notices in newspapers and magazines about the Nazi menace, how the German soldiers were murderous machines. And pictures often showing German soldiers with devil horns sprouting above their helmets. The young man behind the wire fence had said he wasn't a Nazi, and he certainly didn't look like a fiend. His face struck Gem as an open book, and he didn't seem like someone capable of lying *or* murderous acts. She didn't know why such a brief encounter convinced her of this, but it had. And no cat would burble, contented, and cling to a monster like that, even one with food. Cats knew. Cats were smart.

The thrill of talking to the prisoner at the fence thrummed through Gem's mind all afternoon, and didn't once quell.

Knuckles drubbed the office door, officious, dream-snuffing raps.

Miss Fearing opened the door. "Ah, hallelujah, fans at last, girls!" Unpacking the cartons, she explained that she'd filed a request to Ottawa for the fans. "They should bring some relief," she added.

But despite the whirling air the fans eddied around the office, Gem couldn't cool down.

Sadly, the new fans didn't improve Miss Fearing's mood. She was testy through the afternoon, prickly, staying in the lower office with them, bollocking away at her typewriter. It was like being trapped inside a box with a giant wasp.

Gem couldn't focus. Her thoughts kept circling back to the prisoner behind the barbed wire, his cat, and how odious—not to mention unhygienic—it must be, sharing a bar of soap with other prisoners.

Right then she decided to help his soap problem.

The pins had loosened from Miss Fearing's hair, which now resembled a damp mop. At the end of the day, before her habitual dismissal—*Fly away, paper birds!*—she made a speech, drilling her intense eyes into Cora-Lynn, Hester and Gem.

"Another day passes, and still the *Barracuda* ranges freely about the sea—just a matter of time before it attacks our supply ships. I had a telegram from the highest intelligence official in Ottawa: *Any progress at The Cottage, ladies?* He meant pinpointing Krause's U-boat, of course. Other than the directive to send liver paste"—the boss shot a grateful glance in Cora-Lynn's direction—"I had to inform him no."

A sludgy air of despair overtook Miss Fearing. Hester looked shaken. Even the Wonder seemed defeated—a first during Gem's stint at The Cottage. Gem vowed, silently, to do better.

"Thank the stars Ada Swift starts tomorrow. I hope she'll be our saviour, shake us out of this . . . impasse." Then for several more minutes their boss extolled the marvels of this latest hire, calling her "an utter original, a siren of intellect, a regular Mata Hari, our own Hypatia, a regular Hedy Lamarr."

Gem didn't know who any of these people were, except the glamorous actress from a movie magazine.

Then Miss Fearing beamed her eyes over to Ada Lovelace on the wall, and murmured something indecipherable, eclipsed by the fans' bellowing churns. After this, Miss Fearing advised them, "Get some rest, my paper birds. Come back refreshed."

They lost no time in skedaddling out of there, Gem, Hester and Cora-Lynn.

As she hurried along, homebound, Gemma struggled to sift through the events of the day. Cat. Prisoner.

She hadn't even learned his name.

FIVE

AUNT WREN'S SPIRITS were exuberant that night. It was as if her stooped shoulders wore wings. While having her morning oatmeal, she'd drawn the Wheel of Fortune tarot card; the luck that card foretold had been borne out. She'd polished off her crossword in record time, but that was only the start of the day's fine karma, she chirped to Gem while they supped on potato fritters dolloped with applesauce. She'd been able to finish more mending than usual, no headache for a change. She'd found an eye doctor who'd accept payment in instalments, Lyle Fox. He'd placed an ad in the *Lake Shore Dispatch* to this effect. She'd phoned to make an appointment and, just so there was no misunderstanding, explained that her first instalment would have to be paid after Gemma's payday. That was fine, he'd said. After that, Birdie sat right down at the kitchen table and drafted a budget.

What a chatterbox Aunt Wren was that night, and how opposite their poles. In contrast to her, lively and pragmatic, Gem floated, distracted, in a dream world. But it *did* gladden her that her aunt might finally find some relief from her vision woes. While still in high school, Gemma had done her best to help when Birdie was first stricken with her terrible headaches. They stemmed from vision problems, the doctors thought. Often Gem had stayed home from school to take care of her aunt, who, at that time, couldn't mend clothes, or do crosswords, could hardly raise herself from the chesterfield.

Between bringing Birdie cold compresses and soup, Gem had rushed off to the nearby Carnegie Library to see what she could learn. Hours slurped by as she read an encyclopedia. *Oculus*: "eye" in Latin. Early ophthalmologists were called oculists. Her own young eyes absorbed the keratoscope, the slit lamp, the Hirschberg test. She read about Toronto's Dr. Abner Rosebrugh. But he couldn't help Aunt Wren; he'd been dead for over thirty years. And although his legacy no doubt carried on, her aunt wouldn't have been able to afford the treatment; and now, with the war, the hospital at Sunnybrook was for soldiers, even if Birdie *could* afford it once Gem received regular paycheques.

Aunt Wren was serving rice pudding. "Where are you, niece of mine?"

Gem smiled. "I'm here. And I'm thankful your eyes, hopefully, will be in better shape soon."

"New spectacles would bring a new world," Aunt Wren mused between spoons of rice pudding. "I'm tired of seeing this world through a glass spiderweb."

Her aunt meant the badly cracked lens, Gem supposed. She mustered the wherewithal to wash the supper dishes. Soap bubbles. They reminded Gem that she wanted to bring the prisoner some soap tomorrow.

Just when she was about to excuse herself, to go to bed early, Birdie said, "And now, another surprise on this lucky day—I've hit on a solution to lighten my loneliness, since you've started your job, and to bring in extra income. It's a revelation, really, don't know why I didn't think of it sooner. We'll take in a lodger, a girl. She'll keep me company."

The dishtowel still in her hand, Gem leaned against the sink, gawked in bewilderment and waited for her aunt to elaborate, which she did. Aunt Wren had been in Preston's Meat Market with its poster-filled walls—luckily for Birdie, in large fonts—things like *Don't Hoard; Don't Blame the Butcher; We Have the Right to Limit Quantities of Merchandise; Lakeshore Horseshoe Pitching League;*

Recruits Needed for Reserve Army. Then, in an even larger font, red: *Accommodations Needed for Working Girls—Wartime Industries.* Wren had written down the phone number. While Gem still stood, agog with her dishtowel, her aunt, animated, laid out the plan. She'd shift around her sewing room and rent it. "I mostly work in the living room, because there's better light; the sewing room is more of a catch-all than anything."

The lodger's room and board would be a godsend, along with Gem's salary from the office, and the admittedly minimal sums from Wren's own sewing. Putting all this together, they might squeak by with less hand-wringing, less month-to-month worry. And the extra income could go towards the stronger eyeglasses Wren needed. That would speed along her sewing. This wasn't the first time Wren had seen signs posted about lodgings for girls, she told Gem. The newspapers printed stories, too, about girls coming in from all over the province, and beyond, to work in their industrial lakeshore towns. Especially from Ontario's north, Sudbury, Owen Sound, Gravenhurst, North Bay. *A Feminine Infusion*, one article vaunted.

Birdie had already checked with Mrs. Deluca, and their landlady had no objections to the lodger provided she was a good, quiet girl, preferably Catholic. Now all that was needed, for Fortune's wheel to turn, Aunt Wren said, was "a helping hand, niece of mine, to rearrange and clean the sewing room for the new lodger."

Even in her brain-fogged state, Gem detected a few gaps in her aunt's logic. She set the dishtowel aside and sat down at the kitchen table across from Birdie. "I'm all for extra income, but how will the lodger be company for you when, like me, she'll be away at her job?"

Aunt Wren looked downcast, but only for an instant. "Maybe she'll have different shifts. And it'd be hard to think she'd work as late as you do, Gem."

Gemma almost asked, what if the girl isn't the sociable type?

But she held back. She hadn't seen her aunt so optimistic in a long time.

"Then let's get started!" Aunt Wren said. "It's not even dark outside yet. Got to love these long summer nights that stretch on and on."

She'd already propelled herself towards the sewing room.

"Long" doesn't begin to capture it, Gem thought. That day felt like three, so much had happened. The fraught, knotted office, shaming from the boss for returning late after lunch, more shaming from the boss for their failure to uncover information on the deadly U-boat. The cat. The open-faced young man locked behind the tall barbed-wire fence.

And Gemma suddenly felt weary to her bones. Where Aunt Wren burst with energy, Gem barely mustered enough strength to lug armloads of fabric yardage, partly stitched clothes, baskets of sewing supplies and hastily stacked magazines out of the sewing room into her aunt's bedroom, where they piled everything into a corner "to sort later." Gemma hadn't been in Birdie's room in ages; she and her aunt had a privacy pact, to not invade the other's domain. Gem had all but forgotten her aunt's zealous anti-plumage campaign, how she'd lobbied against the slaughter of birds for millinery. Gemma had forgotten, too, the single feather on her aunt's nightstand, from her childhood farm in Etobicoke Township. The framed picture on the wall of Martha, the last passenger pigeon, who'd died in a Cincinnati zoo in 1914. The same year Aunt Wren's sweetheart, Adam Hartsock, was killed in the war. Gem glanced at the shrine to Adam on a shelf above the bed: his photograph, Adam in his military uniform; a clutch of dried flowers so fragile a mere breath might blast them to pieces; a second photograph, grainy, of Wren and Adam at Niagara Falls. Yellowed papers, folded beside the brittle petals, that Gem imagined must be letters Adam had sent home. Gem had known about her aunt's lost sweetheart, Adam, since her earliest days. Her aunt often spoke of him. It was a lot to burden a little girl with all that sadness, how her aunt would never again find love, how her heart was sealed tighter than a tomb. But Wren had no one else to tell, so young Gem became the keeper of her aunt's sorrow.

Gemma recalled, too, how her aunt, during that same period, read the lady poet Edna St. Vincent Millay, over and over, sometimes aloud to Gem, who didn't fully grasp the poems but sensed that their darkness, their gloom, fuelled Birdie's sense of being cheated of love. To this day Gem recalled snippets of those poems. They were gloomy, yes, but there was music in those lines, too. She supposed that dusty volume was kicking around the flat somewhere. Her aunt had set aside those poems in favour of crosswords and tarot. At least with tarot one had a fifty-fifty chance of optimism, depending on which card, and whether upright or inverted.

The opposite wall of her aunt's room had a large shelf with hats Wren had designed during her millinery years. Instead of plumage, which meant slaughtered birds, her aunt's hats were adorned with pops of ingenious beauty, like felted pine cones, woven bows, hand-stitched hearts, whimsical posies. One hat occupied a prime spot on the shelf. She hadn't seen it in ages, the exquisite ivory wide-brimmed one, trimmed with satin and velvet, with a frothy veil, clearly meant for a bride. For Wren herself.

So fully absorbed had Gem been on making it to the finish line in high school, then starting work at The Cottage, that she hadn't thought about her aunt's wedding hat in some time. Or the bedroom shrine. External emblems of Birdie's inner scars of grief.

Gem was so overcome with all of it that she dropped her armload of fabric on the bed and hugged her aunt, causing her aunt, too, to dump several bolts of calico, to accept the hug.

Wren let out a nervous chord of laughter. "What's this about?"

Gem released her aunt's shoulders and stepped back. "Oh, just because. And I'm glad your Wheel of Fortune day turned out so well."

Smiling, Birdie said they'd bitten off a sizable chunk of the sewing room preparation; they'd finish the rest tomorrow night.

SIX

To atone for returning late from lunch the previous day, Gem hotfooted it south to The Cottage so she'd arrive early at work. Her goal was to be as many minutes early today as her tardiness yesterday. A sense of balance like that felt important for a girl on probation. Walking briskly, she clutched the bar of soap tucked inside her straw satchel, as if she feared it would jump from its straw container and run away. She was, in equal measure, excited and anxious to bring this gift to the prisoner during her lunch hour, which felt a thousand years away.

Miss Fearing stood at the small sink, froth-mouthed, scrubbing her teeth. She seemed startled by Gem's entry, but soon recovered her composure and gave a friendly enough greeting.

As Gem settled at her desk, she noted the heralds for that day, writ large, on the chalkboard:

Welcome to the exceedingly talented Ada Swift

Find The Barracuda before more of our sailors die

POWs may escape, walk our very streets. ANY fraternizing with the enemy is punishable

Trembling, Gem palmed the soap through her straw satchel. The word *punishable* roiled around in her stomach. But honestly, she didn't see how anyone would escape from the tall barbed-wire fortress not far from where she and the other girls worked.

"Continue with frequency analysis," Miss Fearing told Gem. "Anything you find could save Allies' lives. Even if it's from a few weeks ago, it's still context, and bits of context can add up to knowledge."

Before Gem could mouse back a dutiful reply, Hester and Cora-Lynn arrived, followed by a third girl who stepped into the office trippingly, with confidence. Her wavy, long platinum hair reminded Gemma of Veronica Lake in *I Wanted Wings*. Her skin was flawless. This new girl looked about Gem's age, or slightly older. She wore the prettiest sailor-collared dress, quite fitted. Daisy earrings dangled from her ears. What was this fashion-plate model doing in a basement in Mimico?

Miss Fearing introduced Ada Swift to the office. "Miss Swift brings fresh air and a wide breadth of knowledge. She's a number girl like you, Cora-Lynn, but she also possesses a strong logical bent like you, Hester. And Gemma, you're not the only wordsmith on the block now. Miss Swift is *the whole package*. And she knows German, which should help us a great deal."

"I speak a little Greek, too," Ada added. "*Steganos*. Covered. *Kryptos*. Hidden." Her smile cast a brilliance through their subterranean office.

Gem wondered if the girl wasn't putting on airs—or flat-out showing off.

Miss Fearing went on. "Ada nailed double transpositions and grille blocks in no time flat—during her interview, no less."

No fumbling after snowflakes or reading Hamlet backwards for Miss Swift, Gem thought, twiddling a strand of her hair as if about to plait a glum length of straw for a dunce hat—for herself.

Hester Hobbs's look was pure awe. Clearly impressed, she smiled at Ada in a kind, welcoming way.

Face pulled corset-string tight, Cora-Lynn Ponder lit a menthol cigarette and huffed a hello.

"Miss Swift will work with us whenever Station M, The Castle, can spare her. She'll go back and forth, for she's indispensable there and we're lucky they agreed to share her talents. She won't need much training—she knows scads already. What little coaching she'll require, I'll undertake myself. Learn from her all you can."

Then Miss Fearing directed Ada to the desk beside Gem's— under the portrait of Ada Lovelace, her brilliant namesake.

They hacked away all morning. Hester and Cora-Lynn carried out their frenetic pencil work. Every so often, one or the other of them hailed Miss Fearing: "I think I've struck on something!" Then their boss would clatter over—she wore real shoes that day, not bedroom slippers—to whichever codebreaker summoned her and twitter joyful fingers like a child seeing her first rainbow, and shout, "Bravo—well done, paper bird!" Gem, though, hadn't detected a single pattern in the cipher groups, not one letter in the same slot twice, which in and of itself surely meant something—but what? It was all so arcane, so esoteric. The numbers and letters burned her retinas, and none of it made sense.

Every so often, to boost her spirits, Gem felt the bar of soap through her straw satchel. At least she could do some good for *someone* that day. Gem thought of the Greek word Ada Swift had spoken—*kryptos*. Hidden. However much meeting the prisoner had stirred Gem, however much his plight moved her, she knew she mustn't tell a soul that she'd met him. Must keep him *kryptos*. Telling anyone she'd been at the enemy camp *fraternizing* would mean losing her job and—she thought of the Official Secrets Act—result in punishment. She was pretty sure she'd been fraternizing. Even if the young man behind the barbed wire claimed not to be an enemy, others might not see it that way.

Miss Fearing clanged the bell to signal lunch hour. She loved that bell. She could have just told them, her paper birds, to fly away, get some fresh air. But no. Always these theatrics. Apparently, she wasn't worried about passersby hearing her bells, or people in nearby houses who might wonder what was going on at The Cottage. But the world was full of bells, the Lake Shore streetcar being only one example.

Gem felt the soap bar again, inside her satchel. She couldn't wait to behold the prisoner's face, the way it lit up like a lantern. The day's herald about forbidden fraternizing gnawed at Gem, but the urge to see him again, give him a gift to alleviate his discomfort in that grim place, pulled at her harder.

But the day had other plans. As they left the basement, Hester beckoned Ada to lunch with them by the lake.

"Coming, Gemma?" Cora-Lynn asked.

"Thought I'd take another walk today," she replied. "Get some air."

Ponder the Wonder said, "Oh, you *must* lunch with us, Gem. Don't you want to get to know Ada, our newest paper bird? It'd be very uncivil *not* to! And there's plenty of air down by the lake."

Not wishing to be uncivil, Gem reluctantly joined them. She was so disappointed. The soap gift would have to wait until the next day. She trailed her co-workers through the ruined garden, then onto the sand, to their fallen-tree improvised bench.

It was impossible to dislike Ada Swift. Everything enthralled her—the silver, weathered lunch log so smooth she could stroke it without fear of slivers. The lake, the mottled clouds, how sunlight broke through in long torches (she said). Gulls skirling about. The way you could see, in the distance along the shore, the towers and spires of Toronto's downtown. Hop vines spuming green heaps over a nearby fence. The sand warming Ada Swift's soles brought forth a squeal of delight—she'd kicked off her platform shoes and burrowed her bare feet into the beach. (One advantage to nylon stockings being scarce; no one missed them in summer.)

Even Ponder the Wonder, who must have felt less wondrous since Ada Swift's arrival, was having trouble disliking Ada—Gem could tell by how Cora-Lynn engaged with her, by how Cora-Lynn, too, kicked off her red sandals, copycatting the new arrival's sand footbath.

Then Hester.

Cora-Lynn lit a cigarette and blew smoke out over her sandy feet. "Sounds like you knocked it out of the park at your interview," she told Ada.

A silken laugh. "I guess. Doesn't hurt that I have the same first name as Miss Fearing's idol, Ada Lovelace." Then she bent to retrieve a tiny whorled shell her feet had uncovered. "Why does Miss Fearing call us paper birds?"

"She's very eccentric," shrugged Hester, unwrapping a bagel.

Gem said, "Likely to inject some levity into our work, which is sombre—war, death all around us."

Ponder the Wonder popped her energy pill and dabbed her mouth with a handkerchief. "Oh, it's more than a comic device to lighten the mood—I'll wager it signals our transience, as women, that after this war we'll be whisked back to the margins, ephemeral as last week's coupon flyer in the mail. They tell us how vital our contributions are, but after all this, we'll be nobodies again. History will forget us. We'll just fly away into oblivion."

"That's very depressing, Cora," Hester groused.

"And exactly why I mean to pursue graduate study in mathematics," said the Wonder.

All this was bringing Gem down, as if being trapped there on the log, prevented from giving the soap to the prisoner, didn't make her crestfallen enough. She strove for lighter talk. "How old is this fallen tree we're seated on?"

Cora-Lynn shrugged.

Thankfully, Hester ran with it. "Maybe the big storm almost a century ago—my grandmother used to regale us with that. When the Toronto Islands became islands. They weren't always alone." A swatch of her dark hair fell over her face as she stroked the broad trunk in a thoughtful way. "Yes, our lunchtime bench might be approaching its hundredth anniversary."

Hester had this way of allowing oxygen into a situation. Twenty-four hours isn't so very long, Gem thought, imagining the bar of soap pass through the barbed wire's gap, into the prisoner's grateful hand. Her next opportunity to bring it to him. If anything, he'd be even *more* grateful, after another day of soap-sharing. She gobbled her sandwich then turned and saw, where sand met stony scurf, the graceful arch of a raspberry cane, its berries well on their way to ripening. On a whim she leapt from the log, plucked a single raspberry and took her place again. She studied the berry closely, as if seeing one for the first time. She imagined that each fleshy, intricate orb of the fruit bore a code. The thing was miraculous, really. A raspberry was a miracle. And when the berries were fully ripe, she'd take some to the prisoner.

"A raspberry is a miracle," she told the other girls.

They laughed.

Hester turned to Ada. "Can you tell us what you do at Casa Loma?"

A breeze riffled Ada's sailor collar; she flipped it back in place. She scanned the beach, the pale-blue sky. A child flew a kite far along the lake's shore. "Since I don't think any recording devices are strung down from the clouds or that kid's kite, and since you've all signed the Secrets Act, so long as it doesn't go beyond this ancient, fallen log, I don't mind telling you."

She stalled until she had the other girls, with their bated breaths, spindled around her finger. They shifted along the log to move closer to Ada, whose platinum hair fell over part of her face, as if on cue, adding allure, mystery.

"I'm a little bit magic," she said. Dropping her voice more, she elaborated. "I'm in the espionage business for the Allies."

"You're a *spy*?" Hester shrieked.

Cora-Lynn went *Shhh!*

"I might as *well* be." Ada crossed her long, slender legs. "Spies need equipment. I make, and train others, mostly girls, to put together espionage kits. We sew face wads, to stuff under the upper lip to change a person's face, pouches for powered ash, to grey the hair. We turn pens into knives, biscuit tins into radios, buttons into compasses. We embed explosive devices in menstrual rags, shoulder pads, cigarette packages. Wireless sets inside paint boxes. Detonators inside bars of soap or shaving brushes. Barefoot covers to disguise boots. You wouldn't believe what we can do with driftwood, with gramophones. We're tackling bigger projects, too: Dummy parachutists sewn from cloth—think flying scarecrow. Amphibian breathing apparatus. My specialty is printing: a map on a scarf, a one-time cipher on a necktie, counterfeit passports, forged identity cards, fake luggage stickers, a hotel here, a pensione there, a grand resort, so it looks like the person is a harmless tourist. Codes stamped on bloomers. They don't call it 'theatre' of war for nothing. Our work at The Castle is producing stage props, to a large extent. Costumes. I do a lot with ciphers and codes, which is why, I suppose, Miss Fearing recruited me. I've just finished sewing tiny leg pouches for carrier pigeons. Now I'm working on explosive books. I hollow out copies of the novel *Frankenstein*; anyone opening that tale will be met with a monstrous surprise."

A feather could have knocked Gemma over, she was that dazzled. Hester beheld Ada Swift with a fandom face. Ponder the Wonder looked even more impressed.

Gem suddenly realized that Ada hadn't eaten anything, so inquired about her lunch.

A simple shrug from Ada. "I forgot."

So, even a magician can't cover every single base, Gem thought.

Hester drew some sweets from her skirt pocket. "Here." She

extended the offering to Ada. "Licorice. Take them—my waistline can live without them."

Cora-Lynn teased, "If you don't eat them, you can always plant tiny explosives in them, or poison pills."

Ada laughed. "Good idea. Maybe to use on the stable boy at The Castle. He's been bothering me."

Before she could elaborate, the end-of-lunch bell shrilled across toasty sand from which they reluctantly unburied their bare feet, wiped them and put their shoes back on.

"Back to Grindstone Cottage," Cora-Lynn said with a sigh.

As they trudged through the humid air towards The Cottage's back door, Hester told Ada, "I feel special now, working with someone so . . . *gifted*. I feel less ordinary—*bigger*."

Cora-Lynn tongued a cluck. "That's because you've just eaten lunch, Hobbs."

Hester took the quip with good humour.

Pawing the bar of soap through her satchel, Gemma said nothing. The truth was, even though she admired Ada Swift in spades, Ada made Gem feel extraordinarily ordinary. In fact, if Gem felt any smaller, she'd be able to squeeze through a space in the barbed wire fence and cross over to the prisoner's side.

Through the afternoon, even with the wheezing fans, the office was a sauna.

Miss Fearing lowered the whip down on their heads. She worked in the lower office, again bollocking away at her typewriter, explaining to Ada some codebreaking methods.

The noise impaired Gemma's concentration. Still, she'd done her best with frequency patterns and uncovered a few fragments. *Proceed northwest. Straggler ship.* Miss Fearing called this useful, but lacking context or specifics. Still, Gem's findings could be part of a bigger puzzle, their boss added, so she'd log this and send it on to Ottawa.

Late that day, Ada Swift plopped her pencil on her desk in a lavish, jubilant gesture. She turned to the others. "I've cracked some coordinates, possibly from a U-boat. Maybe even the *Barracuda*. Forty-three degrees thirty-five minutes North, fifty-six degrees—a bit I can't quite decipher West. Somewhere south of Newfoundland."

Relief flooded Gem, for Ada's discovery made Miss Fearing leave off bashing at her typewriter.

Another day ended, and Gem hadn't heard that her probation was over. She could only assume it wasn't. If she hung on, she'd be paid in two more days, and the rent would be handed over and home secured for another month.

How she wished she could have given the young man the soap.

SEVEN

THE SEWING ROOM was ready. Though small, it made comfortable enough digs for the lodger, Aunt Wren declared. They'd dragged the treadle sewing machine into her own room, the cartons of *Simplicity* patterns. They laid a small rag rug in front of the bed, brought in a rocking chair, folded a clean quilt with soft, faded colours sewn from their own old clothes on the bed. As a finishing touch, Gemma moved the moth orchid from the kitchen and placed it on the windowsill, "to cheer up the room a little more."

The girl who'd answered the ad Aunt Wren placed in the *Lodgings Vacancy Register* arrived that evening. She'd come from the north, Gravenhurst, all her planetary goods, as she called them, stuffed into her suitcase. Her name was Rooney Delacroix. She was seventeen years old, full faced, with a russet braid flowing down over her shoulder, an aquiline nose. Taller than Gemma by a couple of inches. Keen to boost the war effort, earn her own money, she told Gem and Aunt Wren after they'd led her into the living room, to the armchair beside the sewing basket, while they settled across the room on the chesterfield. This Rooney Delacroix was already dressed for work, it seemed, in overalls, blue bandana knotted around her neck, jacket with shoulder pads that jutted like two lofty cliffs. Gem marvelled at how the girl didn't pass out from heat.

The evening was warm. Through the open living room window Mrs. Deluca's heirloom roses musked the air. But after a few minutes the rose scent receded, replaced by something animal, foul. The girl had taken the Muskoka train. Had the malodour that clung to her derived from one of its coaches? Had the girl not bathed in some time?

Maybe *she* needed the bar of soap even more than the prisoner.

Gemma poured the girl a glass of iced tea. Before they finalized things, Aunt Wren asked Miss Delacroix to tell them about herself. Birdie had never taken in a lodger before, so she supposed some kind of audition was in order, she added with an apologetic air.

The girl sat, visibly nervous, with her cold drink. The ice cubes jitterbugged in the glass. It took some doing to draw out this newcomer who, in addition to nerves, seemed shy. Getting her to talk was like priming a pump.

Wren asked why Rooney hadn't stayed and worked in the north, closer to home, lots of wartime work in the shipyards, for instance.

Rooney wanted to see the world. "You know, change of scenery."

"What do you do for fun?" asked Gemma. "Any hobbies?"

"I knit," the girl answered. "For the soldiers."

"That's nice," Gem said. "You write letters to the boys overseas, too? So many young women do, boosts the soldiers' spirits."

The girl took a long slug of iced tea. "No letters. I don't want to give them the wrong idea. I just knit."

They talked some more. The bad smell's source was revealed: Rooney had gone straight from the train station to the tannery, Donnell & Mudge. Left her suitcase in the front office while the foreman took her around the sprawling factory. Right through the beamhouse where the skins were fleshed and unhaired. Past the stinking pits of lime. Past the hand-scudders. Huge, slatted drums. Scouring machines. Past the leg of a small animal, goat-kid likely, bloodied, lying on the floor. Seeing this, the foreman barked for "clean up." He told Rooney if she had the stomach for the job, it was hers; some women worked there. She told him she'd seen her share of gore. The tannery needed help badly. Government contracts for the army, they were backlogged. The foreman told her the salary.

And the better news, that she'd work as a tray dyer. Or presser. So, farther from the hides in their raw state. Most ladies undertook the lighter tasks, like pressing, dye work.

Gemma and Wren found all this, more than they wanted to know, quite gruesome. On the train, Rooney had overheard other passengers say that the tannery paid more than the soup company or Empire State Ice. So she'd gone directly there, to Donnell & Mudge. They kept a copy of the latest *Vacancy Register* in their front office; she found Wren's listing. So their new lodger already had work, and her rank odour didn't emanate from some lapse in hygiene or terrible flesh-eating disease.

Wren asked the lodger if she wouldn't rather work in a nice office like her niece, Gemma. Rooney informed them she'd been raised on a farm; dead animals were common. "Every time you turn around, there's another corpse, haloed by fizzing flies." Besides, she didn't own any dresses or office clothes.

Gemma found the prospective lodger jumpy. She wondered if they'd be friends. Or *should* be friends. Gem wouldn't be able to discuss The Cottage or her work with this new stranger in their lives. Not that she could *anyway*. To steer away from the office topic, Gem chirruped, "Let's get Rooney installed in her room—she's likely tired from her trip."

There was a matter to settle first, Wren said, calling it a "sticking point, though one easily fixed. If Miss Delacroix agrees to it, she has a home."

Alarm shunted across Rooney's bottle-green eyes.

It was this: Wren asked Rooney to deposit her dead-animal clothes in the foyer at the top of the stairs every day, hang them on the coat hooks there, and not bring them into the flat, for they'd smell the place up, killing everyone's appetites for supper. There was a wall shelf in the foyer. Rooney could leave clean clothes on it and slip into them right there in the foyer. No one would see her;

they kept the door between the foyer and the rest of the flat closed. Wren would lay a cloth draught-dodger across the bottom of the door to further block the foul-flesh smell.

Rooney said, "We have a deal. The extra daily rigamarole is a small price to pay for a roof over my head."

That clinched it. Gem took Rooney's suitcase into her room. Then she and her aunt showed the lodger how to toast bread so it wouldn't burn and smoke. The spot on the kitchen floor that wailed in agony when stepped on. How much hot water to use so enough remained for Gemma and Wren. (This applied to handwashing clothes as well.) Which electric light socket didn't work. Which section of the refrigerator Rooney could claim, the top cupboard shelf she could use for her dry goods—Wren supposed Rooney would soon have her own ration coupons, but they'd share theirs until she did. Which days they—Wren, Gemma and now Rooney—were allowed to use the wringer washing machine in the Delucas' basement, and the wash line in the backyard. They warned her to hang her clothes out there for the least possible duration, because they'd soon film with soot from the nearby rail yards. And once Rooney got on her feet, they'd expect her to provide her own toilet paper and soap. In the meantime, Wren said, they had an extra bar of soap. She ducked into the bathroom, opened the medicine cabinet. "We *did* have an extra bar—we must have used it without my noticing. I'm old, Miss Delacroix; I can't keep track of every last atom." Then she laughed. Which opened space for Rooney to laugh—a musical warble. Gem let out a half-baked "*Ha.*"

Wren made pancakes for supper that night. With watered-down honey she served in a small bowl, telling Gem and Rooney to "pretend it's maple syrup." Between bites they conversed more. Which days Rooney would pay rent. How they'd find a rhythm, Wren felt sure, to their daily lives. How Miss Delacroix was free to take her meals when she liked. But *not* free to bring anyone home with her, of course, that went without saying. All those young soldiers looked spiffy in their uniforms, but if Miss Delacroix wanted company, she might head to a diner, or a park. Or, if she could afford it, even into the city, or Sunnyside Pavilion. What she did outside the flat was her business. But if she came in late, to be quiet, and not cook after nine o'clock at night.

"I won't come in late," the lodger told them. "I want to save money. Besides, I don't know anyone. As for soldiers, I'm sure my stink will make them run fast in the opposite direction."

They all laughed.

"You can sit with me while I do my crossword puzzles, if you like," Wren said.

The girl's eyes shone. "Oh, I'd love that, Miss Maw. I'd learn new words. I didn't finish high school. I'll bet the puzzles would be like a *little school*, almost."

Aunt Wren said she'd enjoy the company.

Gem told Rooney there was a bicycle she could use. Leaning against the side of the house.

"Gosh, thanks, but don't you ride it, Gemma, to your office and back?"

"I walk," Gem said. "Helps me think."

Aunt Wren said, "One last thing. We observe a strict code of privacy here in the flat. So, when your room door is closed, whether you're home or out, it's *your sanctuary*—no need to worry about invaders. Same with my niece's room. And mine. A lady needs her hermitage, for sure as anything the world rubbernecks and scrutinizes us all the time."

They finished their pancakes. Rooney Delacroix from Gravenhurst spooned the last of the diluted honey from its bowl into her mouth. This made Gem wonder when the girl had last eaten or had anything sweet.

EIGHT

No amount of coaxing and cajoling from Hester and Cora-Lynn the next noon, that Gem should lunch on the silver log with them, could detain her there. "Need exercise," she breezed. "Taking a stroll."

The day's intense heat didn't hamper her, either, as she hurried along Lake Shore Road, only slowing, every so often, to gobble a bite of her sandwich, or feel the bar of soap through her straw satchel. Luckily, Aunt Wren hadn't made a federal case out of the missing soap—preoccupied with sorting out the lodger, Gem supposed.

Soon she turned off Lake Shore Road into the industrial area. Forlorn earth between factories, it bore a bombed-out look. Chewing, walking, Gem wondered if she'd see the cat, Hedwig, because there was no meat in her sandwiches to attract the creature. They'd run out of canned meat, so it was lettuce sandwiches that day. Lettuce from their landlady's garden she'd kindly given them, even though she still hadn't received that month's rent. Gemma didn't see the cat. Would the imprisoned young man hover near the wire fence? Something he'd said had lodged itself in Gem's mind, how his cat liked pretty girls. *Was* she pretty? Gem hadn't ever thought so, though her long pecan curls and high forehead maybe didn't award her the Plainest Jane in Town Prize. She bolted down the last of her sandwiches.

There it stood—the immense, shambling, bleak structure. Tall fence. Guard hut. She approached, feeling for the hundredth time the soap in her satchel. She tiptoed to the fence, which, she thought, was a daft thing to do, because who'd hear her? A great deal of noise clamoured forth from within the internment facility—thespian shouts, sour music from a squeezebox, melodramatic piano chords, metal striking metal. Gem couldn't make sense of it. And there was no young man at the fence. No Number 1007933. (She'd memorized his number.) She considered pushing the bar of soap through the wire; it would fit. But how would she ever know if he'd discovered it, or another prisoner?

As she turned away from the fence, had already taken several steps back towards Lake Shore Road, she heard, "*Miss!* Miss!"

She turned, her abrupt pivot thudding her satchel against her thigh.

The prisoner stood there. His handsome face latticed with ugly wire. Dressed in the same drab uniform. He saw her hesitancy to walk right up to the fence.

"*Ansatz*," he said, waving her closer. "It's all right." He gestured upwards, towards the guard hut. "*The Happy Gang* is on."

She stepped closer, asking, "What's the other racket in there?"

"They're rehearsing—*Hamlet*—a hideous, outrageously mangled version—Third Reich approved. My mother would retch and reel with revulsion at their vandalizing of Shakespeare's stunning poetry. The thing is fully costumed; the Young Men's Christian Association donates all kinds of clothing, fabric, glittery stuff, craft supplies, for these theatrics. I can't believe they'd trust the men with objects like scissors in here."

"I know the play," Gem said. "A tragedy."

"Yes. Would make more sense to put on *The Tempest*, since most prisoners here are from captured submarines."

"Aren't you in the play?"

He nodded. "I play Horatio—but I'm not in the scenes they're rehearsing just now. So I"—pink stormed his cheeks—"came to the fence to see if"—deeper pink—"*you* might be here. Almost missed you—you'd started to leave."

Gem had saved so many questions she burned to ask the prisoner. Stockpiled them like ration coupons. But now all she could stammer out was, "I'm not supposed to be here."

He sighed. Heavily. "Me neither. As I've said. So that we have in common, Miss—"

The air held his hunger for her name. Like he *starved* for it.

"Gemma. Please don't reveal it," she pleaded.

The prisoner laughed, soft and sad. "No chance of that. I'm an expert keeper of precious information. I'm holding it close, your name." And he patted his heart with the palm of his hand in a way that made her ache for his confinement.

"And yours?" she asked. "Name?"

"I'll swap you a secret, then," he said. "I won't reveal your name if you won't reveal mine."

She stood so close to the fence now, his warm breath pattered against her ear, swooping with the grace of a small bird.

"Toby. Tobias. Albrecht."

It had a lovely ring. Reminded her of *to be*.

"Why is your English so good?"

"I lived in Canada until I was twelve," Toby said. "Then I went to live with my mother in Germany."

"Does she know you're here, in this place?"

His eyes brimmed with anguish. "I doubt it, and I'm crazed with worry over where she is." He pressed his forehead against the wire. "I think they might have rounded her up and done something awful to her."

"Where's your father?" Gem asked. "Germany, too?"

He shook his head. "My parents separated. Father is here."

Gemma stood, stunned. She'd have to dash like fury to make it back before the end-of-lunch bell. She wanted to tell him something hopeful, but there wasn't time. She wanted to ask about the cat, Hedwig. Gem glanced at her feet, an errant shoelace spilled along the ground, almost across the bottom wire, near Tobias's feet in their plain, worn, dusty shoes.

"I wish I could talk with you more," Gem whispered through the wire.

"I wish we could, too," he husked.

"But we can't. I must go," Gem murmured, urgent. Then she jammed the bar of soap through the opening in the wire and into his hand.

Toby's eyes welled. "Thank you, Gemma." He slid the soap bar into his trousers' pocket.

"Don't say my name!" She didn't mean to sound cross, and if she *was* cross, it was at herself. She should have used a fictitious name. Talking to him *was* risky, after all.

Toby still stood there, at the fence, his hands clutching the non-thorn sections of wire, his face taut, pained.

She'd turned to go—again—when an impulse overcame her. She thrust her hand through a space between the thick wire mesh and grasped his hand. It was like part of *her* dwelt within those walls now. His palm, fingers, felt smooth, which surprised her, for working with submarine equipment, she'd have thought, would result in rougher, calloused hands. But then perhaps he'd been locked away so long that the calluses had smoothed.

"You have your own soap now. Do you need anything else?"

The old guard high in the hut must be going deaf, Gem thought, because *The Happy Gang* theme song, impossibly buoyant, blared across the large prison yard. And the *Hamlet* rehearsal must be over, as that racket had ended. This told Gem that other prisoners might appear and catch them communing at the fence.

Toby sensed that, too, it seemed. He grasped her hand harder.

"If you could bring me a book, that would be wonderful. I could escape, through its words, from this place. The Christian Association donates books—I've read them all. Tiresome tales for boys, swashbuckling pirates, frontier adventures. Bibles I can't manage—I struggle to believe these days, with the war and everything."

"You're not the only one," Gem said. "My aunt Wren lost her faith during the last war. Traded Christianity for the occult—tarot. What kind of book, then?"

He brightened. "Anything . . . different. The real gift is *you*, bringing it to me, Gemma."

She blurted, "I usually go by Gem." What a thing to say, when she shouldn't have revealed her real name at all.

Then she turned and ran.

Gemma blustered into The Cottage late. Again. Her thoughts reeled about for an excuse. Lineup at Lake Shore Dairy for ice cream was all she could invent. Weak, and she knew it.

Cora-Lynn and Hester were at their desks, bent over intercepts. Ada Swift was working her spy magic at Casa Loma that day. Her empty desk, Gem felt, missed her spirited presence. From her place on the wall, Ada Lovelace's lips pursed with disapproval.

Miss Fearing scowled. "Late once more and I'll send you packing—and don't think I won't. I have *no respect* for tardy young ladies."

Then the mousetrap under the small, covered window made a decisive *snap*; a tiny, terminal squeak reached their ears. Gem, Hester and Cora-Lynn witnessed the dismal sight of their boss carrying the dead mouse by its tail and tossing it with grim relish out the back door into the forsaken garden's tangled weeds. Then Miss Fearing brushed her hands together in the manner of one who's completed an unsavoury chore.

Gem's afternoon swamped into a murk of jumbled alphabets. It was only late in the day when she redeemed herself, or so she hoped.

Just before quitting time, Hester Hobbs slapped her hand on her desk, cautiously jubilant. "So close! So close! I think I've cracked a U-boat message. Do any of you know what this German word is?" She spelled it, then sounded it out loud. "A-N-S-A-T-Z."

Gem could hardly believe it. Toby had used that word.

"Where's the dictionary?" Hester asked. "I'll look it up. Should have thought of that."

"I took it home with me," Miss Fearing said. "Worked through the evening, even though we're not supposed to take work home. Daft of me. I'll be sure to return it here tomorrow."

Gem said, "I'm pretty sure that word means *approach* or something very close to that."

Hester beat her palms together, applause, appreciation. Swept into the adrenalin of discovery, they didn't ask Gem how she knew the word's meaning.

"And I can tell by the date stamp that this U-boat manoeuvre hasn't yet happened," Hester added. "So, for once, I'm not trolling yesterday's news."

"Good work," their boss said. "Gemma has cracked the door open a little more in this cipher string; we can make an educated guess at the rest." Despite this affirmation, Miss Fearing's tone was restrained, a reminder that knowing one German word wasn't enough to redeem Gem's tardiness.

Miss Fearing went upstairs. The heat in the basement office was suffocating. From her place on the wall, Ada Lovelace delivered Gemma a disapproving look. *The heat must be making me hallucinate*, Gem thought.

"What I wouldn't give for some ice cream right now!" Cora-Lynn brayed. "Lucky you, Gemma, having ice cream at lunch. What kind?"

Gem hesitated for a few seconds. "Orange pineapple."

"Lucky you," Ponder the Wonder repeated.

But the workday, at least, had been partly salvaged—thanks to Toby's help, unbeknownst to him. As Gem trekked home, her satchel lighter without the soap, a rhythmic word pattern danced through her mind: *to be, to be, to be, Toby.*

Already she'd begun to mull reading material for him. *Anything different.* A book borrowed from the library wouldn't work, too unwieldly to move it around. Late fine risk. The book better be smallish, too, to squeeze through a space in the wire fence. Toby mustn't have considered that when he'd requested reading material, and it hadn't dawned on Gem, either. Too absorbed she'd been in his hand's surprising smoothness, silken as the silvered log behind The Cottage.

NINE

THE DAY OF Wren Maw's appointment with the eye doctor felt momentous, suffused with a sense of life moving in a new direction. And the cards she'd drawn lately all pointed towards change, optimism, a turning point. *Wheel of Fortune. Three of Wands.* And it had already begun with the lodger's arrival and, before that, Gemma earning wages to help them along.

Such light her niece brought into Wren's life, and this wasn't the first time the girl had saved Wren. In those bleak years after Adam's death in the trenches, raising her sister's child brought purpose and meaning to Wren's existence. Another of life's cruel twists—her sister Hannah and husband Caleb gone to Muskoka, to the sanitorium, for the "rest cure" that advocated sunshine, fresh air. Swimming in the lake. The word went that one of them had begun to flounder, then pulled the other down under the water. Rescue arrived too late. Little Gem had been left in Wren's care during their sojourn at the sanitorium. The child never left. And Wren, in her later fifties, became a mother. How adeptly little Gem plaited straw, which helped Wren's millinery work. And soon Gem, grown up, employed, would receive her paycheque, solving the July rent problem. To mark this upswing in their fortunes, after her appointment Wren decided to splurge on an ice cream sundae at the Lake Shore Dairy.

So, serendipity shone down on Wren's grey, thinning hair. Soon she'd be gifted with new sight, stronger spectacles with no splintered cracks. This occasion deserved a good hat, Wren resolved. Why not live a little, pull out all the stops? Even lodged firmly, irrevocably, within her eighth decade, and even with all her past sorrows, an irrepressible urge to be happier—*at peace* in some way—grew with each passing moment. *Ah, life's shrinking clock.* How it all dwindled down. Standing before the mirror, Wren planted the hat on her head. Her own millinery hid her frumpy hair. A lady with a mission gazed back at her. Perhaps a bit overdressed for the occasion, with the hat and its large bow sewn at a rakish angle, but the cards she'd drawn lately emboldened her. So, southbound she set out, towards the streetcar stop on Lake Shore Road.

Only later would Wren realize the impracticality of the hat, for it made her hot and she'd had to remove it for the optical examination. So much for hiding her grey, thinning hair.

The optometrist's waiting room featured pictures of bespectacled cats. On a coffee table, magazines: *Optometry and Vision Science*, *British Journal of Physiological Optics*. These sounded hopeful, though *Retinoscopy Fundamentals* made Wren shudder. She wondered why these were left in plain view for patients; these clinical words might scare them away.

The eye doctor's name was Lyle L. Fox. He had a shock of white hair, like Beethoven. He'd studied at Ontario's College of Optometry but often travelled to America for what he called "eye-opening conferences." He'd told Wren all this with her forehead pressed against the boxlike contraption, her eyes staring into its abysses. He swept around beams of light, tested her refractive error (he said). After she'd blundered through the alphabet wall chart, its letters withering to impossibility, he regaled her with trachoma, sarcoma, tarsal cartilage, polar and posterior cataracts, divergent strabismus, Schlemm's canal, things macular, vitreous, venous. Orbital processes. Prisms.

"What colour is the tie I'm wearing?" Dr. Fox asked.

"A rich red approaching maroon." *Likely quite similar to my face*, Wren thought.

"Good, so you're not colour-blind," he said.

"Thank heavens for that, Doctor. Much of my life I've been a milliner, and that wouldn't have happened if I couldn't discern colours."

Wren had been the only person in the waiting room, so, she reasoned, this must be why Dr. Fox didn't rush the examination. There was no receptionist, either; he'd summoned her himself. After the eye tests, he led her to the chair in front of his desk. Then settled into his own commodious chair and thumbed through a medical-looking book, but mostly he talked animatedly—about progress, advances in ophthalmology.

Wren remembered long ago, a farmer near her family's acres. A sightless straw-plaiter. "Do you think someone will ever find a cure for blindness?" she asked.

"Possibly. Though at this point they'd pretty well need to be Jesus."

"Too bad," Wren said. "I don't believe in any of that anymore. Jesus and such. The world is too awful."

Lyle Fox removed his spectacles, laid them reverently on his desk. His own eyes, the palest blue shade of delphiniums, exuded keenness, but also time, expansive swatches of years. "It's so, Miss Maw. But devastating as was the last war—now *this* wretched one—they've pushed our work ahead by light years. The field of military ophthalmology, I mean."

"That's superb—for those soldiers who *didn't die*, who lived to see another day," Wren said bitterly.

"You speak truth, Miss Maw."

Then Dr. Fox explained that her new eyeglasses would be a special prescription he'd formulate himself. She should find a significant improvement, he said, but again emphasized how crucial it was to have patience. The amplified lenses might help her headaches, though if those continued, further investigation would be needed. He dove into more vision science while he wrote in a notepad what she assumed were the specifications for her new eyewear.

Wren liked his patter, even though she didn't understand the words or hadn't encountered them in crossword puzzles. They bore the ring of progress. Lately, he'd been reading about pediatric optometry.

Regretting her bitter retort about dead soldiers, Wren strove for lightness. "Pediatric? Well, you don't need to worry about that in *my* case."

Her ploy worked. Lyle Fox sent up a great laugh, like an exuberant French horn, scaling. He told Wren her new spectacles would be ready in a couple of weeks, he'd telephone her. And after she'd worn them for a while, he'd call again, to check how she fared, whether her lenses or frames might need adjustment.

She checked again whether an instalment plan for payment would be acceptable. Dr. Fox confirmed this.

Now, about to take her leave, she put the hat back on—a pillbox style, cadet blue with a side bow, she'd thrown it together long ago, when Gemma was still in elementary school. She'd fashioned much more elaborate headpieces than this, yet this little blue number fetched attention. As Wren turned towards the eye doctor to thank him, she saw how staunchly his gaze fixed upon the hat, seemed locked in a hypnotic way on its blue bow. It was as though he'd frozen her there, on the spot, and she couldn't move until he broke the spell.

"This hat, Miss Maw, made by your own hands?"

She nodded, her mouth rounding into a smile. This seemed like a peculiar question from a man who'd just spoken of things vitreous, orbital.

"It's quite charming," Lyle Fox said. "Manifests an eye for artistry, surprise within symmetry."

Wren didn't know what to say. He'd flustered her. She hadn't received praise for her hats in some time, except from Rooney Delacroix, the lodger who'd seen a straw hat Wren had brought into the kitchen to repair. A daisy loosened from its brim. People still craved beauty, Wren was convinced—perhaps more than ever, during a war—but were often preoccupied with how many ration coupons they had left. Loved ones overseas. Later, Wren wondered why she couldn't have simply said thanks instead of sending him that silly, embarrassed wave as she stepped from his office into the still-vacant waiting room. Its emptiness puzzled her. But then again, since Dr. Fox looked to be of only slightly fewer years of age than her, perhaps he'd begun to ease his schedule. Either that, or people now chose younger oculists and, despite his breadth of expertise and experience, men of Lyle Fox's ilk moved, like the passenger pigeon, towards obsolescence. Or milliners like herself, whose artistry—he *had* used that word—had been eclipsed, largely, by industrial-made headgear. The old milliner and the snowy-topped eye doctor, both endangered species.

TEN

QUITE THE OBEDIENT mouse, Gemma had been, in school. She'd only missed classes because her aunt, during that awful patch, needed her at home. She'd been studious, truth-telling, law-abiding, an attentive niece, a helpful straw-plaiter, member of Canadian Girls in Training, for mercy's sake! But now look at her—she'd grown brash, emboldened. Brought a gift to an intriguing prisoner who wasn't at all hard on the eyes. And she was about to bring Toby a second gift. This wasn't the Gem of a few weeks earlier, that was certain. Difficult as her work was, the mental strain of it, Gem dared to hope she'd improve. Hester Hobbs had taken Gem aside the other day and said, when you've sunk to your lowest point of misery with the codes, suddenly things will begin to click into place. "You just have to show up *on time*," Hester added, rolling her eyes. And the fact that Gemma still worked at The Cottage suggested maybe Miss Fearing thought she wasn't utterly hopeless at codebreaking.

The immediate task, once Gem arrived home from work, was to find something for Toby to read. She couldn't afford a book. A magazine somehow didn't seem like enough. *Anything different*. An idea struck Gem. Poetry. That was different, all right. She'd feel bad, because her scheme involved stealing—from her *aunt*, no less. But Birdie hadn't read that book, as far as Gem knew, in years. Maybe she wouldn't even notice it was missing. Gem decided to think of purloining her aunt's copy of Edna St. Vincent Millay's poems as a sort of extended loan, an act of mercy. That Toby, locked in that terrible place, needed the book more than Birdie.

Her aunt had left a note on the kitchen table: *At Eye Doctor*. Where the lodger Rooney Delacroix was, Gem didn't know. The girl was typically home by then, and would usually be reading a magazine, drinking tea or ensconced with her knitting needles. Or sometimes, after making herself a peanut butter sandwich, Rooney went straight into her room. Whatever the case, the girl might return at any minute, and Gem didn't care to explain why she was rifling through piles of things in the flat, searching for a book.

Gem rooted through cartons, stacks of newspapers. Birdie subscribed to several magazines, mostly for crossword puzzles. She enjoyed the recipes, too, and never tossed out the magazine. Which was why their flat towered with these yellowing issues, on side tables, in corners. Searching for the book, Gem recalled Birdie's stories about reading the slender volume with her fiancé during their love affair, how they would read the poems out loud to each other. Her aunt derived comfort from Millay's darkly romantic lines.

Did Toby care for poetry? Gem didn't know.

She found the book lodged at the bottom of a basket that held fabric scraps and sewing notions. The fact that crosswords, magazines and tarot had usurped its place in Birdie's days assuaged Gem's guilt a little. And Birdie hadn't mentioned Edna St. Vincent Millay in ages, not like when Gem was little and they still lived in St. John's Ward. It was all "Edna this" and "Vincent that" and "Listen to this, Gem." And surrounded by pieces of millinery, buckram and wire and hat blocks and pliers, Aunt Wren would read from the book with trancelike fervour, and Gem, a mere child, found its heaviness and sorrow too much and wished Birdie would stop. But there was no one else *to* listen, and even at her tender age Gem understood that releasing the words into the air filled some deep, hollowed need in her aunt's heart, so Gem bore it. Lines unfit for a child, like, "Love has gone and left me and I don't know what to do." In the same poem, "Ashes of Life": "And life goes on forever like the gnawing of a mouse."

Later, when Gem was older, it struck her that voicing the poems was her aunt's way of *being with* her sweetheart again, almost as though he were present in their small workers' cottage, like a ghost. It was Birdie's way of bringing him back, at least for as long as those fleeting syllables floated in the air, for she and Adam had read Millay's poems together, just before he'd enlisted, left, died. (Aunt Wren had told Gem all this.) One poem Gem *did* like was, in fact, about a ghost, the little girl in the garden with a high wall and green gate. The phantom-girl in her "broad white hat," hands in lace mitts. She was a friendly ghost, who meant no harm.

Gem remembered all this without even opening the book. But now, hearing the door of the flat open, she scurried into her bedroom with the book. The familiar scuffling noises in the foyer told her Rooney Delacroix had come in and was changing out of her work clothes. Aunt Wren still wasn't back; she must have run a few errands after her optical appointment.

Gem sprawled on her bed and perused Millay's pages. Birdie had underlined in blue ink some sections or starred the margins. Time had mutated the ink into a faded wash, like a pool of ancient rain.

Gem applied frequency analysis to the lines, and then a basic substitution cipher to see if she might unlock some hidden code therein. But little was left to spring, it was all there in plaintext: loss, loss. She hoped Toby wouldn't find the poetry too depressing. That was the last thing he needed in that dreary prison. But perhaps the music evoked by the words would bring some pleasure, help transport him beyond those walls. In any case, it wasn't like she had a library from which to choose.

She heard her aunt Wren come in, singing out a cheerful greeting to Rooney, who must've been in the kitchen. Gemma slid the book under her pillow and joined them there. On the table near the tarot cards was Birdie's hat with the large bow. She hadn't worn that hat in a long time.

Rooney lowered her magazine, sent Gem a cordial hello.

Thirsty, Gem made for the refrigerator, where there was a pitcher of iced tea.

Already wearing her gingham apron, Aunt Wren stood by the sink, more straight-shouldered, un-stooped, than Gemma had seen her in ages. At that moment she appeared as tall as Gemma's earliest memories of her. Birdie's time-worn cheeks flushed from walking outside in the heat, Gem supposed.

Aunt Wren beamed. "A doctor named Lyle Fox is giving me new eyes. I'll be able to finish orders for my customers waiting for alterations and repairs. And I'll be able to see my crosswords better—and *read*. Books, even. I've missed that." Aunt Wren sounded cheerier than she'd been in a long time.

For a moment, Gem worried. With her improved vision her aunt might seek the poetry book, the very one about to be smuggled out of the flat, into the prisoner-of-war camp. But perhaps, Gem thought, catching up on her backlogged seamstress work would preoccupy Birdie, or even some *new* interest sparked by clear-eyed vision.

ELEVEN

MISS FEARING'S STERN stance on tardiness, and the bloodless efficiency with which she'd dispatched the poor mouse, cemented Gemma's resolve to do better. If she was fired, there'd be no new glasses for Birdie—and Gem had witnessed first-hand how even the *prospect* of this brought her aunt joy and renewed vitality. She'd brought the poetry book with her, in her straw satchel, to The Cottage, but she'd have to cool her heels on the gift front. Until she smoothed things over at work and Gem could safely take the Millay volume to Toby, she'd keep it in her desk drawer at The Cottage. How she ached to give him the book. But even more urgent was making things right at work. Which is why she arrived early, to salvage her reputation, make them forget she'd been the tardy girl with her flimsy ice-cream excuse.

As Gem's sneakers brisked towards the lake, she couldn't fathom why it was called "crack" of dawn. There was no crack, rather a fiery eye, a slow blush of claret and tangerine to the east, the soaring buildings of downtown Toronto. A rooster crowed behind a small house Gemma passed, a hacking rattle of lament that hinted at the bird's advanced years. She was glad to have kept the sneakers, for now rubber was in short supply.

Like some reverse mirror, in contrast to its outward-facing, storybook front, the back of The Cottage bespoke neglect. She spied, for the first time, a tipped-over planter near the crumbled lady statue. And now one of the steps down to the basement had a splintered, rotting board.

When she came through the door, Miss Fearing was at the little sink again, frothing at the mouth, brushing her teeth. Her sleep-mussed, spiky hair looked like a chandelier in a brawl. Through the baking soda, she frothed a curdled "Good morning" to Gem, who settled at her desk piled with a loose accordion of papers.

The office felt clammy and eerie with just the two of them, boss and underling. Glancing at the day's heralds chalked on the board, Gem read:

> Ladies, we specialize in intelligence, not stupidity.
>
> "Better three hours too soon than a minute too late." Shakespeare
>
> Who is Karl Krause, U-195 Captain? Get inside his mind.
>
> New intercepts on your desks! High-level code-red material for Ponder & Swift. Hobbs & Sullivan keep plugging away best you can.
>
> Today is payday. Cheques distributed at fly-away time.

Miss Fearing went upstairs. Gem switched on the fans and noticed a cube of cheese in the mousetrap, bait lying in wait for the next victim. Not even dithering over whether to or not, she stooped, opened the trap, took the cheese and popped it in her mouth. She hadn't left time for breakfast.

There. She'd saved a life, a mouse. If she couldn't save a sailor, she could spare a tiny creature. No bait, no lure, no death for that mouse. Gem swallowed the cheese, sharpened her pencil, breathed. Began sussing out patterns among the letters.

Hester Hobbs clattered into the office in new shoes that elevated her.

Cora-Lynn Ponder bounced in a minute later and immediately lit a menthol Kool.

A hair before the hour, Ada Swift arrived. Resplendent in a pink sundress. "The magician has landed," Hester said, all smiles.

"We'll need all the magic we can get today—Lady F has ratcheted things high for you and I," fluted Cora-Lynn over to Ada's desk.

"At least she's upstairs this morning," Ada said. "It's easier to work without boss lady over my shoulder."

"Maybe we shouldn't talk about Miss Fearing," Gem told her co-workers. "I mean, this office might have a . . . recording device hidden somewhere, maybe she's hearing everything we say down here. Making sure we're working, not telling tales out of school."

The other girls snickered.

"When did you become so paranoid, Gem?" Hester asked.

Gem recognized this for what it was—a rhetorical question. She kept quiet.

Cora-Lynn must have swallowed her energy pills. They made her edgy, combative. "And you should brush up on your fibs, too, Gemma. Just so you know, Lake Shore Dairy doesn't *sell* orange pineapple ice cream. I checked on my way home last night."

Gem had no answer for this, either. Her cheeks candled with shame. She hunkered down to the paper stacks of intercepts.

Because Ada and Cora-Lynn had been assigned high-level code-red material, they compared notes in fits and starts. They were working on grouped numbers, grids. They bandied excitedly about numerical combinations. *Divisibility. Primes. Modular arithmetic. Exponents. Variables and constants.* Even though they spoke in low tones, their exchanges broke Gem's concentration, but there was also an intoxicating aspect to listening to the talk. It was as if they dwelt on another planet, spoke a different, highly animated language. There was something magnificent about it. It was like eavesdropping on the eavesdroppers, for hadn't Miss Fearing likened codebreaking to eavesdropping?

"What do you suppose the key is?" Ada was asking Cora-Lynn.

"Book, maybe?"

Ada laughed. "Oh, good. That narrows it right down, to a million possible books."

Gem couldn't resist. "If you don't mind me interrupting, Miss Fearing passed along a wise tidbit to me."

Seeing a scrum of some type forming, Hester popped out her earplugs and sat up straight.

Cora-Lynn stared hard at Gem. "Well? And? Care to share this tidbit?"

Gem spoke slowly, to imbue the information with the solemnity she thought it was owed. "Miss Fearing told me the enemy may grow complacent, lazy even. And, in a rush, the enemy will make mistakes. Take shortcuts. These shortcuts are wormholes our minds can bore through. So, if you were looking for the quickest solution, which book would you choose as a key?"

She had their attention now.

Sweat pearled across Ada Swift's forehead, along her cheekbones, setting them aglow. "Something you'd have handy in your home, I imagine—a typical German home. A family with some education, the sort of family with a naval officer father—like Karl Krause, the U-boat captain."

"You're the German expert, Ada," Cora-Lynn broke in. "Please enlighten us more."

Furrowed in thought, Ada twirled a strand of her platinum hair.

"Don't *think* so much!" Hester urged. "Remember, you're lazy and in a hurry. Spout the first thing that leaps into your mind."

Ada became a doll suddenly animated. "The Bible—in German, of course. *Grimms' Fairy Tales.* Shakespeare."

Gemma studied the chalkboard, the quote about tardiness by the Bard himself. "Go with Shakespeare. Play? Poem, maybe?"

"You're the *word person*, Gem—that's why Lady F hired you, for the linguistic side of things—so you tell *us*," Cora-Lynn prompted.

This was Gemma's *first* real fun in that brain-busting bunker since she'd started. She paced in a small circle. "I'm in a hurry, seeking a shortcut, so while *Hamlet* leaps to mind, a play is too long. So, I opt for something less bulky. I'm a naval captain, which means I'm ambitious. I want my family educated, cultured. To associate with the right people. Read the right books. The Third Reich tells us what to read. I'm a follower, so I obey. Shakespeare has been vetted through official censors. Their translation is approved. I'm in a hurry. I snatch the Bard's sonnets from the shelf; the book falls open at Sonnet 18—because my wife enjoys it, reads it often, so its spine is naturally inclined towards that page. Perhaps this same wife craves a little romance, since her husband is away at sea so much, commanding his U-boat, obsessed with war. And it's summer, after all."

Gem stopped, breathless. Giddy.

Cora-Lynn looked puzzled.

"I'm making all this up, don't you see?" Gem said, darting her gaze in the Wonder's direction. "It's a scenario, a story. I'm *imagining* it. Getting inside Karl Krause's mind like today's herald directed." She jabbed her finger at the chalkboard.

Cora-Lynn, Hester and Ada had swivelled their chairs, facing Gem like predators circling prey, deciding whether to ambush.

"This—Sonnet 18 could be your key," Gem said simply.

"What are the odds?" Cora-Lynn intoned. "One in . . . what?"

"You're the number wonder," Gem replied. "You tell *us*." But she wouldn't stoop to Cora-Lynn's snark-level. "Miss Fearing also told me to lean into every hunch. And I've a hunch about Sonnet 18 and this code-red directive, pinpointing Krause's U-boat."

Ada groaned. "Red, yes. High-level. Now one of us must trot off to the public library to retrieve a copy of Shakespeare's sonnets. More wasted time."

"No," Gem said. "I can recite it. From high school—literature class."

Ada clapped her hands. "Brilliant! Let me grab my paper pad. I'll write it down while you recite, then I'll translate it into German. After that we'll see if your hunch is correct and it's our key."

Gem recited.

Ada wrote, madly.

They returned to their regular work as well as they could, given they were frantic with anticipation, while Ada translated. They could hear her mutter in Deutsch. *Sommertag, Nein, Du bist lieblicher* and more.

After a few false starts—maybe Gem hadn't recalled the poem exactly?—Ada said, "I just might have it. Let's see if it works as the key, Cora-Lynn."

A shot long enough to stretch to another galaxy, perhaps.

It worked. *What were the odds?*

Ada squealed, full delight. "Oh, sweet ambrosia! This is even better than hollowing out copies of *Frankenstein*!"

"Let's get cracking, Ada," Cora-Lynn piped in. "Push the buzzer to call Lady F down from upstairs."

Hester beamed. "You're a marvel, Gem! An absolute Queen of Hunches."

Gem shouldered a small, comic shrug. "Lucky guess."

The buzzer summoned their boss downstairs while the intercepted message, in the number girls' capable hands, was readily decoded now that they possessed the key.

Miss Fearing blew in, aflutter. "Well? What? And? So?"

"I think we've got him—Karl Krause and his U-boat, Miss Fearing. We've decoded an intercept that tells us a lot," Cora-Lynn burst out.

"*Gemma hit upon the key*," Hester announced. "With brute intuition."

"It was just a hunch," Gem said. "I was only following instructions, weaseling into the submarine captain's mind, like you instructed. What would he be thinking, trapped with his men, in that iron coffin for days on end? Missing home, his heart's desire, most likely."

(Here Gem thought of Toby, trapped, too, and the book in her desk drawer, but only for a flash because things now galloped along quickly.)

Miss Fearing implored, "Read your translation, from German into English, Cora-Lynn, or Ada—one of you. No time to lose."

To Gemma's startlement, Cora-Lynn passed their worksheet to her. "Let's hear it from you, Word Girl. You gave us the key, after all."

Gem read: "*Next Milk Cow send applesauce. Tell my wife she is more lovely than a summer's day her eternal summer shall not fade. Let her know Love Karl.*" Gem added, "There are some numbers, too: coordinates, likely, dates, times."

"What's a milk cow?" Ada asked.

"A supply ship that brings fuel and supplies to the U-boats," Miss Fearing explained.

As Gemma lowered the paper, the boss's words reverberated in her ears. *The enemy will make mistakes.* So, in this case, the mistake was love. Knowing this, Gem began to shake. No one noticed; either that or they took her disconcerted state as part of the moment's intensity.

Miss Fearing swooped down on the paper and deciphered the numbers. "Date. With coordinates. The milk cow wouldn't have delivered yet. This might be *it*, girls—enough for our side, with high-frequency direction finders, huff-duffs, to find Krause and his *Barracuda* gang and finish them. I'll wire Ottawa right away—*exceptional* work, girls, especially *you*, Miss Sullivan!"

Their boss bustled back upstairs.

The lower office stayed abuzz with the discovery for the rest of the morning.

It had been a one-in-a-million hunch, Gem knew that. But it had boosted her confidence hugely, fuelled faith in her powers of intuition. Surely, she'd be seen as indispensable at The Cottage now. Her gaffes forgotten.

When the lunch bell clanged, Gem knew exactly what she'd do—her key discovery, she felt, had earned her freedom. She grabbed her satchel, which held her sandwiches, snatched the book from her desk drawer and told her co-workers, "*This* paper bird is flying away."

Fleeing the office, she sprinted along Lake Shore Road, skirt flapping around her knees. Slowed her steps enough to cram bites of sandwich into her mouth. It was tricky to hang on to the book for Toby and her satchel and eat all at once, but she managed it. She'd save the other canned meat sandwich for Hedwig. If she could lure the cat, it might bring Toby to the fence. She jogged across the scruffy field, noting briefly, since her last foray there, a fracas of ox-eyed daisies had sprung from unyielding soil.

She tore along, her thoughts ranging wildly. So, the U-boat captain, with all his murderous patrols, had a romantic streak. Again, the words reverberated through her mind, *The enemy will make mistakes*. In this case, love.

And Gem ran right towards it.

TWELVE

Wren began to worry that she'd misunderstood, that the whole thing had been a mistake. The eye doctor, Lyle Fox, the examination in his office. She'd felt it had a . . . personal cast. Then there was its unrushed tenor, his chatty unspooling of things ophthalmological. Above all, his praise of her "charming" hat. Could all his optometric babble possibly have been him trying to *impress* her? Or was she simply an old woman who'd succumbed to flattery, who'd misread it all? That no one had paid her such close attention for such a long time, she supposed, made her susceptible to flattery.

As she sat, squinting at the kitchen table, one-eyed, through the good lens of her spectacles, patching a pair of trousers for a customer, she was confused. It was true that she'd not received close personal attention in ages. And since her niece began that office job, even less attention from her. Which was why taking in the lodger had been such a brainwave, enhancing the household income but also supplying companionship.

Wren liked Rooney Delacroix. The girl was quiet and polite, and read crossword puzzle clues out loud for her. Because Rooney arrived home earlier than Gemma, she filled that lonely vent of time, that hour and a half or two between late afternoon and supper when one is too tired to start anything new yet it's too early to eat. Rooney made them grilled cheese sandwiches, always saving a couple for Gem. Often, too, the lodger brought a bouquet of flowers to the flat, some wild, like orange hawkweed or devil's paintbrush, and buttercups, and some garden flowers she confessed she'd filched from people's yards—blue bellflowers, pink phlox. Wren told Rooney if snitching the odd posy here and there was her worst demeanour, that made her a very good person.

The girl had grinned, shrugged lightly and said she wasn't so sure about that.

So they began to pass that vexing pocket of time pleasantly, old seamstress and young flower-filching lodger. Wren had noticed how the girl remained vague about her family, her upbringing, even if she had siblings. Wren only knew that Rooney came from a farm near Gravenhurst. "Beside a lonely church on a rock," the girl had said. For whatever reason, she guarded her privacy, and Wren didn't push.

It didn't work the other way, though. The lodger seemed fascinated by Wren's life. That night, after placing a clutch of daisies she'd picked in a vase on the kitchen table, Rooney Delacroix sat, all bright-eyed, bushy-tailed across from Wren at the kitchen table and asked if she would mind telling her some things about her life, like how she'd come to make hats, or live in the city at all. Rooney called Mimico "the city," which amused Wren. So, while Wren would have preferred launching into a new crossword puzzle, the girl had made tea and set a plate of sliced cheese and saltine crackers on the table. And Wren was grateful for the company.

Wren told Rooney about how she'd left the farm—like Rooney herself—when young, much against her parents' wishes, and travelled alone, with only five dollars in her pocket, to Toronto.

Rooney took a slice of cheese. "What year? Did you leave, I mean."

"1890. I was twenty."

The lodger gasped, as if struggling to fathom such antiquity.

"I came to the city, like you," Wren continued, pausing in brief intervals to nibble a cracker. "To find my way. Not an unusual story, girlish wanderlust. Naive as I was, I underestimated what a tough row lay ahead of me, most of us, really—girls working as live-in housemaids for wealthy families, or in factories like my friend Vivian at the corset factory or me at the necktie factory, at first. Hardly able to pay for my room in St. John's Ward near Dundas Street. My parents would have been horrified if they'd known I lived there, a part of Toronto the newspapers reviled as a filthy slum. I rented a post-office box uptown, though I could ill afford it, to hide my real address from them."

Rooney's eyes welled with pity.

Wren realized all this held the tincture of melodrama. "I had grand times, too, when I could spare a few pennies. Enjoying the rooster orchestra, or the albino tightrope walkers, the vaudeville houses, or the boxing cats at the Maple Leaf Theatre, or the beach, or, later, Shea's Hippodrome. The very places my parents, again, would have been appalled by, if they'd known. But I had to be careful, too. The social purity reformers and moral zealots and crusaders against delinquent and vagrant girls were always trolling the streets, eager to round us up. Far as they were concerned, we were all objects of concern."

The lodger winced.

"Being a girl, unattached, in the city verged on being a criminal," Wren went on. "Even someone like me, who held a steady job. A girl like Carrie Davies epitomized this, and when she walked free after shooting her employer, Bert Massey, that was one of the happiest days of my life. With the hordes, I waited in the damp chill outside the courthouse in 1915, and when the timid teenaged girl emerged with her lawyer, I beat my wool mittens together in ecstatic applause and sang out a lusty *Hip-hip! Rah-rah!* along with the buzzing, cheering human swarm. Such a rabble. For, as many of us saw it, a decent, ordinary citizen, a lowly housemaid, had overcome a Goliath of empire. We saw the justice in it, though others no doubt waited outside the courthouse to glimpse a murderess. I did a brief stint as a live-in domestic servant when I first arrived in Toronto; I knew how powerless girls like Carrie Davies were.

"Outside the courthouse, crowds that February day were nearly as thick as the dark, netted clouds of passenger pigeons from my childhood—oh, you can hardly imagine it, Miss Delacroix!—vast flocks moving, airborne, above Etobicoke Township. There'd been even more before I was born, people said. But there were still many, darkening the sky, and people stood outside, watching in wonderment. Or readied, with rifles, to shoot them. And they did. In mass slaughters. Even though it had once seemed like those inky, feathered moving masses would never end. But they did. End.

"As for Carrie Davies, I made her a hat. I'd begun millinery by then. A special, glorious hat to mark her victory, spangled, ribboned, rich with plaited chiffon, brocade and braid, velvet roses tumbling over its brim. A hat to end all hats. Inspired by one I saw in *The Delineator* fashion magazine. Given what the Davies girl endured, I figured she'd earned it. She should hold her head high. I never got to give Carrie the hat." Wren sighed. "Once she'd escaped the public eye, she vanished. Word had it she'd married a farmer and lived out her days quietly, anonymously."

"I still have the hat," Wren said. "I'll show it to you sometime."

"I'd like that very much," said Rooney.

Just then, they heard a noise in the foyer. Gemma was home.

"There's more to the story," Wren told Rooney. "I'll continue another time. That niece of mine is late—she must be starving."

Gemma walked into the kitchen, told them sorry she was late— they'd had some urgent juggernauts to unsnarl at the office.

THIRTEEN

So, Gemma became the girl who'd slain the *Barracuda*, taken down Krause and most of his crew. There'd been a few survivors, scuttled into lifeboats. With the decoded information from The Cottage, an Allied escort ship had been able to locate Krause's submarine. They'd rammed it, destroying it. Krause's crew had been caught off guard, playing cards in the torpedo room, or huddled asleep in the hull; they'd scrambled to fire a few torpedoes, but misfired. This news came to Gem, Ada, Hester and Cora-Lynn from Miss Fearing, whose Ottawa sources had informed her in a telegram ending with *Congrats to the Mimico Dames*. Other lone-wolf U-boats lurked in the Atlantic, but Krause's had long been regarded as the most lethal.

After following her hunch about the key to uncrack the coded intercept that quickly became known as the *Sonnet 18 Solution* or, by Miss Fearing's male superiors, "the hen coop coup," Gemma's status rose in the office, and in addition to Ada the magician, Cora-Lynn the wonder, there was Gem, newly crowned Queen of Hunches. It was Hester Hobbs, now, who wore the dubious mantle of the muddler, the chain's weakest link. No one said this, of course. Like so much at The Cottage, their perceived competencies could shift like cards shuffled in a tarot deck. As with so much at The Cottage, silences became their own codes. But Gem knew one sure thing, and it was this: her star had risen by a freak of luck.

After Miss Fearing tolled the noon bell that day and Gem's sneakers sprouted wings carrying her towards the prisoner-of-war camp as she clutched the book for the prisoner, the thought flashed through her mind that in a sense *she herself* was responsible for ending human lives. And that Krause's wife was a widow now, and he'd never again compare her to a summer's day, and each man in Krause's submarine was someone's son, or brother, or husband, or beau—like Aunt Wren's beloved in the last war. So Gem realized for the first time that a codebreaker was, yes, a trespasser, eavesdropper, but worse, in an indirect way, an agent of death.

That morning, Aunt Wren had drawn the Death card from her tarot deck.

A luxuriant band of nettles had sprung up along the barren field's edge. As Gem slowed a little, to catch her breath, she reminded herself that while her star had risen, a single misdemeanour could gutter it, like being late for work again or getting caught poking around an enemy prison camp. Her star was fashioned from tissue paper, affixed to the sky with soggy tape. She'd better be careful. If the enemy could make a fatal mistake, so could she. But her longing to see Toby overruled any of these considerations.

Toby stood at the fence. Gem's steps sped again, and when she reached the fence, he thrust his hand through the wire to grasp her hand, the one not holding the book.

Still breathless, she said, "I promised you a book. Here it is."

The small volume of Edna St. Vincent Millay's poems, as Gem had hoped, fit through a space between the barbed grid, though it proved a squeeze and the small volume buckled, curved.

Toby seized the book.

"It's poetry," Gem offered. "Not always uplifting, and I'm sorry for that. You'll need to take what good you can from it, what music from its cadence can reach your ears."

Toby had withdrawn his hand from hers, moved it back to his side of the wire, to peruse the book. He turned its pages slowly, with reverence. "The book has been well read, with sections underlined.

And there's a name inside the cover—*Wren Maw*. Then another name, *Wren Hartsock*."

Gemma squirmed. She'd forgotten that Wren's name was written there.

Raucous music from somewhere deep inside the prison reached them. While unpleasant to the ears, it boded well that the other prisoners were preoccupied.

"That's my aunt," she confessed. "This is her book. She and her sweetheart used to read poems from it to each other until he was killed in the last war. Adam Hartsock was her one love. Writing her name as his, she surely imagined her married future which never came to pass."

"How uncannily the last war seeps into this one," Toby said thoughtfully. Then he looked perturbed. "Will your aunt not want her book back? Seems like it's precious to her."

Gemma scuffed the toe of her sneaker into the dust, stalling. "She doesn't read it anymore. It took me some unearthing to find it. I doubt she'll miss it." A new, more redemptive angle bolted into Gem's mind. "And I think it would please her that someone else found diversion, comfort even, in its words."

Toby brightened. "I'll return it to her someday—or to you."

Something—Gem's recent ascent at The Cottage, perhaps—emboldened her. "Do you have a love back in Germany?"

"Yes, I have a love, but it's not a human. It's a boat. A racing shell. For competitive rowing. When not in school I spent most of my time on water, the Elbe River, training, building my strength. Those days were the happiest of my life, and such light, like powdered gold, over the river . . ."

So, he, too, has a romantic streak, Gem thought.

He seemed far away now. "I loved rowing more than anything. I'd hoped to try out for the national team. But the war changed my plans. And here—locked away—my rowing muscles have shrivelled to almost nothing. The calluses on my hands, from the oars, are gone; my hands are smooth as a baby's skin. And I'm so close to the lake, but I can't go there, which makes me very sad. If I was free, you and I might stroll along the lake near here."

She didn't have the heart to tell him about her aversion to water. Instead, she asked, "Where's your cat?"

He shrugged lightly. "Hedwig? Out there somewhere. Doing cat things, I suppose."

Gem laughed. Then asked Toby if he'd had any news of his mother.

"None that has made it past the censors on either side of the ocean," he said, saddened. "I can only hope my father continues to work on this. While not a couple in the conventional sense, they remain civil. And"—he blushed—"they had me together."

Gemma sensed he ached to tell her more. And she was dying to hear. How cruel to say she must leave, but leave she must. Earlier this time—extra insurance that she wouldn't be late returning to work.

He made her promise to visit him soon. "I've talked too much today. Next time you must tell me more about yourself, your work. Everything. I only know you're the kindest girl, who has brought me soap, a book—and the prettiest."

Gem squeezed his hand through the wire, then sprinted away.

The extra time she'd allowed for returning to The Cottage had been generous, so intent Gem had been on not losing the ground she'd gained with respect to her improved status at work. When she arrived back, Hester and Cora-Lynn were still down by the lake, seated on the silver log. Ada was working in The Castle's spy laboratory that day. Not keen to enter the steamy, muggy basement, and feeling she should probably be more sociable to her co-workers, Gem joined them, flopping down on the warm wooden slab. The lake looked varnished, benign blue right to the horizon. The day was very still, so Gem didn't worry about the water. How different, Toby's love for it, her own aversion.

Lighting a menthol cigarette, Cora-Lynn smiled broadly. "Well, if it isn't the Queen of Hunches deigning us with her presence."

Gem squinched her eyes at Ponder the Wonder. Having had no time for a single bite of lunch, she took her sandwich from her straw satchel and chomped on it.

Hester was still eating, too—something round, doughy.

"What's that you've got?" Gem asked.

A minty cloud scudded above Cora-Lynn. "It's the food of Hester's people, a blintz."

Hester grimaced. Between bites, she groused along the fallen tree, "I told you that in *confidence*, Cora. You vowed you wouldn't spill it to anyone."

Cora-Lynn shrugged. "Since it looks like Gemma has earned her place here with us—after her brilliant hunch sank a submarine—I figure we might as well bring her in on it. And sometimes I get tired of being gagged, living in this gaggle of hush."

As if on cue, a Canada goose waddled along the sand near the lake's edge.

The Wonder turned to Gem, blurted, "Hobbs's big secret: Her father is from some British Isles place—his name protects her. And the Celtic cross over her desk, a diversion tactic."

Flummoxed, Gem asked, "Why the need for diversion?"

"Hester is half Jewish," Cora-Lynn answered. "She keeps that side secret."

Now Hester joined the exchange. "You don't get out much, do you, Gem? You haven't seen the signs on the city's beaches about who's welcome, who's not? Never heard of the Christie Pits Riot? Rather ancient history, but prejudice dies slow." She checked her wristwatch. "Even more ancient history—my parents met in a delicatessen in St. John's Ward, downtown Toronto."

"I know that place," Gemma interjected. "I lived there with my aunt Wren when I was little, before we moved to Mimico. I've been to that very delicatessen."

"Then I'm surprised you don't know what a blintz is," Hester mused. "Their families weren't thrilled about them marrying. My father, an Anglican with a fondness for smoked meat. My Jewish mother. You wonder why I keep my mother's side under wraps? Here's a lesson in real life, Gem. Consider who governs us: white, mostly Protestant men. They refused to allow a ship loaded with Jewish refugees to dock here in Canada four years ago. And while Beatrice Fearing might seem like a liberated, even radical, woman, she is, after all, part of the system. I can't risk my job by testing the limits of her beliefs. So, I masquerade as a dark-haired Celt."

Gem wondered, could this be why Tobias was imprisoned?

"I don't understand," Gemma said. "Lots of Jewish boys enlisted, are over there right now, fighting for us."

"Like my cousin, Mitch Waldman." Hester's dark eyes smouldered, acrid. "Our boys are good enough to place in the line of fire yet spurned here at home, where people lounge by their radios, howling with laughter at Louis Weingarten—known as Johnny Wayne—and Frank Shuster entertaining them." She eyeballed her watch again. "We're due back inside soon. I don't know why Fearing insists on ringing that annoying bell—we wear watches. We can tell time."

Cora-Lynn ignored this. "Lady F never eats with us. Too high and mighty. And she works through lunch. So she never sees Hester's bagels, blintzes, cold latkes. If she did, she might figure it out. That's how I did."

"What about winter?" Gem queried. "We won't be able to eat outside then."

"Maybe the war will be over by then," Hester answered. "If we could accelerate our code cracking, we could speed it up."

The bell sounded.

"Back to the daffy-house." Hester sighed.

They rose from the log. As they walked, with the drawn-out, reluctant steps of those dragged indoors at the summer day's pinnacle, Hester asked Gem, "And you'll guard my secret?"

About to descend the steps to the basement office, Gem replied, "Rest assured. Careful of the broken step."

"Thank you. You're all right, Gemma Sullivan."

Cora-Lynn let a few seconds slide by, enough so that Hester had already entered the office, out of earshot. Just as Gemma was about to step down into the office, too, Ponder the Wonder half whispered to Gem, "I know where you go at lunch—you go to see a *fellow*."

It took no codebreaker to decrypt how those words dripped with accusation.

"So what if I *do*? Would that be any of your business?" Gem countered, surprised by her own quick comeback. "Anyway, you're wrong. I go to see a *cat*. It's been abandoned, sticks around the shore. I feed it part of my lunch, poor thing. I don't know who'd abandon such a sweet creature."

"Right," Cora-Lynn said. "Sure."

Vexed, Gem retorted, "Believe me or not, Cora, as you wish."

Hester was already at work beneath the Celtic cross. Her pencil a sabre she wielded fiercely.

Gem glanced at the chalkboard. A new herald had been added:

Reminder of the anti-fraternization policy. Anyone even remotely suspected of being a Nazi should be shunned immediately. Remember the enemy walks in our midst.

Not if they're locked behind barbed wire, with only a book of poems and a cat for company, Gem thought, and a cavern of pity widened within her. No, more than pity, much more.

FOURTEEN

Wren received a letter; her new eyeglasses were ready. She'd thought Dr. Fox would telephone. The letter directed her to collect the spectacles at his office. She wore the same hat with the bow. But a substitute eye doctor met her there. Dr. Fox was out of the office that day, this young optometrist told her. He looked hardly older than Gemma, Wren thought, while he fiddled and adjusted the frames, going on about gradual adjustment. The new glasses were heavier than her old ones—their weight alone would take getting used to. Then the boy-doctor sent her off, emphasizing again the importance of adapting to the glasses in short stints, at home, for the first while.

What a marvel, to see the world in sharp, clear shapes! And she'd been able to pay the first instalment for the spectacles, thanks to Gem's salary. Bless the girl, yet again she'd saved Wren's life. Wren might have died of loneliness in the years after Adam's death if Gem, only three years old, hadn't come under her care. How entertaining the wee sprig had been, always cheerful. Adept at plaiting straw, which helped Wren's millinery. And now Wren took the bulk of her niece's office earnings downstairs to their landlady, Rosa Deluca, who'd invited Wren in for tea by the mantel with the Lady of Guadalupe casting kind eyes down on them. Rosa, aptly named, for she resembled a rose, said how pleasant it was to have Wren's company, for Rosa's husband Dante worked at the rail yards, and her children had grown, moved out of the house—after which they'd converted its upstairs to the flat rented to Wren and her niece. Mrs. Deluca, after tea, gave Wren a bundle of red oakleaf lettuce from her garden. It would stay good for a week at least, in the icebox, the landlady had added.

Now, with restored eyes, Wren studied the lettuce's intricate beauty, its ruffles, frills, green at the heart, fringes the burgundy blush of deep blood. It reminded her of a large rosette, a flouncy skirt. And it was just lettuce. What a sense of wonder for ordinary things those new eyeglasses brought to Wren. And she'd soon be able to resume her mending work full tilt. To show appreciation, she'd bake a cake for her niece, the thrifty spice cake recipe from the newspaper, sweetened with raisins instead of scarce sugar. The lodger would enjoy it, too. Tying on her oldest flour sack apron, to keep her gingham one clean, Wren looked forward to the oven's spicy aromas greeting both girls on their arrivals home. So often Gem arrived home weary; the cake would be a treat. Quite the slave-drivers at that office, in Wren's opinion.

She mixed and stirred, switched on the radio. Mussolini had been ousted. She set the oven timer and worked on a crossword—how vividly the letters leapt out at her!

Soon the raisin-laced, clove-scented batter burgeoned. She should probably remove the new glasses for a while, Wren thought, but she didn't want to take them off, not just yet—just a little longer. She peered through the thick lenses into the bright world of her own kitchen, risen anew in vivid colours and distinct contours. And it would get *even better* than this—both eye doctors had used the phrase "gradual adjustment"—but it was *already* wonderful. She felt wholly reborn. How vibrant the lemons patterned on the curtains over the sink; the small, dancing tea kettles on the wallpaper. She could read the date on the 1943 wall calendar from all the way across the kitchen. The crossword puzzle words on the table marched boldly along their columns. Wren wouldn't need the magnifying glass to read them now, or the lodger Rooney who sometimes read them aloud. (Though the girl enjoyed it, so why not carry on with the ritual?) The new spectacles were a type of magic, Wren felt. How much easier, too, would each day's card ritual be. In fact, why not draw a card right then, while the world opened itself to her and the kitchen grew sweeter and spicier every moment?

The Empress. How resplendent the golden wheat soaring at her feet, behind her, such vigour, how green the forest, how splendid her starry crown, lush gown and fleshly roundness. How opulent her red-and-russet throne. The Empress lived in a world without rations. This card, Wren knew, signalled abundance, fertility, nurturing care. Not pregnancy in her case, Wren thought, laughing to herself, not at her age. But new life, in some way. And how apt, right on the button, the card, for this day of beholding the world through fresh eyes.

With her new amplified vision, things emerged from corners, cracks, little tumbleweeds of dust, smudges on the cupboard doors, a squashed insect on the window, film of soot on the sill, from the rail yards likely. She laughed again, softly; restored eyes viewed the bad with the good, she supposed. She'd do a better job of cleaning now. Speed along with the mending and sewing; her customers had little patience left. But the best glory of all was that getting her sewing work back on track would allow her to buy some millinery supplies—why not make hats again? The praise she'd received from Dr. Fox inspired her.

A few more minutes and the cake would be done. Wren softshoed around the flat; the living room rose, anew, before her eyes. A hole in a doily she must fix. The framed photograph of her and her niece, taken long ago. How happy little Gemma looked, in her straw hat made by Wren, though Gem had plaited the straw. As Wren swiped at a large fleck of lint on a wooden trunk, she thought back to her appointment with Dr. Fox, his attentiveness that extended, she continued to feel, beyond the optical. Was airy flirtation still possible in one's seventies? She knew nothing of Lyle Fox's life, wife, or not. Surely wife. She caught her reflection in the oval mirror on the living room wall. She wasn't *so* very ugly; if anything, her new spectacles, with their heavy frames, lent her aging face a certain *gravitas*, wisdom. Rendered her more owl than wren.

Sharper vision stoked her curiosity, too, about what lay around her. Quite out of character, for normally, Wren couldn't abide snoops. She tiptoed into the lodger's room. Up to that point she'd given the girl her private space, for, really, it was all she had. And the girl had been assured of privacy, after all. Once a week Rooney borrowed the duster and broom and watered the moth orchid. But otherwise kept her door closed. Faint tannery smells lived in the room, chemical, animal. But the girl's bed was made, her scanty wardrobe items either on hangers or folded neatly in the small suitcase, left opened, on the ottoman. The surprise in the room was the rocking chair, piled with yarn, knitting needles jabbed into balls of pink, green, powder blue, a very nice grade of wool. The girl must spend a goodly portion of her salary on yarn. Some evenings she sat in their living room, knitting socks for soldiers. Sombre charcoal or army green. But here in her room were lovely pastel shades. Among this yarn, sweet little knitted caps for . . . dolls? No, too large. Meant for a human baby.

Wren touched the soft fibres, balled worsted yarn, a tiny bootie, a little sweater that matched one of the pink caps. Wren had snooped this far, what could a gander more hurt? Folded papers tucked alongside the yarn. Unfolding them, Wren could read—wondrous!—knitting instructions, casting on, purling, ribbing, casting off. She'd never been a knitter herself. Such detail. Millinery was detail of a different ilk.

Wren leafed through a few random sheets of paper, on stationery, among the knitting instructions, a name handwritten in pen. *For My Wee Cabbage.* What an odd message, Wren thought. She folded the papers back up, tucked them where she'd found them and returned to the kitchen.

Before removing the glasses—the weight of them really *had* begun to hurt—Wren studied the Empress card again. Such fecundity, fertility.

And Wren began to wonder if Rooney Delacroix from Gravenhurst didn't harbour a secret, didn't live daily with the shame that went with it, for girls like Rooney were whispered about in the grocery store, their tendency to take extended trips, or visits with a relative. Wren herself hadn't experienced this shame, but having had a noticeably younger paramour, Adam, she'd endured enough scornful looks of censure to understand the world's cruel judgments when it came to the female sex. And when Wren toted little Gem around the streets with no male accompanying them, critical stares reached her. She'd looked younger than her age for a long time, so these judgy busybodies must have taken Gem for Wren's own daughter. So, if Wren's conjectures about the lodger were correct and the girl was an unwed mother, Wren decided then and there—punctuated by the oven timer going off—that the lodger's secret was safe with her.

The thrifty spice cake had swelled to splendid completion, and Wren, heavily mitted, set it on the cooling rack.

On the heels of the oven timer, the telephone rang. Of all people, Dr. Fox. He was sorry to have missed her, he said, then asked how she was getting along with the new eyewear.

"They've given me a whole new world," Wren said. "I'm *reborn*. Though I confess the glasses weigh heavily on the bridge of my nose."

Lyle Fox could adjust that. He asked Wren to meet him at the Lakeshore Diner in three days' time, noon. "And wear that hat with the bow—please."

FIFTEEN

It wasn't as though their work was finished, Miss Fearing proclaimed. Far from it. "Our efforts have taken out the *Barracuda*. But inside sources inform me the *Kriegsmarine* has already dispatched a U-boat to replace it. New intercepts on your desks, buckle down to it, girls. I'll expect results by later afternoon. And Miss Swift is with us today, devising decoy messages to trick the enemy. Work your magic."

Ada, wearing a stylish ivory peplum dress, raised her arms, palms upwards, as if entreating some sky muse to provide inspiration.

Miss Fearing added, "I'll be on calls upstairs this morning, but buzz if you need me." Then she clattered off, having again traded in her bedroom slippers for real shoes.

Ponder the Wonder began flogging away with her pencil.

The girl-magician had inserted earplugs.

"*Oy vey*," Hester Hobbs said, staring at her paper stack. She grinned over at Gem.

Gemma smiled back, weakly. How exhausted she was, after a sleepless night. She'd lain awake, thinking about her conversations, brief but intense, with Toby. This brought pleasure but robbed her of sleep. Getting up, she had decided doing something with her hands might settle her down. She'd tiptoed into the living room and dug through a basket of Aunt Wren's sewing notions, remnants, scraps, and found some pretty ribbon in a warm shade of amber, and teal yarn, and a coiled hank of thick roving fibre in a bright-green shade. She cut lengths of these, then began to braid. Soon she formed a collar to fit a cat. She rooted again at the bottom of the basket and seized a tiny bell they used as a Christmas tree ornament. She sewed the bell to the cat collar. Now Toby would be able to track his pet's whereabouts more easily. Pleased with her craft, Gem had slept at last, but less than an hour later, her alarm clock had sounded.

At The Cottage, she yawned at her desk. Her eyes drooped. She honed in on frequency analysis. The new respect she'd earned at work was a boon, but it almost certainly had a shelf life and would fade away—forgotten or eclipsed by new conquests from her co-workers. *Focus, Gem.* The pretty woven cat collar was in her straw satchel. More than anything, she longed to return to that fence, give Toby this gift her own hands had crafted. Cora-Lynn's barb—*I know where you go at lunch, you go to see a fellow*—irked Gem. How could Ponder the Wonder guess this? Maybe she was acquainted with the officer Gem had seen near the prisoner-of-war camp. This wasn't out of the question. After all, Mimico was a town. One of those places where many people knew each other.

What irked Gem, too, was that her cat story was *true*; it just wasn't the *whole* story. And clearly, Cora-Lynn hadn't believed the cat story. Gem felt cornered. If she admitted yes, she went to see a young man—*and* a cat—it would only jump-start a new barrage of questions. No one must find out that the "fellow" Gem went to see was locked in a prisoner-of-war camp. So, reluctantly, to staunch the prying, she steered clear of the place. Going there was too risky. Who knew who Cora-Lynn knew? Maybe she'd have Gem followed. From the start, the Wonder had shown a coldness to Gemma—though why? What had Gem ever done to her? Staying away, not seeing if Toby was all right, made Gem withdrawn, heartsick. Downright anti-social. So she worked through lunch for the next few days, not even stepping outside the stuffy basement for a breath of fresh air. Like a prisoner herself.

She glanced across the office. Ada Swift, wearing earplugs

and scrawling madly with her pencil, seemed oblivious to anything but the task at hand; it was like she floated in some alternate stratosphere. Maybe that was what made her a magician, Gemma thought, that ability to block out the world. How Gem wished she herself possessed that same skill.

Ada Lovelace, from her place on the wall, lifted her nineteenth-century eyebrows in an ironic, exasperated way to signal that she too wished Gem had better concentration skills.

The morning wore on. Even the letter *E*, typically the alphabet's most preening flaunter, hid itself like night-blooming phlox.

Maybe, Gem thought, splashing some cold water on her face would help. So, not meaning for her desk chair to make an irksome scraping noise, she rose and headed towards the bathroom at the rear of the office. On her way there, she heard Cora-Lynn mutter, all surly, something about additives, shift codes. Then more chair scraping as Ponder the Wonder rose and began chalking the blackboard where Miss Fearing's morning heralds usually appeared. Chalking with a fury. There hadn't been any heralds that day, leaving the board empty, blacker than a starless night.

When Gem returned from the bathroom, the chalkboard brimmed with Cora-Lynn's computations, things like:

Theorem 3.4: If $a \equiv b \mod n$ then a and b leave the same remainder when divided by n. Conversely, if a and b leave the same remainder when divided by n, then $a \equiv b \mod n$

How Cora-Lynn managed to puff on a menthol cigarette with one hand while the other chalked away madly astounded Gem.

Miss Fearing's earlier words ricocheted back to Gem: You're either a word girl or a number girl, occasionally a hybrid.

Good lord, Gem thought. *No wonder the Wonder needs her brain tea and those pills.* Her symbols and numbers might as well be hieroglyphs on a cave wall. Then, below this mumbo-jumbo, Cora-Lynn had written words in English that Gemma *could* understand:

The Queen of Hunches Never Lunches

And beside these words, no decoding needed, a wicked, mocking cartoon face inside a circle.

Above their heads, the lunch bell clanged tersely. The clangs must have penetrated Ada Swift's earplugs, for she popped them out, heaved a sigh, declared herself famished.

Bleary-eyed, Hester Hobbs reached for her lunch box and readied herself for outdoors by donning a sun hat.

Cora-Lynn stood by her desk, staring, expectant, at Gem. "Not going to see the 'cat' again today?" Her fingers formed little air-quotes around *cat*.

"That's not true what you wrote," Gem said, "that I never lunch. I've been working through lunch; I eat at my desk."

The Wonder's aura softened a little. "You haven't exactly cracked the earth open this morning, have you, Gemma? Staying locked in here isn't doing you any favours. Come on, eat with us down by the lake—we don't bite, you know."

Though Gem wasn't so sure about this last bit, she had to admit Cora-Lynn was right about her morning's work. It had been dismal. She had to escape from the office. Craved oxygen, sky. Even more than these, Toby. She fashioned a hasty fib, telling her co-worker that Aunt Wren needed her at home, that she needed to dash back there during lunch.

A tight-lipped smirk from Cora-Lynn.

Gemma left the office, sped along, leaving behind the grand houses lining the lake's shore, then the smaller ones and entered the industrial waste fields, half-dead sunflowers stooped, withered Canterbury bells, parched vegetable patches. The scorching days were taking their toll. There was no sign of Hedwig, the fluffy, slate-toned cat.

As she neared the fence, she thought how strangely the summer had unfolded. If she had a normal job, one not so entangled with the war, with signals intelligence, the signed Official Secrets Act, she might go where she pleased, live under less scrutiny. And what *of* The Cottage? Why *couldn't* she give it up? The fact was, the challenge of codes wielded a dark power; it was an elixir, a thrill, blood lust, quickening of the pulse the more patterns she pounced upon like some word-panther. And after her hunch had unlocked the Sonnet 18 key, she'd donned a mask of humility, but in truth she'd never felt more alive. The Cottage was a vortex that lured her like a child to a gingerbread house, and she couldn't free herself. Tobias Albrecht was also a vortex, but where The Cottage's vortex had a dark, witching aspect, Toby's was sheer light. How wholly Gem was drawn towards his light.

A silver flash, a mewl. A cat streaked across Gemma's path. Hedwig stopped, meowed as if in greeting. Mewled again, more insistently—*Pay attention! Follow me!* (her feline code quite transparent). Gem held out a bit of jelly sandwich, but Hedwig didn't show any interest, instead padded over the baked earth just ahead of Gemma. They reached the fence. The cat slipped through.

She didn't see Tobias at first. But heard loud cornball music she guessed must be *The Happy Gang* because of how absurdly buoyant it was, with its cavorting brass and clownish organ riffs. So, that meant the usual guard. No prisoners in sight. She did notice, hoisted at half-mast on a pole in the middle of the vast, gloomy shambles, a flag shunting about limply in the hot, intermittent breezes.

Gem's earlier fatigue was gone now, as she stood at the fence, lightly on the balls of her sneakered feet in case a quick retreat was needed. Suddenly, in a rapid flicker of movement not unlike the cat's, he appeared. Thinner than the last time Gemma saw him. His face, still fair to behold, looked malnourished.

His voice was almost a whisper. "You came, finally. I was so afraid I'd never see you again."

Gem asked him how he liked the book she'd given him.

"I like it very much and find something new with each rereading of Millay's poems."

She whispered back, gestured towards the half-mast flag. "What's that for?"

"One of our men died. An infection. The others are at a funeral service for him right now. I was restless, so I left. I'm sorry the poor brute died, but he was no friend of mine. Zealot for the Third Reich, he was. And now Hamburg's been flattened—I just heard. That was my home since I was twelve."

"How did you hear about Hamburg?"

"There's a radio one of the men in here rigged from old parts left from charity donations. Information from other rogue radios reaches us that way, sometimes belatedly. I've been living in constant fear for my mother's safety; now I'm beside myself. She might be crushed beneath a bombed building—if they haven't already carted her away long before this."

The cat wound itself around the prisoner's ankles as if to comfort him.

Gem kept her voice low. "What makes you so sure they've taken her?"

"Because I was there," Toby said. "Not the day they took her, but just before—in her class, at the gymnasium. Sorry, high school, as it's called here in Canada. Mother was also my teacher. She was an independent thinker, lived life on her own terms. And no longer a young teacher in 1937, the year an 'inspector' with a swastika on his jacket barged into our classroom. The Nazis had 'cleansed' the curriculum. 'Carry on, Frau Albrecht, teach your students,' the inspector barked. While Mother tried to teach *Hamlet*, the Nazi officer poked around her classroom, and we were supposed to discuss the Prince's famous soliloquy while the inspector pulled Mother's copies of Marx from the shelves and dumped them in the garbage, while he motioned to her to move aside while he rifled through her desk drawer. 'How am I supposed to teach while you're making all that noise?' Mother said—which infuriated the officer. He kept firing items from her desk drawer into the garbage can. We students sat there, mouths open, while Mother just kept reading out loud. But after a minute or two the Nazi officer raised his flattened hand. "*Aufhören.*" *Stop*, in German. Mother stopped. I felt the entire class hold our collective breaths. With his other hand, the one not palmed into the air like a traffic officer, he raised a magazine he'd yanked from Mother's desk drawer, waved it about, flashing the cover at her. '*Die Freundin*—what's this?' 'A women's magazine,' she answered. He flipped through its pages, then made an ugly, mocking face at her. 'These don't look like recipes, Frau Albrecht.' Then he pitched the magazine in the trash. 'And why do you still teach Hans Rothe's translation of Shakespeare? That trash was removed from the curriculum over two years ago. Why do you not use the approved Schlegel–Tieck version? You're corrupting your students' minds.' Mother was, I'm sure, about to reply that Rothe's *Hamlet* was more poetic—she'd told me that earlier—but the officer in his heavy boots stomped from the classroom."

The cat mewled and Toby picked it up. It circled his neck like a scarf.

Gemma fingered the collar inside her satchel, absorbing the prisoner's story.

"I didn't grasp the seriousness of that day at first," Toby said. "I just saw it as a rude intrusion. And I confess my mind was on other things."

"Girls?"

He laughed faintly. "Rowing. As I think I've told you. Mother used to joke that I spent more time on the Elbe River than at home. Rowing was my dream." His face shrouded. "That dream vanished. The day the inspector came into our classroom, Mother told me at supper that night, 'I might have to go away, Toby.' She told me where she'd hidden some money, that I needed to put it somewhere safe; they'd likely ransack the apartment. The next morning, when I woke up, she was gone, and I haven't seen her since. To this day I don't know how they took her away without me even waking up, though rowing did exhaust me to my bones and caused an almost unhumanly sound sleep."

Gem noted again how thin he looked. Her satchel still held her jelly sandwich. She offered it to him.

He shook his head. Sweetly. Saying he wouldn't feel right stealing her lunch.

"You told me you're not supposed to be here," Gem said. "What did you mean?"

"I meant I'm not one of them."

He pressed his face so close to the wire she worried it might cut his skin. She could feel his breath against her cheek. Just then a loud, rousing song came from within the walls, the voices of men singing.

"What's that song?" asked Gemma.

"'Lili Marleen.' If I hear it one more time, I'll shoot myself."

"Oh, *don't* do that," Gem pleaded.

"I jest, partly," Toby replied. "They sing it because it was the dead prisoner's favourite song."

Gem checked her watch. "I must go soon."

Hearing this, Toby looked so miserable. But then she recalled the gift. She reached into her satchel, took out the cat collar with the bell and passed it through the wire. "I made this—it's for Hedwig. It has a bell so you can hear where she is."

He took the cat collar and slipped it on his wrist, like a bracelet. "It's wondrous. The weaving, colours. I love it."

Gem wanted to know, "What will you say when your . . . fellow inmates ask where it came from?"

"There are bits of cloth and such, from the *Hamlet* play. I could have crafted it from those. And you'd be surprised what some men in here wear. Some have developed surprising . . . sartorial habits. But the *real* gift would be if you returned here."

"I'll try," she said. "I wish *I* wore a bell, so you'd hear me approach the fence."

"I wish you did, too," said Toby. "I'll dream the sound of you, ringing, as you waltz in your canvas shoes towards me."

She laughed. Suddenly everything inside the walls went silent. The funeral must have ended, *The Happy Gang*, too.

A man's loud summons reached them—"Tobias Albrecht"—then cross German words slung through the air. This frightened Gemma, and scared the cat, too. Hedwig leapt off Toby's shoulders onto the ground and scurried off somewhere inside the prison. Gem looked behind Toby and saw the shouting man approach, lumbering in large, rapid strides towards Toby. His voice louder with each step closer to the fence, to them.

"Gemma—*run!*" Toby urged.

She tore across the barren field, her satchel slapping madly against her ribs, back to where the houses began, then she crossed Lake Shore Road. She turned around, didn't see anyone trailing her. She ducked behind a shrub to catch her breath, to think. She panted there for a couple of minutes. Thinking food would steady her, she stuffed her jelly sandwich in her mouth. When she reached

The Cottage in her dishevelled state—almost but not *quite* late—Miss Fearing was there, to take note. Hester, Cora-Lynn and Ada were already at their desks. Cora-Lynn pointed at Gem's mouth. She swiped some jelly away with her finger and slumped down at her desk.

Miss Fearing went upstairs.

The close call at the prisoner-of-war camp had shaken Gem. Badly. She didn't know if she'd ever be able to return there. The rows of codes blurred before her eyes. She fought to steady her breathing. Her hands shook. Ada Swift must have sensed Gemma's distressed state and appeared at Gem's desk, a small, intricate object resting on her palm.

"You look like you could use a bird," Ada said. "Here, take one of mine."

Gem looked more closely at the object—it *was* a bird, exquisite, formed from folds of paper. Paper covered in pencil—numbers, code groups. So elegant, this bird, a tiny miracle really. It reminded Gem of her aunt's hats, festooned with felted birds. But Aunt Wren's were more hand-cut-looking, more charmingly folkloric; this paper bird was pure artistry. *Only a magician could make something like this*, Gem thought.

"Here, it's yours now," Ada said. "It's origami."

With great care and delicacy Gem set the gift on her desk. "It's the most elegant bird I've ever laid eyes on."

"I make them from my coding scrap paper," Ada explained. "Folding helps me think. And there's more where this one came from." She swished her shapely arm towards her desk, on which a small flock of paper birds had gathered. Gem had been so distracted by the debacle at the barbed wire fence, she hadn't noticed them. Cora-Lynn and Hester seemed not to have noticed Ada's birds, either.

Now Cora-Lynn and Hester chippered up, admiring Ada's papercraft. The Wonder took a bird from Ada's desk, turned it over in her hand, more admiringly with each passing second. "This is amazing," Cora-Lynn said. "Paper folding is used in geometry."

Ada said, "Yes. And we've done some spy-craft items with it at Casa Loma. Cora, have you read Houdini's work on paper folding that draws on mathematics?"

"Houdini? As in Harry, the magician?" Hester asked.

Ada nodded. "The very one."

"Sure, I've read it," breezed Cora-Lynn. "Also, Margherita Beloch's fold, what a swell engagement with axiom theory and cubic equations."

"The enemy may be, as we speak, sending codes folded within origami," Hester said. "We'd better get back to work."

"You can be a real killjoy, Hobbs," Cora-Lynn said. But heeded this directive.

The others followed suit.

Gem wished she could shape an exquisite paper bird and send it flying over the tall fence at the prisoner-of-war camp. And somehow Toby would catch it, and read the words of comfort, cheer and affection she'd have penned on its wings. Maybe Ada Swift would teach her paper folding, Gemma thought, maybe a little of Ada's magic would rub off on her. She could really use some right about now, at this juncture when she didn't know if she'd ever see Toby again. For a return to the fence was surely unwise, dangerous even, now that they'd been caught. If only she could fold herself, like origami, and slide through the gap under the fence, like Hedwig the cat. Or, better, fold Toby to fit under the fence, release him from his prison. Then unfold him, in her arms. Turn paper back to flesh.

SIXTEEN

How fleeting, short-lived, the accolades earned by a job well done. Just before lunch, Miss Fearing took a telephone call from Ottawa in which she was informed that "the Mimico Dames" had done well, but they expected more from them very soon. As Miss Fearing stood before Gem, Hester, Ada and Cora-Lynn that morning, she told them how repugnant she found this moniker, "the Mimico Dames," and how the newly tightened thumbscrews ramped up the pressure on all of them.

Then she tramped back upstairs to her office.

Gemma's hair had been falling into her face all morning. The night before, she'd dreamed that she'd struck upon another key—much bigger than her Sonnet 18 hunch—*so* big, it sped the Allies to victory, the war ended, prisoners all released. And she and Toby could be together and really get to know each other. But she woke up, as usual, in her bed and she knew the dream had been a ludicrous flight of fancy. But it carried forth into her day. It inspired her. If she could immerse herself more deeply, she might solve more conundrums. Annoyed by the hair sliding down over her eyes, impeding her work, she took the scissors from her desk drawer, went into the bathroom, fisted her long hair into a ponytail and hacked away with the scissors until her pecan curls fell around her feet. Then she gathered the fallen locks and threw them into the wastebasket. Returned to her desk. Gem's co-workers, facing the wall at their own desks, didn't notice her shocking transformation. (She had, briefly, looked in the mirror, but it was too late. It couldn't be undone.)

Shortly after this, Miss Fearing trekked back downstairs. Hearing her descending footfalls, Ada, Hester and Cora-Lynn turned away from the wall, saw Gem and her radical new haircut. Gem simply said her hair had been interfering with her work. Miss Fearing remarked on "Miss Sullivan's very severe shearing," and asked, "Is this some new victory hairstyle?"

"I'm trying to get my brain closer to the codes. My hair was in the way," Gem said.

MISS FEARING SPENT the morning in the lower office with them. Worked in a state of great vexation, inhaling Pall Malls with such intensity she seemed in danger of igniting herself into flames, between "fiddlesticks," "darnation," "damn this algorithm," and "*Fig!*"

Gemma still didn't have earplugs. Their boss's outbursts hampered her thought. The constant smoke made breathing a chore.

Noon was a blessing. Gem beat it outdoors with her co-workers, equally desperate for oxygen.

The day was sunny. Lake gulls wheeled overhead. Sunflowers nodded over tall fences backing other summer homes along the shore. Farther down the sandy beach, children cavorted. The four codebreakers, ensconced on the old silver log, dug into their lunches. It had rained the night before, and the air held a tropical after-smell along with the peppery scent of wild carrot, that frothed, leggy weed.

After a few minutes, Ada remarked, "The lake looks so lovely today—hard to believe a frightening creature, serpent-like, dragon-like, dwells in its depths. There are Indigenous stories about it."

Pensive, Hester crunched on her apple, contemplating this.

Cora-Lynn looked skeptical.

"It's not hard for me to believe at all," Gem said. "Water holds a monstrous energy, death dwells within its currents and swells. My parents drowned in a lake when I was three, hence my fear of water. It was all I could do, at first, to eat lunch out here."

There was a chorus of sympathetic clucks from the others.

"I can't imagine serving duty on a submarine," Gem added. "Surely it must feel like being trapped in an underwater grave. Even trying to picture it makes it hard to breathe."

"I've heard it's very rough," Cora-Lynn weighed in. "They can't bathe or change their clothes for days on end."

Looping back to the monster topic, Hester lamented, "Miss Fearing *herself* is turning monstrous. She's so grim, it's dragging me down."

"And she's stopped awarding bonuses," Cora-Lynn grumbled.

"Even when she works upstairs, I hear her tramping about, huffing and puffing," Hester griped. "It's like working beneath a thundercloud. Thank golly for earplugs. I'm worried Lady F may be slipping off sanity's ledge—into madness. And that affects us—hugely."

Ada Swift sprang off the log and stood, wide-eyed, elated, before them. "I've *got* it—a brainstorm to make our lives here easier—it's *genius*." A thespian's pause. "Lady F should get out more. She needs some fun. What if *we* take her out *dancing* this Friday night."

Hester laughed.

Cora-Lynn lit a cigarette and blew out a befuddled smoke ring.

"Socialize with the *boss*?" Gem squeaked. "We don't even know if she dances."

A Canadian goose performed a rumba along the shore.

Gem pressed on. "Would a lady with a motorcycle *also* be a dancer?"

Ada replied as if this was the daftest thing she'd ever heard. "*Everyone* dances, Gemma. Even that *goose*, as your own eyes now behold."

"Ladies, we have two minutes to clinch this wild scheme," Hester announced. Ever the timekeeper.

"We'll go to the Palais Royale," Ada declared. "The group of us. I'll bet our boss never has any fun. We tell her she's been working too hard. Which is true. All she does is work."

"She even *sleeps* at work," Gem said. Then a worrisome thought struck her—there might be police at the Palais Royale. Not long ago she'd heard a random, passing remark in the drugstore that the Palais swarmed with undercover police—looking for spies. Or fraternizers. Would her short hair be a disguise? It wouldn't be a good idea for her to go. "The Palais costs money," Gem said. "Admission. Then there's streetcar fare, sodas, the cost of dance tickets."

Ada shooed away these protests. "Admission is twenty-five cents cheaper for ladies. They want us there, so they give us a break. It's a small price to pay for our . . . *well-being*, Sullivan! Consider it an investment in your job security. And looks like it wouldn't hurt *you* to enjoy yourself for a change, too."

"I can't dance," Gem protested.

"You'll attend Swift's Dance Academy, right here on the sand, tomorrow—lunch hour. I'll teach you. Besides, what will you do this Friday night? Sit at home like a thousand other girls and write letters to soldiers?"

"I'd rather you teach me origami than dancing," protested Gemma. "Then I could make my own lovely birds."

Ada ignored this.

"Don't we need escorts for the Palais?" Gem dithered. "You know, fellows. They might not let us in without escorts."

Ada swatted this housefly of a concept. "My cousin is a bouncer there. He'll make sure we get in. Besides, do you really think they're going to turn away a flock of skirts? You can bet there'll be single guys there."

"We're not supposed to talk about work outside the office,"

Gem interjected. "Another reason to avoid the Palais. We probably shouldn't even yack to each other out *here*, at lunch. We exist in a cone of silence."

Ada fly-shooed these words away, too.

"What if the Cipher Queen says no?" asked Hester.

Ada Swift had an answer for everything, had nailed every angle before it even occurred to the rest of them.

"If she says no—which she won't," Ada went on, "I'm very persuasive—*we* say we'll all *quit*, and she'll have to waste time training new girls."

"I don't *want* to quit," Hester whinged.

"I'm saving for school tuition," said Cora-Lynn.

"My pay goes for rent," said Gem. "I—I can't afford to not work."

Ada scowled. "We *all* go to the Palais—otherwise it won't work. Office solidarity—"

"The co-operative spirit," Hester ballyhooed, clearly warming to the scheme. "Miss Fearing likes that."

"So you can't use entry-fee pittance as an excuse, Gem—that's unacceptable," said Ada.

Gemma could tell she'd lost the debate. (Even though admission, sodas, streetcar fare were *not* a "pittance" to her.)

Ada went on. "Look, I'll make sure she says yes. I'll even pay your entry, Gem, if that's what it takes. Bert Niosi is the king of swing—what a dream, his orchestra will transport us to a magic land! We'll lindy-hop, we'll swing, we'll fling! We'll breathe the same air as Cab Calloway, the Dorsey Brothers. We'll feel the night breeze off the lake against our bare shoulders—we'll *live*!"

The lunch-over bell caterwauled.

"When do we . . . broach this?" Cora-Lynn asked.

"Leave it with me," Ada said as they trudged out of the sunlight, into the burrow of codes.

SEVENTEEN

AUNT WREN WAS aghast, seeing Gemma's shorn, boyish look. "Whatever possessed you, niece of mine? Your tresses were your crowning glory—you've ruined your beauty—what are they doing to you at that office? You resemble some sad, disfigured marionette now."

Gemma allowed her aunt to vent. At some point Birdie would surely leave off with her lamentations.

Thankfully, the lodger, Rooney Delacroix, diverted attention away from Gem. That night at supper, the girl was the most animated they'd ever seen. Supper's fare had been boosted, too. The lodger's rent, Gem's wages and Wren's sewing had placed a pot roast on the table, and they tucked into it while, between bites, the lodger chattered about news at the tannery.

"Some men from the Mimico prisoner-of-war camp work at the tannery now—*enemy merchant seamen*," the lodger added.

The girl had their attention, especially Gem's.

"They've been there for a while, I just haven't had a chance to share this."

"Tell us more," said Wren.

"The tannery is backlogged on a military order for aviators' boots. Mornings, the prisoners are driven to the tannery, and taken back to their camp at day's end. Escorted by guards. But they eat lunch with us."

Aunt Wren poured gravy on her mashed potatoes. "How odd, that the enemy helps make equipment for the very people against whom they fight."

Gemma's heart thrummed. She laid down her fork. "Have you talked to any of these prisoners, Rooney?"

The girl scarfed down a slice of roast. "We're not supposed to speak to them. The tannery walls are plastered with *anti-fraternization* warnings. But the men have aroused oodles of curiosity. Like, maybe we're working with Nazis. And we eat outside, behind the factory, under this huge, rough-hewn picnic shelter, and I can tell you there's a *good deal* of fraternization in play. Odd how few words they know of each other's language and yet can communicate."

"How do they look?" Aunt Wren asked.

"German-like," Rooney said. "Some remind me of circus strongmen, from pictures I saw in a book," she added. "Like they could lift three of us with one hand. Because of their strength they were given the worst jobs. But one young man is very thin. Thankfully, they didn't send him to the beamhouse or lime pits—it's gut-wrenching work, he wouldn't last."

Now Gem was so roused she had trouble remaining in her chair. She had a strong hunch that the thin prisoner was Toby. To appear casual, she served herself more mashed potatoes.

On the table was the tarot card Aunt Wren had drawn that morning. *The Lovers*. Heat rushed to Gem's cheeks.

Rooney continued. "They gave the thin young man a heavy apron and brought him to the finishing room, not far from my pressing table. Only a few feet away, in fact. We tried not to stare at him. Bent to our work—the mallet workers walloped, the trimmers trimmed, the resin-workers resonated, I pressed—while the foreman showed the prisoner how to apply the brush. I suppose they won't let prisoners use any sharp objects. He works away quietly."

Still burning, Gem had to confirm his identity. This meant taking a risk; her need to know trumped caution.

"What does this prisoner look like, Rooney?"

Aunt Wren's brows tipped upwards.

"I don't look at guys much," the lodger said. "But occasionally I stretch my neck and shoulders at the same time as him. He's sandy-haired. And handsome if he wasn't so frail, his eyes so sad. But I saw him laugh once—the first time he saw me wear the clothespin I use to pinch my nose shut, to block the foul smell. I laughed, too, realizing how silly I must look. And I wondered, if two people laughed over something, does this count as fraternization?"

"Coming at this question from my advanced age," Aunt Wren said, "I'd say *everything* does."

Rooney's face clouded.

Gem began to serve apple cobbler in three bowls. Silently cussed the serving spoon trembling in her hand.

"There's more." Rooney sighed. "I might land in trouble because I talked to him—under the picnic shelter behind the plant, at lunch. I asked him if he'd like me to bring him a clothespin, for his nose. We bantered back and forth a little. But other women yack and laugh with the prisoners of war during lunch, too—a lot more than me, because I don't have much to do with guys anymore."

"Did this fellow tell you his name?" Gemma probed.

Rooney lowered her voice, as if she feared a recording device had been planted somewhere in the flat. "Toby. I probably shouldn't talk to him anymore."

The serving spoon dropped from Gemma's hand and clattered to the floor. What if Toby, perhaps out of loneliness, told their lodger about a girl who'd been coming to the fence to visit him? A girl named Gem.

Gem took the spoon to the sink to rinse it. "That's probably a good idea, Rooney—I wouldn't talk to him after this if I were you."

After supper, they retired to the living room. Still in a sociable mood, despite the fly-filled ointment of fraternizing with the prisoner at the tannery, Rooney knitted socks for soldiers. With her improved eyesight, Birdie reclined in the floor lamp's beam, doing a crossword puzzle. Gem had, with shaky hands, poured herself a glass of iced tea and rested on the chesterfield. The Palais Royale matter perturbed her greatly. Whatever Ada Swift had said to persuade Miss Fearing to go, it worked. Gemma sipped and stewed. She considered telling Ada and the others that her aunt wouldn't let her go to the Palais, but this flimsy excuse, Gem sensed, would be sussed out quickly enough.

So, Gem had no choice but to broach it. At first, Aunt Wren protested vigorously.

Rooney interjected with, "What's the Palais Royale? I'm new to the area, you know."

Aunt Wren had set aside her crossword puzzle. "Dance ballroom by the lake," she answered. *"Sin Palace."*

Gemma explained. "I'm meeting my work chums there, Auntie. Our boss will even be there, so how bad could it be?"

I'm painted into a corner, Gem thought. *If I go, I'm in hot water at home. If I don't go, I'm in trouble at work.*

"I don't want you out on the streets alone at night. It's not safe, niece of mine."

Gem recalled Ada Swift's notion that dancing helps a person leave their troubles behind. If dancing truly did have that kind of power, how grand it would be to ease the worries that had been plaguing her. Whether her visits with Toby would land her in trouble, or him. The arduous codebreaking work. How she'd love to float above it all, even for a few minutes. The Palais visit began to appeal to her. And if being arrested for fraternizing with a prisoner of war was inevitable, didn't she deserve a few final moments of happiness? And now Aunt Wren was throwing a wrench in things.

"I'm nineteen," Gem countered, rattling the ice cubes around in her empty glass.

Suddenly, for whatever reason, Rooney leapt to Birdie's defence.

"I went to a dance hall once, up north—with no chaperone. You're right, Miss Maw, it's not safe."

"Then I rest my case." Aunt Wren looked smug, resuming her crossword puzzle.

There had to be some solution. Gem longed to feel free, if even briefly.

"Wait," Gem said. "Rooney, why don't *you* come to the Palais Royale tomorrow night as well? Then there'll be two of us on the streets to fend off pirates and demons in the dark."

"That's not funny," Aunt Wren rumbled.

Gem pretended not to hear her aunt's remark. "And you've been working so hard, Rooney—wouldn't a break be nice?"

Rooney's expression was hard to decipher. A stew of confusion, sadness, laced with something like longing.

Gem felt a pang of regret. She'd wedged their lodger into an awkward spot, stranded between her landladies. Still, Aunt Wren hadn't vetoed this latest proposal.

But now it was Rooney who hesitated. "I *do* love music. But I have something going on tomorrow night . . ."

Both Wren and Gemma waited to hear.

"Knitting," Rooney continued. "Also, I can't dance, and I don't have a nice dress to wear to a fancy place like that."

Gem brightened. "Knit before we leave. You can borrow one of my dresses. And don't worry about dancing—I can't, either."

Aunt Wren sighed heavily. "Perhaps a night with music and dancing will restore your femininity, Gemma, after what you've done to yourself, *ruined* your looks. Rooney, if you accompany my niece, she—you, Gemma—may go to the Palais Royale."

Now everything rested on Rooney's decision.

"You can even keep the dress," Gem added.

"No need," replied Rooney. "I wouldn't get enough wear out of it. I'll go if it helps you out. You and your aunt were awful nice, giving me a place to live. I owe you a favour back. I could have ended up with *much* worse landladies."

Aunt Wren and Gemma laughed.

"And *we* could have taken in a much worse lodger," Gem declared. "Though, Rooney, if I may ask this, please wash your hair before the dance. A dead-sheep smell wafts from it, and no one wants to swing with a deceased ewe."

Thankfully, the girl took this remark in a spirit of humour and promised to shampoo her hair.

Gemma didn't know how the others at The Cottage would react to a stranger joining their group, but codebreaking talk was out of bounds anyway. If the topic of work arose at all, they'd play their parts as ordinary office girls. And Miss Fearing? Who knew? Gemma couldn't form any notion of her eccentric boss outside work; it was as if Miss Fearing faded into smoke at each day's end.

Aunt Wren looked up from her crossword. "What's a word for 'concessions made by both sides'? Ten letters."

The lodger surprised them both. "*Compromise*?"

She'd been helping Birdie with crossword puzzles, and her vocabulary bloomed more briskly than Mrs. Deluca's trumpet vines.

EIGHTEEN

THE CODEBREAKERS TREADMILLED through the morning.

"Must have changed the dratted key again," Hester Hobbs griped. Cora-Lynn scratched with her chalk madly on the blackboard, more equations. Ada drubbed away and hit upon a "null" symbol, a discovery that inched her forwards. Gem found a pair of words, *Apfelmus*, that the girl-magician translated: "*applesauce*." They sent this upstairs to Miss Fearing, who said, "Could be something—a supply order from a U-boat, the name of an operative. Or could be nothing."

At the noon bell, they scurried outdoors like schoolchildren at recess.

Ada led the way. "Step on it, Grindstone girls!" she ballyhooed. "Hurry and eat your lunch—no time to lose. Swift's Dance Academy is open for business."

Ada formed the improvised sandy theatre stage between the log and the lake again. She conjured a whole world from air. She wore a dress with a daisy pattern that day. Its fitted bodice made her waist look tiny. They stared at her from their places on the log. Then, with a smooth, graceful gesture, Ada pulled a long silken scarf from the dress's sleeve. As suddenly as it had appeared, the scarf vanished. Before they could marvel at this—even Cora-Lynn's mouth gaped in wonderment—Ada snapped her fingers, like a hypnotist bringing her subjects out of a trance, and sallied forth.

"Get your admission money ready, girls! Soon enough we'll be in big-band paradise, the Palais. Our hearts overflowing with sheer pleasure; it's our chance to lift our boss from the depths of despair.

Which will help all of us. Music is the ultimate magician! The dancing will do us good. Our bodies shrivel while we overtax our brains."

Scuffing up sand with her bare feet, Ada sashayed over to the log, to Gemma, and stuck her porcelain-skinned face directly, nose to nose, in front of Gem's. "Stop eating those stupid boiled eggs, Sullivan, and get down here."

Gem rose from the log slowly, reluctantly. She stood beside Ada on the improvised stage.

"I guess you can leave those on," Ada said, pointing to Gem's canvas sneakers. "I, however, prefer to dance in bare feet. I'll give you a lesson. You"—she pointed to Hester and Cora-Lynn—"watch and learn."

"What's the point of teaching her?" Cora-Lynn honked. "Nobody will ask her to dance, looking like that."

"Just *dry up*, Ponder—*cork it*," Ada replied.

Hester Hobbs applauded.

Gem stood in the sand, helpless.

Then Ada faced Gemma, placed her arms in the correct position, and laughed. "You look terrified. Don't worry, Sullivan, I won't flip you into the air. I'll teach you a basic swing step, so you won't embarrass us—or whatever poor sod ends up as your partner. Now, imagine a band playing. I'll lead," Ada said. (As if there was any doubt on that score!) Then she began to propel Gem around in the sand. "Side, together, side. Now other direction, side, together, side—rock, step, back, replace. See, not so hard, is it?"

Gemma, who stumbled through the sand, felt her cheeks flare with shame. High school physical education had revealed how clumsy she was; this only reinforced it.

They paused. Always intuitive, Ada read Gem's thoughts. "It's just a pattern, Sullivan. Like a code. Let's try again."

They moved with less jerking and sand-dragging this time, then again, more smoothly. After a minute or so, they were dancing.

"Five-minute warning," Hester declared.

"That will have to do, then," Ada said, releasing Gem. "Ponder, Hobbs, do you understand this basic swing step?"

Hester nodded.

Cora-Lynn, over whom smoke still hovered, jerked her head up, down.

"There's so much more—the shag, the stomp, the camel walk, the shuffle. Old stuff like the foxtrot, the tango. No point teaching the jitterbug, no time, and anyway not allowed, the Palais's rule, too many injuries. I've even got a dance of my own invention—the Mimico goosestep. But there's no time for that, either."

They polished off the rest of their lunches.

"Two minutes," Hester mewled.

Slowly, she and Cora-Lynn rose from the log and stretched their limbs.

"We meet at the Palais's front doors, under the arch, eight p.m.," Ada said. "Dress fancy. I'll convey this plan to Miss Fearing. My cousin Happy—Nick is his real name—works at the door. If anyone gives you trouble, you tell them talk to Hap the bouncer."

As they traipsed back to their desks, Gem realized she hadn't let them know about Rooney Delacroix. There was no time for that now. They'd just have to accept the girl, and, hopefully, be cordial.

NINETEEN

Dr. Lyle Fox leaned across the table in the booth he shared with Wren at the Lakeshore Diner. He removed her weighty spectacles. Though this was purely a professional gesture, she was irked at the girlish jitters that rippled through her. She'd worn the hat, as he requested, and he'd given her praise again for its artful style. He didn't wear his eye-doctor suit, but a dress shirt with a collar clip and, though she'd only caught a glimpse as he seated himself, pleated trousers. He'd tamed his Beethoven hair.

He opened a small velvet case with eyeglass instruments, tweaked Wren's spectacles this way and that, and, placing them back on her, said, "I think you should find this more comfortable. I've tried to distribute the weight more evenly."

She thanked him.

He gazed at her earnestly. "Yes, they appear balanced on your face."

He ordered grilled trout for himself. Wren, a western sandwich.

"Wouldn't you rather have something more, like a minute steak, Miss Maw? Or the broiled flounder special?"

Too embarrassed to reveal how closely she guarded her pennies, Wren pleaded a late breakfast. And she certainly wasn't about to tell this professional gentleman how she'd scrimped and exercised thrift her entire life—even during her years at Munro's Millinery, where the bespoke hats she'd designed flew off the shelves despite factories' assembly-line headgear—for in those years she had little Gemma to feed and raise, and who knew how long the craze for personalized hats would last? So, penny-pinching was, by now, baked into her bones.

Since Wren hadn't answered, and the waitress stood waiting for the order to be finalized, Lyle Fox said, "Make that two grilled trout lunches. What the lady can't finish can surely be boxed to take home later."

Wren was crestfallen, for there went the week's budget for coffee, All-Bran. Money thoughts never failed to fluster her; she mustn't forget the envelope in her purse with the next payment instalment for the eyeglasses. She'd meant to give this to Dr. Fox, but the moment, somehow, didn't feel right.

She'd noted his intent stare at the waitress's name badge, or at least that *seemed* the focus of his gaze. He was, after all, a man.

"Are you acquainted with the waitress, Dr. Fox, or perhaps been served by her before? You noted her badge quite closely."

He looked wistful. "Mildred. Same name as my wife."

Wren didn't know what to say.

Lyle Fox added that he'd been a widower for ten years.

Wren told him she was sorry.

"And you?" he asked.

She so rarely spoke about Adam; it was difficult at first. "I'm a widow—even though we never officially married. We were engaged. But my fiancé enlisted, never returned. After that I designed hats and raised my niece. The years passed, as they do. We moved to Mimico in '36. My niece is nineteen now, with a clerical job in a government office. I take in mending and sewing, and thanks to your optical care I can see much better to work."

The Andrews Sisters' harmonies wafted from the jukebox.

He listened, she thought, with exceptional attention. Perhaps he specialized in ears as well as eyes. Then it all spilled forth from Wren, the story of Adam Hartsock, her fiancé. How she'd pleaded with him not to enlist. His letters, heavily scratched through by censors. Then the silence, until the official condolence arrived. She told Lyle Fox, too, how she'd refused feathers, in her millinery, due to the atrocities committed against birds, and how she'd forged her own path, hearing her lady-customers' stories and building the core elements of these stories into hats that brought respectable profit, though she split the proceeds with Adeline Munro, her boss who'd allowed Wren to run a little cottage industry within Munro's Millinery.

She stopped. No doubt told him much too much. Yet she sensed no disapproval; he sat quite still, listening with that acute attention of his, every so often taking a swallow of coffee.

The waitress set plates of steaming grilled trout before them.

In truth, Wren was famished. She reminded herself to eat slowly, in measured, ladylike bites, to not contradict her earlier remark about a late breakfast.

Lyle Fox set down his fork. "I'm very sorry for your loss, Miss Maw. And I must say I admire you greatly, for your fortitude and courage to be an independent thinker, and artisan."

Fishbone caught between her crooked front teeth. She'd no choice but to pick at it with her fingernail, for the bone impeded her meal, like trying to chew with a needle in her mouth.

He watched this awkward bone-removal.

"I'm sorry, Dr. Fox."

"We're human, Miss Maw. And fish are . . . fish."

They laughed.

Years slid from her like great ladled scoops of hand-churned ice cream.

After the trout, he ordered hot fudge sundaes. There went more of her budget, but a mood of reckless abandon overtook Wren. Why should she not, once in a periwinkle moon, be extravagant? She'd poured opulence into her hat designs; why shouldn't she, for once, lavish a little on *herself*? One of Edna St. Vincent Millay's poems flared through her mind, about seizing life by the jowls, living dangerously, even, burning one's candle at both ends, how soon its light would snuff out. There, in the Lakeshore Diner, she, Wren Maw, in her seventy-fourth year, burned her candle at both ends. Her habitual lunch, at home in the flat, was a slice of dry toast.

Lyle Fox studied her closely across the table. Just then an inkling, a hunch, struck Wren, that *he*, too, sensed the allure of a candle burning at both ends.

"What do you do when you're not mending other people's clothes?" he asked.

She shrugged. "Crossword puzzles. Groceries. Dabbling with tarot cards."

A swooning, crooning song played on the Wurlitzer, "Dream a Little Dream of Me." Wren began to find all this too much.

"I'd like to do a crossword puzzle together sometime, with your permission," Lyle Fox said. "But even before that, dinner—the two of us."

Wren was stunned into silence. Lately her life had been disjointed, in small, domestic ways. A bar of soap missing. A new boarder. Her niece's increasingly odd behaviour, since starting that office job. And now this eye doctor who wasn't acting doctor-like in the least. It was as though they'd both forgotten the original purpose of the meeting—the eyeglass adjustment.

This reminded Wren of the envelope in her purse, which she handed to Lyle Fox. They'd had what could only be called a personable lunch, but she still owed him a debt.

"I'll have the next instalment in two weeks," Wren said.

"That will be fine," Lyle Fox said. "But our dinner I'd like to happen before that. I'll ring you."

Then he paid for the coffee, grilled trout lunches, hot fudge sundaes, and a tip for Mildred.

PART TWO
....

THE *NORTHSTAR*

Love said to the wind, Be still;
To Time, Be merciful;
To Life, Be sufficient.

—MARJORIE PICKTHALL

TWENTY

In the flat on Pidgeon Avenue, Aunt Wren perched atop a high stool, seamstress's pins pinched between her lips poking forth like a porcupine, tape measure noodled over her stooped shoulder. New owl-spectacles bridging her nose. Gemma stood nearby, dressed in a rose-pink spun rayon dress with a bow at the neck that had not been worn since her high school graduation.

Aunt Wren had altered one of Gem's dresses for Rooney Delacroix. After Birdie hadn't managed to quash the Palais Royale scheme, she leaned into it, muttering that there was no point in "her girls" looking shabby.

She removed the pins from her mouth. "Turn," she told the lodger, wiggling her finger in a circular motion. "So I can check the back."

Rooney had, as instructed, shampooed her hair, and styled it in a pretty roll. She turned.

"Good, now face me," Aunt Wren instructed.

The girl turned, smiled. The pastel-blue dress, full skirted, brought out the russet tones in her rich auburn hair. Seeing her standing there, no one would guess she lugged around animal skins all day.

Gem could only jab a barrette into her cropped hair. Later, she would wonder why she hadn't asked to borrow one of her aunt's hats. But Birdie hadn't mentioned this, either. So much millinery around the flat, yet neither had thought of it.

Pleased with her alterations, Aunt Wren pronounced Rooney's dress passable and remarked how much her new eyeglasses helped—especially after Dr. Fox's adjustment of the frames.

"Gemma," Rooney urged. "If we're doing this, we need to leave."

Aunt Wren told them to enjoy themselves, reminding them to stay on the alert for flim-flammers and rounders and wastrels and grifters and hooligans and soldiers who might be on the make for a quick night of pleasure before shipping out, and of course she wouldn't sleep until they'd returned, safe. Quite the send-off.

They made their way out of the flat. The last thing Gemma saw, on the kitchen table, was a tarot card. *The Moon*. A stern lunar face scowled down on a dog and a wolfish animal with bared teeth, also something clawed and scorpion-like, crawling up from the watery depths. Venomous-looking mushrooms sprouted along the water's edge, and the image was flanked with two cold, grey pillars. She shuddered, hoping this wasn't a harbinger of the evening.

Rooney tugged at her sleeve. "Gemma—come on—you talked me into this, so quit dragging your heels before I change my mind!"

She was right again, and Gem trailed the girl in the blue dress out into the summer night. The solstice had happened a few weeks earlier, but evenings remained lit, in that dreamy twilight way, into the later hours.

THE OTHERS WERE there already, waiting near the Palais Royale's front archway, when Gem and Rooney arrived. Parked cars everywhere, roadsters and coupes and sedans, and men, ladies, leaning against them, smoking, gabbling animatedly. A bus spilled eager passengers, dressed to the nines, from its open doors. Music, strings, horns sounded from inside the ballroom, propulsive riffs, saxophones' mellow swells, trombones' impish, sliding growls, crooning clarinets.

"We thought you'd never get here, Sullivan," Ada Swift warbled while her feet in flirty open-toed sandals shuffled out dance-like steps. Then, swishing her hand in Rooney's direction, she asked, "And this is . . . ?"

Gemma introduced Rooney Delacroix. "I had to bring her. Otherwise, my aunt wouldn't let me come tonight." The look of hurt on Rooney's face made Gem regret what she had said. "But you'll see she's all right," Gem blundered.

Cora-Lynn Ponder took over as social convener and carried out introductions. Her words spritzed forth a mile a minute, making Gem wonder how many of those little pills she'd swallowed. Cora-Lynn's polka-dot dress was a tiny size; her melon lipstick shade matched it perfectly. Her ponytail swung while her hands spun through salvoes: *this is . . . meet . . . here's.*

Gem scanned the parking lot, no sign of police—unless they were disguised in plain clothes, posing as Palais guests. Even with her newly shorn hair, she worried, for how much of a disguise were shorter locks, really? Gemma felt suddenly shy. This was the first time she'd ever seen her co-workers outside The Cottage or their lunch-hour log. How different they appeared at night, dressed fancy. Hester Hobbs looked perky in her frock with its print of tiny ferns. Ada smoked a cigarette, her lipstick rouging the end of it. Gem couldn't imagine where someone would find a dress like hers, with its mermaid sheen. Certainly not at Silvert's in Mimico. Same went for her beret, which was spun gold, with a bow.

But it was Miss Fearing whose transformation surprised Gemma most. Their boss had been standing in the background. She'd marshalled her hair into a latticed clockwork of waves. She wore shoes with heels that amplified her height even more. But it was her dress that gobsmacked Gem. Kelly green with a full shirred skirt, crossover bodice. Gemma hadn't known their boss had . . . a bosom. And, the icing on the sartorial cupcake, a matching sequined green belt.

Miss Fearing seemed caught in an awkward conundrum. Her lavish dress, on the one hand. On the other, the way she shrank back, as though trying to conceal herself in smoke.

"You're dressed quite ... strikingly tonight, Miss Fearing," Gem said.

"Thank you. Tonight, I'm just Beatrice. I thought it might be interesting to see what the world does, after hours."

Gemma still felt bad about her gaffe with Rooney Delacroix, who stood, one glove off, one on. She'd set it right later. Who could predict how sensitive the girl was? Rooney might do something rash, like move out of the flat. And Gem realized, there in the parking lot, that she knew hardly anything about the lodger besides her tasty grilled cheese sandwiches, her obsessive knitting habit, how she came from up north. But so did Santa Claus.

Now Rooney asked, "So, do you *all* work in an office, like Gemma?"

Hester shuffled her shoes against the pebbled gravel. "Sure, we know each other from work."

Ada Swift tipped her golden beret back off her face a little. "Are we going to waste time out here in the parking lot like a bunch of clams? Let's go trip the light and rule the night!"

They agreed.

Ada Swift handed each of them a few dance tickets. Miss Fearing said the others should take her share. "Just getting out is enough," their boss added.

"Someone else can have mine, too," Rooney said. "I can't dance, and I don't care to try."

Ada issued orders. "From time to time we'll need breaks. We'll regroup. When you see me raise my beret, head out behind the Palais, to the terrace along the lake. We can congregate out there, compare notes. Otherwise, we'll lose each other. There are hundreds of people in there. Remember, the golden beret held high is your sign, all right?"

They agreed again.

Then Ada whistled—an eardrum-drubbing blast, her fingers at her mouth. This piercing summons, then her equally shrill call over to the sturdy young man, her cousin, at the door. "Hap! Happy! Me and my friends, we're going in now."

He waved them over, took their admission money.

Just before they stepped inside, Miss Fearing told them, "Remember, loose lips sink ships, ladies."

But Miss Fearing didn't really have their attention at that point.

They entered a dream, the Palais. Just inside the door, a large photograph of the big band. Its leader, Bert Niosi, stood, moustached, in the centre with eleven band members flanking him. All wore suits, dress shoes, and their leader stood out with his shoes' white tops. The swanky ballroom was enormous, starrily lit beneath its barrel-vaulted ceiling. There were elegant light sconces on the walls and a constellated cluster of large, round pendant lights suspended at varying heights from the ceiling rafters, like the prettiest glass moons. The expansive band filled the stage. As if timing the downbeat to their entry, "In the Mood" launched, its da-da-da-*dutt*-da opening bars in equal parts celestial, visceral, and the crowd squealed and applauded, dance tickets flurrying like confetti as everyone leapt to life, jostling, bumping Gem, Rooney and the others as the dancers angled for the best open spots on the packed floor.

The six of them stood at the dance floor's crowded perimeter. Cora-Lynn twitched about, enlivened by the music. Ada tapped her foot, snapped her fingers. Gem glanced over at Rooney and read, in the lodger's eyes, an admixture of awe, nerves. Hester and Miss Fearing stood a bit behind Gemma, but she guessed they, too, were impressed by the dancers. And the band—so divine. Glittering horns. Wild-haired piano player rippling his arpeggios into tomorrow. What a mélange of smell! Cologne, shave lotion, dandruff antiseptic, faint tinctures of whiskey, even though the bystanders, Gem noted, held bottles of cola. The dancers' bliss blitzes were palatable. Soldiers in uniform, other men in starched white shirts, ties, pressed trousers, ladies in the sweetest styles, dresses surely from Toronto shops. They all moved as if this was their last night on earth and they'd dance until their feet fell off. Unlike so many other things, dancing wasn't rationed. The ripple, the jump, they wanted it all.

Ada Swift had already spun away from them; a soldier waved a dance ticket, extended his arm, and she entered the fray, her dress billowing as she twirled, flashing her shapely legs. Somehow, the golden beret, worn at a rakish angle, stayed on her head. Then a young man with a chin cleft so deep a coded message might be tucked within it ushered Cora-Lynn onto the dance floor. Turned out Ponder, the high-strung, pill-popping university student, had some decent moves. Another soldier swished his dance ticket at Hester Hobbs, and she slouched onto the dance floor in a posture of mock resignation. She held her own. Miss Fearing and Rooney Delacroix had retreated, closer to the wall, and chatted. Gem turned quickly to glimpse them there. So she stood pretty much by herself, wedged between other spectators on the sidelines who bopped to the music, sipped sodas, taking in the whole spectacle.

The regular beat of dancers' feet vibrated under her own soles in a pleasant way. There were some real high rollers on the dance floor now, fellows tossing their partners into the air, sliding them along the floor between their legs, then flipping them back up. Jitterbugging wasn't allowed at the Palais, but wasn't this just as wild?

Miss Fearing said she'd buy a soda and take it outside to the moonlit lakeside terrace.

"What a good idea," said Rooney. "I'll go with you. It overwhelms me in here."

Such an odd combination, Gem thought. *Mathematical genius and tannery grunt.*

They tripped away.

A hand on Gem's shoulder startled her.

It was only a girl, about her age, holding a bottle of soda pop.

"Having a good time?" the girl asked. Her lipstick deep sumac red.

Gem nodded.

"Lots of dishes here tonight, eh?"

"Dishes?"

"Yeah, cheesecakes. Stacked dream dolls among the seaweed. And Casanovas. Cads. Some real hunks of heartbreak, and swoonies, but some void coupons and pathetic Peters, too."

Gemma scrambled to decode this lingo; to nod again seemed the best course.

"What's the dope?" the girl asked. "You can't talk?"

"I can talk," Gem said.

The girl blithered on—loudly, to be heard above the orchestra—about her work over in Long Branch, how she'd built hundreds of Bren light machine guns. How, if you worked out in Ajax, your residence had its own beauty salon, imagine! She'd glanced at Gemma's head, saying this, but thankfully didn't remark on the lumpy haircut. Instead, she asked about Gem's work.

"Office," Gemma answered.

The girl raised her bottle, as if about to make a toast. "That's what they all say. Like a swig?"

Gemma shook her head and, shrugging, sumac-lips ambled off, across the ballroom. A relief to be free from this chatterbox and her dizzying idioms.

A man called over to Gem, "Hey sugar, are you rationed?"

Disliking his brash tone, she ignored him. He spun away in another direction.

Awkward as Gem felt, standing completely solo now, on the sidelines, she wasn't alone for long. A young man crossed the floor and strode towards her. This ticket-bearing young man asked her for a dance. His face spangled with freckles, smile eager. She gulped, telling him she wasn't sure she knew how; she'd only taken one lesson.

"Then we'll learn together," he said. "Come on, don't be a cold fish."

They fumbled through basic swing steps. Tromped on each other's feet, then laughed apologies. His name was Archie, he said, as their arms crossed awkwardly over. He remarked on her hair. "You look like a pixie."

Gemma didn't think it came across like an insult, and he left it alone after that. One of the trumpets broke from the pack, a rogue solo, then the drummer seized the spotlight and bashed out a storm of cymbals. When the song ended, Archie told her it was his last dance ticket. Gem said that was likely a good thing, that his feet must be sore from her tromping on them.

"Quite the opposite. My feet were never happier, Miss," he said, giving her a comical salute.

Finding herself partnerless on the dance floor, and the next tune, a slow, swooning "Moonlight Serenade," already under way, Gem felt a hand, gentle but firm, on her arm.

She turned—then blinked, gasped—to face Tobias Albrecht, dressed in a nice suit, not the ugly uniform with the number on its back. Not behind barbed wire. But how . . .

He looped Gem's arm through his and steered her into the song's swells, blending them both into the dance floor crowd.

They danced. This time Gem felt no awkwardness, her feet, somehow, knowing where to place themselves. She pretty much forgot she *had* feet, she near floated. He led well, not bossily but with an intuitive directional flow. Through his suit she could feel his upper arms; they'd taken on muscle. It hadn't been so very long since she'd last seen him. How fast, this change. His face had filled out, too. Still dumbstruck, Gem couldn't speak. But then neither did Toby. There was only the music, and the two of them. Moving. Touching.

He twirled her, which pulled up his shirt sleeve, and Gem glimpsed the bright woven coil she'd made for his cat—it flashed on his wrist.

Toby saw her notice. "I never take it off," he said.

He removed his hand from her shoulder long enough to smooth a short strand of her hair. He'd noticed her new hairdo.

"I like it," he said. "It brings your face into the light even more."

The band's playlist slowed again, opening more space for them to finally talk.

"I told you I wasn't supposed to be in there," Toby said.

"Are you worried about... running into anyone here?" asked Gem.

"Seeing you here swept me off to another world," Toby said. Then he lowered his voice, which brought his breath right into her ear. "You're right, Gemma. I need to keep my eyes open in case a guard from you-know-where is here."

"I'd better keep my eyes open, too. I don't want the girl who came with me to see you—it would confuse things a great deal." Her heart pattered the way it always did when she fretted. "They—the group I'm with—might start wondering where I am and send someone in to find me. They must have stepped outside onto the terrace."

She felt Toby's hand grip hers more firmly. He asked, "Does this 'group' include your beau?"

The question released laughter in Gem. She shook her head.

He spoke, close to her ear. "If I should turn my head, that your sweet eyes would kiss me from the door—"

His words tumbled, dizzied her. "What did you say?"

"Lines from the poetry book you so kindly brought me," said Toby.

Just then something—someone—caught his attention. He kept his voice low. "One of the guards from the camp may be here. I glimpsed the chap from a distance, so can't be sure. But to be on the safe side, I'd better make myself scarce." His face then filled with a similar anguish as at the barbed wire fence those times she'd told him she had to leave.

"Gemma, meet me at Wild Pigeon Park on Sunday at dusk. The bench beneath the willow tree. Please. I'll explain everything then."

She agreed. She sensed the reluctance with which he released her hand, shoulder. He skittered away through the dance floor crowd. Another man in a soldier's uniform stepped up to take Toby's place, but Gem shook her head and hurried off the dance floor. Meeting him there, looking so fine, had been like a dream. A reckless but beautiful dream.

The reverie now over, Gem hurried out onto the back terrace. She could only hope that Rooney had been there the whole time, that she hadn't seen Gem dance with Toby, whom she might well have recognized from his brief stint at the tannery. The expansive lakeside terrace was strung with lanterns. Right beside the lake on which moonlight crested little dragonflies. Part of Gem remained in the dream, dancing with Toby, because the lake, mere feet away, didn't scare her much; it looked more like a setting from a romantic movie.

A familiar voice called out to Gem. "*There* you are, Gemma!" said Ada. "We were about to send a search party for you. Where've you been all this time? Obviously, you missed me waving my gold beret, the signal to convene outside."

The others stared at her, awaiting an answer.

"I . . . was just in the ladies' room, freshening up," Gem said, meeting their gazes the best she could.

Cora-Lynn laughed. "You don't look very 'fresh' to me—in fact, the opposite. You're sweating, Gemma Sullivan. You look like the cat who swallowed the canary."

Gem ignored this. "It's hard to see with the hordes in there. But here I am now."

Gem wondered where Toby had gone, whether he'd evaded the possible guard. She breathed a silent prayer for his safety.

Thankfully, Miss Fearing shifted the subject, remarking how pretty the lanterns looked.

Ada fished a flask out of her handbag, unscrewed it and drank.

"Soda is a snore-fest, ladies. The stuff of treadmill tongues. This moonshine is much better, corn liquor of the gods."

Cora-Lynn had been resting against the railing, tipping her face to the moon. Ada passed the flask to her, and Ponder the Wonder took a hard pull. Cora-Lynn handed the flask to Hester Hobbs, who'd been fanning herself with a folded snack bar menu. Hester's eyes held a faraway look.

Presented with the flask, Hester glanced over at Miss Fearing, as if seeking permission.

"It's all right, Hobbs. Remember, tonight I'm just Beatrice. Why don't you have some . . . *judicious fun?*"

Hester laughed, and said, "Yes, why don't I?" She drank from the flask, then passed it among their group.

"There's more where that came from, too," Ada brayed. "My cousin Happy will keep us happy. Or Jack, the swain who used all his dance tickets on me—he's shipping out tomorrow and means to have a good time tonight. He's practically proposed to me. I imagine he'll be out here soon enough, looking for me, for more dances."

She handed Gemma the flask. What harm in a tiny sip? Gem took one, then realized someone was missing. Rooney Delacroix. She craned her neck to scan the terrace.

Rooney reappeared. She must have slipped away to the ladies' room. When Ada offered her the flask, she shook her head.

"You must be in training for a nun," Ada teased, but then let it go, as Rooney's unease was palpable.

Happy the bouncer came their way and handed Ada another flask. "You should get back in there and dance," he said. "We like to keep this place jiving hot."

She took the flask. Waved him away. "All in good time. Right now, we're out here having a meeting of . . ." She tried to think of what.

"The covert coven," Cora-Lynn interjected.

The overgrown boy Happy shrugged and left.

The new flask circulated among them.

"I thought you were going to say Imperial Order Daughters of the Empire," Hester quipped.

"The empire is mostly rubbish," Miss Fearing blustered, sparking a cigarette that smelled so odd that when the others detected its spice, they swivelled their heads in her direction. "It's one of my special clove cigarettes," she explained. Then she removed her shoes and stood, barefooted, on the wooden terrace. "Lord, I hate lady-shoes." She exhaled exotic spice.

"Whatever do you mean, Miss—Beatrice—what you said about the empire? After all, you *benefit* from it, do you not?" Hester appeared deeply puzzled, asking this.

Miss Fearing had been reserved all night. Now it was as if a bottle top had popped open. Between drags on her spicy, burning stick that flared down very quickly, she spoke: "The empire is a colossal monster of inefficiency, a dead letter office vaster than any of you can imagine, a planetary theatre of male egos vying for recognition—and while their cocky games play out"—she tossed her cigarette butt into the lake—"terrible things are happening to people—unspeakable things. The newspapers censor it out."

Even though Miss Fearing had said she wasn't the boss that night, she *was* the boss, and now she took a handkerchief from her dress pocket and dabbed in a distraught, angry way at beads of sweat on her forehead. Witnessing the crack in her usual armour was unsettling for Gem, and the distressed stares of her co-workers indicated they felt the same. No matter how annoying her bell ringing, how eccentric her office habits, the way she called them paper birds, what an egg beater of a boss she could be, she was the paste that bonded them.

Rooney Delacroix gave Miss Fearing several comforting pats on the arm. "It's all right."

"But it's *not*," Miss Fearing stormed. "Not even close. I've had no letter from Peggy in weeks. I don't know what to make of it—whether the mail censors are bogged down or something much worse has happened to her."

The others had moved closer to Miss Fearing, too, weaving a little tent of privacy around her, though Gem noticed stares from other couples and clusters of people also out on the terrace.

"And Peggy is?" This came from Cora-Lynn.

"Margaret Fricker," Beatrice said. "She's a mechanic, might have been sent closer to the front line. I'm desperately worried about her. I thought coming tonight might take my mind off things, but"—she dabbed at her forehead again—"clearly it hasn't. Please forget what I've said—I prefer keeping my life private. But since we're here and I've said this much, I'll tell you—she's my heart's other half."

"Take some of this." Ada offered their boss the flask.

She took a swallow and passed it to Gem.

Gem didn't see the harm in another sip. A warmth akin to sunbathing settled over her, deepening the feeling already there, since dancing with Toby.

Gem's hunch was that now they needed to divert their boss from her troubles.

Ada sensed this, too, it seemed. She swept her arm towards the moonlit water. "Do you think there are U-boats out there?" She seemed to ask everyone at once, and no one.

"I hope not!" Cora-Lynn wailed.

"They're here, you know—in Canada," Hester said. "Skulking like giant, deadly eels in our waters—Gulf of St. Lawrence. Who knows, even closer."

They fell quiet, standing clumped beneath the summer moon.

"How's the cat, Gemma?" Cora-Lynn asked.

A marvel how the Wonder could smirk and smoke at the same time. At first Gem didn't know what she meant, took her a moment to recall Cora-Lynn's taunting accusation about where Gem sometimes spent lunch hour.

"The cat is fine," Gem said.

Rooney looked puzzled.

"It's just a cat I feed. A stray."

"Does your aunt know?" Rooney probed.

"What does it matter? Why would my aunt care about some random stray cat?" Too late, Gem realized she'd been snappish.

Rooney looked hurt. For the second time that night. "Only about the wasted-food part."

Out of blue yonder, Hester said, "Rooney, I didn't see you dance once—quite the wallflower."

"I can't dance," Rooney said, simply. "And you never know who's in there—I don't want to risk fraternizing. Talking to someone I shouldn't. There are posters about it everywhere." She added: "Seems like quite a lively office you ladies work in. I spend my days with dead sheep, they can't talk. Neither can pigs."

"Stop!" Hester pleaded. "Don't mention pigs, please. You'll make me sick."

"What's wrong with *her*?" cawed Ada.

"Pigs are against her faith," Cora-Lynn blathered. "Not kosher."

Hester groaned. "Cora, why do you have such a big mouth?" Verging on tears, Hester asked Miss Fearing, "Will I . . . be . . . fired now? You must have seen the signs on beaches, about us. They call us 'the unwanted.' Our government doesn't want us here, so now that you know what I am, why would I be allowed to keep my job?"

"Because you're *good* at it," Miss Fearing answered flatly. "And because I know what it's like, being among the 'unwanted.'"

"I shouldn't even be here," Hester added. "After sunset, it's the Sabbath. If my parents find out, they'll be very mad at me. I could only come because they're away, at a cottage. My brother knows I'm here—he's my chauffeur tonight, and hopefully he won't blab."

"Your secret is safe with me," Rooney said.

The melodic strains of "Chattanooga Choo Choo" rippled forth from inside, rich with clarinets' whimsied diddles.

Ada Swift sang along for a few bars. Then turned sulky. "Girls, we came here tonight for pleasure—to fandango the night, bust some moves. I go to all this effort, and what do I get instead? Confession hour. I've had *enough* gloom, *enough* true confessions."

A sturdy fellow approached their group and invited Ada to a turn on the dance floor.

"Jeepers, thanks for rescuing me from these Negative Nancys," she said, trotting away on his arm. She'd tucked her golden beret in the little purse hooked over her shoulder. So it seemed that her signal system had ended for the night. She'd had enough of them.

Rooney turned to Gem. "We need to catch the last streetcar. We should leave."

She was right. Time, somehow, bent differently in that pleasure dome, had flown.

Hester Hobbs bid the others good night, too. She'd arranged for her brother to pick her up at eleven, the hour had come. Cora-Lynn said she'd walk with Gem and Rooney to the streetcar stop—a rare stroke of thoughtfulness, for the Wonder. Rightly or wrongly, no one worried about Ada Swift. She orbited an alternate stratosphere. Possibly her cousin would drive her home. She'd have more suitors before that night ended, likely, than the rest of them for the remainder of their days, Gem thought.

Beatrice Fearing took a key from her dress's pocket. "My chariot awaits."

"You're riding your Norton home?" Cora-Lynn asked, astonished. "In that sparkly dress and those shoes?"

"Why wouldn't I?" the boss bristled, her characteristic edge back. "My boots are in a kit bag strapped to the beast. I'll bin these nasty heels. And when I'm home, I'll write Peggy, go on the faith that the letter will one day land in her hands. That's the only way now. If I lose faith, that's the end of me."

She slipped away.

By the time Gem, Rooney, Hester and Cora-Lynn deked around the dancers and exited under the front door's archway, Miss Fearing's motorbike had already growled off into the night.

THE STREETCAR RIDE home was quiet for Gemma and Rooney, each in her own thoughts. The only sounds, as they walked from Lake Shore Road a few blocks north to Pidgeon Avenue, were intermittent late night crickets and the occasional car passing them. Deep darkness saturated everything. Gemma was glad for the lodger's company but also, now that the moonshine had worn off, remorseful. She needed to set things right. "I didn't mean that about 'having' to bring you, Rooney—what I said earlier. And I'm sorry I snapped at you about the cat."

"It's all right," Rooney murmured.

They neared the Delucas' house. Pungent squash blossoms and dusky perfume from other vined vegetables from Rosa's front-yard garden reached them. This was the first time Gemma realized that a night garden possessed its own essence, different from daytime.

When they tiptoed into the flat, Aunt Wren's snores reached them. She hadn't waited up for them after all, weariness had gotten the better of her. But she'd left a light on in the kitchen for them.

"Good night, Rooney," Gem whispered.

"Night, Gemma."

In bed, Gem thought about her time on the dance floor. Toby dressed so fine, looking so well. So different. A more divine version of himself. As she drifted into sleep, seven words wafted, banner-like, across her mind: *Wild Pigeon Park, willow tree, Sunday, dusk.*

TWENTY-ONE

"WE ALL SAID too much at the Palais Royale last night," Miss Fearing harped, voice rife with chagrin as she stood, pale-lipped, in the lower office, beside her desk. The retching fan kept shunting a strand of hair in her face and she whacked it back in place repeatedly. It was obvious she'd slept on the cot in the corner; her beige slacks were rumpled, a coffee stain blossomed on her wrinkled blouse. She must have gone straight from the Palais Royale to The Cottage. Kept a change of clothes by the cot. Her employees stood, too, at droopy attention, beside their desks, like other mornings, awaiting the day's directives, its onslaught of data. But their boss didn't launch into that right away. Instead, she said: "We've been fools. I count myself in that."

As much as Gem needed wages, she resented working on Saturdays. But nearly everyone else did since the war began, and Miss Fearing had told the girls, tartly, when one or the other of them had broached this topic, to "quit whining. At Bletchley it was non-stop, day shifts, night shifts, seven days a week." Strange to think that mere hours earlier they'd been listening to a big band, dancing, and passing a flask on the moonlit terrace behind the ballroom.

"With all due respect, Miss Fearing," said Cora-Lynn, "I can't imagine what we said that was so very harmful or incriminating."

Hester Hobbs side-eyed Cora-Lynn warily.

With a single soured gesture, their boss lit a Pall Mall. "*Really*, Miss Ponder? Words like *U-boats* flew from our moonshiny mouths—not to mention my spilled beans about Peggy." Miss Fearing went on. "And your—friend, Miss Sullivan—that girl Rooney, sweet kid, but who knows who her loose lips might flap to?"

Ada Swift stepped into the fray. "The girl struck me as very shy, so she might not talk."

"I'll . . . ask her not to," Gem stammered.

"This whole fracas is *my* fault," Ada said. "I just thought getting out would do you good, Miss Fearing, and as for the rest of us, we work together, and some social time seemed like a worthwhile project, might help us bond, help these hangdogs ginger up." She pointed to Gem, Hester and Cora-Lynn.

Their boss's stern aura softened. Her voice, usually so steady, so procedural, quavered. "Your motive derived from kindness, Miss Swift. It's done now, and all we can do is take a lesson from it, how easy it is to let one's guard slip. I for one will be less of a fool after this."

The very tarot card Aunt Wren had upturned that morning. *The Fool*. Gemma had glanced at it while grabbing a cookie from the jar then rushing out the door. She recalled that Aunt Wren had once recounted that *The Fool* means reckless folly, poor judgment. Had it been folly to dance with Toby? This question wasn't worth considering, really; the instant Gem saw him, running away was never an option.

Wild Pigeon Park, willow tree, Sunday, dusk.

Miss Fearing brandished bundles of intercepts. "I've scanned this latest infusion of code strings—they're brutal. They've obviously reset the key. Now, get to work, paper birds."

Gem strained for a pattern—anything—in the alphabet freight trains. A dull headache throbbed in her temples, likely from the moonshine.

Hester isolated a symbol that, she felt pretty sure, was a space between words.

The beast of a morning dragged on and on.

At the noon bell, they dropped their pencils, relieved, and went outside. Gemma rose, stiff, and followed the others to the shoreside log. She didn't feel talkative, or even particularly hungry. She longed to sprint across Lake Shore Road, through the factory lots, the arid, cracked-earth field with its rogue tufted grass, to the barbed wire fence to make sure Hedwig the cat was all right. She loved the furry creature who'd led her to Toby. If Hedwig hadn't beckoned so persuasively that first time, Gem might never have ventured so near the tall, formidable fence.

Her co-workers ate their lunches quietly, Cora-Lynn sipping from her thermos. Gem took her tuna sandwich from her satchel. While she nibbled the sandwich, she thought about Toby. He *had* said he wasn't supposed to be locked in the prisoner-of-war camp. He'd sounded so truthful, she'd believed him. For the first time, it struck her that he might have taken the cat with him. If he'd had to leave her behind, would she be cared for by the other prisoners?

Ada Swift chomped on an apple. She'd scuffed her shoes off into the sand. Her bare legs gleamed with some kind of lotion, a medicinal though not unpleasant smell.

Hester brandished a blintz. "Might as well eat what I enjoy now that everyone *knows*." She glared at Cora-Lynn, who sat cross-legged on the log in a recent style of pants, culottes, reading a *Maclean's* magazine she held higher than necessary, a wall between herself and the others.

Whether the morning's difficult work had worn them out or the awkwardness from the Palais exerted a lingering effect, for whatever reason, each girl kept to herself during that day's precious noon break. Along the shore, sandpipers skittered, pecking at microscopic food. Lake gulls trolled the air not far above the girls' heads, waiting for crusts, crumbs, cores. The scent of tiger lilies and pinks wafted from nearby gardens.

Ada broke the silence. "After you girls slugged yourselves home, I had some fine fun, dancing. *Closed* the place, in fact."

Cora-Lynn slapped her magazine down on the log. "This *Maclean's* is dull. Tell us more, Ada. What happened after we left?"

This question piqued interest and drew each girl out of her private bubble.

"I don't mind spilling. My dancing partner was . . . *fascinating*. And a gentleman. After the dancing ended, we sat in his Packard convertible under the stars and talked for ages. His name is Edison—Eddie. After stargazing, he drove me home."

Quite brazen, Gem thought, *taking a ride from a stranger*. But she kept this to herself.

"What's so fascinating about Mr. Eddie?" asked Cora-Lynn.

Ada pushed herself off the log and stood, turning to face her audience still seated on the log, as she'd done during previous lunches, turning the swatch of sand into an improvised theatre stage.

"Lots of things make Eddie fascinating," she began. "First off, his job. He works in that prisoner camp near here—as a guard. Can you imagine?"

Gemma nearly choked on her last bite of tuna. Hester had to hump along the log quickly to slap her on the back several times.

"Did he tell you anything? Like, what it's like in there?" Cora-Lynn asked.

Ada, in her element, shone. If she didn't do spy work at Casa Loma or codebreaking at The Cottage, she could, Gem thought, land a movie role, or at the very least model for the T. Eaton Company.

"He told me lots of things," she said.

Gem flattened her hands on the log, worried they might start to shake. Maybe this Eddie was the very guard Toby worried about running into at the Palais. She felt like *The Fool* on the tarot card, at the edge of a cliff, part of her dying to know more, part of her *afraid*, for what if she was about to learn something terrible about Toby?

Ada, with her peerless instinct for drama, had paused. "To begin on the bright side, the Red Cross and other charities bring the prisoners all sorts of books and sports equipment. Musical instruments. They put on plays. That's why people on the outside gossip and gripe about the place being like a resort. But it's no resort," Ada said. "Some men suffer from nervous illnesses or are physically sick, or diseased. More men have died in this camp than others in Canada, Eddie told me. The toilets are always backing up, the place reeks. But worst are the divisions between the men themselves. Not all prisoners support Hitler—some quite the opposite. One arch-Nazi is a strapping brute who beats the poor lads who don't toe the party line. There are other abuses, like nasty things slipped into their food or in their beds—and worse, so bad Eddie couldn't mention them. The prisoners get away with a lot because the guards can't watch them every second. And who knows, maybe certain guards are in cahoots with them?"

"Eddie told you *all this*?" Cora-Lynn buzzed. "Isn't he under some kind of gag order, like us?"

Ada shrugged. "Probably. But"—her eyes playful—"I think he was trying to impress me, and maybe some rye whiskey we shared loosened his tongue."

Inhaling heavily, as if to breathe courage from the summer air, Gem ventured: "Did Eddie tell you about any *particular* prisoners?"

"A few colourful characters, sure, who enjoy wearing dresses in the theatrical plays. The camp bully I've mentioned." Just when it seemed that was all Ada had, she tacked on, "Oh yes, and this sweet-tempered young man who speaks fluent English, and who's taken the brunt of the bully's nastiness, so Eddie watches out for this fellow the best he can."

Then an awful notion struck Gem. Had Eddie seen Tobias Albrecht at the Palais? If so, what would happen to Toby?

She knew she shouldn't push things too much more. But she couldn't stop, not yet.

"Do the prisoners ever talk to regular people, you know, civilians? Did Eddie mention that?"

A gull wheeled close again. Ada flung her arm high, faked a toss, like she'd thrown something, sending it on a wild gull chase.

"You're in there long enough, you pick up a little English," Ada replied. "And vice versa. The prisoners gab with the guards all the time. Though they're not supposed to. The prisoners aren't supposed to talk to regular people, like, outside the camp—though I don't see how they *would* anyway. Eddie described the tall barbed fence. But he said up in Muskoka, where most of the officers are, they get away with murder, even swim and sun with local girls. The prisoners sign a pledge that they won't speak with civilians, but Eddie said it's not worth the paper it's—"

The lunch-end bell clappered, insistent. They gathered their things, purses, lunch wrappers, *Maclean's* magazine. Ada sighed, slipping her sandals back on her feet.

"You didn't tell Eddie anything about *our* work, did you, Ada?" Hester asked in anxious huffs as they gaggled their way back to the basement office.

"Oh phooey, of course not, Hobbs. What kind of witless Wilma do you take me for? I told him, when he asked, that I work in a beauty parlour. 'Of *course* you do,' he said, 'because you're beautiful.'"

When they settled back at their desks, Miss Fearing, newly animated, announced that they'd been given a "special assignment" from Ottawa. She was thrilled about the vote of confidence in them, she said, and she'd soon unveil it all. Whatever the assignment was, it boosted her mood a great deal.

TWENTY-TWO

Perhaps it was age, Wren thought, a creeping daily absent-mindedness. Small things at first. A bar of soap, misplaced. A book of poetry lost somewhere in their flat; they only lived in three rooms plus a kitchen, living room—how far could it have gone? Her new eyeglasses proved a great boon, but sometimes she needed glasses to find her glasses. Out on errands, she'd twice forgotten to buy All-Bran. And she kept misplacing things.

She laid down her needle. Of the various misplaced, or lost, items, the book of poetry irked her most. She hadn't read Edna St. Vincent Millay since losing her fiancé to the war; it would have been too painful. But now, years later, she craved those poems once more, to again see their words set the page aflame. The attention lavished on her by the eye doctor confused her, too. Yesterday, he'd phoned, asked Wren to make him a hat. She'd been honest: She had left millinery behind long ago. But Dr. Fox wouldn't take no for an answer. In that case, she'd need to take measurements. So he'd reminded her of the dinner —he didn't call it "supper" as she did—a few days hence. His hat-order timing had been canny, for she had, in fact, toyed with the idea of restarting millinery with her improved vision.

WREN ROSE, CREAKILY, embarked on a full-out hunt for the book. She even overturned the chesterfield pillows. She rifled through her dresser drawers. Closet shelves. Under her bed. Still feeling guilty for her earlier trespass into Rooney's bedroom, she didn't enter it. But it did occur to Wren that both the soap and book had disappeared after the lodger moved into the flat. No, Wren wouldn't snoop in the girl's room a second time, but she'd find an opportune moment, and muster all the tact she had, to broach the missing items with Rooney. For though in many ways Rooney Delacroix was the ideal lodger—pleasant, quiet, paid her room and board on time, knitted, went to church on Sundays, a crossword companion—the girl *was* capable of deception or, at the very least, withholding information. Here Wren recalled the knitted baby clothes in the girl's room. Wren would continue to give the lodger her privacy but would secure a chance to inquire after the soap, the book.

Wren gave up searching for the book and took up her needle, thread, again.

A knock at the door startled her badly. She jabbed her finger, winced, and went to answer the door. The landlady Mrs. Deluca stood there, holding a long-stemmed red rose.

"This just arrived," the landlady said with an arch expression. "Looks like someone has an admirer. I must go, my radio program is on." She trundled back downstairs.

Wren took the rose into the kitchen, where she could now inhale its perfume.

Attached to the rose's stem was a note, with a single hand-printed word: *Upstairs*. That meant their flat.

She placed the rose in a water-filled vase on the kitchen table. Still wearing her new spectacles, she studied the rose carefully; it really was a splendid specimen. Hothouse, most likely. Purchased from a florist. Not cheap.

How hard vanity dies, Wren mused. For she dared to think that perhaps, *possibly*, Dr. Fox was the floral giver. He knew where she lived. He must have been working in his office and paid to have the rose delivered. She found it amusing that he hadn't written his name on the note. His way, perhaps, of seeming mysterious, playful.

Well, *two* could play. *She* could be enigmatic, too. A more predictable lady would ring him at his office, to thank him. But Wren decided to stay mum about it until their upcoming dinner.

Now more than ever, she wanted to find the lost book. Poetry and roses fit well together.

She heard some scuffling noises in the foyer. Rooney Delacroix was home from the tannery.

Entering the kitchen, the cheerful girl remarked on the rose. "How grand, so plump!"

Asking her right then, with even the gentlest tact, in the most casual way—*Say, did you happen to see my copy of Edna St. Vincent Millay's* Renascence, *or the soap?*—was the wrong thing to do, Wren decided. So, while the girl put the kettle on, they conversed amiably, then tackled a crossword, and decided on a supper of scrambled eggs when Gemma arrived home. Wren would store the uncomfortable questions about the book and the soap in her mind a little, though not much, longer.

TWENTY-THREE

That Sunday, the day she'd agreed to meet Toby in Wild Pigeon Park, it felt to Gemma as though dusk would never arrive. She washed her hair, which took hardly any time at all, then spent much of the day in her bedroom, wanting to be alone with her thoughts, hopes. Dreams. She'd padded into the kitchen in her slippers long enough to make toast and look at the pretty rose in the vase on the table. The lodger sometimes brought flowers to the flat, wild blooms snitched from local gardens. But this was no rose snitched from a garden; its luxuriance bespoke florist shop.

Rooney munched toast at the table, saw Gem eye the rose.

"I wonder who your aunt's admirer is," the lodger said. "It's all very mysterious."

It certainly was, and Gem would think about it—later.

That same Sunday, Aunt Wren knocked on Gemma's bedroom door, asking if she had seen the book of Millay's poems. Pressing a pillow over her head for a few seconds so her aunt wouldn't hear her groan, Gem had called back, "Maybe, Birdie, I'll take a look later." Why *now*, of all times, did Aunt Wren want a book she hadn't shown any interest in for years?

After returning from church, Rooney knitted in her room all afternoon. Then she emerged and made fried potato pancakes for their supper. Aunt Wren, in high spirits, enjoyed them "profusely," and over her empty plate declared to Gem and Rooney that she was thinking of returning to millinery. "Now that my eyes are so much better." She beamed, glancing at the tall rose.

Gem picked at her pancakes.

"Are you quite well, niece of mine?" asked Aunt Wren.

"Fine," Gem said. "Just not that hungry—no offence to your cooking, Rooney. A walk will do me good. I spend so much time in the office, I feel like I'm missing out on summer."

Rooney said, "Can I have the rest of your pancakes?"

Gem nodded, then rose from the table.

"But it's almost dusk," Aunt Wren protested. "You'll end up walking home alone in the dark."

"I'm not afraid of the dark, Birdie, and I'll take a flashlight. Don't worry, I shouldn't be long, just really need to stretch my legs."

So Gem left the flat, flashlight in hand, wearing a blouse with a mosaic pattern, and slacks. As she walked briskly towards Wild Pigeon Park, she wondered if she should have dressed up more. Maybe she should have borrowed one of Birdie's hats to obfuscate her terrible haircut. But asking Aunt Wren if she could borrow a hat would have spiked more fuss, more questions, when she wished to slip quietly away.

The park was near the lake, but Gem was too excited to fret about water. Dusk would soon descend, and the park's ragged grass was a deep, velvety green. The day's last shadows quivered, and as Gemma neared the willow tree, she saw Toby, seated on a bench. Noticing her, he stood, like a soldier almost, straight, at attention. There didn't seem to be anyone else in the park.

And now Toby was right there before her, no fence between them. There, wearing civilian clothes, plaid shirt, trousers. His proximity seemed strange to Gem, and it was stranger still to have become habituated to that hostile barbed wire barrier and his awful uniform with its prisoner number.

As if reading her thoughts, Toby, still standing in that stiff, formal posture, said, "It's so odd that we can walk right up to each other with no wire thorns blocking our faces. Oddly nerve-racking, yet marvellous."

He motioned for her to sit on the bench beside him.

They sat and he took her hand. Gem set the flashlight down on the bench beside her.

"I'm so glad you came," Toby said. "Gem, you seemed rather—afraid when you first saw me at the Palais. You were shaking."

"It was the sheer surprise of seeing you there."

"Why? Were you with a . . . beau?"

Gem fiddled with the flashlight. "No." She was pretty sure she'd already mentioned this, at the Palais. Maybe he needed reassurance. "Were *you*?"

He shook his head.

"How did you escape from the camp, Toby?"

He laughed. "Escape? They'd have captured me quickly enough, and I wouldn't be here, sitting with you in a park. Even if they couldn't find me, I'd be swimming for my life or hiding in a shed or barn."

She still didn't understand.

Toby's hand pressed her own more firmly. "I'll tell you everything."

Gem waited.

He shifted closer to her on the bench. "I work for Allied intelligence. For the past several years I've been what's called a 'listener within the walls.' Basically, an eavesdropper. It's well-known that prisoners of war are valuable sources of information. So, day after day, in the guise of a fellow prisoner, I listened to the other men, to see what I could glean. My superiors gave me a script, basic information to maintain my disguise in the camp. I asked the prisoners questions. Maybe *too* many, for they began to distrust me as time went on, sensing I wasn't one of them—though I was treated the same way, to maintain the ruse. It wasn't like I had extra bars of soap or food rations slipped my way. Which was why your gift of soap was a godsend. As were *you*. Then I was sent to work at

Donnell & Mudge—the prisoners might disclose different things there. And while the tannery was a vile place—I don't eat animal flesh—even my brief stint there helped restore the muscles rowing had once built."

His face had that open, earnest look Gem recalled so well, making it hard not to believe him.

"So, is none of that true—about your mother, living in Germany and all that?"

"It's all true," Toby said sadly. "Everything I told you. I was born in Canada. My father is Canadian. And since my hometown, Hamburg, has been flattened, I still don't know where the Nazis have taken my mother, or if she's even alive. And I was worried enough *before* that."

Gem gave his hand a sympathetic squeeze. "Have you even been inside a U-boat?"

Toby shook his head. "No submarine, only my racing shell—for rowing."

Gem worried she wasn't worldly like he was. Maybe she was even naive. Maybe she should be more cautious. "Is Tobias Albrecht your real name?"

"It is."

"Your superiors gave you a script, a story of your life to follow. Why didn't this script also include an assumed name?"

"Fair question," Toby said. "We were mainly numbers in the camp. My number was 1007933. The other men dubbed me Puny 33 because I'm—was—thinner than most of them, except the sick ones."

Darkening, the grass's deep colour took on a blackened blood hue.

"So, those times I visited you at the fence, the guard wouldn't have done a thing because he, presumably, knew about your . . . role? And the whole time I was scared to death that the guard might see me?"

Toby squeezed her hand. "I'm sorry, Gem. It wasn't like I could tell you. And there *was* risk if the other prisoners saw me talking to you—and in fact one *did*—that day you ran."

Gem noticed the woven cat collar around his wrist, minus the bell. "What happened to Hedwig?"

"When they reassigned me, it was hard for me to leave her," Toby answered. "I can only hope she attaches herself to another prisoner, one kindly predisposed to cats. Or that she finds a new home outside the camp."

"What's your new . . . role? If you can tell me," Gem asked.

"I feel that you won't disclose any of this. I trust you, so I'll tell you. I go where they send me. Lots of us are dispatched from assignment to assignment, place to place, as we're needed."

Gem thought of Ada Swift, working some days at Casa Loma, others at The Cottage.

Toby continued. "I'll be in this area for a while, but I don't know for how long. The sooner the war ends, the sooner I can find out what happened to my mother. And live a normal life."

"There was a guard from the prisoner-of-war camp at the Palais Royale the other night. Eddie somebody. Does he know about the special assignment you had there?"

"I don't think so. Not all the guards knew about me. The idea was that I'd be treated like the other prisoners. A sympathetic guard might slip and make a mistake. I spied Eddie in the crowd and hoofed it out of there after I danced with you. I don't think he saw me."

Gem was relieved to hear this.

"I need to tell you this, too," Toby said. "Those times you visited me, and brought soap, and poetry, and your sweet, kind face, you saved my life. I'd started to lose myself. While I wasn't a real prisoner, I was still a prisoner in my *mind*. If it hadn't been for you, and my cat . . ." He trailed off.

Glancing at the bright coil around his wrist that she'd woven, a sudden, deep sorrow suffused Gem. "They'll send you somewhere else, far away from here."

She was glad, now, for the dark, as tears sprang onto her cheeks. Toby took a handkerchief from his trousers' pocket and wiped them away.

"Not right away, Gem. In the meantime, we have time to get to know each other more." He grasped both her hands.

There'd be limits to how much she could tell him, Gem reminded herself.

"My aunt will be very worried by now—I must go," Gem said.

"Meet me here next Sunday—please. But earlier. To give us more time. Three o'clock?"

"What if you're sent away before then?" she asked.

"I'll find a way to get a message to you."

She wrapped her arms around him.

Then, as Gem let go and began to walk away, Toby said, "Did you like the long-stemmed rose I left for you?"

What? *Oh, poor Birdie*. But what could Gem do, at that moment, but turn and say: "It's lovely, thank you."

TWENTY-FOUR

THE NEXT DAY, Miss Fearing entered the basement in a pressed blouse and skirt, in her oxford shoes. This meant, Gem knew, something serious was about to happen. The girls turned from their desks to look at her, their faces expectant. Ada Swift was working at her other job that day, installing grenades in briefcases, knives in fountain pens, maps on silk scarves. Spy-craft. At Station M the rest of the world knew as Casa Loma.

Miss Fearing began. "As I'd alluded to previously, they've sent us a special assignment. In several weeks an Allied supply ship called the *Northstar* will set sail for England. Except this is no ordinary supply ship. It will carry supplies, yes, but also top intelligence documents. We can't be one hundred percent certain there hasn't been an intelligence leak; the enemy may have been informed of the singular nature of this operation, which means their U-boats will be circling like sharks, in the Atlantic. They will attack the *Northstar* and try to seize the documents before it sinks to the bottom of the sea and everyone on board drowns."

Gemma cringed. That same terrible, agonizing fate that had befallen her parents.

"We need all hands on deck here. Before the *Northstar* sets sail and during its passage, you'll turn your full attention to breaking codes that might reveal the enemy's attack strategy. We must protect this Allied ship at all costs. I can't overstate how momentous this operation. If successful, it could move the world closer to ending this ghastly war, bring our loved ones home sooner."

Miss Fearing paused to light a cigarette. Then continued.

"They're placing huge trust in us. Paper birds, we need your minds now more than ever. You'll have to work together collaboratively." She inhaled her Pall Mall. "A little competitiveness is healthy, it spurs us, but for this operation you'll become *a single machine* with all its moving parts in a synergistic flow. Ponder, your numbers must talk with Sullivan's words, Hobbs's logic must engage with Swift's magic, Sullivan's hunches must cohabit with stone-cold certainties. You won't be able to huddle in your silos on this one. You'll need to meld with each other's psyches. Get inside each other's minds to open the widest conceptual spaces possible. I'll fill Swift in tomorrow when she returns. Questions?"

"Why doesn't Whitby take this on?" Hester asked. "Their equipment is so much more sophisticated than what we do here in our little office. They have *technology*, while we're armed only with pencils and paper."

This struck a nerve. It launched Miss Fearing into a tirade. "Humans in ancient times acquired language with nary a pencil *or* paper. Yet still, progress in communication evolved. Prometheus stole fire from the gods, and he had neither pencil nor paper. I *very much doubt* he whined about this deficiency. We learned to tell time by studying shadows. Even now I sound the bell to signal your lunch breaks; again, meaning without pencil or paper. Therefore, if so many advances in human history took place *without* pencils or paper, think, my paper birds, what you might achieve *with* such tools at your disposal."

To punctuate her speech, Miss Fearing bashed out her Pall Mall.

Their boss had reached a level of true magnificence, or terror.

They cowered like frightened voles at her oxford-shod feet. She began to shuffle around the office, distributing the day's intercepts. Then she went upstairs.

"Guess she told *you*, Hobbs," Ponder the Wonder carped across the office.

Hester looked shaken. Shamed. "That was harsh. Lady F could have simply accused me of whining instead of delivering a lecture on advances in human history that didn't involve pencil and paper."

They set to work. Gem hadn't slept much. She was still stirred up from her meeting with Toby at the park. The disclosure about the long-stemmed rose had rattled her. He said he'd "left it," meaning he knew where she lived. But then, he worked in intelligence. He was trained to discover information. She worried that he might somehow find out about her work. Then there was the thorn at home, Aunt Wren believing the rose was for *her*. If it had proven true, what Rooney said, that Birdie had an admirer, how greatly that might help her to get over the tragedy of Adam Hartsock at last. As for Toby, what if he asked to *visit* Gem at the flat on Pidgeon Avenue? Then how would they explain to Rooney Delacroix that, yes, he'd worked with the other prisoners at the tannery but now he didn't, now he walked about free, and even brought roses there—for Gem?

The best solution was to keep Toby under wraps. And the rose? How disappointed Birdie would be, if she knew it hadn't been meant for her.

LAKESIDE LUNCHES WERE less lively on the days Ada Swift worked at Casa Loma. Hester sat sullen on the log, still reeling, Gem supposed, from the dressing-down Miss Fearing had given her. Cora-Lynn smoked a menthol cigarette and gazed out at the lake. There was no reason for Gem to sneak away to the prisoner-of-war camp now, though she still worried about the cat. She glanced along the log at Cora-Lynn. Their boss had directed them to "meld with each other's psyches." Gem shuddered. She couldn't imagine what went on in Cora-Lynn's brain, the formulae she plugged away at that filled the chalkboard. Gem didn't see how any meeting of minds, hers and Ponder the Wonder's, could ever happen.

"Why do you like numbers so much, Cora-Lynn? Mathematics, I mean," Gem asked.

The Wonder blew minty smoke out over the sand. This question seemed to throw her off, but only for a few seconds. Looking at Gem square-on, Cora-Lynn answered: "Numbers are precise. Numbers don't lie. Few things are more elegant than a well-rendered formula. Math is a distillation so pure, so beautiful. I'd give anything to have known Ada Lovelace, Roger Cotes, Leonhard Euler, whose famous equation taps into the very essence of life, equal to the greatest work of art. And someday, if I can continue my studies, I'd love to devise an equation of my *own*."

This seemed a day for speeches. And certainly, this was more than Cora-Lynn usually said to Gem in one sustained chain of smoke.

"Whereas *words*," she went on, "are murky, with gaps in interpretation you can drive a lorry through. Words mislead, dissemble. When it comes to falsehoods, lies, words propagate faster than rabbits. Word people like you, Gem, and sometimes you, Hester, traffic in semantics which are sloppy. Number people like me deal with symbols which are purer forms. I'm closer to Ada Swift, we're both steeped in magic. My version of magic is ciphers that use algorithms to transform symbols."

Hester yawned.

But words can be symbols, too, Gem thought. She didn't have the nerve to challenge Cora-Lynn; Gem sensed she'd lose. That girl's mind dwelt on some higher plane Gemma's would never reach. How could she ever be comrades with their resident word-hater? But just then Gem's stubborn streak reared its head.

"Not *all* words are lies," Gem protested. "Many are not."

Cora-Lynn seemed not to hear.

Breaking out of her funk, Hester interjected, "And measurements can be wrong, Cora. There can be inaccuracies. Misfires. Miscalculations. Misconstrued angles. Flawed ratios. Your system is far from perfect, Clever Britches."

"Well, yes, mistakes happen—made by dullards," snapped Cora-Lynn.

Gemma couldn't fathom how they were supposed to get inside each other's minds, so inured they were, each to her silo. They were far from compatible. She could only hope that Ada Swift would exercise some sort of levelling effect.

The sound of the bell reached them. Needing no pencil, paper, numbers or words to tell them that lunch was over.

TWENTY-FIVE

"THERE HAVE BEEN some puzzles around here lately," Wren said after dinner. "And I don't mean crosswords. I'd like to clear the air about a few things."

Rooney turned away from the sink, where she was scouring the pots, and stared anxiously at Wren and Gemma, who were both still seated at the table. Gem had been scanning the newspaper. The long-stemmed rose still graced the table's centre.

Wren gestured to Rooney to sit back down at the table. "The pots can wait."

The girl obliged. She looked nervous, Gem thought. But then so was *she*. Took one to know one.

Wren began. "You're likely wondering where that rose came from, for clearly it's a hothouse variety, and not one of Rooney's mostly wild, pretty offerings."

Gem coughed.

"Unlikely as it may seem at my age," Wren said, "I have an . . . admirer. I believe this rose was sent by Dr. Fox." She picked up a flyer insert from the newspaper and, as if stricken by a sudden flash of heat, beat the paper back and forth, fanning herself.

Another cough hacked from Gemma's throat as if she'd choked on something. She studied her beloved aunt, sitting there half flustered, half proud, but fully, Gem could tell, delighted. Birdie had been sad for so long, for most of her life, really, but now she was joyous. Gemma shared a small portion of her aunt's glow, if only for a few moments. She realized that the misunderstanding about the rose was useful, because it kept Toby out of things. Gem wouldn't set the record straight. It would crush Birdie to learn the rose wasn't meant for her.

"Dr. Fox would like me to make him a hat," Wren continued. "To discuss the details of it—and other things—we'll be out at a dinner tomorrow night, so you girls will have to fend for yourselves. The eye doctor and I have moved beyond a strictly professional relationship. And no one is more surprised than *I* am."

Gem said that proved it was never too late for love.

Rooney added, "Everyone deserves a second chance—except a criminal, I guess."

"A valuable shred of wisdom, Rooney," Wren remarked. "And Carrie Davies back in 1915—that whole Massey murder debacle—is a case in point. Thank the stars that girl, after what she endured, all to preserve her virtue, was given a second chance at life." Then Wren's tone became more hesitant. "A couple of things have gone missing from the flat—a bar of soap, but more importantly, a book of poems, of which I'm quite fond, by Edna St. Vincent Millay. Up until lately the poems stirred too many memories, I couldn't bear to open the pages. I'm in the right frame of mind for poetry again. It's been a long time. And seeing much better also whets my appetite for verse. Do either of you girls know anything about the missing soap or book?"

She steadied her owlish gaze on the lodger.

Rooney said she'd no knowledge of the soap or the book.

The owl-eyed interrogator probed deeper. "It's better to confess than not, Rooney. And if you promise it won't happen again, you won't be evicted. We rather like having you here. Perhaps you'd taken the book into your bedroom to read and simply forgot to return it?"

"I'm sorry those items are lost," Rooney said. "In truth, I don't care much for poetry, so wouldn't have any use for such a book. As for the soap, maybe I use more than other people—the tannery odours are intense—but I don't believe I've gone through a whole bar since I moved in here. If I have, I'm sorry. I'll replace it right away."

Aunt Wren seemed satisfied with this. Her owl-gaze now shunted over to Gem. "Anything you'd like to tell me, niece of mine?"

"All right, Birdie. Yes, I took your book to my office, to read at lunch. I should have told you—but you hadn't dipped into its pages in ever so long."

Rooney looked relieved by Gem's disclosure.

"All right, then. It is solved," Wren said. "Perhaps you need it worse than me, Gemma—that office job has really set your nerves on edge. But I'd like it back very soon, please."

Gem nodded in slow motion.

Wren turned to the lodger. "Don't bother yourself about the soap. I've made too much of it."

"All right, Miss Maw," Rooney said. Then, after finishing the pots, she padded from the kitchen to knit in her room.

TWENTY-SIX

MISS FEARING WASN'T exaggerating about her paper birds becoming *a single machine* for Operation Northstar. When Gemma and the others arrived at the office the next day, they found their desks moved from their spots facing the wall. The desks now formed one large square in the middle of the room, a single massive surface. So now they'd work around one table, facing each other, and, Gem thought in dismay, cigarette smoke would waft right into her face.

Their boss advised them to think of it as a banquet table laden with the food of knowledge.

The rest of the office stayed the same, Miss Fearing's desk in its usual spot.

Or Gem *thought* it remained the same, until she glanced across the room and where there'd been one mousetrap planted below the window, now there were two traps. The mice problem had worsened of late, and their boss had been grumbling about it; her theory was that the girls' lunches enticed the pests. But there seemed no solution to the lunch storage. The office didn't have a refrigerator.

Ada Swift was back with them and, seeing the new desk configuration, said, "How did you move all this furniture, Miss Fearing? You must be very strong."

"Luther, the messenger lad, came early and helped me," their boss said. Then she informed them that the moved desks were merely the *start* of their "bonding regime. Instead of idling away your lunch hour dreaming down by the lake," their boss asserted, "use that hour to get to know each other more fully, use it to build trust, be at one with each other, try devising some bonding exercises."

Gem's heart balked. "Bonding exercises" better not mean that awful activity they'd made them do in physical education class, falling back into someone's arms, trusting that person to catch you. How she'd dreaded that, the letting go.

"You were four islands, now you are one," the boss said, piling a stack of intercepts on the middle of the large, newly formed megadesk, and advised they "dig into it." Then she ascended the steps and returned to her office.

Puffing on a menthol, Cora-Lynn sorted through the intercepts, dividing the papers between them.

Miserable minutes passed.

Gem coughed on the smoke that clouded across the gargantuan desk. The change in the physical space was more disorienting than helpful, she thought. And she sensed her co-workers felt the same.

After some pencil drubbing, Hester wailed, "This is terrible. Why did Lady F have to upset the apple cart? Who knew having one's desk in a different spot would be so disruptive?"

"I miss the wall," said Gem. "A long crack ran down it, right over my desk, and somehow that crack helped centre me. I miss the crack."

"I hate this new set-up," Cora-Lynn groused. "And sifting through endless papers. I'm dying to work on my equations."

"Just what kind of patriotic spirit is that, Cora?" Hester nettled across the huge block.

"I'd rather be back at The Castle, doing invisible ink," Ada whined.

"But we have to *try*," Gem insisted. "Each of us is a gear in a bigger machine."

"I'm not a gear, I'm a *girl*," carped Hester.

The morning went on like this. It was a genuine disaster. They weren't even listening to each other.

At noon, the four of them traipsed out to the silvery log. Into the scorching day.

They ate their lunches morosely. Except Cora-Lynn, who nursed her thermos, immersed in thought. Then she said, "Lady F has the whole thing wrong. What this *Northstar* operation requires is the *opposite* of her directive."

The others pivoted their attention on her, awaiting elaboration.

"Our boss wants us less siloed, tells us to bond, but in fact we should be *more* siloed, allowing each of us to lean deeply and utterly into her area of expertise. That would mean leaving me alone with my number theory, equations, algorithms, Sullivan to wield her hunches and play with her beloved words, and so on. As for moving our desks, Lady F might have *asked* us first."

Ada Swift stepped into the mediator role. She clapped her hands loudly, thrice, as if releasing the others from a trance. "Stop this! I don't care for the new system, either, but we must try. And trying begins now."

"Just how do you propose we bond?" Cora-Lynn asked. She said *bond* like it carried a foul odour.

"I've got just the thing," Ada said. Reaching into her purse, she flourished a bottle of nail polish.

They stared.

Ada knew she'd stumped them. "It's a symbol—we work with one mind, and one hand. This isn't ordinary nail polish—it's special. I concocted it myself, a special formula used as a signal, for spies. *Look for the woman with blue nails*, you get my drift." She unscrewed the small bottle's top with an air of ironic intrigue, as if she were uncorking some potion.

"What's special about it?" Gem asked.

Ada beamed. "It glows in the dark. I call it *Midnight Lake Ontario Mermaid*."

"That's a *very* long name," said Cora-Lynn.

"Cora, do you have to ruin *everything*?" said Hester. "And I've never seen *anyone* wear blue polish, ever. We'll be stared at."

Shrugging these words off, Ada said, "Who wants to go first?"

Perhaps to atone for her critical remark, Cora-Lynn, to their surprise, moved closer on the log to Ada, and held out her hands. "Paint away, magic one—make me glow blue in the dark."

In no time, Ada had painted Cora-Lynn's nails.

Gem stepped up next. "Heaven knows what I'll tell Aunt Wren and Rooney," she said.

"You're a word girl, make up a story," teased Cora-Lynn. "Just be sure your blue-tipped fingers don't scare the *cat* you visit during lunch hour." She laughed.

That again.

"I haven't seen the *cat* in a while," Gem snapped back.

"Hobbs, you're next."

It was a pretty shade, Hester had to admit.

Ada painted her own nails quickly, expertly. She let them dry for several minutes, riffling them about in the air. Then she tucked the bottle of polish back into her purse.

They fluttered their hands, too, to hasten drying.

"Now we'll work as a single hand," said Ada, triumphant. "All blue mermaid hands on deck! Just be careful not to scare yourselves, if you wake up in the middle of the night and look at your hands."

They all laughed.

The bell summoned them back to the office.

Suddenly nervous, Hester asked, "What do we tell Lady F?"

Ada laughed lightly. "The truth. We did a bonding exercise during lunch. Who knows, maybe *she'll* want glow-in-the-dark mermaid fingernails, too!"

As they trailed over the sand, Cora-Lynn said she very much doubted it. And if anything, their boss would think them a bunch of freaks.

"At least we did something *together* like we were directed," Hester said.

TWENTY-SEVEN

WREN DIDN'T RECOGNIZE half the dishes on the menu, they were like crossword clues that befuddled her. The truth was, they intimidated the hat right off her head. *Snails in Pernod served in profiteroles. Salmon quenelles with Pinot Noir butter.* French accents on platters. And birds. *Pheasant sautéed with chanterelles. Duck with pink peppercorns. Ballotine of duck.* She could read all this clearly enough and normally enjoyed word puzzles, but here, now, in the restaurant with its white linen tablecloth and candle and Dr. Fox in his suit and ascot seated across from her, studying his menu, she felt fully out of her depth. Her secret heart would have given anything for a bowl of mushroom soup and a glass of ginger ale to soothe her flip-flopping stomach, then a nice hot beef sandwich. Lyle Fox had announced the dinner as "my treat" and Wren breathed more easily as she glanced at the prices on the menu. Her purse held another instalment, too, for her glasses.

"Who knew there were so many types of lettuce?" Wren said. "Boston, Belgian endive, romaine, red leaf." Silently she craved a simple iceberg lettuce salad. And her hidden thought, as she plumbed the bewildering bill of fare, was, *You'd never know there were rations*.

She ordered the dish she best understood. Beef tenderloin.

"Are you sure you wouldn't like the pheasant?" Lyle asked.

"When it comes to birds, I only allow myself chicken."

"In deference to you, then, Miss Maw, I shall have the scallops, and as an appetizer we'll share the snails." He closed the menu and smiled across at Wren.

The waiter hinted at a bow, then left them.

Wren gazed out the dining room window at the Humber River flowing along its course. She couldn't fathom her nervousness, likely due to the ostentatious grandeur of the dark, half-timbered dining room, the clinking of fine cutlery around them. Her tape measure lay coiled in her purse; she'd take his measurements after their meal, for the hat. But she worried she should have worn a less plain dress, or her blue suit. She supposed she should say something beyond the inanity of lettuce. She'd said little, too, on their drive to the restaurant after he'd picked her up in his posh coupe.

She sipped water from the fine crystal goblet. "Thank you for the rose you had delivered—a very fine specimen." *Specimen? What was she thinking?*

Lyle stared back, blank.

And Wren knew in an instant. The rose wasn't meant for her. She choked a little on her water as the waiter flourished the snails in front of them. She'd never eaten a snail and wasn't sure she wanted to start now.

Now Lyle looked fully confused.

"I'm sorry," Wren said. "I've created an awkwardness. I live with two young ladies—my niece, who I've already mentioned to you, and a lodger, a quiet girl who works at the tannery. One of them has a secret admirer, it seems. No note or card accompanied the flower."

The eye doctor looked pained, but then brightened, as if struck by a revelation. "Think nothing of it, Miss Maw."

"Wren."

"Wren. You *do* have an admirer; he's directly across the table. And you *shall* have a rose, and more—just wait. Now try these snails."

She tasted earth, near a mushroom patch perhaps, earth infused with butter and something exotic she recalled from an herb garden long ago, in her youth—anise. Overall, it was a subtle, mysterious and, at the same time, homey taste that was pleasing to the tongue.

They were light years better than she'd imagined. Lyle ate his snails with gusto. Then asked Wren how she liked them.

"I like them very much," she said. Meaning it.

During dinner, which enchanted her mouth, and his by the look of him, he asked, taking pauses from his plate, about Wren's avoidance of birds as food—except chicken. "You've alluded to this, but tell me more."

It was as though a garden hose had been opened, and out rushed the details of her anti-plumage crusade and her millinery years.

"It all began with the passenger pigeons, I suppose. When I was very young, the vast flocks of them overhead, moving like a single dark veil that filled the whole sky, on their migrations, which sometimes lasted for several days."

"I remember them," Lyle mused.

"Of course, they wreaked great damage to the trees, and the soil, by their sheer numbers," Wren continued. "But did they not deserve to live? How awful, the shooting matches that brought them down by the thousands. All that carnage for sport. They were also sold for meat. There were so many, then they were gone. Then, in 1904, when Currie's neckwear factory burned down, I was out of work. I was seeking a job and I went into a bookseller's and browsed, thinking a novel might divert my mind. But instead of fiction, I squeezed enough coins from my purse to buy Hornaday's book *Our Vanishing Wildlife: Its Extermination and Preservation*. I may not be recalling the exact title correctly. But the book caught my notice because I thought it might help explain the tragedy that unfolded with passenger pigeons."

She allowed more tenderloin to melt in her mouth.

"I began to read more, whatever I could get my hands on, mostly at the library, about the feather trade. It was slaughter on a global scale, and it aroused such fury in me. The feather industry claimed that hats were trimmed with moulted feathers, but pamphlets and articles I consulted disproved this. Feathers were ripped from living birds. The birds were killed, tortured, and all for fashion. I was familiar with Miss Dickinson's poem about hope, the thing with feathers. But no hope remained for those tragic birds, their quills and down ripped from their bodies. All this brought me nightmares.

"Around that time, I began an apprenticeship with a milliner on College Street, Mrs. Adeline Munro, a singular, imposing woman with a fountain of thick braids spraying from her head. She had an otherworldly appearance and, as I later found out, dabbled in divination cards. I begged her to give me a chance. It was rough at first, as she watched me fumble with buckram, with wire. I'd always loved looking at the pretty hats in downtown department store windows, some with brims so wide they reached across and touched the hats beside them. They were breathtaking, but decked with death, feathers. So it wasn't long in my employment at the millinery shop that I told Mrs. Munro I couldn't in good conscience use feathers on hats any longer. I wouldn't participate in the cruelty. She'd laughed at first, sure her 'protegé' joked—for what good was a hat without plumes? Who'd pay for a plain affair like that? She'd have to let me go, she said—quick enough, she'd find a new girl to apprentice. *And*, Adeline Munro had jabbed, like a pin into a hat, word would spread that I was uncooperative, single-minded—and no other milliner would hire me.

"Again, I begged to be given a chance. I'd make hats with no plumage that—and here I flew wildly by the seat of my bloomers—ladies would buy, perhaps even gentlemen. And I did. My designs veered towards the whimsical, even the outlandish—a shock of deep-purple, folkloric flowers, mock pine boughs, a jester-like mustering of ribbons, miniature dolls, topiary, even a tiny book. Hats with little dioramas, hats that told stories. Formed from felt, cloth. Mesh and stories and straw. Their sheer originality enticed customers for my designs. I'd build a lady's dreams into a hat's design; no other hat like it would exist anywhere. Indeed, when a prospective customer came to the shop to order a custom-made hat, I first interviewed her. What were her dreams, her nightmares, her worst fears, her deepest hopes, and which did she wish externalized, worn atop her head for the world to see? And in my work apron stuck with pins, I'd sketch madly as my customer spoke. One lady longed to lounge by the seashore, so I affixed small felted sea horses and azure ribbons that rippled in wavelike patterns. The lady was enchanted. And paid handsomely. Sometimes I suggested that turning the dark things outwards could be the first step to facing them.

"The business grew, and over time Mrs. Munro, with her otherworldly bent, wasn't averse to her shop becoming partly, as she put it, 'a therapeutic oasis.' And she received a goodly portion of the profit—I worked and sold out of her shop. She even added a gilt-edged sign to the front window: *Personalized, Bespoke Head Splendour. Special Orders Taken.*" Wren was determined that not a morsel of tenderloin be wasted, so she finished her meal. "Heavens, I'm talking in excess."

"Not at all," Lyle Fox countered.

"Anyway, there's not much more. The upshot of the whole thing was that for thirty years I was Adeline Munro's right-hand woman, designing my feather-free, bespoke hats. Even through the darkest times, ladies wanted hats—through the terrible flu epidemic, the war, last one. The Depression years. Steadfastly, I made all manner of hats, for funerals, weddings. Until the last apocalypse, ladies will want hats, it seems. In '27 my niece came to live with me, after her parents drowned; the child soon proved very adept at plaiting straw, which also aided my work."

The waiter removed their empty plates, gave them a dessert menu.

"But like the passenger pigeons, all things end. And factory-made headgear expanded and was cheaper than hats from millinery shops. Women were lured by the glamour of T. Eaton and other lavish arcades. They might have their hat instantly, not wait days for their order. Even with raising my niece, I'd been frugal, and in '36 had saved enough to leave St. John's Ward and rent the flat in Mimico. The millinery work had been hard on my eyes, but now, thanks to you, that's improved—which is why I might just return to millinery work."

"Beginning with *my* hat," Lyle jibed.

"Oh yes, I almost forgot. Let me take a few quick measurements—if you don't mind." She drew the long tape from her purse and moved it around. Eyebrow ridge. Crest. Occipital bone. She brushed her fingers against the tops of his ears.

A few diners at nearby tables watched these odd proceedings.

"It's not what you think," Lyle called over to them in the manner of a joke. Caught ogling, the other diners returned to their meals.

He asked her advice on style. Wren proposed homburg. It would take her a couple of weeks, she said, longer than usual, adding, "I'm rusty."

"I'll look forward to it immensely," Lyle said.

Wren said, "Now you know why I only eat chicken, for never have I seen a hat trimmed with chicken feathers."

Hearing this, he sounded that French horn laugh of his, then reached into his pocket and fingered a roll of bills. He gave Wren ten dollars "for materials." As for the hat itself, they'd settle up later, he said.

She called the ten dollars too much.

He said they'd sort it out down the road. Then he ordered dessert.

The waiter brought their dessert and, brandishing a torch, lit it on fire.

TWENTY-EIGHT

With her shorn, jagged hair and now bright-blue manicure that made it appear as if lake dripped off her fingertips, Gemma looked, she thought, downright *odd*. Birdie saw her garish manicure but didn't say anything. Same with Rooney. And Ada Swift was right, her nails glowed in the dark, which was eerie to say the least. She wondered what Toby would think, next time they met.

That day, just before lunch, Gem told her co-workers she couldn't eat with them; her aunt needed her for an errand. So Gem skipped off before they had a chance to probe this. She'd known, the instant she woke that morning, what she must do that day: try to find Hedwig. She could have told her co-workers, those Nosy Parkers, that she meant to visit the cat, but what if one of them, like Cora-Lynn, offered to go along with her? That wouldn't do. She'd say that sitting at the large table with them was fine for work but sometimes during break she needed some time alone, something like that.

Forty blue-tipped fingers, hers among them, had plugged away hard all morning at the giant table. When the clock struck noon, Gem sprinted along Lake Shore Road in the prisoner-of-war camp's direction. The urge to find out if Toby's cat was all right had been pulling hard at her. She wanted to confirm the cat's well-being so there'd be good news to tell him beneath the willow tree. She hoped Hedwig was safe for Toby's sake, and of course the cat's sake, and she herself was quite fond of the creature. Hedwig would be left to her own devices, catching field mice, voles, whatever else. But Gem's real worry was that if the prisoners found out why Toby had been in the camp, they might, out of spite, harm his cat, torture it even. Gem had to make sure Hedwig was safe.

She turned towards the scruffy, wild field, towards the prisoner-of-war camp. As she loped along, the old fever she'd felt on her previous forays there returned, those moments with Toby at the fence when she'd felt things, aching, acute, that never before coursed through her.

The prisoner-of-war camp was about a baseball diamond's distance away now. A tender burdock tickled her ankles. She didn't see anyone at the barbed wire fence. She'd packed a tuna sandwich in her satchel. In case the cat was in the vicinity, she unwrapped the sandwich, bit into it. And—*huzzah*—in a sudden though decisive advance, low to the ground, Hedwig ran towards her. More like trundled, like some furry trolley, for the cat's girth was rotund.

In muted tones, Gemma beckoned it. "Hedwig! Come here, I've missed you. Well, they certainly haven't been starving you in there—either that or you're an excellent hunter."

Gem crouched on her haunches. The cat nuzzled her hand and pawed at the sandwich. Hedwig must have a belly full of mice, Gem thought, but nevertheless the cat gobbled up pieces of the sandwich; she was ravenous. Gem called her a little glutton and frizzed the fur between her ears and enjoyed the cat's obvious pleasure in sating its hunger. Then she headed back to The Cottage, pleased that she would be able to tell Toby she'd seen his cat.

At day's end, she tore out of the office the instant Miss Fearing released them with her habitual sign-off: *Fly away, paper birds!* Gem needed no prompting. She dashed home and found Aunt Wren humming at the kitchen table, which, instead of crossword puzzles and tarot cards, was laid out with millinery tools: rounding jack, brim cutter, block, pliers, chalk, bodkin threader, foot tolliker, rolled wool felt in a rich shade of charcoal—not unlike Hedwig's coat. Gem recalled these tools from her aunt's previous life in millinery. The long-stemmed rose in its vase was still on the table, only moved to the side, in full bloom now, a gorgeous red chalice.

At Gem's arrival, Birdie looked up from her work. "Wren Maw Hats rises again," she said, cheerful. Then added, "No feathers, of course. This hat is for Dr. Fox—he's commissioned it."

Gem detected a rosy splash across her aunt's cheekbones.

Shuffling in the foyer. Then Rooney entered the kitchen, greeted them, and remarked good-naturedly at the kitchen's transformation into a hat shop.

To avoid clearing the table, they ate their supper of baked beans on trays balanced on their knees in the living room. Aunt Wren recounted, with wonder, her dinner with Dr. Fox—a dessert that burst into flames, imagine! Then she asked if Gem had thought to bring the poetry book back from her office. It had slipped Gem's mind.

After that, Aunt Wren looked at both Gem and Rooney, saying, "One of you girls has an admirer. The rose on the kitchen table wasn't meant for me at all." She fixed her gaze on the lodger. "Rooney?"

The girl's face went flat, suddenly drained of blood. "I don't have any admirers. I avoid conversing with boys, as I've said. And that prisoner I talked to at the tannery doesn't work there anymore. Besides, a prisoner couldn't send a rose."

Then Birdie turned to Gem, expectantly.

Gem deflected. "Why are you so sure the flower wasn't for you, Birdie?"

"Heard it from the horse's mouth, more or less. But not to worry—there are other currencies, other sorts of gifts. It was vain and foolish to think an old woman like me would be sent flowers, even one bloom."

Rooney looked a little hurt. "*I* bring you flowers, Miss Maw—I pick them myself."

Sensing her misstep, Wren said, "Indeed you do, and they're so pretty and we enjoy them very much."

Gem wasn't in any mood to be grilled about the rose. She announced she was going out for a walk. The evening's damp though not unpleasant smells wafted in through the open window. Aunt Wren remarked that her niece's recent strolls at dusk worried her.

"No need, Birdie—I'll make sure the nocturnal moths don't bite me."

Gem took a quick stroll, inhaling the gorgeous night-scented flowers from residents' gardens, and thought with fervent anticipation of her next meeting with Toby. She looked forward, too, to giving him reassuring news about his cat. Then, as she turned for home, she looked down in the darkness at the iridescent blue lake drops on her fingernails.

ON SUNDAY, AUNT Wren worked busily at the kitchen table. A man's hat had begun to take shape. Gem had always found this process fascinating, but she had another, even more exciting, prospect. Before Birdie could ask a string of questions, Gem zoomed out, towards Wild Pigeon Park. The day was fine, pinnacle of summer. And Toby was there, waiting, on the bench under the willow tree. Some kids threw a ball not far away. Families picnicked.

She reached the willow and he hugged her. He noticed her blue fingernails. "Why does it always have to be red or pink? There are too many red nails in this world." He liked the blue.

"Just a bit of fun at lunch break—in the office," Gem said.

As she walked towards a bench, Toby told her, "Don't get too settled. We're not staying here today. I've missed the water so badly. I know a fellow with a small motorized boat—I'm taking you for a ride."

He was proposing being not near but *on* water. *In* water.

"Oh—I can't," Gem protested. "I get seasick."

"You won't today," Toby said. "I just came back from the shore—it's calm today. Perfect day for a cruise. Just imagine, the two of us—in a boat." He beamed, and even with her fear, it struck her, how alive with light his handsome face.

Gem's mind raced. She could sit there on the bench and keep making excuses. Or she could tell Toby the truth about her water phobia and the reason for it. So she took a deep breath and told him the truth, the whole story about her parents' deaths in the Muskoka lake.

Toby reached for her hand, stroking her blue fingernails. "I'm sorry that happened to you, Gem. It must have been terrible. I haven't experienced such a devastating tragedy, but I do suffer day and night, not knowing where my mother is, or if she's even alive."

They sat together silently. Gem gazed around at the grass, the willow's long, trailing branches. He was right—the air was utterly still, no breeze. He'd prepared this gift for her, and she really didn't know if she could do it. She'd spent the last number of weeks beside water, but not on it.

"Will you at least come to see the boat? It's moored a short distance from here. The fellow loaned it to me for the afternoon. Please, Gem?"

"All right, but only to look."

As they walked towards the boat, she realized this was the first time she and Toby had ever gone anywhere together. Now, if only she could muster the strength to face her fear.

The boat was, she had to admit, charming. A runabout (he told her), in a rich honeyed shade of wood, with red trim.

He saw the colour drain from Gem's face and took both her hands. "Gem, do you think you can try it? You won't believe how glorious it will be out there on the water today. I'll hardly rev the motor at all. We'll wear life jackets. If you feel even a little frightened, we'll come back, I promise. Can you trust me that much?"

She gazed at Toby. If there was ever a chance to overcome her fear of water, it would be like this, with him.

He reminded her that he was a seasoned sailor. "Won't you try it, Gem?"

She'd embarked on so many new things this summer. Why not one more?

"All right," Gem said shakily. "But we have to return to shore if it's too much."

Delighted, Toby helped her into her life jacket, then donned his own. He extended his hand to steady her into the boat. Her legs were jelly. She sat on the bench-like seat, trying not to look at the water. Instead, she imagined they were on a soft mattress somewhere.

Gulls capered above their heads.

Toby started the engine, the boat purred to life.

Gem clung to the edge of the bench. True to his word, Toby kept the boat's speed very slow. She scanned the bottom for leaks. She'd noticed a bucket, presumably for bailing water, affixed to the inside of the boat.

Toby's sandy hair shunted around his face as he turned every few seconds to make sure Gem was okay. She relaxed—a little— enough to gaze around her, at the shore. The world appeared boundless, expansive. They cruised near The Cottage. She bet Miss Fearing was in there now, working, even on Sunday. How unique it was to see that place where she'd been spending her days from a new angle.

"You all right, Gem?"

She nodded. "It's almost . . . nice," she called back. Then tipped her face towards the sun the way Cora-Lynn had done so often, at lunch on the log.

How different the shore, the town of Mimico, looked from the boat. Toby pointed east, where the tall buildings of downtown Toronto peeked above the horizon.

He cut the engine and moved next to her, as close as the bulky life jackets would permit. He placed his hand on her shoulder. "Thank you for coming with me, Gem. This is my first time on water in several years. And it's the best day of my life, and *you've* made it so." He leaned over and kissed her.

This was the finest day of Gem's life, too. Her first kiss. And first time in a boat. She'd even allowed herself to look down into the water. Still, she wasn't entirely comfortable yet, she'd need to get used to water in a gradual way.

"Can we go back now, Toby?"

He agreed.

They returned to shore and Toby docked the boat at the same small, boarded slip where they'd found it.

They sat close together on a large rock, holding hands, while the boat bobbed gently a few feet away.

"Oh, I almost forgot. I've got good news for you, Toby. I saw Hedwig!"

"I was so worried. How is she?"

"She was glad to see me, and looks well-fed. In fact, she's portly. Yet gobbled my sandwich like a starved creature," remarked Gem.

"Hedwig may be pregnant. Eating for two—or three—or four—or *more*."

"I hadn't thought of that. *Oh jeepers.*"

Toby grew agitated. "Can you get her out of there, Gem? The sooner the better. If those Nazi brutes find out about me, they will exact cruelty on Hedwig and her kittens. I know those men. I know how they think. I've eavesdropped on them for three years. I know, too, they have canny ways of getting information, so there's a good chance they've already learned about me, they have their channels."

"How will I catch her?" Gem asked.

"Lure her with food, then pop her into a loose-woven bag, sturdy one, or a basket."

She moved a strand of his hair, still blown from sailing, back in place. "But *then* where do I take her—*and* her babies?"

Toby withdrew his hands and sank his face into them, as if racking his brain. "Almost anywhere is better than that prison. Post a notice for free kittens in the grocery store? If Hedwig is that hungry, and that pregnant, you only have a short time to find a solution."

"Why can't you take her?" Gemma asked.

Toby's eyes flooded with anguish. He palmed his hands against his face as if stricken by a bad headache. "I can't take the cat *or* her brood—I'm shipping out, Gem."

"As in, leaving?"

He nodded miserably. "My next assignment is to take high-security documents on a supply ship to England. I shouldn't tell you that, but knowing what *you* do, I'm confident this will stay secret."

He was telling her so many things at once. "Wait—how do you know what I do, Toby?"

"The military intelligence community isn't that big, Gem. And it's tight-knit. I know where you work, who you work for, what you do."

Gem was shocked, but it also made sense. "And I suppose that's how you knew where to send the rose."

He shrugged. "Yes. I'm a regular Sherlock Holmes."

Then, what he'd said a moment earlier suddenly dawned on her. "When?" she asked.

"When what?"

"When do you *leave*, Toby?"

"A month."

No no no no no no no.

"Any chance you'll sail on the *Northstar*?"

Now it was Toby's turn to be flummoxed. "How do you know about the *Northstar*, Gem?"

"As you said, our intelligence branch isn't exactly vast. My colleagues and I are tasked with tracking signals from enemy predators that might harm it—and you—and the ship's crew."

"So, you're my guardian angel, Gem."

She smiled at him. "Something like that. We'll give it our all—and then some. What will you do after you arrive, Toby?"

"If I can make it over there without getting blown up, I'll deliver the documents then go underground to Germany, try to find my mother."

"This doesn't sound very safe," Gem whimpered.

"It isn't. Especially sailing through the Black Pit, the part of the ocean beyond Allied aircraft's range. Will you rescue Hedwig? Please?"

"I'll try," Gem said. "And I'll strive with every fibre of my being to keep you safe." Then he put his arms around her. The bracelet's soft yarn and cloth coils brushed the back of her neck. They embraced on the rock until they began to hear thunder in the distance, and Gem said she'd better go home.

Before she left, she recalled Aunt Wren's book of poetry. "When can we see each other next?"

He told her to meet him beneath the willow in two weeks' time. Sunday. Dusk. It couldn't be sooner—he sighed—because he would be preparing out of town for the special assignment.

She mulled this, distressed at the length of time. "When we meet, can you bring that book of poems, please? My aunt would like to read it again." Then Gem blurted, "I think she's in *love*."

"She's not the *only* one in love," Toby said, and kissed her gently again. He assured Gem he'd bring the book.

"What will I do after you've left?" Gem asked, beginning to cry. "I'll be so worried about you."

He wiped away her tears. "Look up into the night sky, at the stars, and you will see me."

The sound of thunder closed in on them.

Gem kissed him again, then ran, trying unsuccessfully to outrun the rain. *Raining cats and pitchforks*, Aunt Wren used to say. Gem's hair soon soaked into a short, sodden mop, and when she opened her mouth for air, her mouth became a cup filling with water. Now she *was* water, aqueous, surrendered herself to it and felt fully alive.

TWENTY-NINE

Ada Swift could make even peeling a banana fascinating. The dramatic way she brought sections of it down to the stem in slow motion amused them as they lunched on the silver log. She was putting on a show and she knew it. She had this *smoulder*, doing even the most ordinary thing. Cora-Lynn had been scribbling away on a pad of paper and laid it aside, unable to resist Ada's charisma.

The day's heat shimmied the air like a mirage and made them lethargic, all but Gem. She'd been chiding herself inwardly for stalling with the cat rescue. Toby's words rang accusingly in her ears. *You only have a short time to find a solution.*

After polishing off the banana, Ada smoothed her floaty skirt and declared, "You wouldn't believe the absolute dreamboat fellow who came to my other job, to inspect some of our work and file a report. Tall, muscular. And eyes I could just crawl inside."

Hester snapped her lunch box closed and listened.

Gem finished her hard-boiled egg. She'd been plotting the cat's capture. But now Gem listened more closely. The more Ada described the "dreamboat," the more Gem was convinced she was describing Toby. She knew he was preparing documents for his mission on the *Northstar*. And he'd pointed out that the intelligence community was small. So maybe it wasn't such a coincidence. But she had to find out for sure.

"What was this dreamboat's name?" she asked Ada.

"Tobias Albrecht. Special Agent." Ada pattered her blue-tipped fingers over her heart.

Of course.

This made Gem uneasy. She surveyed Ada's flawless skin, long platinum wavy hair, trim figure. Ada wore her gold beret that day, the one from the Palais Royale. Gem didn't know how anyone could look more beautiful, unless some beauty-queen mermaid arose from the waters of Lake Ontario. Gem thought about her own appearance, with her hacked-off hair, an infuriating new pimple on her nose, and her old cotton sundress, its torn strap held in place with a large safety pin because Aunt Wren hadn't gotten around to mending it.

The other girls chattered about heartthrobs from movies, but Gem was too distracted to be interested. Things were different now that Toby was out in the world. But he'd said he was *in love* last time they'd met. He still wore the braided cat collar around his wrist. The thought of this bright, soft circle and how Toby said he never took it off calmed her. A little. If she trusted Toby in a *boat*, of all places, she should trust him in the world.

Shouldn't she?

Pondering Toby's departure, and on the *Northstar* no less, filled Gem with dread. She might never see him again. She recalled what he'd said about the "Black Pit" of the Atlantic; she couldn't imagine anything worse.

The morning had been rough. Hester unlocked a few weather cribs, Cora-Lynn cussed, and Ada threw her hands up in exasperation more than once. Gem leaned into every hunch, but none panned out. Any intelligence they could unlock before the *Northstar* sailed, Miss Fearing had stressed, was as crucial as during its crossing. The mousetrap under the window went *pock* and a tiny creature, emitting a terminal squeak, suffered an agonizing death.

Since their new "banquet table" desk configuration, no one wore earplugs—Miss Fearing had stipulated this, saying they must learn to listen to each other.

Cora-Lynn wailed, "Will someone take the damned thing outside? I can't work with a *dead mouse* a few feet away!"

"Then you wouldn't like *my* job," Ada jibed. "Grenades stuffed inside corpses of rats."

Hester winced.

Gem glanced up at Ada Lovelace, high on the wall, felt sure the lady genius inside the frame squinched her eyes into a visage of pained repugnance. Dead rodents.

Ada dispatched the mouse.

Partway through the afternoon, Miss Fearing tramped downstairs and told them that a simple mousetrap had done more effective work that day than *they* had. Then ordered them to fly away, go outside, take a break. Maybe it would revive their efforts.

They left the office.

"You've all worked here before I came," Ada said as they walked to their lunch log. "Can you tell me why Miss Fearing calls us 'paper birds'? What in Jupiter is that about?"

Hester Hobbs had taken a tube of lanolin cream from her purse and smoothed it onto her hands. "I take it as an . . . idiosyncrasy—a quirk, a random sort of thing."

Cora-Lynn sat on the log, and began writing in a notebook, but set it aside to biff at a dragonfly. "You're off target there, Hobbs. It's *much* more than that. *Fly away, paper birds* is a philosophical predictor variable—plainly put, a visual projection, through imagery, of what will happen to us girls when the war ends. We'll be tossed, like a crumpled sheet of paper, into the air, the waste bin—melted by rain, erased by time. We're expendable, don't you see? That's why we need to stay relevant, why I'm bent on becoming a mathematical scholar, or engineer, after the war."

The Wonder sure knew how to bring down a break meant to be restorative.

"So that, then, is why you scribble away on that pad, things numerical, I assume?" Ada asked.

Cora-Lynn nodded. "I've been wasting too much time. I need to use breaks to advance my education, to *think*, rather than gawk at that dumb lake and dream. What I've been working on is a replica of Scherbius's cipher disc—here, see for yourselves."

She turned the pad of paper and they beheld three discs labelled *keyboard, scrambler, lamp board*. Then she explained how wires entered the scrambler, did about one-sixth of a revolution, how a current lit a lamp and a new letter emerged, different from the original one struck on the keyboard. Then Cora-Lynn praised the virtues of a cipher machine with two scramblers, or rotors, or even a third, which made—easy math—26 by 26 by 26, or 17,576, arrangements. "And that's only the *start* of it," she vaunted.

"Cora, do you have *any* friends?" Hester asked warily.

Cora-Lynn ignored her and lit a menthol cigarette. "All this . . . mechanical magic is why I'm reaching the end of my rope with The Cottage. There's no equipment here in this two-bit, rinky-dink office except chalkboard, paper, bloody pencils. I'm just so . . . bored with it all. I'm desperate to get hired on with Camp X, to work with Hydra—I've heard some girls do that. What a thrill to be in the same room as that wondrous transmitter, named Hydra because of its many moving parts, like the mythical swamp snake with multiple heads." She puffed furiously on the cigarette.

Their moods, it seemed, ran along a thin, frayed wire. "And I suppose you're bored with *us*, too, Cora?" asked Ada.

"Don't be silly," Cora-Lynn replied. "Don't take it so personally."

"Should you be telling us this stuff about Hydra?" Hester asked.

This question spiked Cora-Lynn's cranky mood. "I'm tired of *that*, too," she groused. "The myth that we're all *such good girls* with our mouths welded shut, the perfect patriotic citizens."

"Honestly, there's no talking to you sometimes, Cora," said Hester. "You can be such a *kvetching little trout*."

"A regular sourpuss," lobbed Ada.

"Maybe you should cut back on your cranky pills," Hester footnoted.

They couldn't have said it better in Gem's view. But to be fair, the pressure cooker they'd been placed in, the tightened thumbscrews with respect to the *Northstar*, had set them all on edge, none more than Gemma herself.

THIRTY

WREN COULDN'T HAVE been more surprised when Lyle Fox pulled up in a convertible coupe in front of the house on Pidgeon Avenue. For their heavily accented dinner beside the Humber River, he'd picked her up in this same car, but now, with its top down, it transformed into a snappy roadster that looked like something from *The Great Gatsby*.

It was much hotter outside than Wren realized; she'd had the fan blowing upstairs in the flat. She'd worn her peep-toed shoes, so at least her toes wouldn't swelter. Why hadn't she chosen her striped rayon dress with the keyhole neckline? It was more slimming than the suit. Less stuffy. Wren turned, once, before stepping into the eye doctor's car, to see the landlady, Rosa Deluca, peering out her front window.

"I thought we'd take a cruise with the top down," Lyle said as Wren settled into the passenger seat. "Such a splendid day."

Wren told him she'd never ridden in a convertible car. Which was true.

"Then you're in for a treat," he said.

And it was. It was, in fact, glorious. The only downside being Wren had to remove her straw hat; she worried it would blow away. She felt self-conscious about her grey, thinning hair that blew in wispy strands out behind her. She'd rather hoped to keep her hat on during this outing. But the air, lush with lake smell, felt wonderful and she abandoned herself to the wild convertible ride.

She asked Lyle where they were going.

"It's a surprise," he said, gearing down.

She regretted again that she'd overdressed. The doctor's attire was more attuned to the climate—linen trousers and a light shirt a golfer might sport. She loved the sensation of freedom the convertible brought, and she complimented his car, reiterating that this was her first ride in an automobile with the top down. She didn't mention the horse-drawn wagons of her rural childhood; that would only accentuate her age.

"I bought this coupe in '35," Lyle Fox said. "It'll have to last me a long time, the way things are going. I don't drive it much—I walk to my office and home—trying not to waste gas. But today, like our recent dinner, is a special occasion. It feels good to be behind the wheel again, though I'm still rusty."

"I'm rusty, too, Doctor. Rusty at life." *What a ludicrous thing to say.* Wren felt herself blush.

He turned the coupe into the lot of a marina and parked. Wren read, with difficulty without her glasses, the wavering sign: (something) *Yacht Club; Open-Air Dancing, Tea Room, Flotilla Amusement Ride* (could that be right?).

He cut the engine. "Before we do anything else, put your glasses on, please. I'd like to check them, Miss Maw."

It amused Wren how he switched back and forth in his mode of addressing her, sometimes more formal, other times less. She took the spectacles from her purse and settled them on her face. She didn't even want to *imagine* how abysmal her scraggly, blown hair must look, so didn't.

He fussed with the temples. Advised her that nose pads would help. "You can put the glasses away now. Keep growing into them gradually. In brief bouts."

Wren placed them back into her purse. "A useful reminder. I've been overdoing it, I think, wearing them too much, too soon. But it's hard to resist the near miracle they brought me, seeing more clearly—even though I don't always like or understand what I see." Having no idea why she tacked on these last few words, she chastised herself again silently.

To his credit, Lyle Fox didn't draw her out. Instead, he said, "I don't have any nose pads with me today. I'll bring them next time."

"I've always liked this tea room," he said. "It has a fine view of the lake. I haven't been here since"—a pause, a cringe on his part—"Mildred and I used to enjoy it here."

Wren sensed his discomfiture over this. She decided the best course was to forge onward. "Should I leave the hat I made for you in the car? Until later?"

Good idea, he told her. It would be quite safe there.

The rustic tea room had an outdoor deck, where they sat, nibbled on scones and sipped tea. The deck overlooked a splendid, panoramic view; and lovely as it was, taking in the lake, Wren couldn't push a recent tarot card she'd drawn out of her mind. Her troubles had whisked away into the wind during the ride in the convertible, but now her thoughts returned to plague her. *The Moon.* Instability. Insecurity. Wolf and dog, howling at the scowling nocturnal moon. An ugly crayfish or lobster crawling up from the watery depths. Not a reassuring divination. There on the shore, a new, troubling question struck Wren: Might not Dr. Fox's professional status be compromised by fraternizing with a patient?

"What's the matter?" Lyle Fox asked. "You're all keyed up, more ruffled than a grouse."

She fibbed. "Oh, nothing. I'm just—you know, giddy—from tooling around in a convertible."

He stared at her, unconvinced, not hiding it well.

So she came out with it. "Am I still your patient?"

He burst out laughing. "After I affix the pads to your eyeglasses, you can fire me—as your eye doctor. And hire me as—your humble servant, companion. More than I think you know yet, or perhaps still don't believe. Right now, I'd like you to tell me more about your life."

So, he'd intuited her need for clarity.

"I brought Mildred's ghost here today, unwittingly, with my earlier remark," Lyle said, more seriously. "That gives you permission, Wren, to invite a second ghost to this tea table. One who's been loved."

Relief suffused Wren's bones, and after another scone she told him more about Adam. Having someone listen to her story, her life, someone who cared, felt so freeing, so fine. She relayed that Adam worked as a designer at Grip Ltd., how talented he'd been, though he'd always sluffed that off. She told him the tragic rest of it—which he already knew, but it felt necessary to Wren to bring her time with Adam, in this telling, to completion. Lyle allowed her story to breathe, let it waft, rife with memory, along the willowy shore. Somehow, speaking of Adam instilled a calm in Wren. A sense of peace that made the malevolent Moon card, with its sinister images, recede into the abyss.

After a few laps by a trolling gull nearby, Lyle said, "How hard that must have been. But it was so long ago. Do you mean to tell me that *all* these years you've not"—his tone unsure, cautious—"had *any* suitors?"

The word *suitors* brought a small, stuttering laugh from Wren. "I didn't have the interest, or the time. I was making hats. Raising Gemma."

He said she'd endured plenty of hardship. And added that she deserved a medal.

Wren swatted away the accolade. "I was just doing what anyone would do, trying to make it through the Depression years and give the child the best I could." She finished her tea. "It wasn't all bad. I loved millinery. I found solace in making beautiful things. It brought much pleasure."

"If not a medal, Miss Maw, then a scone," Lyle Fox said, passing the tray.

They sat in quiet contentment for a while. Really, few things in life were lovelier than the shores of Lake Ontario in summer. Wren was reluctant to puncture the moment, which felt like a movie, with business. But she did. She reached into her purse and gave Lyle the envelope of money.

"The last instalment, Dr. Fox. Now my spectacles are paid in full."

He placed the envelope in his trousers' pocket and smiled at her. Then he paid for their scones and tea, and they sauntered back to his coupe.

As they stood for a moment beside the fine automobile, a butterfly flitted by.

Wren should have revelled in the moment, her debt having been paid, but doubt again crested, like a whitecap on the lake. "Do you think it's wrong, Dr. Fox, that—let's be honest—an old woman like me should, especially in a time of great suffering, of war, indulge in a . . . convertible cruise? Quite *hedonistic*, really. Am I not . . . *past* all this?"

His gaze was steady, serious. "Past pleasure, you mean? And joy?"

She nodded.

"As in, too old for it?"

Again, Wren nodded.

Lyle studied her in that intense way he had. "You're not dead, are you?" he asked.

"I think you know the answer, Dr. Fox. For here I stand, animate."

"Yes. And by the way," he said, "I'm only five years behind you—in age."

She supposed he knew her birthdate from his files.

"You're never too old for joy, Miss Maw. And, as far as I can tell, in the Bank of Pleasure, you're in a deficit position. Deep in the red, so to speak."

Wren was relieved to have him confirm that she was not past joy.

She reached into the car and took the hat out of the brown butcher paper she'd wrapped it in. Then, smoothing Lyle's snowy hair, she placed the homburg on his head. To her it looked dapper, distinguished.

He looked at himself in the side mirror.

"I hope the hat is to your liking," Wren said.

Lyle turned to her. "*Liking?* It's perfect, and soon we must negotiate my payment for it. I've paid you for materials, but not labour."

Before she could demur on this score, he opened the car door for her and she got in.

When Wren returned to the flat, a long-stemmed red rose lay, funnelled in paper, in the foyer. She released the exquisite flower from its paper coil, and a note shook out: *For Wren no mistake this time about who sent this and who it's for—and you shall have one every week henceforth. Lyle F.*

She held the fragrant velvet petals against her cheek. How lovely, not being dead.

THIRTY-ONE

GEM HOPED SHE wasn't too late to rescue Hedwig and her litter, which might well be birthed by now. She'd promised Toby and meant to keep her word. The following lunch hour, offering no explanation to her co-workers, Gemma took the large woven willow basket they used as a trash bin, dumped its papery contents on her chair and hurried off with it. She heard Cora-Lynn yelp, "Hey, where are you taking the wastebasket?" as she rushed out the door.

Gem retraced her familiar steps to the prisoner-of-war camp. She'd placed a pungent tuna sandwich in her satchel. Hurrying along with the basket, she soon found herself in that barren field, in the factory district.

A sudden movement through the scraggly grass startled Gem. *Hedwig!* A silvery dab of white fur offside that pink nose was a giveaway. There was also something familiar in her feline gait. Joy engulfed Gem, and she called out. "Hedwig! I've brought you a treat!"

She set the willow basket on the ground and took the tuna sandwich from her satchel. The cat ambled eagerly towards her, then throat-thrummed madly. She ruffled the cat's fur between its ears. Then brandished the tuna sandwich in front of Hedwig, in temptation. The cat sent out a shrill meow that sounded like a summons, and sure enough, Gem spied a rustling movement through the ragged grass.

A kitten ran in a comedic, lopsided way towards its mother.

The grass rippled again and another appeared. This one lustrous black, amber-eyed.

Kitten three followed on the heels, a tiny calico.

A final miniature feline, smoky like its mother, was the last to arrive.

"*Four* babies—no wonder you're so hungry, Hedwig," Gem said. A mewling, happy family reunion ensued. Now the trick was how to get the whole family into the willow basket. Food, of course. Gem broke the tuna sandwich into small pieces and placed it in the basket. Then she scooped the mother cat and lowered her into the basket. While Hedwig chomped tuna, Gem, in a smooth motion, turned the basket, still on the ground, on its side until it formed a kind of circular door level with the earth. With the gentlest hands, she propelled the kittens into the basket. They were soon nestled next to their mother's soft, milky belly.

Gemma lifted the willow basket carefully. It was quite heavy now, with its furry load.

Huffing, her arms full of felines, Gem made it back to The Cottage, with difficulty. She honestly hadn't thought through this next phase of things. *You've done it now, Gemma Sullivan*, she told herself. But she'd kept her promise to Toby. Still, she'd have some explaining to do. Just a nick shy of being late, her three co-workers already seated at the behemoth desk and Miss Fearing standing nearby, stick of chalk in one hand, cigarette in the other, their eyes all turned to Gem when she trudged back into the office, puffing, damp with sweat, and laden with the willow wastebasket that now resounded with *meows*.

Gem sensed the importance of getting the upper hand in that moment, before anyone else piped in. "I brought some help," she declared. "For our mouse problem. And as keepers of secrets, these furry creatures are *unparalleled.*"

It proved a rare moment when Miss Fearing didn't know what to say. Finally, their boss walked over, stood over the basket and said, "Miss Sullivan, *what on God's computational earth?*"

Hester, Ada and Cora-Lynn swooped in, each picking up a mewling kitten and swaddling it, lovingly, near their faces. Even Cora-Lynn, that kvetching little trout, had a look of wonderment. Only one kitten remained, unswaddled. The smoky one. So Gem took the wee creature from the basket and stroked it. Hedwig, the mother, remained in the basket, curled up, likely glad to be relieved of her maternal duties for a minute or two. Miss Fearing then reached into the basket and picked up Hedwig. She cooed, actually *cooed*, over the mother cat she now cradled in her arms like a baby.

"Well, you *are* a fine puss, aren't you?" their boss murmured to the cat.

So, there stood the boss, talking to Toby's cat. And the other codebreakers, each coddling one of Hedwig's offspring, were clearly smitten as well.

But it didn't take long for Miss Fearing to return to herself. Still holding, petting, the mother cat, but back to herself. "How did this . . . feline situation come about, Miss Sullivan?"

"I—I rescued them," Gem said. "And as I've already mentioned, brought them here to address the office's rodent issue."

"One cat is one thing," their boss said. "But five cats? *Quite another.*"

But as their boss continued to murmur into the cat's furry ears, it was clear that she was flat-out smitten with Hedwig.

Slowly, with reluctance, Miss Fearing gently placed Hedwig back in the basket. Gem, Cora-Lynn, Ada and Hester followed suit, placing the kittens back with their mother, whose soft belly the tiny ones burrowed against.

Miss Fearing took a few bills from her desk drawer and directed Hester to go and buy cat food. There was an empty crate with low sides upstairs in her office that she'd bring downstairs. Cora-Lynn was directed to take it outside and fill it with sand, for a litter box.

"The family will stay downstairs during the day, to give the mother access to mice. At night I'll take them upstairs. I mostly sleep up there now. The cat family will amuse me, keep me company. But"—a shadow crossed her face—"when the kittens are older, we'll need to find homes for them. Start working on that, Miss Sullivan. For now, they still need their mother."

"Yes, Ma'am," Gem said. Adding, "If it's all right, the mother cat already has a name—I've named her." (Minor fib.)

They all stared at Gem, waiting to hear it.

Gem said, "Hedwig." A bolt of revelation struck her. "After Hedy Lamarr."

"Good choice," Miss Fearing said. "In addition to her beauty and acting prowess, a wonderful mechanical mind. A genius with radio waves. Not much she couldn't invent—rather like you, Miss Swift."

Ada made a quick curtsy. Not trying, even a little, to hide how fully this compliment pleased her.

Hester nipped out to buy cat food. Miss Fearing went upstairs, returned with the carton and two bowls, then retreated back upstairs. Cora-Lynn was dispatched to the sandy beach. Leaving Gem and Ada in the office.

Ada took the tiny midnight kitten with huge amber eyes out of the basket, placed it on her knee and dangled one of her origami birds in front of it, in play. The kitten swatted at the paper bird.

"I *adore* the tiny black cat," she twittered.

THE AFTERNOON'S WORK carried forward with ramped intensity. The unspoken aura around the desks was that Gem, Ada, Hester and Cora-Lynn needed to hop up their codebreaking efforts to compensate for time lost with the cats' arrival. Meows from a folded blanket Miss Fearing had placed on the floor in the corner affirmed this. At intervals Hedwig would stand, stretch and roam around the office, as if on patrol.

Cora-Lynn lifted her pencil long enough to say, "I dare any mouse to come in here now."

At day's end, just before Miss Fearing came back downstairs to check their progress and tell them to "fly away," Gem turned to Cora-Lynn and said, "I *told* you I went to see a cat at lunchtime."

And Cora-Lynn looked, for the first time, chastened.

THIRTY-TWO

THE PAPER BIRDS worked like never before. The *Northstar* would soon set sail; any intelligence they could glean at this juncture was critical. Rain ponged The Cottage's small windows. There were no more mousetraps. Hedwig proved an adept mouser, leaving her trophies under chairs, so each day, before the girls took their places, they checked before seating themselves. Over the past few days, late summer rains had set in, presaging autumn. During these noon hours, the codebreakers were content to eat their lunches at the large desk and play with the kittens. Now, added to the chalkboard, all concerning the *Northstar*, was the directive *Feed the cats*.

Fervently as they tried, there were no real breakthroughs in their assignment. Cora-Lynn floundered. Ada Swift worked full-time at The Cottage now, during this special assignment. Usually unflappable, even she seemed at her wits' end. "I *hate* failure. I'm not used to it."

The telephone rang—it was Miss Fearing from upstairs. Hester answered, took in their boss's words, then hung up.

Hester looked shaken. "Lady F wants us upstairs. Now."

"Oh lord," Cora-Lynn wailed. "Maybe she's going to sack the whole lot of us, for our lack of progress on Operation Northstar."

"I don't think so," Hester told them. "I didn't get that from her tone. In fact, Lady F said she had a surprise for us."

"We've *never* been invited to the upper sanctum," Cora-Lynn said. "It's forbidden territory, *terra incognita*."

"Well, we are *now*," Hester said. "And she said to bring Hedy with us and for Gemma to lock the downstairs door behind us."

So Gem scooped up the cat in her arms and locked the door, and they set out, for the first time, to the main floor of The Cottage.

On their way upstairs, Ada said, "I've often wondered what she's got up there, like Frankenstein's laboratory or something."

The silence of the others conveyed that they, too, had wondered.

MISS FEARING'S OFFICE, as it turned out, wasn't in the least sinister. In fact, it looked very much like an office anywhere. Except nicer. There were polished hardwood floors with a Persian carpet. A few items from the previous occupant remained: a chintz loveseat, coffee table, lamps, tall hutch with a glass front that now held files instead of teacups, an upright piano. Then Miss Fearing's desk, littered with papers, ashtray, typewriter, telephone. There must have been a kitchen in the adjoining room, and a bedroom above, beneath the gabled roof, but their boss didn't give them a tour. Rather, she bid them to seat themselves. Cora-Lynn and Hester took the loveseat. Miss Fearing brought three folding chairs and set them up around the coffee table. Ada took one chair, Gem the other. Chair three remained empty. The coffee table was bare but for two books, *The Letters of John Keats* and a volume of Keats's poetry.

Hedwig explored the large room's nooks, crannies.

How different it felt, being above ground. From her chair, Gem could see the green world outside—someone whizzed along Lake Shore Road on a bicycle, then, a few seconds later, the streetcar. The top of the upright piano was empty except for a large photograph of a striking young woman in military garb. That must be Peggy, Gem supposed.

Then their boss said, "You've all been working so hard. As a reward, you're about to meet someone very special."

As if on cue, the doorbell rang.

Miss Fearing answered it. A young man dressed in a dove-grey suit entered. He carried a briefcase.

An involuntary squeak arose from Gemma's throat. Toby. How badly she wanted to dash over to him and wrap her arms around him.

There might have been more attention paid to Gem's squeak if Ada hadn't called out, purringly, "Oh—Mr. Albrecht—*we meet again.*" She batted her eyelashes at Toby.

He wasn't looking at Ada Swift, though. His eyes were fixed on Gem, and something she read there warned her—strongly—against revealing that they knew each other. This had to do with the prisoner-of-war camp, Gem reasoned. She recalled that Ada knew a guard there, so Toby's assignment behind the barbed wire fence must stay vaulted. What an oddly knotted universe they inhabited. So, as painful as it was, Gem played her role, as a stranger. She was looking forward to their next meeting. He was obviously back from Whitby and—how awful to contemplate—would soon sail far away from her.

Ada told everyone that she'd already met Toby at her other job.

"Ah yes," Miss Fearing said. "That makes sense." Then she introduced Toby to the others. He nodded politely. Gem noted a flush across his cheeks when their boss said her name, adding, "Miss Sullivan is our word girl. Our Queen of Hunches. Miss Ponder, all about numbers. Miss Hobbs tackles anything, and Miss Swift, who you've already met, is a chameleon. So, I've an excellent range of skills here."

Then, with a lusty mew, Hedwig dashed across the room, right to Toby's feet.

He laughed. And Gem's heart melted.

"Our cat—*my* cat," Miss Fearing said, "is wild for you, Mr. Albrecht. Gracious, I've never seen anything like it. Do you carry treats in your shirt pocket, perhaps?"

Toby picked up Hedwig, beaming. "I'm very fond of animals—*especially* cats." His hand fuzzed the fur on the cat's head, and Hedwig looked, as much as a cat can look, ecstatic.

"We call her Hedwig," said Hester.

Toby said he thought that a wonderful name.

Miss Fearing scurried into the next room that Gem supposed was the kitchen and carried back a plate of sandwiches. She set them on the coffee table and invited them to help themselves. She invited Toby to sit on the empty folding chair. He sat, keeping Hedwig on his lap. They now formed a loose circle around the coffee table.

Gem chomped hard on a watercress sandwich to restrain herself from saying anything that might reveal their secret. Toby, she could tell, worked at distributing his attention evenly among them.

Their boss cleared her throat. "Mr. Albrecht works in high-level intelligence. In fact"—dramatic pause—"he'll be carrying the documents on the *Northstar*."

They gawked at him in hushed awe.

"These four young ladies," Miss Fearing told Toby, "have been toiling away for me all summer. Toiling, I might add, in the dank basement beneath us. They work in isolation, so I thought they deserved a glimpse of what goes on at top levels. And they've all signed the Official Secrets Act."

"I commend you ladies on your work here at The Cottage," Toby said, as Hedwig, her attention diverted by a dashing shadow on the living room floor, hopped down from his lap. "It must be so challenging. You must at times be stumped?"

"Often," Hester said.

Cora-Lynn chimed, "Rarely."

"We rather *are*—stumped right now," Ada interjected.

Gem wanted to throw a sandwich at her. This sort of remark was *not* reassuring to Toby. He seemed unphased, though, curious, engaged. "What do *you* do, Miss Fearing, when you've hit a wall? You've so much wisdom and experience with cryptanalysis."

Their boss seemed hesitant at first, but then, with an air of throwing caution to the wind, answered, "Fair question. Sometimes our ciphers and formulae and substitution keys and algorithms and columnar transpositions and navigational tools of our own devising, even our hunches, let us down—*then* what frontier remains? How *then* do we navigate? Only by where we've been—a kind of dead reckoning of mind and heart. Circling back to what we've done that worked. And my other passion—I doubt sharing this violates any state secrets—I read John Keats. His poems, letters." She pointed to the volumes on the coffee table. "Keats's poems shift the lens for me, shake up my usual patterns of analytical thought. As for his letters, what cryptanalyst doesn't enjoy reading someone else's mail? His letter about *negative capability* I find especially inspiring."

They nibbled their sandwiches, intrigued.

"What the poet means with respect to *negative capability*," Miss Fearing went on, "is that we simply can't know everything, yet we must carry on in the face of doubts, uncertainties. I present a mangled version, but this is the gist."

"Fascinating," Toby mused.

Gem caught him staring at her and averted her eyes.

Checking her watch, Miss Fearing said, "You girls can ask Mr. Albrecht a few questions, if you like."

Ada burst out, "Do you have a girlfriend?"

The room erupted in nervous, twittery laughter.

Hedwig pounced on moving shadows, tree branches buffeted by wind, checkering the floor.

Gemma couldn't breathe.

Her co-workers stared at Toby, as if on the edges of their seats. Miss Fearing's face was amused, indulgent.

"As a matter of fact, I *do*," Toby said. Studiously not eyeing Gem. "She's smart, pretty, sweet, kind."

Ada looked crushed. Hester, too.

"Is it serious?" Cora-Lynn probed.

Miss Fearing chided, "Now, I think that's Mr. Albrecht's business. I didn't bring him here for a personal interrogation." She gave them all a look that said *enough*.

Toby must have had an itchy neck; he raised his arm to scratch, and the woven bracelet flashed before Gem's adoring eyes.

"It must be exciting, Mr. Albrecht," Hester ventured, "to be always on the move, from one assignment to another, instead of staring at reams of paper, racking one's brain over what messages they might hold, and sitting still all day, like we do, which often is very dull. Your work seems so . . . glamorous."

"Sometimes," answered Toby thoughtfully. "But your assignments, while quieter, yes, and more sedentary, are no less important. The truth is, my line of work is often quite lonely." He glanced over at Gem. Then carried on. "Taking on various identities, you can forget who you really are—and sometimes you long, badly, to just be *yourself*."

"The secretive part is something we understand well," Miss Fearing said.

Again, he praised their work, the tenacity it took, adding, "And what a tight-knit team you are. Right down to your matching bright-blue fingernails."

They laughed.

The only one not blue-fingered, Miss Fearing, interjected. "Much of what my paper birds do here at The Cottage involves heavy doses of *negative capability*, for codebreaking often feels like groping in the darkness for a tiny wedge of light, crack of illumination, frequently flying by the seats of our hunches, prevailing through uncertainty." She gestured towards the books on the coffee table.

"Not *me*," Cora-Lynn said. "I'm not negatively capable—I'm *highly* capable."

At first no one seemed sure if she meant this as a joke, but laughter erupted soon enough.

Miss Fearing continued. "My other project, when I need inspiration, is a code I'm devising so I can write letters that extend beyond platitudes, to my sweetheart overseas. To outpace the censors, I mean." Her gaze flickered over to the upright piano, the photograph. Then, almost as if she were alone in the room, she said, musingly, "Love will find its language."

She stopped suddenly. Flustered. Then switched topics again. For the next few minutes Miss Fearing regaled Toby and the rest of them with her thoughts on the shamanic agency of numbers: variables, stacking concepts, transpositions. Then she stopped. "I'm sure I'm boring you, Mr. Albrecht."

"Not at all," Toby said. "I could sit here all day." He cast wistful eyes in Gem's direction.

"Alas, *we* can't," Miss Fearing said. Eyeing her wristwatch, she blazoned that "her girls" had to return to work. "But it's been grand, Mr. Albrecht, to have you visit our little office."

Hester beamed. "*Really* swell. You're the only celebrity I've ever met."

Toby shooed away the compliment.

Ada asked for his autograph. Inked on her arm.

He laughed. A kind but dismissive laugh. He then stared at Gem.

"*Unforgettable*—to meet you," she blurted.

Then Miss Fearing extended their gratitude for his visit, expressed their utter devotion to Operation Northstar, and their deepest hopes and prayers for his safe voyage.

Afraid she'd start to cry, Gemma excused herself. Muttered that she'd go ahead of them and unlock the downstairs door. Back in the basement office, she scurried, almost tripping over a kitten, into the bathroom. For a few long moments she leaned against the wall and fought to slow her breathing. By the time she'd calmed down enough to return to the large desk, her co-workers had settled back into their jobs but were still jawing about "the heartthrob" they had just met. While the four kittens scurried around the room, like tumbleweeds in a desert.

"Didn't you think so, Gemma?"

She'd been mapping the letter *L* in an intercept. "Think what?"

Exasperated, likely by the lack of attention coming her way, Ada turned dramatic. "*Tobias Albrecht!* Isn't he one of the most divine male specimens you've ever seen? And so charming! Even the *cat* went *gaga* for him!"

Gemma smiled. "He seemed very nice."

"Maybe you need glasses, Gem. Never has such a hot pepper crossed my vision," brayed Hester.

"*Stop it*, all of you," Cora-Lynn demanded. "Easy on the eyes, yes. We all liked him. All the more reason to focus more, focus better. Keep the U-boat sharks away from his ship. Now, for the sake of Pythagoras, get to work!"

"She's right," Ada said, subdued now.

And Gem? She didn't hear any of this, her pencil speeding quicker than a meteorite. If she really *was* the Queen of Hunches, she'd better take the throne.

She stayed late at the office that night. After the other paper birds had flown away, she hunkered, still, alone, over work. She'd telephoned her aunt to say she'd be late. Birdie didn't have any way of tracking The Cottage's phone number. Miss Fearing brought her the rest of the sandwiches from Toby's visit, then went back upstairs. So Gem slogged away at frequency analysis long after supper.

When at last she locked the office door and emerged into darkness, the deep navy sky canopied over Lake Ontario was bejewelled with pulsing, dazzling stars. She gazed high into the firmament. One star blazed more brightly than all the spangled others. A lodestar. Surely the northern. And Toby's words, that last time they were alone together, returned to her: *Look up into the night sky, at the stars, and you will see me.*

"I see you," she whispered.

THIRTY-THREE

THE *NORTHSTAR* SET sail. Before Toby left, there'd only been time for one more meeting, beneath the willow at Wild Pigeon Park. A letter had arrived at the flat, from Toby, directing her when to meet him. He'd slipped it into the mailbox himself because the regular post would have taken too long. As they sat on the bench, holding hands, they replayed Toby's visit to The Cottage, how murderously difficult it had been to hide their feelings and play-act the roles of strangers.

Wren had worried about her niece's brooding moods of late. Unable to staunch her curiosity, she had steamed the letter open—an envelope with no stamp drew attention to itself—and read the cryptic missive: *Park. Sunday. Love NS.* No doubt related to that first rose, Wren thought. The one not meant for her.

As for Gem, despite her work as a codebreaker, it had taken her a skip of time to realize that Toby used *NS* as his alias, for North Star.

While Gem fiddled with the woven bracelet on Toby's wrist, he remarked on how wonderful it had been to see Hedwig. And how pleased he was that his cat had been adopted by a lady mathematical genius.

"Now I just have to find homes for the kittens," Gem said.

"I'll pray you do." He shifted a little on the bench. Enough to put his arm around her. "Sadly, no boat ride today, Gem. Today is the worst. I have to say goodbye—for now."

Gaunt mauve clouds scudded overhead, like wispy herring

bones. They reminded Gem of how thin Toby had been when first they'd met at the barbed wire fence.

Gem's tears began.

"I don't know if I'll make it across the Atlantic," Toby said, "especially through the Black Pit, and if I do, I can't say how long it will be before I can get another message to you. If I make it, once I've delivered the documents, I'll go underground for a while, in search of my mother. But they may have another assignment for me, too. I must go where I'm sent, until this war ends. You might not hear from me for a long time," Toby said. "But I'll find a way, somehow, to get a message to you."

"I worry you'll forget me, Toby."

He looked into her eyes. "No. I won't. You're my North Star, Gem. My Polaris, my guiding light. One never forgets one's guiding light."

Somehow, this made it worse. She sobbed. Was this how Aunt Wren felt when her sweetheart enlisted? And never returned. Gem began to fathom how deep Birdie's wound, how unending her grief.

"I almost forgot," Toby said, reaching into his jacket pocket. "Here's the book, your aunt's volume of poetry. I've memorized many of Millay's poems." He slipped the book into Gem's straw satchel. "Remember, there will be a message from me, one way or another," Toby murmured.

"I'll look for any signal that you're alive and haven't forgotten me," Gem whispered. "We don't even have a photograph of each other."

Toby cursed his wristwatch, then kissed her gently. He backed away from her slowly, taking her in one last time before his departure.

"Thank you for rescuing Hedwig—and her family," Toby said.

"I'm attached to Hedwig, too, you know. After all, she brought us together. I'd keep her myself except pets aren't allowed in our flat."

Toby walked her to the park's edge. They stood there, embracing, for several minutes. Then he kissed her goodbye.

The next day, he'd be gone.

THIRTY-FOUR

ALLIED INTELLIGENCE SOURCES learned that the *Kriegsmarine* had ramped up their U-boat fleets, Miss Fearing informed them. If that wasn't enough, the Germans had also engineered new glider bombs. She also told them that the *Northstar* had been directed on a zigzag course, a strategy thought to make tracking it more difficult, so its crossing would take longer. The sea was unusually rough that summer, so weather was another factor. But Miss Fearing's supervisors' best guess was that it would take two to three weeks for the *Northstar* to complete its voyage, possibly longer.

They leaned into their work like never before. They continued to lunch at the oversized desk to maintain morning's flow. They talked about Toby, worrying, collectively, out loud, while Gem worried about him silently, frantically, day and night. Chewed her blue fingernails to the quick. She obsessed over the crew, too, right down to the last man flushing the bearings, maintaining the generators, polishing the signal lamps, the aproned cook. Every day, she arrived early at work and toiled after hours, after the other girls had left, until Miss Fearing ordered her to "go home, for pity's sake, spend some time with your aunt, get some sleep."

As if Gem could sleep. Her nightmares were of fire, paralyzingly cold water, *what-ifs*. What if the watchman, in an instant's distraction, missed the periscope of a U-boat? What if Toby died? There were always U-boats lurking out there. Gem knew a single lone wolf could be as deadly as a whole wolf pack. Their boss also informed them that signals from *Caledonia Rose*, the ship escorting the *Northstar*, might have been picked up on a German radio. This hadn't been confirmed, but it hadn't been discounted, either. Ominous news piled onto ominous news.

The only bright spots in those gruelling days were Hedwig's kittens, those little balls of fluff. On their breaks, Gem, Hester, Ada and Cora-Lynn coddled and played with them, dangling strips of paper, string. And Hedwig continued her rodent patrol in the lower office.

Hedwig's prowess as a mouser was matched by Gem's skill at frequency analysis. She now could scan a raft of intercepts and piece things together quickly. Ada's fluency in German was a boon, and fast as Gem could piece together words, Ada translated: *angriff*—strike, raid, attack; *auftauchen*—take boat to surface; *betriebstoff*—fuel; *kugelblitz*—an excessive serving of noodle pudding, was Hester's guess. Far from it, Ada Swift said: fireball. Miss Fearing's paper birds worked together like never before. Gem sent her hunches across the large table to Cora-Lynn, who factored them into her hypotheses. Miss Fearing moved Ada Lovelace's portrait to another part of the office to make room for a larger chalkboard, where Hester, under Cora-Lynn's tutelage, chalked inside three squares: *key*, *plaintext*, *ciphertext*. When Hester was stuck, Cora-Lynn suggested applying Rejewski's constraint.

One day, when they *did* take their lunches outside, Ada placed a stone on the silver log and stared at it in silence through the entire noon break. The others didn't question this, for who knew where it could lead? Another day, Cora-Lynn took twenty-six small stones, more like pebbles really, marked a letter on each with a soft pen, and laid this improvised Enigma keyboard out on the sand and walked, barefoot, between the letters. Hester wondered aloud if they were all going mad. Gem had little doubt of that.

At the end of her stone meditation, Ada urged Cora-Lynn to gather her "alphabet stones" so they didn't arouse suspicion. There was a tavern, the Windsor Public House, in Mimico, not that far from The Cottage, and Ada had heard from her cousin in Halifax that the worst place for flapping lips was bars. "So, get rid of the evidence, Cora," Ada warned. Cora-Lynn knew Ada was right, so collected the small stones and took them into the office, where the kittens enjoyed scooting them across the floor, creating new letter combinations.

They listened more and more intently to each other. Hunches hummed alongside logic. Letters waltzed with numbers.

Ada Swift had been marking up a set of intercepts at her corner of the table. "I *have* something," she shrieked. "Buzz Lady F right away!"

Hedwig and her kittens had been lounging, curled in the improvised bed fashioned from a large feather-stuffed cushion under the map of the North Atlantic. The mother cat, hearing Ada, looked up, bemused.

Gem pressed the buzzer wired to the upstairs office, a signal that Miss Fearing was needed downstairs. Their boss soon appeared, disheveled, in bedroom slippers, which reminded Gem of the first day she'd met her for the interview. How long ago that seemed.

Even Ada's incandescence had suffered from the brain-wrenching toil and long hours. Darkness shadowed her eyes, her complexion was dull. "This needs no translating," she told the others. "It came in from one of our own listening posts, in plain English: '*Northstar* now enters the Black Pit.'"

Miss Fearing sank down at her desk. "*Confound it!*"

From its bed, the cat family registered alarm, ears erect, ten semaphore flags of concern.

Gem shook. Frightened by what their boss might reveal.

Hester turned a lock of hair nervously in her fingers.

Even Cora-Lynn was rattled, her quaking hand lighting a menthol cigarette.

They waited for their boss to elaborate.

"This is *bad*," Miss Fearing said. "Someone has slipped up

grievously—this message isn't even coded. It only takes one idiot's mistake like this to blow everything up. Why would some imbecile use *plain English*? If the enemy gets their hands on this, it will lead them right to the *Northstar*, or in very close range." A sound of angry frustration arose from the boss as the cat family shrank into the pillow's feather depths as far as they could.

Cora-Lynn snatched the paper from Ada's hands. "There's no date stamp. *Now* as in 'now enters the Black Pit' could mean anything, it's vague."

It was Hester's turn to snatch the paper. She ponied up support. "The Black Pit is no small area. And the missive, however ill-conceived, did not give coordinates, at least."

Miss Fearing still looked disconsolate. She was about to speak when a knocking reached them. She rose to answer the door.

Luther, the messenger, delivered a new package of documents.

Miss Fearing emptied them in the middle of the large desk. "Sift through these as expeditiously as you can. They may contain details related to the incompetence we've just witnessed. Some needle in this new haystack may tell us if the enemy has picked up the uncoded message."

They stared at their boss, who'd been gesticulating so much that her hair now appeared electrified.

"What are you waiting for, paper birds?" Miss Fearing vaunted. "*Hurry!* I'll take some of the newest material over to my desk. I'll work down here with you for a while."

Gem sat, nauseated. All she could think was that his ship was in the most dangerous part of the Atlantic Ocean.

As if gleaning her thoughts, Hester said, "Poor Tobias. Poor *all of them*."

Cora-Lynn had worn her bossy britches that day. "Pity won't save them, Hobbs. Hunker down."

"She's right," Miss Fearing said, spreading papers over her desk.

Hedwig jumped up onto the desk, walked over the papers. Their boss gently lifted the cat back down onto the floor.

Suddenly, a light switched on in Gem's addled brain. "Wait—why don't we devise a decoy message, that contradicts the other one and throws the enemy off course, *away* from the *Northstar*?"

Hearing this, their boss rose and joggled on her heels like an excited child with a secret. "*Yes*—disinformation, decoy news to steer them off the scent. That's using your head, Miss Sullivan!"

Even though they'd been working together, each a cog in a greater machine, Ada Swift couldn't hide her dismay that *she* hadn't struck upon this strategy first. "One of the oldest tricks in the books—it's done all the time," she burbled.

"That's because it *works*," Miss Fearing said. "Write it, Miss Sullivan, and I'll convey it to my superiors, and have it disseminated far and wide."

Gem was nervous. What she wrote could mean seeing Toby again or *never* again, depending on the fate of his ship. She'd be writing for his life. Many lives.

Miss Fearing came over and stood next to Gem. "This doesn't have to be Sonnet 18—don't overthink it, just write."

They all waited.

Fast as her fingers could move, Gem wrote, then handed the paper to their boss.

Miss Fearing read aloud: "'*Engine problem NORTHSTAR must deviate far north off course turn back for repairs REPEAT turn back now aim for Station Ice Cap.*' Not bad, Miss Sullivan. Where is Station Ice Cap?"

"Nowhere but my imagination," Gem said. "Though I was thinking of Greenland."

Miss Fearing left to dispatch the message *post-haste*—her word.

THIRTY-FIVE

THE KITTENS GAINED strength rapidly, proportionate to their mother's growing impatience with them. Hedwig pushed them towards the bowls of solid food laid out for them both downstairs, where the girls worked, and upstairs, in Miss Fearing's domain. "No rations for *these* Mimico meowers," the boss proclaimed. As for Hedwig, she was quite taken by Miss Fearing and, as if to gain accolades from the Priestess, continued to catch mice with enthusiasm, dropping these trophies at whoever's feet were closest. Hedwig still often nuzzled at Gem's neck when Gem picked her up, but Toby's cat was undeniably drawn to Miss Fearing. A cat will choose its favourite, it seems.

So it was cemented in stone now: Miss Fearing would take "the mother" and each of them in the office would adopt one kitten, or at least promise to find it a good home. This plan made Miss Fearing quite happy; the mother cat was a stellar mouser, and good company. "I enjoy her except when she walks across my papers, and a cat will make a fine companion until Peggy comes home—and after that, Peg likes cats." So Hedwig would live at The Cottage for the foreseeable future.

Ada, Hester and Cora-Lynn each took a kitten home.

Gem had a dilemma, given the no-pets policy at their flat. Still, she hoped Mrs. Deluca might be persuaded. Gem chose the tiny Hedwig, the smoky one with the white-splotched nose and creamy tuxedo. As she carried the kitten, tucked inside her straw satchel, north along Church Street, Gem realized she'd no better plan now about what to do with the kitten than she'd had the day she loaded the family into the willow basket and carted them back to The Cottage. That hadn't turned out badly at all, so now Gem could only hope her luck would spill over into the home front. Perhaps the landlady's position could be softened. Aunt Wren was in a buoyant mood these days, which boded well, and Rooney had no real say in the matter—unless she had a deathly allergy to cats or something like that.

If only Gem could let Toby know that everything had worked out with Hedwig's brood. How he'd love to hear that.

Birdie was cross at first. They *weren't* allowed pets, so she told Gem it would be her job to go downstairs and beg Mrs. Deluca to keep the kitten.

Gem went downstairs and told their landlady about the poor homeless creature. Rosa Deluca fingered her rosary beads and thought, then said they could keep the kitten for now but if it made bothersome noise or caused any damage in the upstairs flat, it had to go.

Gem danced back upstairs and relayed the good news. It didn't take much to bring Aunt Wren around. "You've been so nervous and sad all summer, and if this little bundle of fur lifts your spirits, niece of mine, it earns its keep."

The kitten delighted Rooney, too. Wren gave her some money to go out and buy cat food and litter, and she tore off on Gem's bicycle to pick up the supplies.

WREN LOVED THE kitten immediately. She adored it from the pearl of its nose to the tip of its tail, which reminded her of a tarot-card sword. The kitten, still unnamed, was very entertaining. Between sewing and millinery work, Wren fed the kitten and played with it. And laughed. Its naughtiest trick was climbing the living room drapes. Luckily, the drapes didn't belong to Mrs. Deluca; Wren had sewed them long ago, from fabric a customer never picked up—sheer fabric like a wedding veil.

That Sunday, Rooney agreed to babysit the kitten while Wren went for a late breakfast then a movie with Dr. Fox—a double-bill matinee in an *air-conditioned theatre* in Long Branch.

Gem had asked to be let into the office to work that Sunday, but Miss Fearing said, "No, you need a day of rest. I see how hard you've been working, how you've lost weight, how sallow your look. You're no good to me if you're sick. Stay home, or go out and do something you enjoy."

Gemma didn't know what to do with herself. So she decided to go for a walk. Wherever her feet took her. It was frustrating that Miss Fearing wouldn't allow her in the office. Some intercept papers remained on her quadrant of the table that she hadn't finished before their boss ordered her paper birds to fly away. Could the key to everything be in those papers?

Aunt Wren had noticed, too, how thin Gem had become, how little she ate, and setting out for breakfast then the movies, she made Gem eat a bowl of porridge, and watched to make sure she ate it all.

Even though she'd have preferred to work, it felt good to break free of their small flat, and The Cottage.

She stopped in front of a church. Gem had never been part of a congregation, couldn't recall ever setting foot in a chapel of any sort. Aunt Wren had lost her faith years ago, after her fiancé died, and once told Gemma she'd find it hypocritical to send Gem "into that charade." "But surely some people find it a comfort?" Gem had suggested, but her aunt only said Gem could go on her own when she was older if she felt so inclined.

Gem wanted to see the stained glass windows, hear the organ, so she entered the church. A service was underway. She slid quietly into a back pew—a bit surprised someone churchy didn't come and eject her, for the ladies seated around her wore lovely hats and, a glance told Gem, their best summer dresses. And there was she, in her sneakers, a short-sleeved, striped knitted sweater and, of all things, Bermuda shorts. There were a few sidelong glances, but nothing more. So Gem settled back, as comfortably as she could, into the hardwood pew.

She bent her head, then whispered a prayer for Toby and his ship. Gem couldn't really form an image of God; all that came to her were the robed figures from Birdie's tarot cards, with their swords and wands. Or the Magician, in a flower garden. She prayed the best she could, plumbing her mind for the words. The large arrangement of blue delphiniums in a chalice on the altar reminded her of the chalice on a tarot card.

The choir sang "Amazing Grace." Gem had heard this hymn before, the radio sometimes played it. But that day, she truly listened. Exalted organ swells rolled over her, engulfed her. The lyrics, too, swept her away, their grandeur, epic scope, vast as the sea through which Toby's ship now forged its ragged course. The sermon's theme was goodness and truth, how in this time of war, goodness would one day prevail, if they remained steadfast believers. The theme pivoted to compassion, kindness. Which made Gemma realize that she'd not always been kind to Rooney Delacroix.

"Compassion and kindness are forms of grace," concluded the sermon.

The offering plate circulated. Gem hadn't a single coin to drop in it. She felt so ashamed about this, she rose and fled from the church.

In a few minutes she reached the flat. Rooney was in the living room, dangling a string that the kitten chased. "It's not easy trying to knit with this little one close by," she laughed.

Gemma took two glasses of iced tea into the living room. She gave one to Rooney and settled with the other one in the armchair.

Rooney sipped thoughtfully. Then said, pointing to the kitten, "You haven't yet named this little rascal."

"How about Grace, because she graces our flat with humour?"

"Sounds good to me, Gem."

Gemma rattled the ice cubes in her glass. "I haven't always been kind to you, Rooney. And I'm sorry for that."

This sudden sombre turn unsettled Rooney, or seemed to. "Why, *sure* you have—you and your aunt have been very kind to me. You let me take meals with you. I've learned so many new words doing the crossword puzzles with your aunt. You even loaned me your bicycle to ride to my work. You've given me a cozy home life—I haven't had that in ages. And even if you knew the truth about me, I dare to hope you'd *still* be kind—forgiving, even." Then the girl slammed her hand across her mouth in a gesture of one who has over-shared.

The kitten, now Grace, had curled up in her lap.

"*Truth*, Rooney?"

Rooney sighed heavily. "I got into trouble. Up north. One night at a dance hall. I was much too young to go, but I sneaked out of the house. There was a girl there I knew, so it wasn't like I was totally on my own. But that girl soon enough vaporized into the night. And a soldier enticed me to dance. He had a flask of whiskey he shared with me out back. I made a terrible mistake, Gemma. A nine-months mistake. I'll spare you the details. But that's why I don't talk to men now. They can trick you, don't always tell the truth. My parents disowned me, the shame of it."

The kitten awoke, stretched, still in Rooney's lap.

Gem asked, dumbfounded, "You mean all this time you've been living here you've had—have—a child?"

"Yes. A girl. If I can prove myself a fit mother, I stand a chance to get her back. A couple up north is taking care of her until then."

"That must be hard," Gem said.

Rooney was on the verge of tears. "It's awful. I knit caps and sweaters for her and send them. Fall will be here soon, she'll need them. Thought I'd die, giving birth to her, but I miss her terribly.

Have you ever missed someone you love, Gemma? It's its own kind of agony."

"Yes," Gem said, setting her glass on the side table lest she drop it.

Rooney must have intuited a reluctance on Gem's part to elaborate, so she didn't press. Instead, she said, "So, now you know. And I feel suddenly much lighter, releasing my secret. I only hope your aunt is as tolerant as *you* seem to be."

"Aunt Wren is kind. But you've entrusted me with a very personal secret, and I won't tell her if you'd rather I didn't."

Rooney thanked Gem. "I imagine she'll find out at some point. Hiding a baby is hard, even one who's not here. I'm sorry I kept this from you both, but it's so difficult to trust anyone these days what with the government's endless spiels about spies and enemies in our midst, and of course the young man, the soldier, who said, that whiskey-sodden night, it would be all right, that I should go ahead and enjoy myself. And look what happened. But I'm hopeful my situation will change. After all, there's your aunt Wren, raising you on her own—she's an inspiration, a guiding light that it's possible."

"I've every faith you can do it, Rooney," Gem said.

Rooney danced a long strand of yarn across the living room floor again, and Grace scurried around after it. "I've one more confession, Gemma."

A pang of alarm struck Gem. What could be "more" than a baby?

"I must have ridden over something sharp. Your bicycle has a flat tire. I'm sorry."

That's all? A flat tire? This revelation stood so starkly removed from Rooney's previous disclosure that Gem erupted into much-needed laughter that lifted her on invisible wings, like a bird, high over her earthbound worries, and even the nearby lake.

THIRTY-SIX

Rain fell steady and thick the next day. And the mood inside the office matched the weather. They drubbed away through the morning with their pencils. How Gem hoped an update on the *Northstar* might be forthcoming, but Miss Fearing remained upstairs.

At noon, she carried Hedwig down to the lower office. While the cat patrolled, their boss rolled her office chair over to their large table and sat with them. "We can't confirm this, but Miss Sullivan's decoy message may have sent enemy U-boats off track, which gives the *Northstar* a leg-up on making it safely through the Black Pit."

Their eyes lit with hope.

"*But*"—their boss went on—"as you probably realize, the decoy code is only a temporary fix. For one thing, the enemy may suspect that it is, in fact, a trick."

The hope in their eyes dimmed.

"So," Miss Fearing intoned, "as much as I'd like to eat apricots and smoke Pall Malls on the beach when the sun returns, I must put the whip to you harder than ever, my paper birds."

They ate their lunches indoors. Gem missed the sky, the reeling gulls, the sandpipers foraging on the narrow ribbon of beach.

The afternoon only grew darker, more overcast, the codes more obscure. Gem despaired that her previous success with Sonnet 18 had been nothing more than a sheer fluke, a once-in-a-lifetime stroke of random luck. Ada Swift crumpled one of her origami birds and threw it, in a high arc, into the wastebasket. Hester's air was despondent.

Even Ponder the Wonder neared her conceptual rope's end. "My teachers, including Lady F, said don't discount the past. Look to history. Knowledge is a long, winding conversation that often as not extends backwards." Then Cora-Lynn sparked a cigarette and inhaled deeply. Tossing her ponytail, she continued. "I've gone back to the 1700s, the Pigpen Cipher, I've tried Playfair's digraphs. I've gone homophonic, polyalphabetic—*pathetic*! I might as well be at the mad tea party in Lewis Carroll's story for all the sense I, even with my University of Toronto education, can make of this pile"—she grabbed the heavy stack of papers—"of stuff."

The papers made a loud *thwack* when Cora-Lynn dropped them back down on the desk. The thud frightened the cat, who mewled and scurried into the corner, under the cot.

"Now you've gone and scared our resident mouser!" Ada chided.

Gem thought again of the boat ride with Toby. How the lake's water that day had been the same intense blue as her fingernails.

She looked down at her hands, the very ones he'd held.

His memory hovered around her like a ghost.

THIRTY-SEVEN

"CALEDONIA ROSE, THE escort ship, has lost radio contact with the *Northstar*." This was Miss Fearing's grim herald the next day. She stood before them in the lower office, her tone tight-wired, her face showing clear signs of sleeplessness. She held Hedwig in her arms, stroking the cat's fur as if this action steadied her nerves.

Seated around the large desk, the four of them took in this grave news.

Gem slumped forwards in her chair as if someone had punched her squarely in the stomach.

Hester gasped.

Ada's face wore full defeat.

"Does this mean what—heaven forbid—I *think* it means, Miss Fearing?" asked Cora-Lynn.

Their boss lit a Pall Mall. "It could mean a number of things. Rough weather may have pushed the *Northstar* out of range; or one or the other ship's radio might have a malfunction or need to be recalibrated; or the *Northstar* picked up U-boat coordinates and adjusted its course but couldn't risk radioing the escort ship through TBS, *Talk Between Ships*, lest the enemy overhear the strategy; or—"

"It could be *anything*, in other words," Gem wailed. "The *Northstar* could have simply been blown to bits and . . . *sank*."

Her co-workers stared in alarm.

Puffing hard on her cigarette, Miss Fearing said, "Until we hear otherwise, we assume it has *not* been hit—we need to stay calm. The *Rose* will keep attempting contact, even if it must resort to flashing lantern flares, which is not ideal, since prowling U-boats might see these signals, or fog may compromise their effectiveness. The *Rose* is equipped with the latest high-frequency direction finder equipment. I *will* say that the radio man on board *Caledonia Rose* is highly skilled, having trained at *St. Hyacinthe*'s signal school. I know him. Right now, we must tally every point in our favour, to maintain morale."

"But the high-frequency gizmo is only for our ships locating U-boats, and *not each other*." Ada tapped her pencil a mile a minute against the desk.

Their boss bashed her cigarette into the ashtray. "Girls, *please*—you're not being helpful. Go back through yesterday's intercepts with a fine-toothed comb. I'm heading upstairs to work in a calmer, less hysterical setting. I'll inform you of any updates—and remember, that ship is *above* water until you hear otherwise!"

As soon as their boss departed, leaving Hedwig downstairs, Gemma burst into tears.

The others stared.

Ada swanned a handkerchief out of nowhere and fluffed it over to Gem.

"No one has the *slightest idea* where that ship is," Gem blustered. Then snorted into the handkerchief.

"What *is* it with you?" Cora-Lynn barbed. "You and the *Northstar*? There've been lots of other ships before this one."

Gem sniffed, sat in pure misery. Strove to muster a convincing response. "It's just that—don't you find—it's *different* when someone we know is on the ship. It makes all this even harder because it's"—she sniffled—"*personal*."

Cora-Lynn sent a knowing look around the table before her gaze landed on Ada. "Seems like you're not the *only* one with a crush on Tobias Albrecht, Ada."

"Drop it, Cora," Ada said. "I'm not in the mood for it."

Gem took a deep breath.

Through lunch they laboured, spilling crumbs that Hedwig gobbled from the floor.

Somehow, Gem had recovered enough to work. Losing her wits wouldn't find Toby's ship. She sliced away with her pencil as though she wielded a knife, carving up parchment.

Hester hit on two consecutive letters: *NS*. She beelined this discovery upstairs.

Ada composed a new decoy message that, she said, taxed her imagination to the nth degree.

Cora-Lynn laid long, scissored strips of paper over a grid she'd devised.

Gem cracked two words: *W-E-R-D-A-M-M-T* and *N-O-R-D-E-N*, which Ada confirmed were German for "damned" and "north." Panic ripped through Gem. This might mean a U-boat had located the *Northstar*. And that Toby's ship was doomed.

"But it could also mean merely that the U-boat is still *searching* for it," Ada argued. "Like the submarine captain ordered them, 'Find the damned *Northstar*.'"

"Meaning it's still *above* water," Cora-Lynn piped. They phoned this latest information upstairs to Miss Fearing.

Near day's end, Cora-Lynn's ashtray overflowed. Hester rubbed her eyes and drained the last coffee from her thermos. Ada thudded the desk with her palm and declared herself "fresh out of magic tricks."

Just then, Gem found something, a number, amid a string of coded letters. At that same moment, Miss Fearing descended to check their progress, and Gem revealed the number—53097. "It's just a number," Gem said, sighing.

Miss Fearing lifted Hedwig off the floor and hoisted the cat high in a gesture of triumph, then set the bewildered cat gently back down. "53097? This *isn't* just a number, Miss Sullivan—it's the numerical code for the *Northstar*, which is 5309."

"But what of the '7' tacked to the end?" asked Ada.

"That's probably a null," Cora-Lynn said. "Numerical symbol for a space."

Their boss told Gem, "Give me your stack of intercepts, I'm taking them upstairs to work through them. Combined with the earlier *NS* discovery—which I'm sure means *Northstar*—we may have something."

Even in their bedraggled state, they brightened. Their boss eyeballed the clock on the wall.

"You girls haven't been outdoors in hours, and it's late—I need you back here, fresh, tomorrow—now fly away home!"

"Can I please stay and work longer, Miss Fearing?" Gem begged. "I'd like to learn what you discover about the number."

Miss Fearing gazed at her sympathetically. "No. You *in particular* need to go home, Gemma Sullivan—rest, eat something. You look terrible."

The other girls were already gathering their things on their way out. Gem trailed them, trudging outdoors, along Lake Shore Road.

When Gem arrived home, Aunt Wren, Rooney and a distinguished white-haired gentleman in a homburg hat were seated around the kitchen table. At the centre of the table was a fresh long-stemmed red rose in a vase. Near the rose, a crystal wine decanter. She'd completely forgotten that Birdie's eye doctor was dining with them that night. Aunt Wren had mentioned it earlier, saying, "It's high time my girls met Lyle." Gemma had been distracted; this supper was the last thing on her mind.

They'd been waiting for her. The table was set; Aunt Wren had brought out the good dishes, with the delicate floral pattern. Their best silver, freshly polished (Birdie had bought it years ago, as an engagement gift to herself, with her millinery earnings). A mélange of appetizing smells reached Gem—roast beef, turnips, fresh homemade rolls, apple pie. Birdie must have been cooking and baking all day. The kitchen was very hot, and Rooney fanned herself with a piece of paper.

A nervous hush fell over the table when Gem walked in. She was quite late, she knew that, and she apologized.

"This is Dr. Fox—Lyle," Aunt Wren said to Gem.

They greeted each other. Gem took a seat at the table. "Quite the spread, Birdie."

Her aunt's fingers fluttered away the compliment. "I'm glad you're here, niece of mine. If you didn't turn up soon, I was going to send a search party out for you. Finally, we can eat."

Rooney helped Aunt Wren serve the blade roast, turnips, potatoes, gravy, trimmings.

Dr. Fox brought wine and poured them each a glass.

Gem tried to settle her mind from its onslaught of frantic worry about Toby's ship. The pleasant chatter around the table helped—a little. The wine, too, helped—a little.

"Young Rooney has been telling me about her work at the tannery," Lyle Fox said.

Aunt Wren reached over and slapped his wrist—in a loving way. "Not the best topic for dinner," she teased.

"Oh, it wasn't about the gore and blood," Rooney said. "We were talking about the prisoners from the internment camp who work at the tannery."

"Indeed, I've been in that camp. I treated some prisoners for various optical ailments," said Dr. Fox.

It dawned on Gem that he might have met Toby. "How was it, Dr. Fox? Any of the prisoners stand out in your mind?"

He adjusted his hat a little. Gem found it curious that he wore it at the supper table, but that was the homburg Birdie had made for him, and he kept it on as a courtesy perhaps. "I'm not sure what you mean by 'stand out,' Gemma, but I did learn that those men can't all be painted with one brush. Many are far from the Nazi monsters the newspapers go on about; some don't ascribe to the Third Reich at all. And others are simply detained there for capricious reasons, some are civilians. It's a hodgepodge. And the facility is badly overcrowded and ineptly managed."

"Mostly young prisoners, I guess?" Gem asked, picking at her meal.

"About the range you'd expect," Lyle Fox answered. "One mild-tempered young fellow about your age, Gemma, perhaps a bit older, tall and slender. But he's gone now."

"What happened to him, Dr. Fox?" (She knew, but was curious whether other accounts were in circulation.)

"No idea," the eye doctor said. "They don't tell us those things. I found the chap very likeable, I recall, but pitied him, for he was racked with worry about his mother back in Germany."

Yes, Toby. Gem observed her aunt while Dr. Fox had been speaking. Birdie's eyes *danced* with keenness and light as she gazed adoringly at her companion in his homburg hat. How fine it must be to dine with a loved one, to have that person so nearby, a mere touch away. Not a churning sea away, in a Black Pit of peril. Doomed, possibly. She took another swallow of wine; its musky heft snapped something, already frayed, within her.

"I suppose you like my aunt?" Gem asked their hatted guest.

Lyle Fox looked taken aback. "I like her a—*great deal*."

Birdie turned scarlet.

Gem forged ahead. "You *care* for her, then?"

The eye doctor's steady gaze squared off against Gemma's scrutinizing look. "If you want to know, I care for her like my own life."

Rooney seemed about to choke on her potatoes, reached for her water glass and sipped, rapidly.

Aunt Wren began to fan her face with her napkin, a floppy, improvised fan.

Why stop now? Gem thought. "So, you *love* her?"

From under the table, Grace the kitten mewed.

"I would not hesitate on that score in the least," Lyle said.

Gem grew vehement. "Do you know Birdie's birthday?"

Their gentleman guest shook his head.

"What's her favourite colour?"

"I really couldn't say for sure," he said.

"What kind of food does my aunt like best?" Gem lobbed across the table.

Aunt Wren began to intervene. "Niece of mine, I think—"

"Let him *answer*!" Gem blared.

"That I *can* shed some light on," Lyle began. "Your aunt prefers simple, homey fare—like this, before us on the table—over fine dining."

Birdie's face, so bright earlier, folded into wrinkles. "Please excuse my niece, Dr.—Lyle. She hasn't been herself since starting her office job. Her job is terribly stressful, it seems—it even drove her to chop off her beautiful hair."

Right there, at the kitchen table, Gemma realized how supremely tired she was of *not knowing*. Of guesses, hunches. So much for the poet Keats's *negative capability*. She raised her fork, in the manner of a musical conductor. "So, Dr. Fox, you don't know when my aunt's birthday is, or her favourite colour. Were you even aware, before I called her Birdie, that Birdie is her moniker of affection?"

She seemed to have gotten to him. This time Lyle Fox looked genuinely ashamed. "I did not know this, the Birdie nickname."

"Yet," Gem pressed on, "you love her. Even *not* knowing these things."

"Yes, I love Wren. And what I don't know of her, I'll enjoy learning, over time."

Wren stood, rickety. "I'm serving the apple pie now."

"I'll help," Rooney said. Adding, "You *do* know, Dr. Fox, what fine hats Miss Maw makes, I guess?"

His face registered relief brought by the lodger's intervention. "I know this through and through, for proof of it rests upon my very head."

When it seemed as though the topic had run its course, Gem said, "With such partial knowledge, Dr. Fox, when did you first know you loved our Birdie?"

The apple pie was being circulated, on the good dessert plates.

He smiled, like this was the easiest question in the world. "You ask 'when'? Why, the instant, in my office, when I first gazed into those exquisite purple irises of hers, and what radiated back to me was the purest form of light. *That's* when. And in my line of work, I've seen a lot of eyes—but *none* like Wren's."

He tucked into his apple pie.

Gem understood this because she'd experienced the exact same thing when she first beheld Tobias Albrecht through the barbed wire, the way his eyes radiated light back to her.

Complimenting the cook on the apple pie, Dr. Fox lifted his fork, as if in thought, and said, "And yet, there's something *ineffable* about it, about loving her right away, something that eludes logic, a mystery to my very old bones—and I don't feel the need to go chasing down mystery."

Wren glanced over at him, said teasingly, "Your 'very old bones,' Sir, aren't as old as mine."

He laughed. And Gem thought again how sweet it must be to have the one you love at your side, a mere breath away.

THIRTY-EIGHT

THE NEXT DAY, Miss Fearing met them in the lower office. Good news. "The number Miss Sullivan uncovered is indeed the *Northstar*'s code, and we—working through the night in tandem with Whitby and a brilliant young woman in Ottawa—have reason to believe the *Northstar* is intact. It has at least made it through the Black Pit and is now within protective aircraft range again, on the final leg of its journey. Excellent work!

"But the *Northstar* isn't out of the woods yet. Though it may be closing in on its voyage, more than one of our ships has been taken out heartbreakingly near their destinations. We can't let our guard down too soon. The enemy will make mistakes, but so will we. And guess what? It's not the only ship of ours out there, so you're a long way from finished. Come, Hedwig."

Toby's cat trailed devotedly at her heels as she returned upstairs.

WHEN SHE RETURNED home that night, Gem apologized to her aunt for her rude behaviour over dinner. Gem then rang Dr. Fox at his office, to apologize directly to him as well. The way she'd carried on at the dinner now rankled her with remorse.

Taking the phone call, Dr. Fox had been kind. Humorous even. Gem could see why her aunt was so fond of him.

And he had a long-stemmed red rose delivered every week to their flat on Pidgeon Avenue. The same note attached each time: *Make no mistake, for W. xo L.*

But more amends waited to be made, things that needed

mending. Gem offered to go with Rooney to have the bicycle's flat tire fixed; they could take turns pushing the bike to the repair shop. Those chores were more enjoyable with two people, Gem said, so they walked to a weather-beaten garage with a crooked shingle that said *Tires Repaired*. The grizzled garage man removed the tire and tube, then rooted through cartons. "Strange state of affairs, isn't it," he yammered. "Goodyear factory a pebble's toss away, yet I'm forced to scrounge for a scrap of rubber for your bike. But the military needs every shred of rubber."

Gemma and Rooney stood nearby, smiled and waited while he patched the tire.

"Work at the tannery, do you?" The mechanic eyeballed Rooney. He must have smelled her; she hadn't washed her hair in a few days. For her part, Gemma had gotten oddly used to the way she smelled.

Rooney nodded.

The mechanic turned Gemma's way. "And you, young lady? What do *you* do besides bike over nails?"

"I work in an office," Gem said.

"Right."

"It's actually me who cycled over the sharp object," Rooney said.

The man pumped air back into the tire. "You should be all set now, girls."

They asked how much they owed for the repair.

"Not a cent. It's not every day I get to repair a bike brought in by two pretty girls."

THE NEXT SUNDAY, Gemma retraced her steps back to the church where she'd sat, without a penny in her pocket, while the offering plate was passed among the congregation. St. Leo's was a short distance from the flat. Gemma had slept late, rare for her, but codebreaking took its toll, just as Miss Fearing predicted. By the time Gem arrived at the church, mass was over and people had left. The church doors remained open. In that reverent space of solace, Gem's sneakers treaded softly down the aisle. A choirboy was snuffing a candle by the altar and the priest himself stood, still robed in his cassock, at the front, nearby, gathering some papers. Gem steeled herself, for she'd never spoken to anyone this lofty—she thought of Dorothy and her compatriots, creeping up to the Great and Mighty Oz.

Gemma cleared her throat.

The priest regarded her with curious, obliging eyes.

She explained that she'd been there not long ago but hadn't any offering for the plate.

"I remember you," he said.

Gem reached into her straw satchel. "Will you accept this late offering?" She handed him a dollar bill. Then a large portrait on the wall caught her eye. On the metal plate under the saintly figure it said *St. Leo the Great*.

The priest saw Gem look at the portrait.

"Why was he great? Saint Leo, I mean," she asked.

"Lots of reasons," the priest replied. "He was known as a peacemaker. Renowned for his prowess with words, his inspiring sermons. Even now we read from his words, at Christmas for example. He believed that we serve best when we try to ease the suffering and pain of this world."

"He *does* sound great," Gemma said, then, for whatever impulse possessed her, saluted, and left the church. She wondered what Aunt Wren, so immersed in paganism, tarot, so disaffected from traditional faith, would think of her chatting with a priest in a church. This visit would remain her secret, Gem decided.

After that, she walked to Wild Pigeon Park and rested on the bench in the exact spot where she had sat with Toby. She still felt Toby's presence there under the willow tree even though he'd now receded into mystery, the unknown.

A train clacked along the overpass, reminding her of the teleprinter's steady mechanized noise at The Cottage, a local listening that returned her to the moment, the world.

WHEN GEM REACHED the flat later that afternoon, she found the kitchen converted fully into a millinery workshop. Aunt Wren was cutting and gluing madly, and there were a couple of hats on blocks. Rooney was home from church, not St. Leo's, wherever she went, and sat, knitting, near the kitchen table. "She's keeping me company," Birdie said, not looking up from the square of blue felt she was cutting into the shape of a bird. Luckily, Grace the kitten couldn't yet jump as high as the table; otherwise, all the small pieces of hats-in-progress would be scattered asunder.

Aunt Wren was thrilled to be back at millinery. "This is so much more artistic than mending holes in trousers," she chirruped. "I'm so grateful to Lyle for lighting the hatter's fire under me with his homburg order."

Then Gem noticed a small, sweet cap, clearly meant for a tiny, tender head. Felt, in a bright periwinkle. She reached for it and turned it in her hands. "I believe this will be much too small for Dr. Fox," she said. "Or any of us."

Rooney's knitting needles ceased their clicking. She sent a sideways glance over to Wren.

"Much too small, yes. This is for"—Wren side-glanced Rooney back—"the little northern one who waits for her mama."

Gem stroked the small hat, a very fine one it was.

"I'm about to stitch some bluebirds to it," Wren said.

"Miss Maw, this is the darlingest cap I've ever seen," Rooney said.

"Birdie, how did you know?" Gem fished.

Aunt Wren straightened her back, suspended her scissors midair. "Just a hunch," she said.

And they left it at that.

THIRTY-NINE

They'd had confirmation, Miss Fearing said: The *Northstar* had made it. Ada, Hester and Cora-Lynn applauded when their boss made the announcement. Gem clapped, too, but strove to mute the ecstasy that swelled within her. She couldn't even think at that moment how she'd celebrate; she'd find a way. She knew, too, that the ship's safe passage was only the beginning of Toby's journey. Next, he'd search for his mother. That would be difficult and dangerous, too, he'd told Gem. But her heart soared with hope. Aunt Wren had drawn the Star card earlier that morning, an emblem of possibility, fulfillment. A card of blessing. "It reminds us to trust in the cosmic universe, " Birdie said to Gem.

Miss Fearing also informed them that the numerical code Gemma cracked, along with the letters *NS*, had been the key. Their boss had delved into it through the night, with several of her associates, and the message turned out to be the German high naval official ordering his men to abandon pursuit of the *Northstar*. His message, Miss Fearing said, translated into "The damned *Northstar* got away from us."

Laughter filled the lower office. "Let's celebrate at Ramona Dance Gardens at Bloor and Durie this Saturday night," Ada said. "Ralph Blinkhorn and his orchestra are playing. They're *dreamy*."

"No more dance halls for me," said Miss Fearing. "Once was enough."

The others decided to discuss the possibility at lunch. That morning demanded renewed focus, their boss told them; she'd brought a fresh onslaught of intercepts she dumped onto the giant desk.

"Can we move our desks back to their original spots now?" Cora-Lynn asked.

Miss Fearing eyeballed her sharply. "Let's make that voluntary. Those of you who wish to resume your original workstations may do so. Those who don't, leave your desk in the middle of the room in its current group configuration." Then she drew a deep, smoky breath and returned upstairs.

The four girls looked around the large table at each other, as if they were strangers who'd just met.

Hester spoke first. "You know, with one desk removed—yours, Cora—this large central table will seem very off balance, asymmetrical, ugly even. Hard to work with that one piece missing."

"There's a beauty in a perfect quadrant, I must admit," Cora-Lynn remarked. "All *right*. You win. I'll leave my desk here. It'd bother me, too, to disrupt the quadratic symmetry."

"That's the collaborative Cora we all know and love," Ada teased.

At lunch, out on the silvery log, the four of them sat, oddly quiet. The day's light bore that lemony cast of late summer, softer, less urgent. Gardens had reached their zenith, the long grasses turned to straw. Gemma picked up some blades of grass and, after finishing her sandwich, plaited them into strands. The others looked on with interest.

Ada asked, "What are you up to, Queen of Hunches?"

"I'm making a straw hat," Gem said, simply.

Cora-Lynn set her thermos of brain tea on the warm log. "For a *beau*?"

Gemma smiled. She was used to her co-worker's teasing by now.

"Oh, our enigmatic Gem," Hester said.

Ada launched herself off the log and did limbering-up stretches, like a dancer, in the sand. "So, who's in for the Ramona Dance Gardens? We can let our hair down after all that *Northstar* stress."

Hester and Cora-Lynn said maybe, they'd see.

Ada said, "And Gem?"

"I'm busy—with my aunt that night," she replied. "Maybe another time."

Ada didn't press.

And suddenly Gemma knew *exactly* what she'd do on Saturday night, to celebrate the *Northstar*'s safe arrival. She would lie on the grass in the Delucas' backyard and gaze up at the constellations. She'd locate the most dazzling within one of them and know it was Toby, her North Star.

FORTY

Over time, Gemma's hair grew long enough to braid or tie back into a ponytail. And, to her surprise and Rooney's, Aunt Wren began wearing a wig, a new head of lustrous hair, soft grey, like a dove, flecked with auburn. It transformed her. "I've never splurged on anything in my life—for me, I mean. So why, for once, should I not? How many more chances will present themselves, to spoil myself? For many years I crafted beauty from coils of wire, rolls of wool felt, blooms sculpted from cloth. All for others. Perhaps the hour has arrived for my *own* beauty. Why shouldn't I have one last hurrah on that front?"

Wren's new millinery enterprise, undertaken from her kitchen table, had begun to catch on in Mimico. "Now the ladies don't have to travel into the city for their hats," Wren said one night over a spaghetti dinner Rooney had cooked for the three of them.

"Your hat enterprise will need a name, Miss Maw," Rooney had remarked amid a cloud of steam while straining the noodles. Mrs. Deluca had given them a cauldron of rich tomato sauce, made from her own tomatoes, which were abundant that summer.

"She makes a good point, Birdie," Gem said.

They twirled spaghetti on their forks and thought about this.

"Second Chance Millinery?" Wren floated across the table. Hard to discern whether she meant this in jest.

"The name should, I think, reflect something local," Gem proposed. "Here we are, living in the town named after wild pigeons. So, why not call your new venture Wild Pigeon Millinery?"

"That's *it*, niece of mine. Though I'll make it clear to my customers that no birds are harmed in my hat-craft."

IN HER MORNING walks to The Cottage, sky scarlet with sunrise and the ragged rooster on Church Street hacking out its aubade, Gem thought about Toby, how badly she longed to know how he fared. To buoy her spirits, she reflected on things that brought comfort—how Birdie now thrived in millinery and love, how Rooney moved about more lightly, no longer under the burden of secrecy about her child. The pleasure brought by cats. Gem had the company, too, of older, wiser women, her aunt, her boss who'd mellowed some. Even Cora-Lynn's moods held fewer nettles.

September arrived, heat lingered, and the towns along Lake Ontario's shore were washed in a translucent amber light. There hadn't yet been frost. Rosa Deluca's front yard rioted with zucchini, squash, pole beans, caged tomatoes, fennel, kohlrabi, gold-haloed sunflowers taller than her. The front yard was sun-soaked, the backyard cast in shade, far from ideal gardening conditions, which was why the backyard was populated only with a wash line and a bench.

Gem would sit back there on the bench sometimes. And dream. She'd stopped going to Wild Pigeon Park to sit on *their* bench; it had somehow become too sad, made her feel even *more* alone.

One autumn Sunday, Gem had taken the newspaper to the backyard and settled with it on the bench. She'd begun to peruse its stories when a distinctive *click* reached her ears. The familiar *click* of the mailbox lid by the front door being opened then closed. But it was Sunday, no mail delivery. She rose to investigate, and just as she rounded the corner of the house, she saw the back of a man striding away quickly.

She dashed out to the sidewalk. "*Hey!*" she hollered. "Mister!"

But the man didn't turn.

Gem considered chasing him, but her curiosity about what he'd left in the mail slot overtook her, and she went to retrieve it. She already knew it wasn't the long-stemmed rose Lyle Fox had delivered for Wren every Monday, a loving launch to the week, Birdie called it.

So Gem reached into the mailbox and plucked out an envelope, her name on the outside.

She returned to the bench in the backyard, where the breeze flapped the newspaper's pages. Gem sat on the newspaper to still it, tore open the envelope and read:

Shining Gem, I've landed and whatever hand you and your associates played in this, I'm forever grateful. Found Mother. Still many obstacles. Will return even if I must row myself across the ocean. Please don't forget me. I'll bet your hair is long by now. I hope Hedwig and the little ones are well.
Love, T.

Toby hadn't forgotten her.

That evening, her mood was so jubilant, Aunt Wren asked Gem if she was quite well. "Your lacklustre disposition this summer, niece of mine, had sadly begun to seem normal."

Gem assured Birdie that she was fine, *beyond* fine.

That night after dinner, Gem splayed in the armchair with the letter, stroking it like a cat. Thankfully, no one asked about it. Her aunt and the lodger were absorbed in their after-dinner projects of crossword puzzles and yarn. And Grace the kitten bounced around between the three of them.

Looking up from her knitting, Rooney scanned the living room, their tableau of contentment. "We should be on a Christmas card," she said.

Aunt Wren went *mmmm*.

Gemma smiled. Marvelled, silently, how this girl from the north who'd once been a stranger in their home wielded such a comfortable presence now. Like kin, almost.

FORTY-ONE

Several weeks later, the man dropped off another letter at the house on Pidgeon Avenue. This time Gem wasn't home. But Aunt Wren, who'd been working on a hat order, heard the mailbox open and close. Autumn had settled in, but the days were still warm enough to keep the windows open in the upstairs flat. The mail had already been delivered that day, so she wondered what was going on, laid aside her millinery and tottered downstairs to the front door. She reached into the mailbox and found a sealed letter addressed to *Miss Gemma Sullivan*. No stamp. Wren took the letter upstairs, left it on the kitchen counter, and all afternoon its contents itched at her. Her guilt over steaming open the cryptic note her niece had received a while ago still prodded Wren's conscience—she'd no business doing that!—so this one she left sealed. Private.

When Gem returned home from work, Birdie said, "A letter came for you—kitchen counter."

Gem snatched the letter and took it to her bedroom.

Rooney had just blown in, with a bouquet of flowers, chrysanthemums the shade of gold coins. As she arranged them in a vase, she quipped that she'd been feeling outpaced by the gorgeous weekly rose delivery.

"Not at all," Aunt Wren said. "Your rustic bouquets balance the formal elegance of a rose perfectly—and one can't have too many flowers."

Rooney beamed and took a seat at the kitchen table. Wren had shuffled things around to free up space on its surface.

Just then Gemma emerged, rosy-cheeked, from her bedroom. She made toast and joined them at the table.

Winking at Rooney, Wren said, "Seems our Gemma does indeed have an admirer. Fan mail arrived for her."

Rooney's eyes widened.

Crunching toast didn't hide Gem's annoyance at being exposed so . . . openly. But she needed to find out more. "Did you notice who delivered the letter, Birdie?" she asked.

"By the time these creaky old joints of mine made it downstairs and reached the mailbox, the delivery person was far down the street. Maybe your admirer is someone from your office?"

"Then why wouldn't that person just give her a letter at work?" asked Rooney.

"And why no return address or stamp?" This from Aunt Wren.

All Gem managed to say was, "Can't a girl have a pen pal?"

Her tone, acerbic, deflecting, stoppered both of them from pressing further.

Gem went to bed early. Cocooned in blankets, she read the latest missive again:

> G. The good fight continues. Hope you are well. Look up into the night sky, to the most luminous star, and remember the one who loves you. Yours, T.

Scant on information. It was a security risk to disclose too much, Gem supposed. She grew more convinced he'd had to scale things back, for safety. Gem understood this, but a pang of disappointment surged through her nonetheless. How she'd enjoy an effusive, soul-baring love letter that went on for pages. But she'd have to make do with scraps, like the cribs and stock phrases in her codebreaking work. Then, switching off her bedside lamp, she chastised herself, thinking about all those waiting to hear from a sweetheart overseas and who received nothing at all.

On the verge of sleep, it struck Gem that if she could discover the identity of the messenger who dropped the letters, it might shed some light on Toby's situation. Because, presumably, Toby and the messenger knew each other.

The next morning, Birdie was already at work at the kitchen table when Gem shuffled, in her bathrobe, to put the kettle on the stove. Rooney's cereal bowl, washed, rested on the drying rack; she'd already left for the tannery. Gem bid her aunt good morning. Then, while the water heated, said, "Auntie, if someone delivers another letter for me—just saying if—can you try to engage him, please, ask who he is and his business, in bringing these letters. I want to know where they are coming from."

Aunt Wren fiddled with the partly felted posy in her hand. "I'll try, but last time he bolted with almost superhuman speed."

The kettle squealed.

Gem stirred her instant coffee, blew on it then drank it, hurriedly, leaning against the counter. She observed how expertly her aunt cut a leaf from felt.

Wren laid the leaf down and regarded Gem with surprise. "You mean *you*, the recipient of this mail, know neither its sender *nor* source, and this mail is a complete mystery to you?"

"*Lots* of things are mysteries, Birdie," Gem said. "Keats the poet tells us we should accept this, and forge onward in the face of these unsolved elements. But my craving to know, and understand, dies hard. So, will you be vigilant on the letter delivery front, for me, and try to find out who's bringing this mail—if more mail is forthcoming?"

"I'll do my best," Wren said. "But my old legs don't move as quickly as they once did. Often I play the radio while working, in which case I wouldn't hear anyone drop a letter in the mailbox, so to help you solve this puzzle—and I confess I'm curious myself—for the next while I'll keep the radio off and my ears open. Unlike my eyes, my ears are strong; I hear like a midnight owl."

Gem thanked her aunt, kissed her cheek lightly then washed and dressed for work.

THROUGH AUTUMN'S DAYS of dimming light and drifting leaves, an unstamped letter came for Gemma every two weeks like clockwork. Yet no one could apprehend the messenger. Aunt Wren and Gem prevailed upon their landlady, Mrs. Deluca, to ask this fellow his name and where he came from if she saw him approach the house or heard him at the mailbox. Because she lived downstairs, she'd be more likely to reach him quickly. She'd heard the mailbox's lid open, close, and peeked out between the curtains, saw a tall man on the front porch, but by the time she'd put on her slippers, thrown her shawl around her shoulders and made it to the front door, he was gone. It would have been pointless trying to chase him, she added.

To inject some levity into the postal situation, which was, in certain respects, downright eerie, the inhabitants, both upstairs and downstairs, of the house on Pidgeon Avenue began to call the mysterious messenger, instead of the postman, the *ghost-man*.

I suppose if you're going to be haunted by a ghost, a ghost who delivers love letters beats most other kinds of hauntings, Gem thought. Each letter she received was the same as the one before. Still, Gemma saved them all. Quite a stack accumulated, and so she tied them with a special length of coloured yarns she'd woven, much like the cat collar Toby wore as a wristband.

When snow began to fall lightly over their town, the letters still arrived. One Sunday, Gem thought she heard a *click* and, not even throwing on her wool coat and scarf, dashed downstairs in her pajamas, bathrobe and slippers, and of course the messenger had eluded them yet again. But he'd left footprints—large ones—in the snow. Gemma trailed these prints along Pidgeon Avenue, but after about a block they dwindled, and she'd lost him.

Aunt Wren hadn't held back in telling Gem how foolish she'd been to go tearing outdoors with no coat, boots or scarf. And slippers in snow, of all things! To reinforce this scolding, Gem caught a wretched cold, which kept her home from work, and as she sniffled, sneezed and sulked in her bed, she wondered if she should start folding the letters into birds. Ada Swift had taught her this craft during lunch hours at the office, the cold season now confining them indoors. She could take string and hang the birds from her ceiling, and if she folded them *just so*, it might be possible for the word *love* to display on one or the other wing. And when she cast her eyes upwards, she'd see this word, peppering the air above her everywhere, in its own firmament. But she thought better of it, secreting the letters away.

Grace, the erstwhile kitten, had grown, sleek and lithe, into their adored cat who enjoyed perching on the windowsill, watching birds perched in the backyard trees.

As one season shunted to the next, and an Allied victory began to look more assured, Gem's letters continued to be delivered but said very little of Toby's circumstances. But so long as they existed *at all*, Gem felt quite sure Toby was alive. Loving him spurred on Gem's work at The Cottage, too, because how many *others* must be praying for a father or son or sweetheart or mother or daughter or someone else to be safe while crossing the Atlantic Ocean? Not to mention all the other war zones. She'd known this, of course, but since Toby came into her life, she'd felt it on a much deeper, more visceral level.

So Gem bent into her work like a fiend, to keep safe so many who were loved. No one would ever know about their work. Code-breakers having been sworn to secrecy, their working days would fade away like paper birds dissolving in the rain. They'd meld into the streets, ordinary women doing ordinary things. Though perhaps not Beatrice Fearing—she'd *never* be ordinary, would likely become a renowned lady mathematician. And, if she had her way, Cora-Lynn Ponder, too, following in her mentor's footsteps.

On clear nights, in all seasons, Gem often stood in the Delucas' backyard and stargazed. The galaxy never disappointed her, and she'd become adept at locating the most dazzling star, the North Star, blinking down at her, pulsing reassuring signals. One such night, Gem felt a hand's light touch on her shoulder. Startled, she turned. She hadn't heard anyone creep up behind her. It was Aunt Wren, bundled in scarves and her overcoat.

Gemma pointed to the North Star.

"So very *luminous*," remarked her aunt.

They stood there, not speaking. Their breaths frosted plumes in the cold night.

Then Aunt Wren said, "It's *gone*, Gemma."

Alarm stabbed at Gem. "Oh dear, *what's* gone, Birdie?"

"The millstone, sorrow, bottomless chasm of loss—Adam—that's lived within me for so many years, that weighed me down, that wound, like iron. But just today I thought, *Something is missing*—and it was that. The old, habitual, gnawing grief. I *had* drawn a good tarot card this morning, but this new feeling in my core transcends any message from the tarot deck."

She stepped away from Gem, as if doing so would facilitate words she'd yet to speak. "To have the old sorrow vanish is"—Birdie's voice suffused with astonishment—"liberation. I feel so light, niece of mine, I'm like a balloon, and I might lift off right this minute—and fly away!"

Gem reached out and grabbed her aunt's hands. "Oh *no you*

don't, Birdie. You'll stay right *here*, on earth. We need you here. Dr. Fox needs you. Grace the cat needs you. All your hat customers need you—your craft brings them joy. You can be free, and light, on earth, *right here with us,*" Gem said.

"All right, I'll stay," Wren said, laughing. "For as long as I can."

They stood together, looking at the night sky, their arms entwined.

DECEMBER 1945

WILD PIGEON MILLINERY, Wren Maw's enterprise run from her kitchen table, couldn't keep up with orders, especially for men's hats. Returning soldiers clamoured for them. Things were haywire busy at the train station, too, Mr. Deluca reported, filled with frenzied souls greeting returned soldiers. Bewildered brides stepping onto Canadian soil for the first time. Saddest of all, those being helped down from the train because they navigated crutches, missing limbs. Earlier that year, Canadian soldiers had freed prisoners from camps in Europe and the world learned of unspeakable horrors. The earth heaved with graves, the catastrophic shadow side of a near-global tempest. To honour those who returned home, town halls, city halls, all erected the biggest yuletide trees ever, for the first peacetime Christmas in years. The world was free again, but those days weren't all glory and bunting and tickertape. Grief hadn't gone on furlough. Shortages and rations persisted. Many people remained missing or lost.

The Mimico prisoner-of-war camp had closed more than a year earlier. Wren and Gem read this in the newspaper. "Hallelujah," Birdie had intoned over a hat block. She worked so much now, while Gemma didn't work at all—rather, went to normal school, training as a teacher. "Doing something normal at last," Aunt Wren joked while they decorated their Christmas tree, making sure to hang the milk-glass ornaments high enough so Grace, grown, but still with the mischievous spirit of a kitten, couldn't reach them. They'd finish the tree trimming on Christmas Eve, when their guests arrived. "I always suspected what you did at that office wasn't normal," Birdie said. "Typing, filing, shouldn't stress a girl that much. Which is why I'm so glad you're doing something . . . transparent." She paused, holding a blown-glass angel, then added, "And for what it's worth, niece of mine, I don't sleep as soundly as you might think. The times you cried out in the wee hours, in states of dream, or nightmare, gave me a few clues about your job. But your secret is safe with me."

Gemma decided to leave this last remark in the vault and gave her aunt's shoulder a loving squeeze. She told her aunt what a surprise it was, even to *herself*, that one subject she'd teach was mathematics. Cora-Lynn Ponder was coaching her, and the experience was quite tolerable. Fun, almost. Gem would teach literature (her favourite), too. Domestic science as well (her least favourite). It was cozy being there, with Aunt Wren, in the living room, like old times, only with a cat. And Gem would have felt close to contented except for her nagging worry that it had been nearly a month since the last ghost-man's postal drop. And more than two years since she'd seen Toby. She'd kept the letters in her nightstand drawer.

The Cottage in Mimico closed as a Signals Intelligence Office. Miss Fearing sat with them, tearful, on their final day of work. So much for *no crying at The Cottage*. She'd brought a bottle of champagne into the downstairs office, uncorked it and handed out glasses while Ada Lovelace sent an approving smile down on them. Miss Fearing raised her glass to "Ada Lovelace, Enchantress of Numbers." Then their boss turned to the four of them.

"My dear paper birds. I know I've been an ogress sometimes. I'm sorry for that. I don't know what I'd have done without you intrepid young ladies. Keeping so tight-lipped all the time and no one to talk to about what I do all day at work, and Peggy far across the ocean—I'd have gone mad, I think, without you all. Now, for one last time, fly away! Make the most of your lives and, it hardly bears repeating, never tell a soul what you did here at The Cottage. Which will, once again, be simply a cottage on Lake Ontario's shore."

Miss Fearing never *did* tell Gem when her probation ended. Walking home on that last day, Gem chuckled to herself about that.

Soon after The Cottage was decommissioned, Peggy came home. Miss Fearing rang each of them to relay this good news, and to see how they fared. Operations had been scaled back in Whitby, she said, so she'd return as a mathematics lecturer at the university in Toronto. Cora-Lynn Ponder carried on with her studies. Hester Hobbs met someone at Ramona Dance Gardens, fell desperately in love, married and moved to Hamilton. And Ada Swift, the magician? Ada Swift simply vanished—*poof*, like a puff of vapour. But sometimes Gem, who wasn't afraid of the lake now, would amble along the shore, and she'd see a girl in a summer dress dancing there, in the sand, would be about to hail her, for surely it was Ada, but at that very instant the dancing, spinning girl would wisp back into air like some reverse funnel cloud faster than blazing light.

CHRISTMAS EVE. SNOW fell softly over Lake Ontario, and the flat on Pidgeon Avenue resounded with chatter, laughter and song. Lyle Fox gave Wren and Gemma, as a gift, a record player in a handsome wood cabinet with carved doors—on one side a radio, on the other a record player. "The latest Magnavox model," the eye doctor said, smiling, from the armchair, while stroking Grace the cat, who'd installed herself on his knee. He was spoiling them, Wren said, but didn't protest too much.

Bing Crosby's voice wafted through the flat. Salty, sugary aromas drifted in from the ivy-and-mistletoe-garlanded kitchen; a ham decked with pineapple rings and drizzled with maple syrup baked in the oven. They'd have their turkey feast the next day. Earlier that afternoon, between culinary bouts, Birdie and Lyle tackled a crossword puzzle together. Gem had retreated to her bedroom to read a romance novel but enjoyed hearing Birdie and her companion's affectionate, competitive jibes at each other. Earlier, Aunt Wren had shown Lyle some aspects of tarot cards. At her bidding, he drew a card: *The World*, upright.

"A very good card to draw," Wren remarked.

That evening, there was knocking at their upstairs door. Gemma scurried to answer it. A young, rosy-cheeked woman stood there, dressed in a smart wool coat. Crystalline flakes of snow melted on her shoulders. She held a small suitcase. Her other gloved hand grasped the mittened fingers of a little girl, perhaps three years old, whose beret was heavily powdered with snowflakes. They must have walked from the train station. That would have been difficult for the child; perhaps the mother carried her, as well as the suitcase. But she showed no signs of strain, only beamed at Gem, who couldn't believe she hadn't recognized Rooney at first. Their erstwhile lodger was so stylish now, and radiated confidence, and the small girl was cute as a kitten.

"This is Julia," Rooney said, introducing the child. "My little cabbage."

Gemma still stood gobsmacked. Rooney had moved back to Gravenhurst a year and a half earlier—not as long as Toby had been gone, but still, she'd undergone such a transformation in that time.

"I guess I don't have to leave my clothes in the foyer tonight," Rooney said.

Her quip broke the ice, and Gemma brought the guests inside, where Birdie and Lyle greeted them.

"Nice to see you're still knocking about this flat, Dr. Fox," Rooney said.

The eye doctor laughed. "Just try keeping me away."

Rooney remarked on "how very plump and grown Grace had become," and how quaint it would be to sleep in her old bedroom again, where she and her daughter would stay that night. Wren gave everyone a glass of warm cider, hot chocolate for Julia, and set them to work, to finish decorating the tree. The lights already glowed, pastel shades. Some decorations filled the upper branches. Rooney draped strung popcorn around the tree's sweet piney boughs, while Julia hung paper stars as high as she could reach. Lyle Fox said he'd supervise from his armchair. Church bells tolled outside, likely mass at St. Leo's. Gem stood on a small stool and installed the large star tree-topper while Birdie busied herself in the kitchen. Sounds of mirth radiated up through the floor, the Delucas' children home for Christmas.

The days grew dark early now, but that same night, while some dim, watery light remained, Gemma had, on a whim, gone downstairs to check the mailbox. Empty.

To clear the table for the Christmas Eve dinner, Wren had moved her hat-making supplies into her bedroom. A long-stemmed red rose graced the centre of the table. Birdie corralled their guests around the table and a cheerful rabble ensued. Gem tried not to think about the empty mailbox, but it was hard. The others' festive spirits helped. They heaped their plates with sliced ham, fresh rolls, cranberry sauce, stewed apricots and prunes. Boston cream pie on side plates. Condensation fogged Aunt Wren's spectacles, and she laughed, wiping them with her apron. Julia very much enjoyed the cat, though they had to deter Grace more than once from leaping onto the table.

"How often have I sat at this very table. This flat is like my second home," Rooney reminisced.

"And you must regard it as such," Wren said. "And visit more often, bring your little one."

A deep accord suffused the kitchen as they ate, conversed.

After the meal, Birdie moved everyone into the living room. They'd clear up the dishes later, she said. As they sat around the tree, Aunt Wren reached under it and brought forth a package wrapped in tissue paper. She gave it to Rooney, who unwrapped it, blinking wide in disbelief. For inside the wrapping was the loveliest hat, cloche-style, a rich ruby shape, trimmed with felted roses.

"Try it on," Gem urged.

Rooney obliged and it sat perfectly on her head. She made no effort to conceal her tears. "It's beautiful, Miss Maw."

Wren smiled brightly. "It's old, like me. I made it even before Gemma was born. Truth be told, I made it for Carrie Davies, the servant girl who was given a second chance at life. But I never could find her. So, now I'd like you to have it, Rooney."

A tear plopped onto Rooney's houndstooth tweed dress.

"This shouldn't be a night for crying," Birdie said gently. She then gave Julia a doll she'd made from cloth. The girl shrilled with delight.

"Lyle and Gem will receive their gifts tomorrow," Wren said. "You'd come all this way, Rooney and Julia. I decided that you shouldn't have to wait."

For Birdie, Gemma and Dr. Fox, Rooney presented thick scarves she'd knitted.

Then there was a gentle knock at the door. Then a second knock, more insistent.

Gem said she expected that Mrs. Deluca had come upstairs to wish them a happy Christmas, and she set out to answer the door.

A young man in a thick coat, muffler, stood there. His nose and ears were red from the cold. He wore no hat. He must have been out walking in the elements for a while—he was shaking.

"Gem."

That *voice*. Gem threw her arms around Toby.

"The downstairs door was unlocked, so I let myself in. I hope that's all right," he said.

"You look so different," Gem whispered. "Good, I mean. Even

more filled out." She stepped back an arm's length to better see him. "But you look half frozen, too."

Aunt Wren called from the living room. "Who's at the door, Gemma?"

"Oh, heavens. Come in. Please," she told Toby.

Gemma led him into the living room, and introduced Toby to everyone.

Rooney's face paled with disbelief. "I—know you—I *think*. You worked at the tannery, only looking so different now, yet your face I remember. Same cheekbones, eyes."

He nodded. "And you're the girl from the tannery, though much more ... elegant. And no clothespin pinched on your nose."

This whole time a cat whisker could have knocked Gem over. She stood there, kneading Toby's arm through his coat as if to make sure he was real.

Then Lyle Fox's face lit up. "I *also* remember you—I believe I tested your vision. We talked. You were very worried about your mother back in Europe."

Gem appreciated Lyle and Rooney's tact, not mentioning the prisoner-of-war camp.

Toby nodded, looked at Gem and said, "Yes. I can see very clearly."

Wren trilled, for heaven sakes, why was their guest still wearing his coat? She took it and made up a plate of leftovers from dinner. After he'd removed his coat, Toby lifted his arm and Gem saw it— the bright coil she'd woven, dulled now by wear and time. But still on his wrist.

He saw her note it. "It's never come off my wrist," he said to her.

Toby ate the food in the living room, conversing as much as he could between bites. Grace padded up to him, no doubt interested in scraps from his plate.

"That's Hedwig's progeny," Gem said. "Her other kittens also went to good homes."

Aunt Wren stared at Toby, then Gem, back to Toby. "So, how did you two meet?" she asked.

Gem hardly skipped a beat. "At—work. But then Toby was sent to a different work location."

"Ah," Wren mused. "I suppose, then, that's what all those mysterious letters were about?"

Toby glanced at Gem.

"Yes," she said. "I needed a little . . . intrigue in my life to, you know, brighten my days in the office."

Her aunt left it at that.

Toby had finished his food, and Wren took his empty plate back to the kitchen. They settled, and he tried to condense the last two years into a story. How adept he was at spinning a romantic tale that held truth yet didn't break any security protocols. Gem kept staring at him in disbelief, blissed to her very bones. Aware that only Gem knew his background, Toby told the group he'd worked in communications for the Allies throughout the war. Dr. Fox and Rooney both looked puzzled, hearing this, but stayed quiet, waiting to hear more.

Toby turned to Gemma. "I found my mother. She'd very much like to meet you and your aunt someday."

Aunt Wren interjected. "It's nice to finally meet the chap who sent all those letters. We never could catch the messenger. We were convinced he was a ghost."

Toby laughed.

"We haven't received any letters in a while," Gem said.

"And you likely thought I'd forgotten you," Toby remarked. "The lag in postal deliveries had to do with the complexity of my getting out of Europe," he added. "During that tough patch I was unable to arrange to send you even a few words."

"The messenger?" Aunt Wren probed.

"Ah, yes. My father. I reunited with him before I left on an overseas operation." He turned to Gemma. "I'm sorry the letters were so . . . repetitive, but I wrote some of them hurriedly, before I left, so you'd have regular missives The main object was to get any sort of word to you at all. And for security reasons, I had to be careful."

"Your father certainly moved rather quickly," Wren said.

"No question. He used to be a marathon runner. This served him well in his role as a messenger of love. I asked him to simply deliver the letters, not get tangled up in things. In this whole stealth operation, he aided me a lot."

Aunt Wren had been twitching nervously. Then she said, "We didn't know you'd be joining us, Toby—but . . ." Brightening, she hoisted herself from her chair, trundled off to her room and returned with a hat, a fine man's hat, with a small, fringed trim crafted from felt and meant to emulate a feather, sprouting from the rim. "I'm sorry it's not wrapped. But I see you wore no hat here; your ears must be near frozen. This hat has a special design feature of my own devising—retractable earflaps for warmth. You'll need them, especially if you plan to remain in this frozen neck of the woods."

Toby put on the hat and looked quite dapper. "Thank you, Miss Maw. As a matter of fact, I *do* plan to remain," he said, looking directly at Gem.

Gem felt her cheeks redden.

Then Rooney rummaged through her suitcase on the floor beside her. "You'll need this, too." She handed him a folded scarf. "Much thicker than the one you were wearing. I didn't know how many guests there would be this Christmas, so I brought an extra gift, just in case. Knitted it myself."

Toby wound it around his neck. "It's wonderful," Toby said. "The muffler I wore here tonight is indeed worn thin."

Gem strove to steady her voice, but her words came like a broken tambourine. "I—don't have a present for you, Toby."

Hearing this, he couldn't stay in his chair. Leaping from it, he squeezed onto the chesterfield beside her, took her hands while the others stared. "Gem"—hands pressing hands—"*you* are the present."

Lyle Fox cleared his throat. "I brought a rum pudding. Why don't I serve it? And Wren, you could take Rooney and Julia into their bedroom and get them settled."

Everyone cleared out of the living room, leaving only Toby and Gem. Even the cat padded out of the room.

The snow thickened, and now formed white magnolias against the dark window. Gem glanced away from Toby long enough to behold those snowy blooms and think how this moment felt as though she were being held within the prettiest snow globe. But even the sweetest snow globe couldn't capture her attention for long.

While dishes clinked in the kitchen, and amiable chatter came from Rooney's old bedroom, Gemma and Toby sat facing each other, unable to tear their eyes away. Then he leaned over and kissed her. After a moment or two, they needed to catch their breaths. Toby glanced at the deck of cards on a nearby coffee table.

"What are those, Gem?"

"Aunt Wren's tarot deck. Why don't you pick a card?"

He drew a card, and turned it upright to display it.

"It's *The Lovers*," Gem said, smiling. "An excellent card," she added, teasingly.

Toby laughed, laid down the card and grasped her hands. "I hope to never leave you again."

"I won't *let* you leave me again," Gem replied.

The cat soft-pawed her way back into the room.

And the world held its breath.

AUTHOR'S NOTE

WHILE *THE PAPER BIRDS* is a work of imagination, many sources provided inspiration and foundational material. These include not only published works but also material housed in archives and museums, and disseminated across various media including films, television series, podcasts, scholars' digital commons, radio, websites, art installations and much more. The scope of writings on the Second World War, both non-fiction and works of imagination, is formidable. Writings on Second World War military intelligence, indeed Bletchley Park alone, have proliferated in the past few decades. While considerable scholarship exists on women's wartime work in Canada and elsewhere, their contributions as codebreakers have only recently begun to emerge. CBC News, for example, featured "A Secret No More: Canada's 1st Codebreaking Unit Comes Out of the Shadows" (August 7, 2022). There are other, similar Canadian news stories, such as Fred Langan's piece in *The Globe and Mail*: "Code-breaker Sonja Sinclair Kept Her Wartime Work a Secret for Nearly 75 Years" (June 5, 2024). Liza Mundy's bestselling book *Code Girls: The Untold Story of the American Women Code Breakers of World War II* (2017) is a standout example, within the American context, of this emergent topic. Doctoral theses by Annie Burman (University of Uppsala, 2013) and Bryony Norburn (University of Buckingham, 2021) add to our understanding of gendered labour in intelligence during the war, with a predominant focus on Britain. A recent scholarly addition to this subject is Helen Fry's fascinating book *Women in Intelligence: The Hidden History of Two World Wars* (2023).

AUTHOR'S NOTE

Primary research sources for *The Paper Birds* were Ted Barris's *Battle of the Atlantic: Gauntlet to Victory* (2022), Mark Bourrie's *The Fog of War: Censorship of Canada's Media in World War Two* (2011) and Kirk W. Goodlet's article "Number 22 Internment Camp: German Prisoners of War and Canadian Internment Operations in Mimico, Ontario, 1940–1944" in *Ontario History* (Vol. CIV, No. 2, Autumn 2012). The Official Secrets Act (1939) was accessed at https://historyofrights.ca/wp-content/uploads/statutes/CN_Official-Secrets-Act-1939.pdf. Leo Marks's *Between Silk and Cyanide: A Code Maker's War 1941–45* (2007), especially Marks's famous "code poem" "The Life That I Have," inspired me with respect to the role of literary texts in cryptography.

In addition to several informative books about Camp X in Whitby, Ontario, such as Lynn Philip Hodgson's *Inside Camp X* (1999), other noteworthy sources I consulted include: Joel Greenberg's *A Feathered River Across the Sky: The Passenger Pigeon's Flight to Extinction* (2014); Jennifer Wilcox's *Sharing the Burden: Women in Cryptology During World War II* (1998); David Stafford's *Camp X; How to Become a Spy: The World War II SOE Training Manual* (2015); John Bryden's *Best-Kept Secret: Canadian Secret Intelligence in the Second World War* (1993); Stephen Budiansky's *Battle of Wits: The Complete Story of Codebreaking in World War II* (2000); David Kahn's *The Codebreakers: The Story of Secret Writing* (1967, 1996); Simon Singh's *The Code Book: The Science of Secrecy from Ancient Egypt to Quantum Cryptography* (1999); Peter Matthews's *SIGINT: The Secret History of Signals Intelligence in the World Wars* (2018); Paul Kemp's *U-Boats Destroyed: German Submarine Losses in the World Wars* (1997); Helen Fouché Gaines's *Cryptanalysis: A Study of Ciphers and Their Solution* (1939, 1956); *The Book of Codes: Understanding the World of Hidden Messages*, edited by Paul Lunde (2009); James W. Essex's *Victory in the*

St. Lawrence: Canada's Unknown War (1984); Georg Simmel's *The Sociology of Secrecy and of Secret Societies* (1906, 2023); Stéphane Lefebvre's "A Brief Genealogy of State Secrecy" in *The Windsor Yearbook of Access to Justice* (Vol. 31, No. 1, 2013); *Material Traces of War: Stories of Canadian Women and Conflict, 1914–1945*, edited by Stacey Barker, Krista Cooke and Molly McCullough; Miranda Seymour's *In Byron's Wake: The Turbulent Lives of Byron's Wife and Daughter: Annabella Milbanke and Ada Lovelace* (2018); Peter Young's *Let's Dance: A Celebration of Ontario's Dance Halls and Summer Dance Pavilions* (2002); Ellin Bessner's *Double Threat: Canadian Jews, the Military, and World War II* (2019); *The Ward: The Life and Loss of Toronto's First Immigrant Neighbourhood*, edited by John Loring, Michael McClelland, Ellen Scheinberg and Tatum Taylor (2015); Jason Fagone's *The Woman Who Smashed Codes: A True Story of Love, Spies, and the Unlikely Heroine Who Outwitted America's Enemies* (2017); Jeffrey A. Keshen's *Saints, Sinners, and Soldiers: Canada's Second World War* (2007); Sarah Baring's *The Road to Station X: From Debutante Ball to Fighter-Plane Factory to Bletchley Park: A Memoir of One Woman's Journey Through World War Two* (2020); K.D. Alden's *Lady Codebreaker* (2024); Michael Smith's *The Debs of Bletchley Park* (2015); Kate Quinn's *The Rose Code: A Novel* (2021); Molly Green's Bletchley Park fiction series; Sara Ackerman's *The Codebreaker's Secret: A Novel* (2022); Chester Nez's *Code Talker: The First and Only Memoir by One of the Original Navajo Code Talkers of WW II* (2012); Charlotte Gray's *The Massey Murder: A Maid, Her Master, and the Trial That Shocked a Country* (2014); Tina Bates's chapter "Shop and Factory: The Ontario Millinery Trade in Transition, 1870–1930" in *Fashion: A Canadian Perspective*, edited by Alexandra Palmer (2004); William Temple Hornaday's *Our Vanishing Wildlife: Its Extermination and Preservation* (1913); Carolyn Strange's *Toronto's Girl Problem: The*

Perils and Pleasures of the City, 1880–1930 (1995); L. Webster Fox's *A Practical Treatise on Ophthalmology* (1920).

Toronto artist Nina Levitt's art installations on female spies in WWII, especially "Relay," based on Camp X (Robert McLaughlin Gallery, Oshawa, 2008), proved fascinating. David A. Hatch's lecture "Black Code Breakers in WW II at Arlington Hall," which I viewed via Zoom on February 8, 2024, presented by the Arlington Historical Society, contained useful insights. My tour, in 2023, of the tunnel under Toronto's Casa Loma where Allied spy work took place (Station M) was an interesting, if claustrophobic, experience. The lobby area of Casa Loma contains a relevant display on the same topic. The Polybius square that Gemma tackles is taken from Peter Matthews's *SIGINT: The Secret History of Signals Intelligence in the World Wars,* page 48. The text of the signs on The Cottage wall are adapted from a tea towel I purchased in the gift shop at Bletchley Park in 2023. The formulae and problems Cora-Lynn writes out on the chalkboard in *The Paper Birds* are loosely adapted from syllabi posted online, for math courses at NYU, in the areas of number theory, quantitative reasoning and cryptography.

The epigraph to this novel, Lisel Mueller's poem "Sometimes, When the Light," is taken from *Alive Together: New and Selected Poems*, Louisiana State University Press, 1996. In addition to the beauty of Mueller's verse, it was poignant to me that her family fled the Nazis when Mueller was a teenager. The quote from *Hamlet* in Gem's job interview is taken from the Oxford Shakespeare edition, Oxford University Press, 1987. In *The Paper Birds*, Wren and her sweetheart Adam Hartsock would have been reading from Edna St. Vincent Millay's poetry collection *Renascence and Other Poems*, published in 1917. I have taken a small liberty with dates, in that Adam was killed in the First World War before Millay's book appeared in print. However, Millay was well-known prior to 1917, when she won a prize for her poem "Renascence." A digital facsimile of *Renascence and Other Poems* is available at https://www.archive.org. Much of Millay's poetry is also on https://www.public-domain-poetry.com. It should be noted, too, that William Temple Hornaday's book appeared in print a few years after Wren discovered it in a bookshop. The excerpt from Marjorie Pickthall's poem "Love" was sourced from https://www.gutenberg.ca.

ACKNOWLEDGEMENTS

AGAIN, I AM incredibly lucky to have worked with my clear-eyed and generous editor, Janice Zawerbny, whose insights made this story stronger and whose engagement with its subject matter combined with her editorial prowess made work on this novel a deeply pleasurable experience. I'm also indebted to John Sweet's copy-editing expertise. Thanks to the wonderful team at HarperCollins Canada. An Access Copyright Foundation Marian Hebb Research Grant administered through SK Arts in 2023 enabled me to undertake research at Churchill Archives, Cambridge University, UK, and National Archives, Kew, UK. I'm indebted to the super-helpful archivists at these locations. This grant also enabled me to visit Bletchley Park, a memorable and moving experience. The guided tour was brilliant. Toronto's Palais Royale granted me access to the premises, which helped bring my characters' evening there to life. Thanks to everyone at the Canadian War Museum in Ottawa during my visit there in April 2023. I also wish to acknowledge the Etobicoke Historical Society and the Toronto Reference Library. Ted Barris and Mark Bourrie were generous with their time in answering questions and offering their expertise. Thanks to Victoria C. Herrmann at Louisiana State University Press. Numerous individuals—friends, colleagues, former students, family members—provided insights and information, and took an interest in this novel, even if it was just listening to me go on about it. Much thanks to Leona Theis for the gift of a pristine *Maclean's* magazine dated during *The Paper Birds*' era. Thanks also to: Pat Heffernan, Kim Galway, Tracy

Goulding, Simon Boehm, Tracy Hamon, Joanne Rochester, Mari-Lou Rowley, Sheri Benning, David Bateman, Kathleen Whelan, Heather Berkeley, Christopher White, Mark Myers, Frank Klaassen, Sharon Wright, Ruth Panofsky, Rod Michalko, Tanya Titchkosky, Paul LePage and Charles Mims. My students and colleagues at the University of Saskatchewan continue to inspire me. No one withstood the inevitable ups and downs of any long-haul writing project more than Mike Heffernan, who, in addition to his love and support, listened and engaged in lively conversations that often wove together stories and music. As far as soundtracks for the writing of this book went, Mike's exquisite, haunting keyboard artistry on the recording of Gordon Lightfoot's "Shadows" wafted through my mind often, as did Lightfoot's "Summer Side of Life," as well as much music from the World War Two era.